Jeremy: For Theo and Heather

Hermione: For my dad, because he is the BEST!!!! Oh my goodness I love him so much. He is talented and very, very clever. Wow. What would I do without such an amazing inspiration? He's just so cool! How did I get so lucky? Beats me. He definitely did not type this dedication himself when I wasn't looking. So, in conclusion: this book is dedicated to him (my amazing father).

YORICK AND BÖNES

Friends by Any Other Name

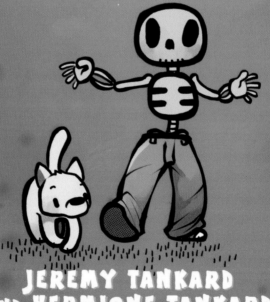

JEREMY TANKARD
AND HERMIONE TANKARD

Quill Tree Books
Imprints of HarperCollinsPublishers

HARPER
alley

Quill Tree Books is an imprint of HarperCollins Publishers.
HarperAlley is an imprint of HarperCollins Publishers.

Yorick and Bones: Friends by Any Other Name

For information address HarperCollins Children's Books, a division of HarperCollins Publishers, 195 Broadway, New York, NY 10007.
www.harperalley.com
ISBN 978-0-06-285433-9 — ISBN 978-0-06-285434-6 (paperback)
The artist used Clip Studio to create the digital illustrations for this book.
Typography by Chris Dickey
21 22 23 24 25 EP 10 9 8 7 6 5 4 3 2 1
❖
First Edition

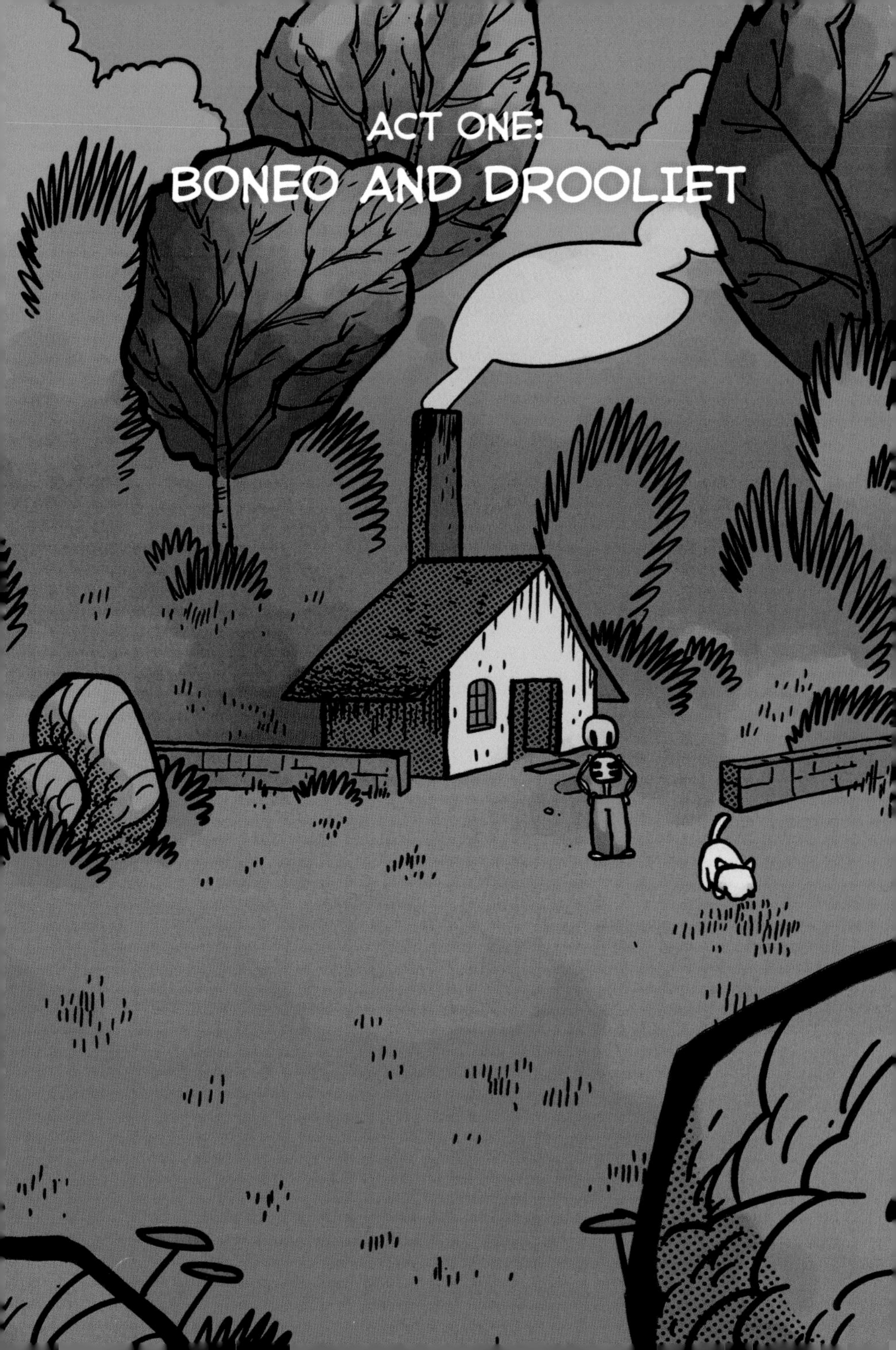
ACT ONE:
BONEO AND DROOLIET

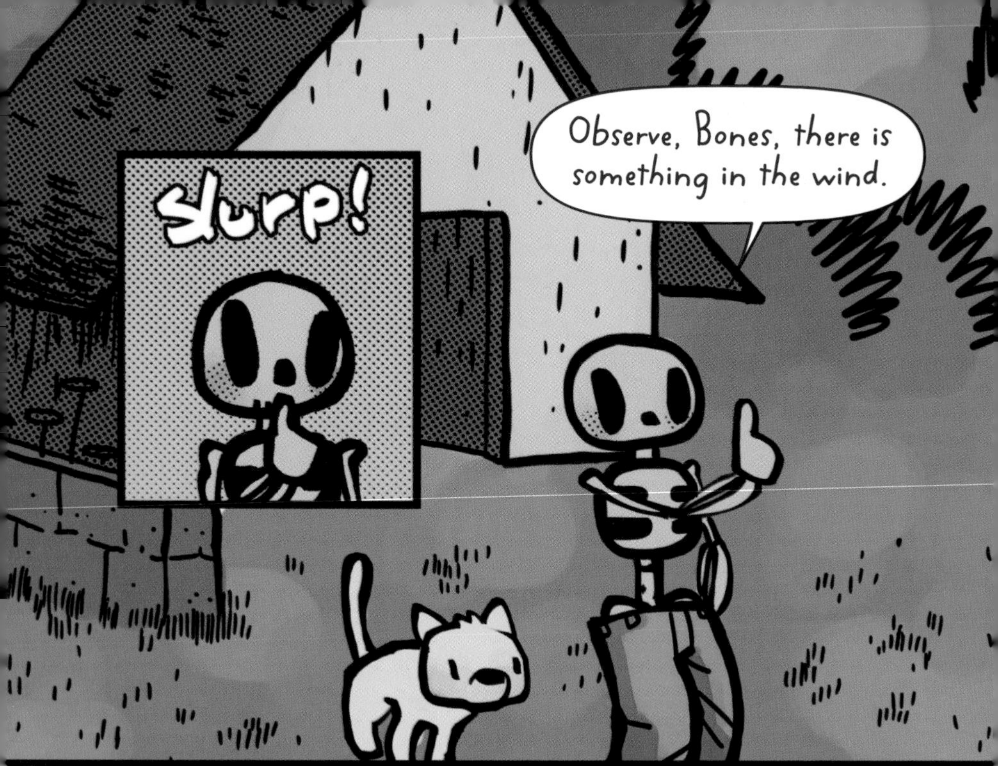
slurp!
Observe, Bones, there is something in the wind.

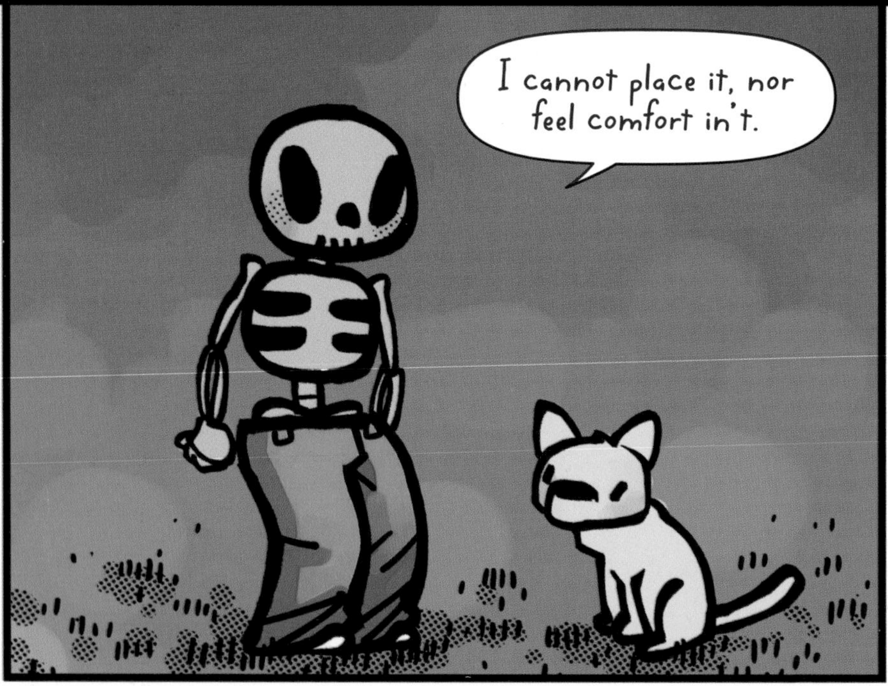
I cannot place it, nor feel comfort in't.

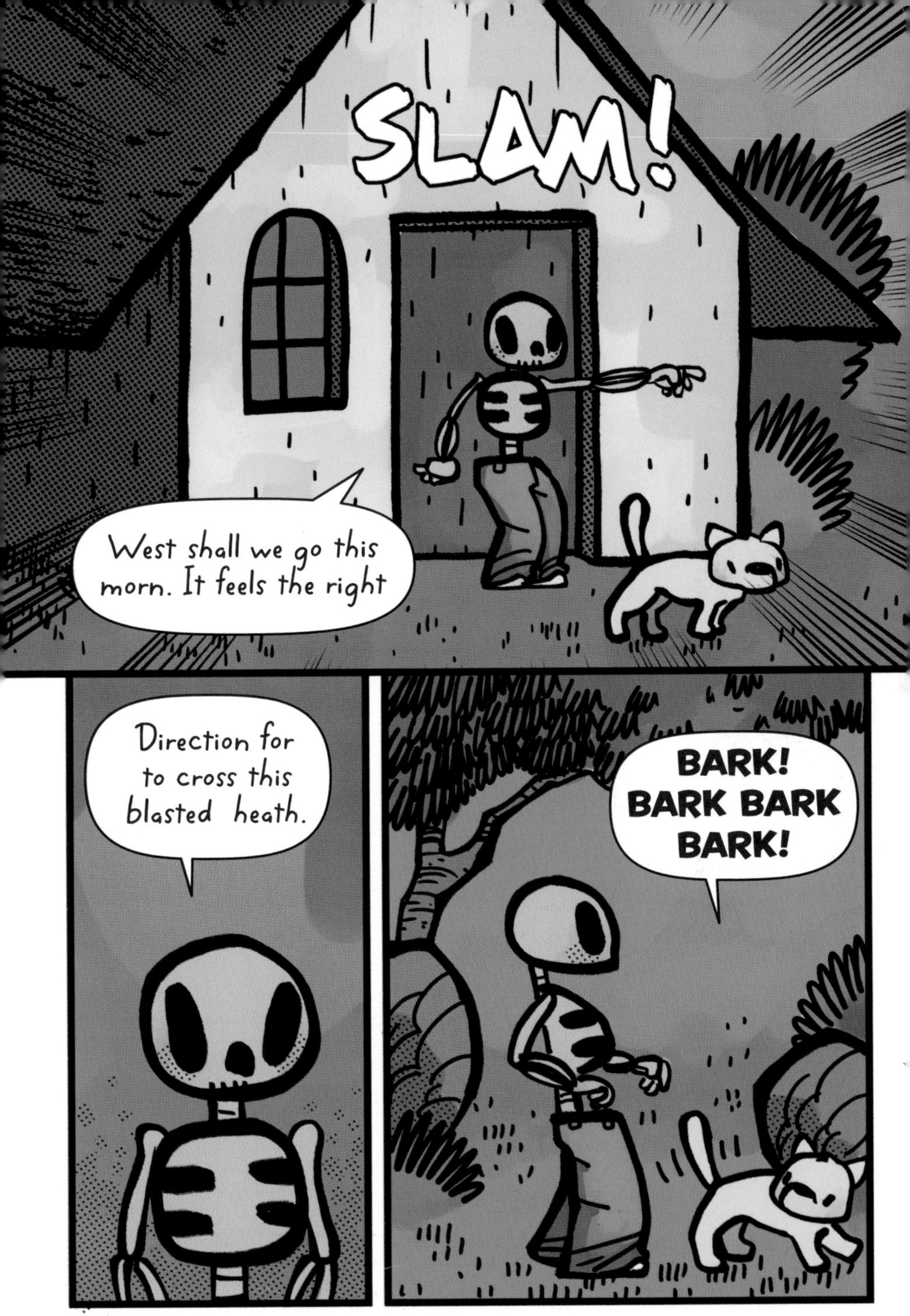
SLAM!
West shall we go this morn. It feels the right
Direction for to cross this blasted heath.
BARK! BARK BARK BARK!

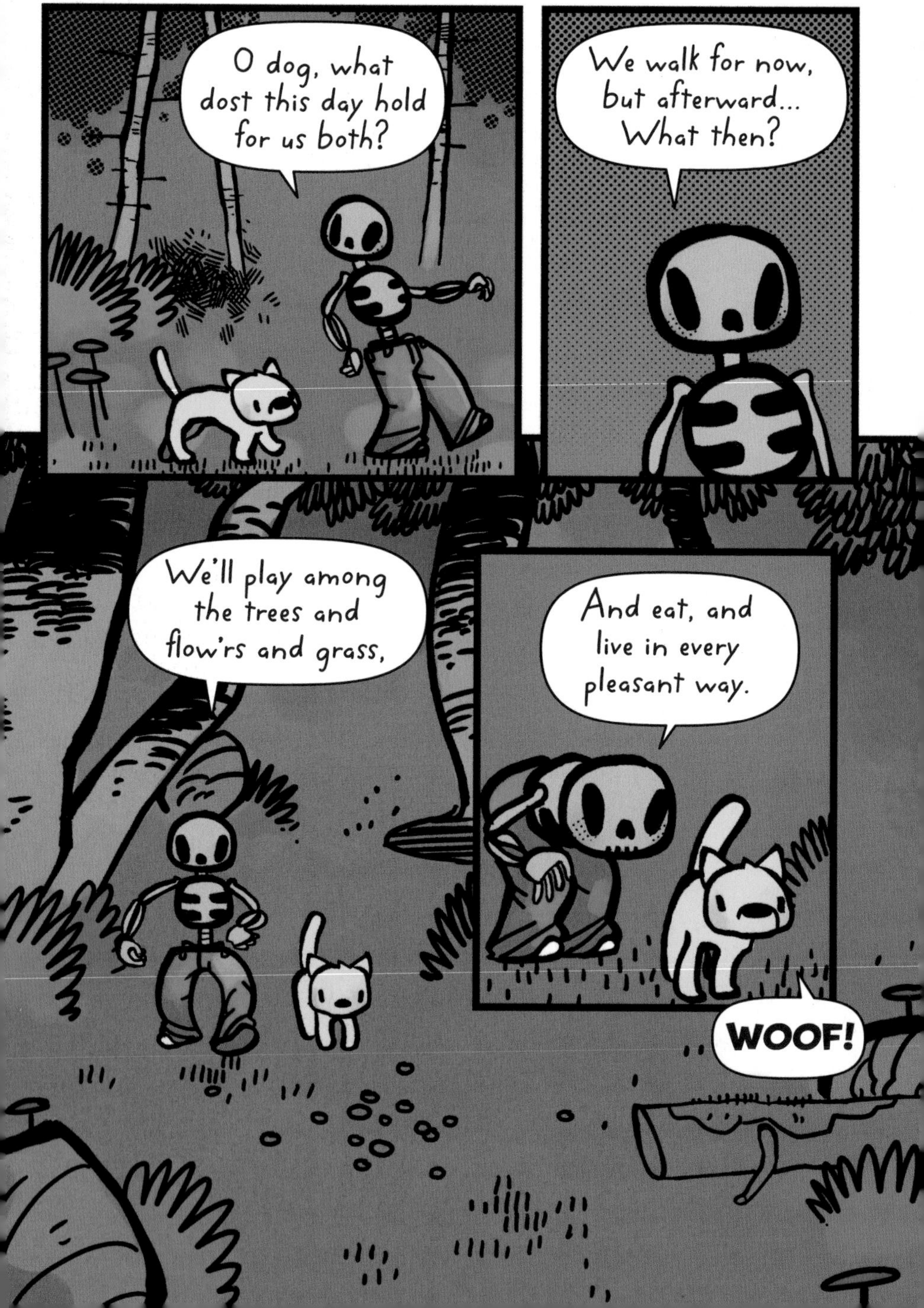
O dog, what dost this day hold for us both?
We walk for now, but afterward... What then?
We'll play among the trees and flow'rs and grass,
And eat, and live in every pleasant way.
WOOF!

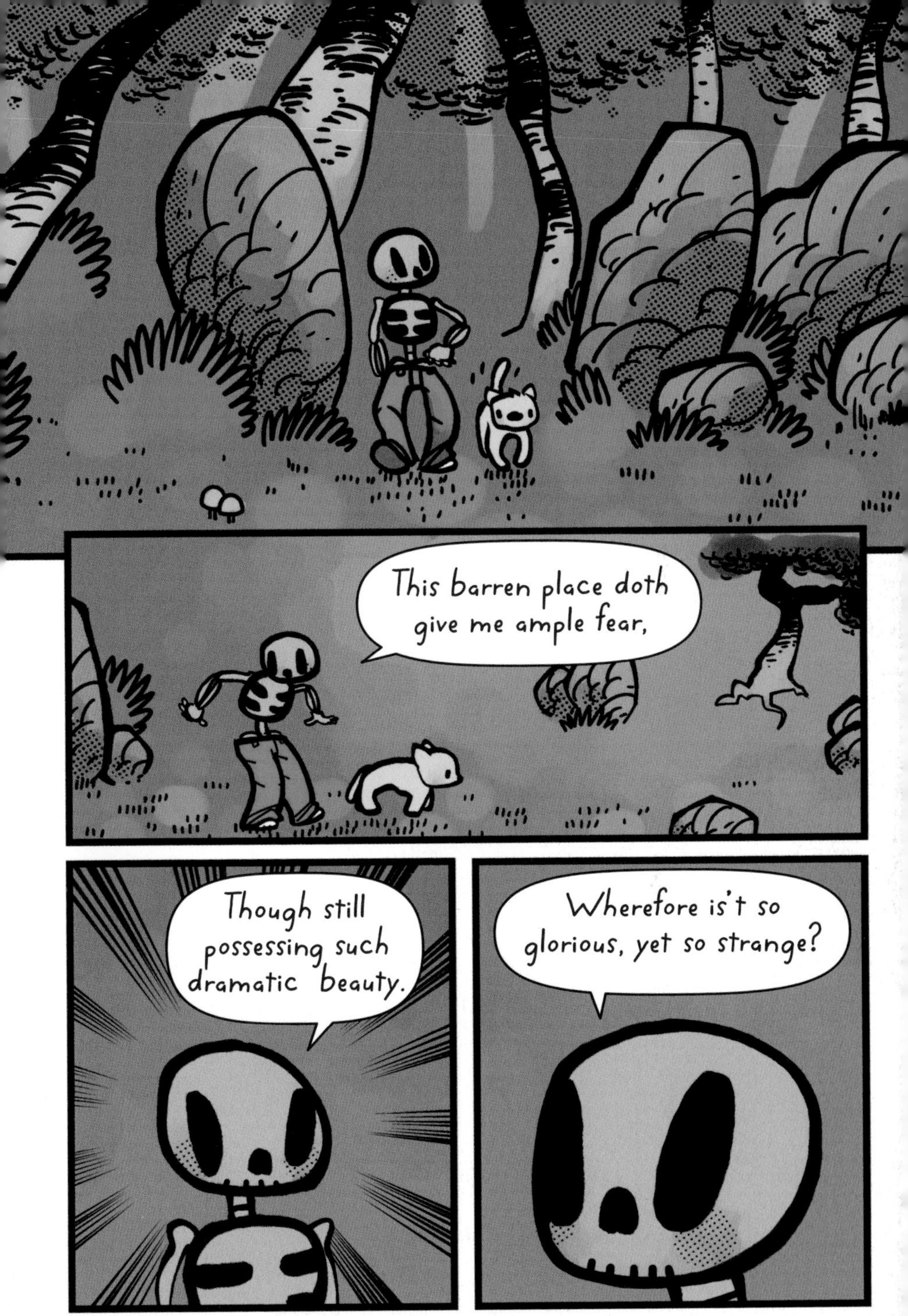
This barren place doth give me ample fear,
Though still possessing such dramatic beauty.
Wherefore is't so glorious, yet so strange?

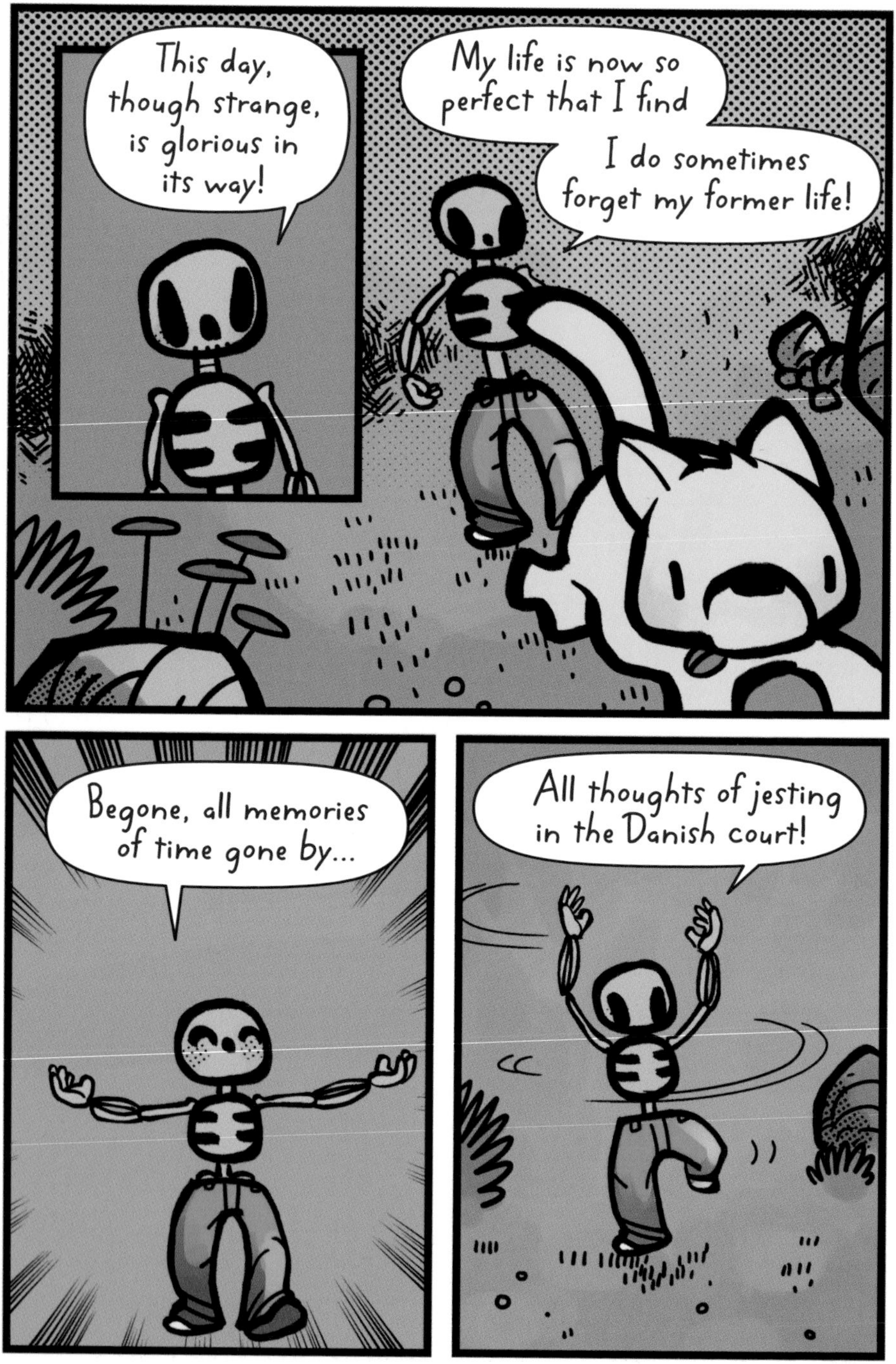
This day, though strange, is glorious in its way!
My life is now so perfect that I find
I do sometimes forget my former life!
Begone, all memories of time gone by...
All thoughts of jesting in the Danish court!

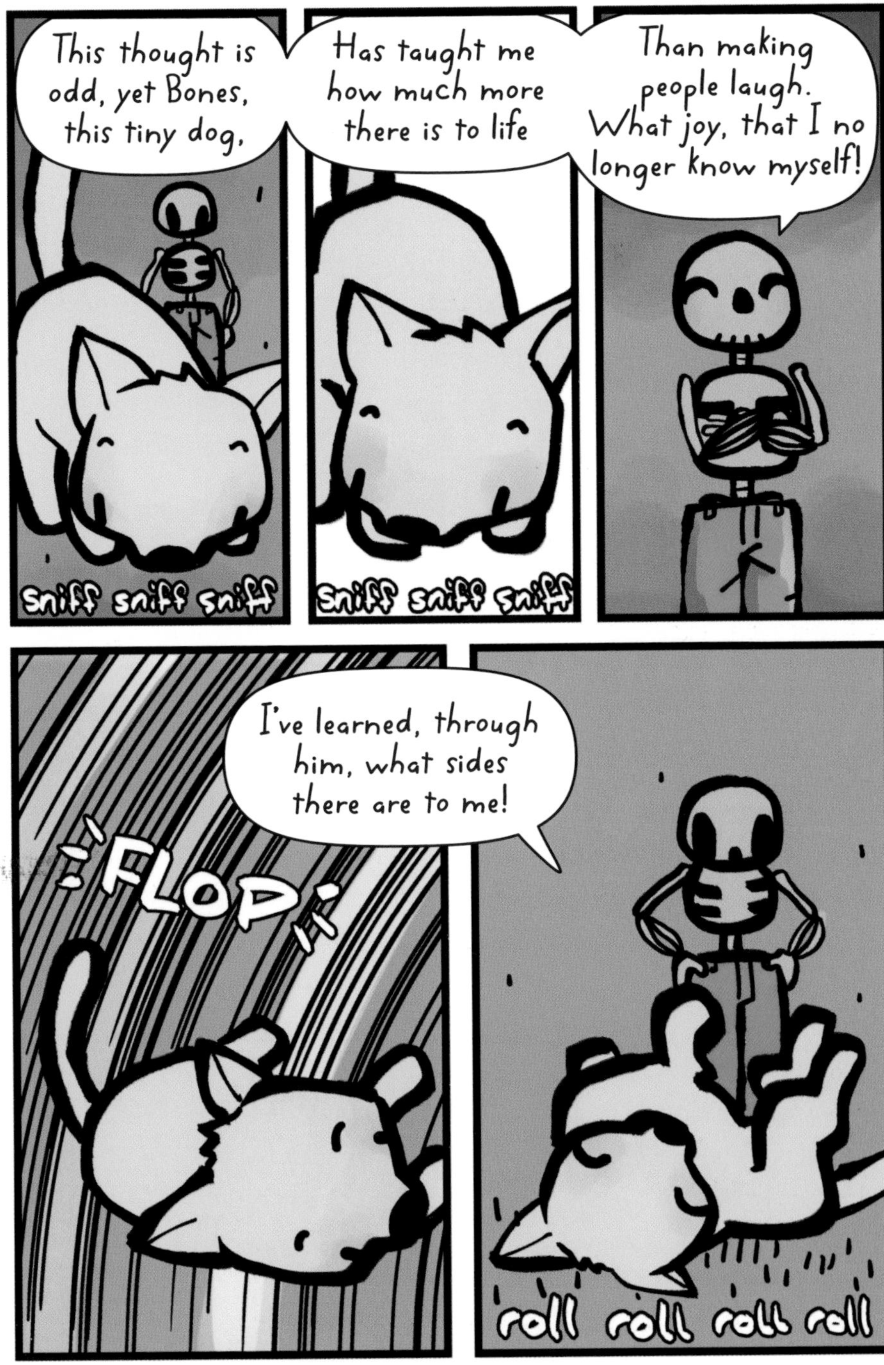
This thought is odd, yet Bones, this tiny dog,
sniff sniff sniff
Has taught me how much more there is to life
sniff sniff sniff
Than making people laugh. What joy, that I no longer know myself!
FLOP
I've learned, through him, what sides there are to me!
roll roll roll roll

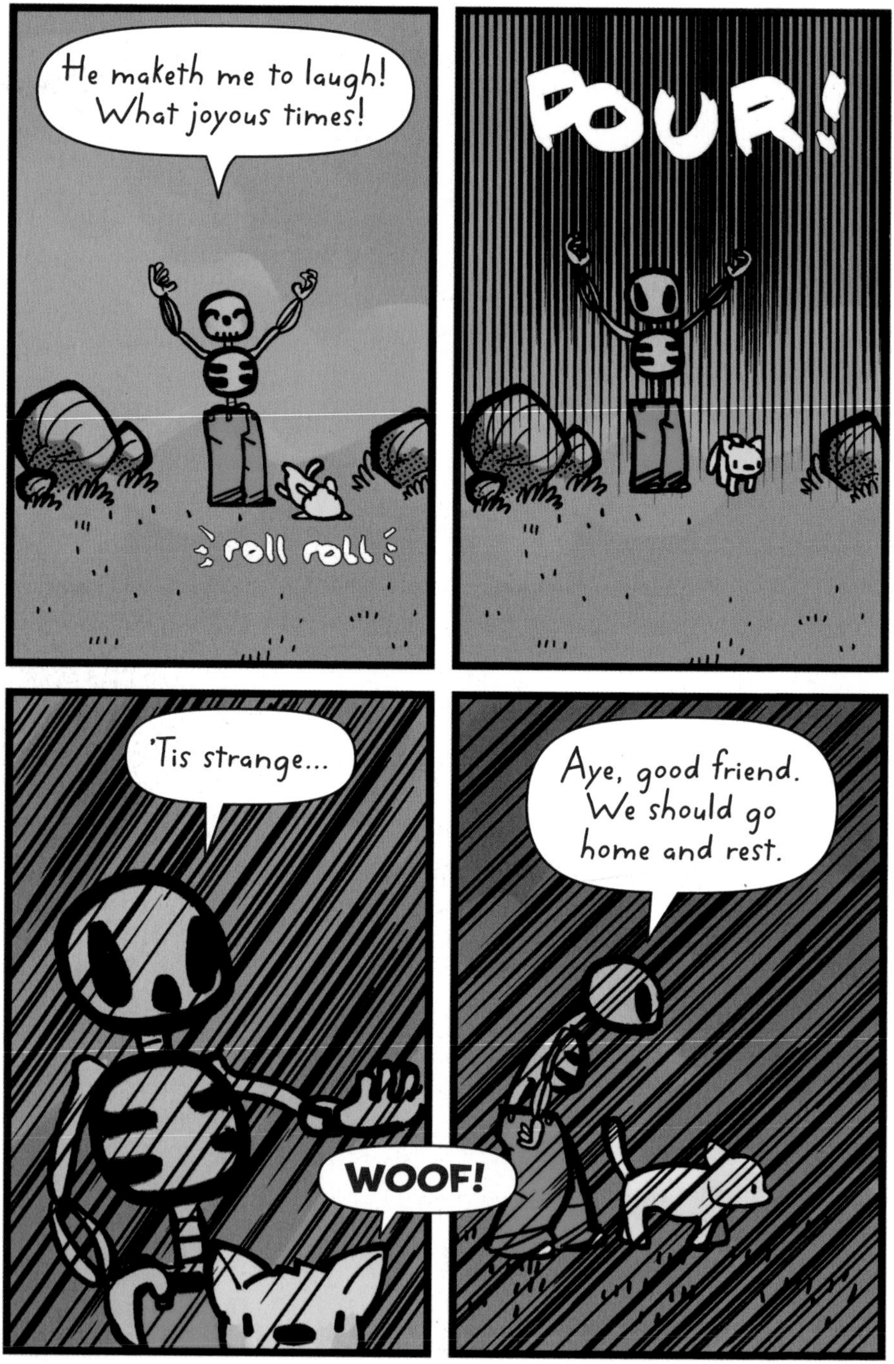
He maketh me to laugh! What joyous times!
roll roll
POUR!
'Tis strange...
WOOF!
Aye, good friend. We should go home and rest.

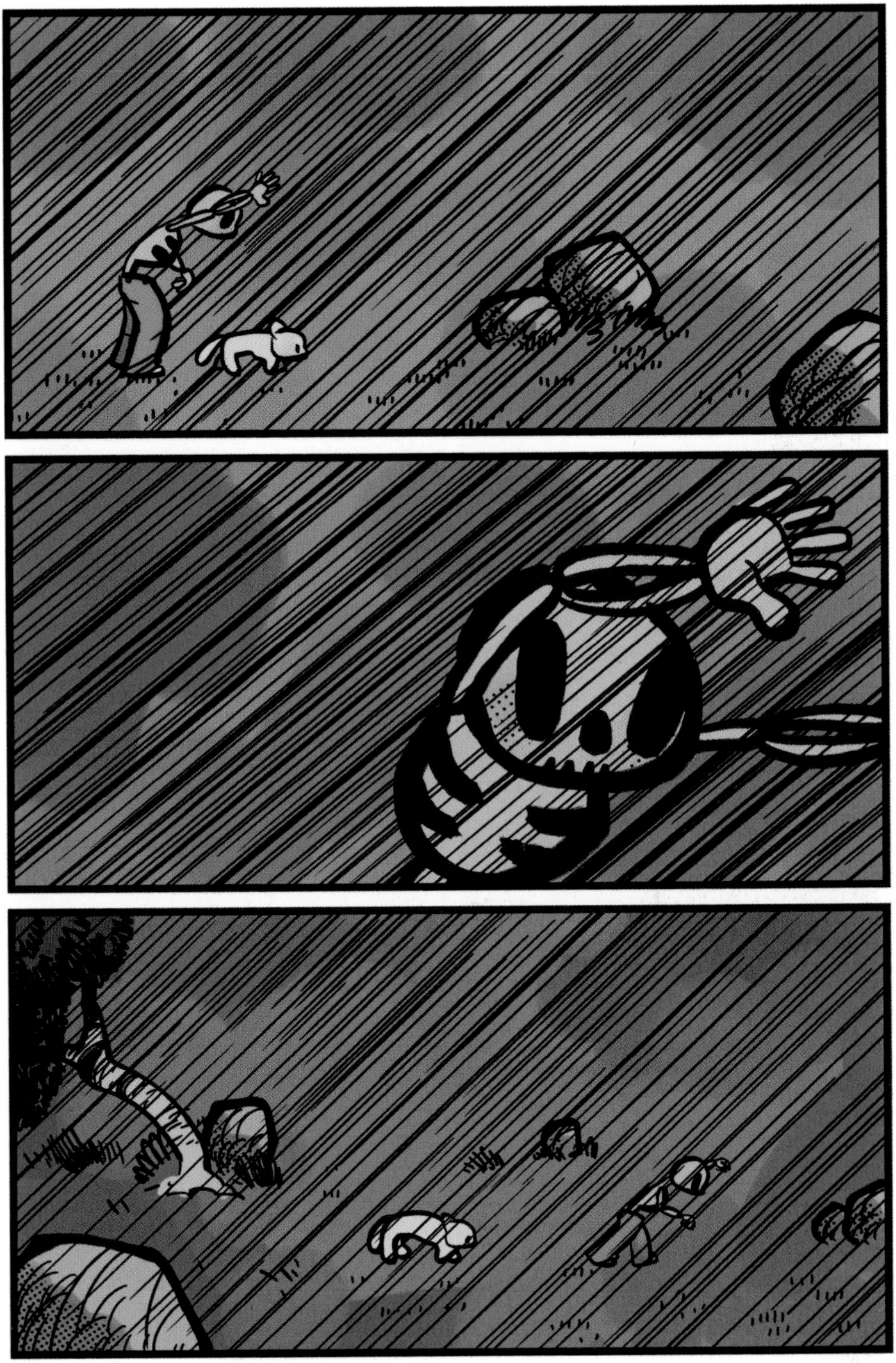

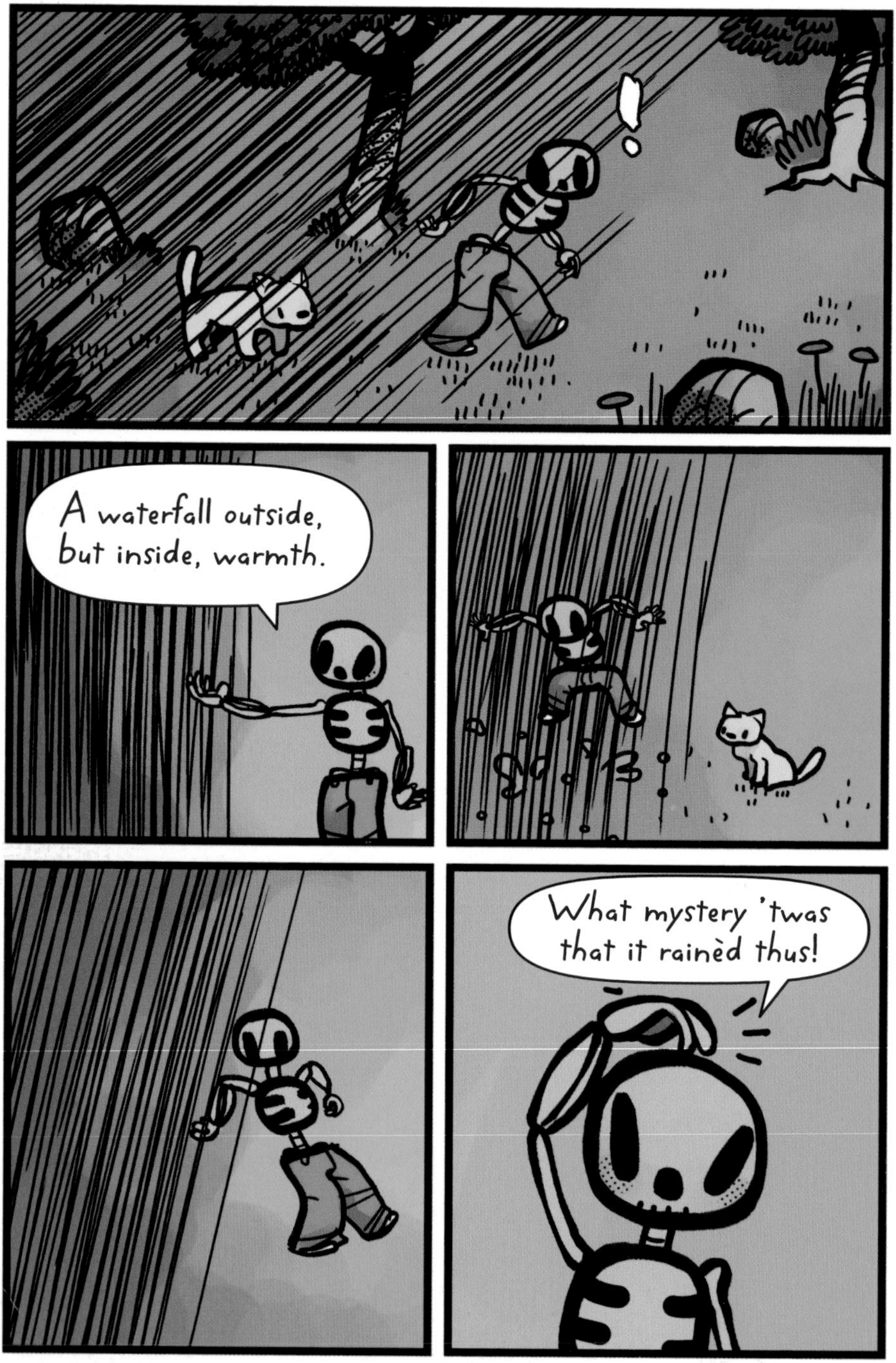
!
A waterfall outside, but inside, warmth.
What mystery 'twas that it rainèd thus!

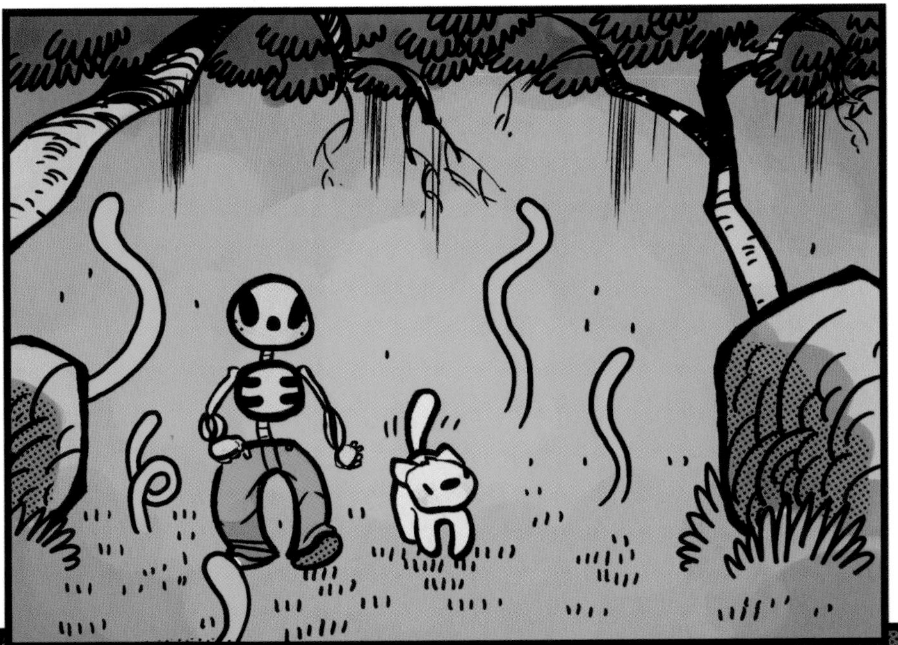

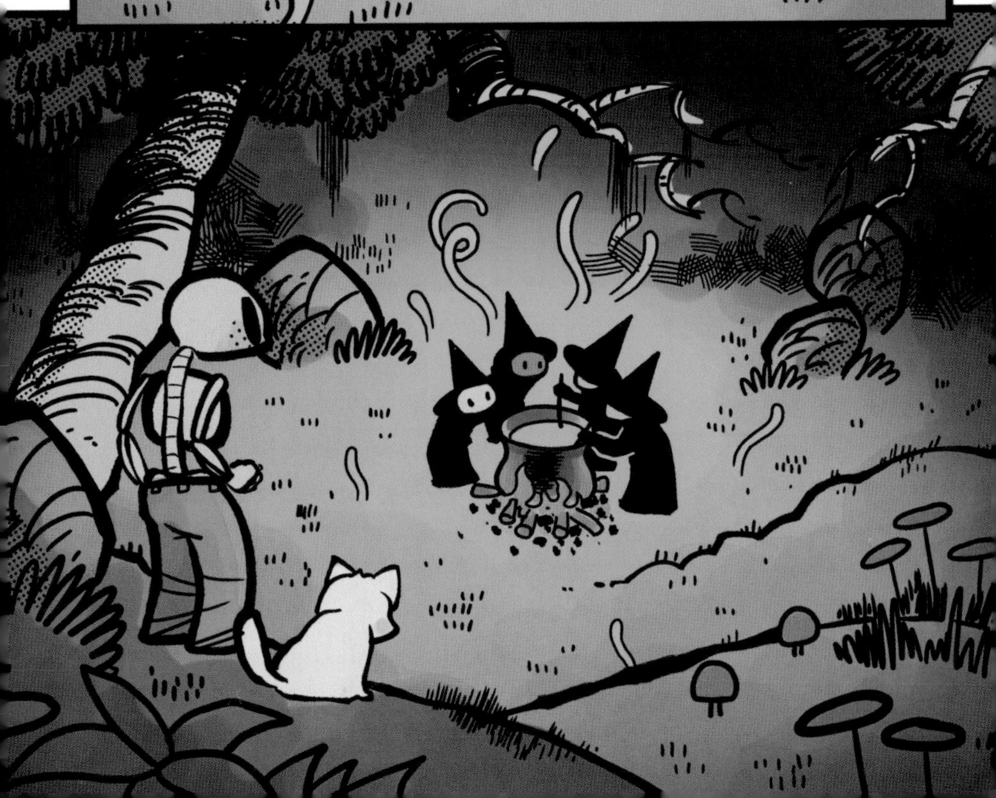

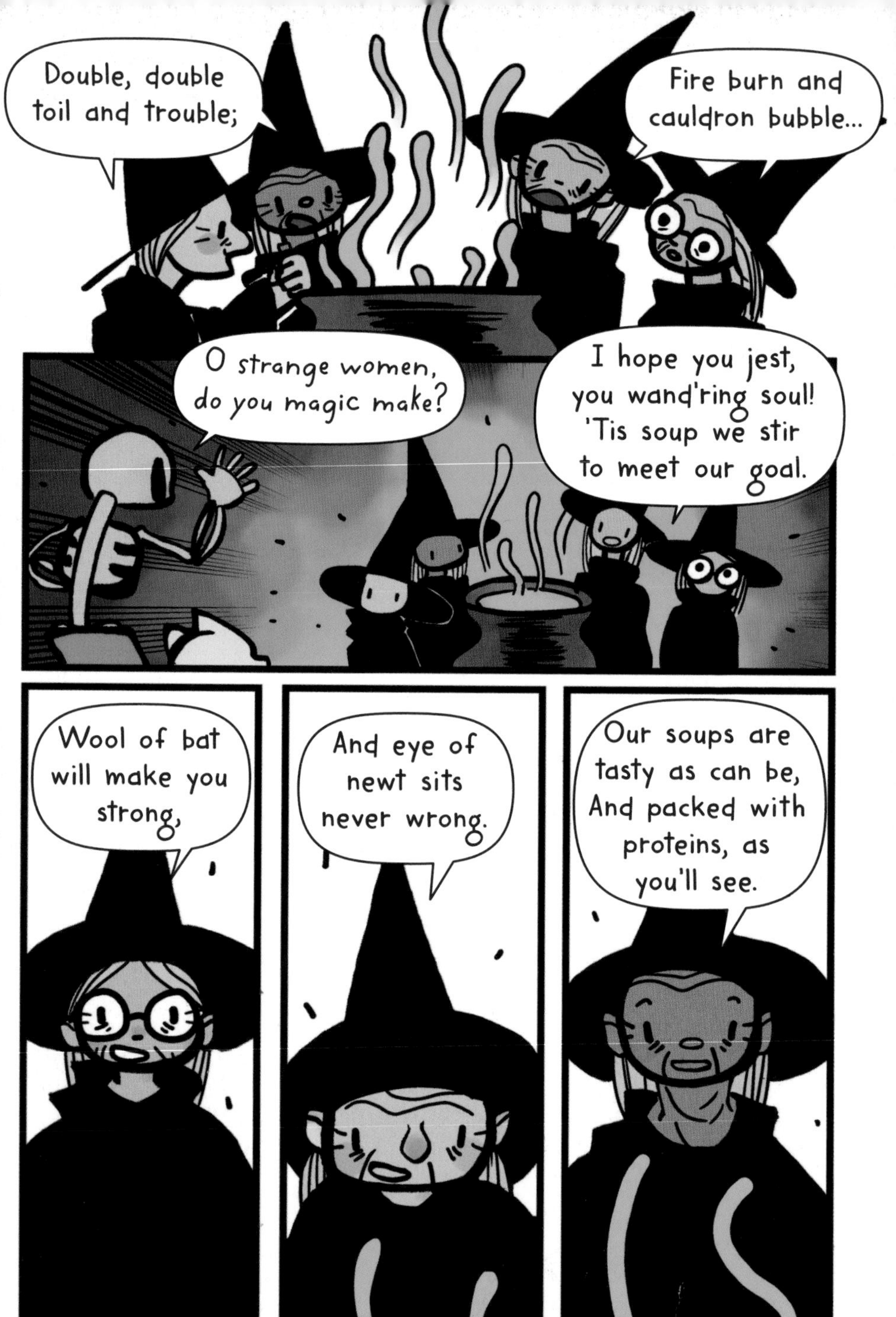
Double, double toil and trouble;
Fire burn and cauldron bubble...
O strange women, do you magic make?
I hope you jest, you wand'ring soul! 'Tis soup we stir to meet our goal.
Wool of bat will make you strong,
And eye of newt sits never wrong.
Our soups are tasty as can be, And packed with proteins, as you'll see.

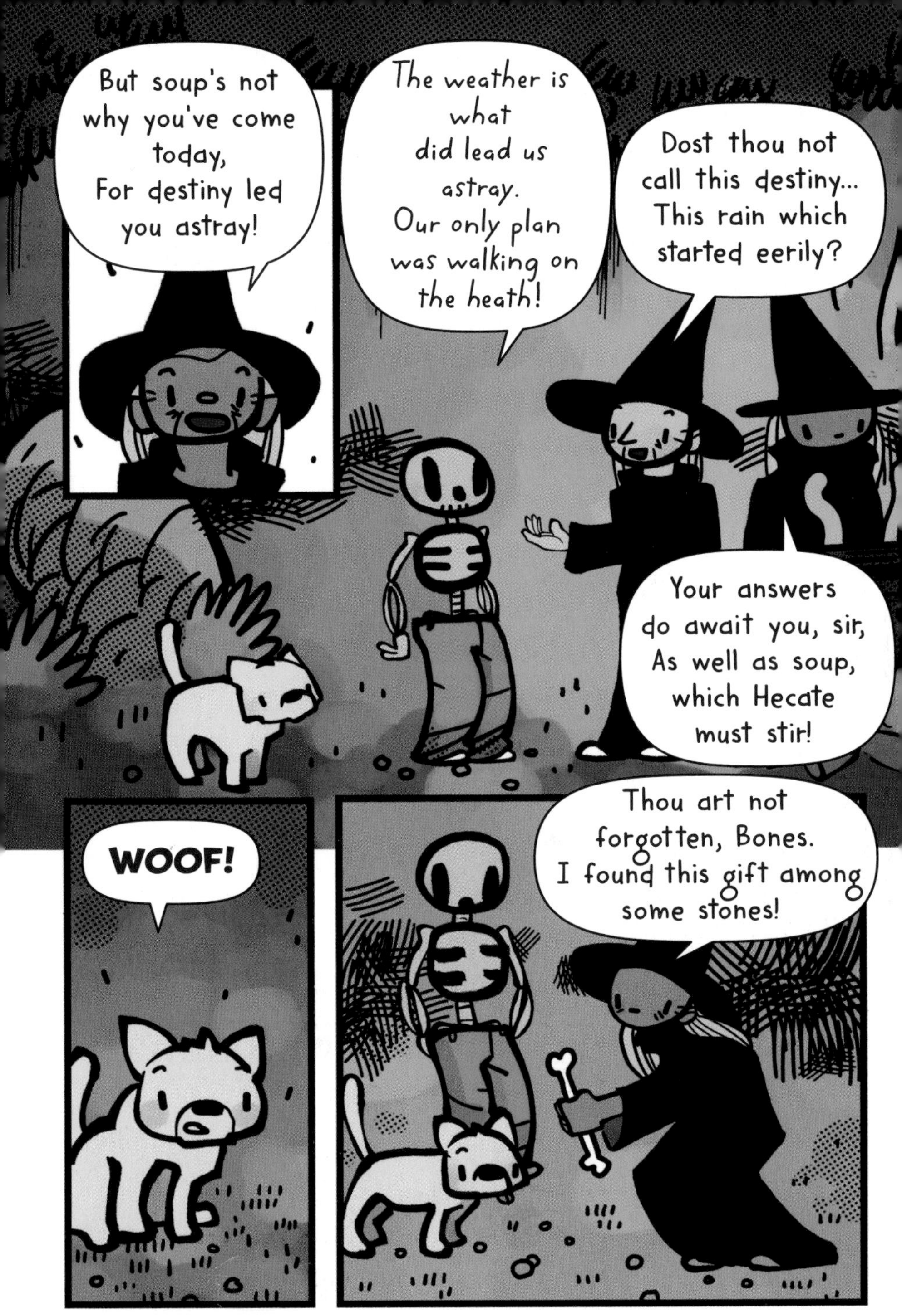
But soup's not why you've come today, For destiny led you astray!
The weather is what did lead us astray. Our only plan was walking on the heath!
Dost thou not call this destiny... This rain which started eerily?
Your answers do await you, sir, As well as soup, which Hecate must stir!
WOOF!
Thou art not forgotten, Bones. I found this gift among some stones!

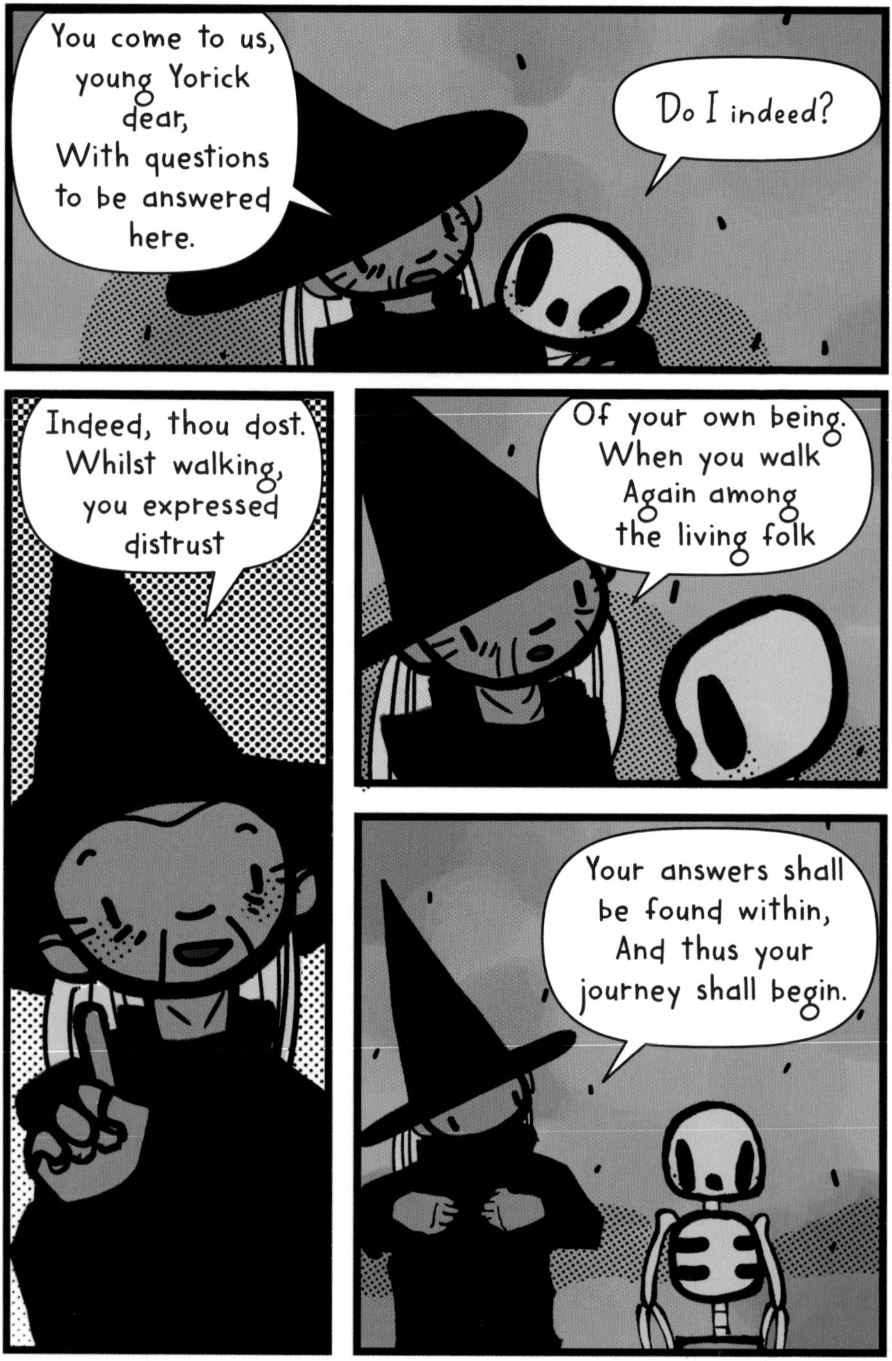
You come to us, young Yorick dear, With questions to be answered here.
Do I indeed?
Indeed, thou dost. Whilst walking, you expressed distrust
Of your own being. When you walk Again among the living folk
Your answers shall be found within, And thus your journey shall begin.

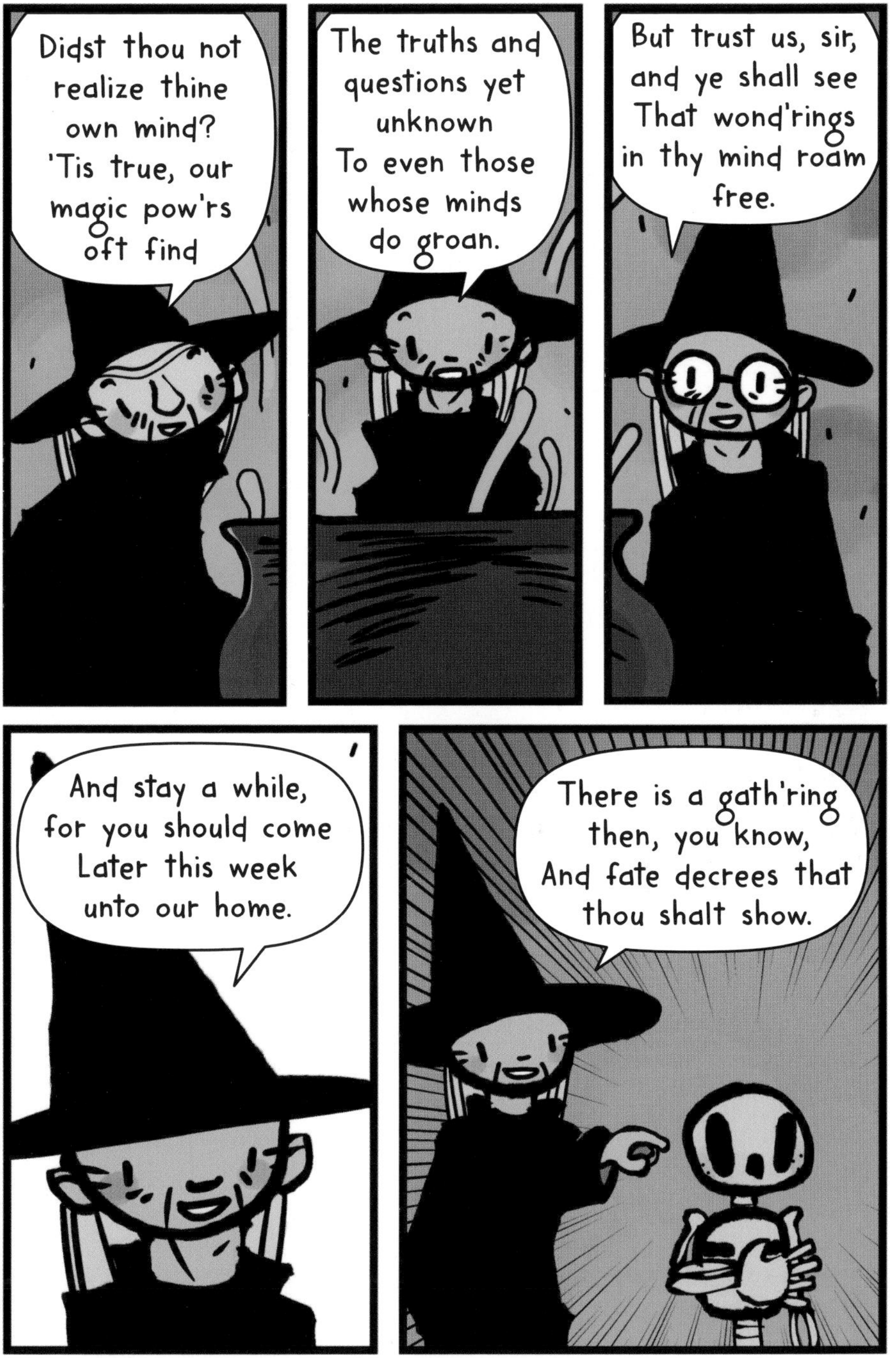
Didst thou not realize thine own mind? 'Tis true, our magic pow'rs oft find
The truths and questions yet unknown To even those whose minds do groan.
But trust us, sir, and ye shall see That wond'rings in thy mind roam free.
And stay a while, for you should come Later this week unto our home.
There is a gath'ring then, you know, And fate decrees that thou shalt show.

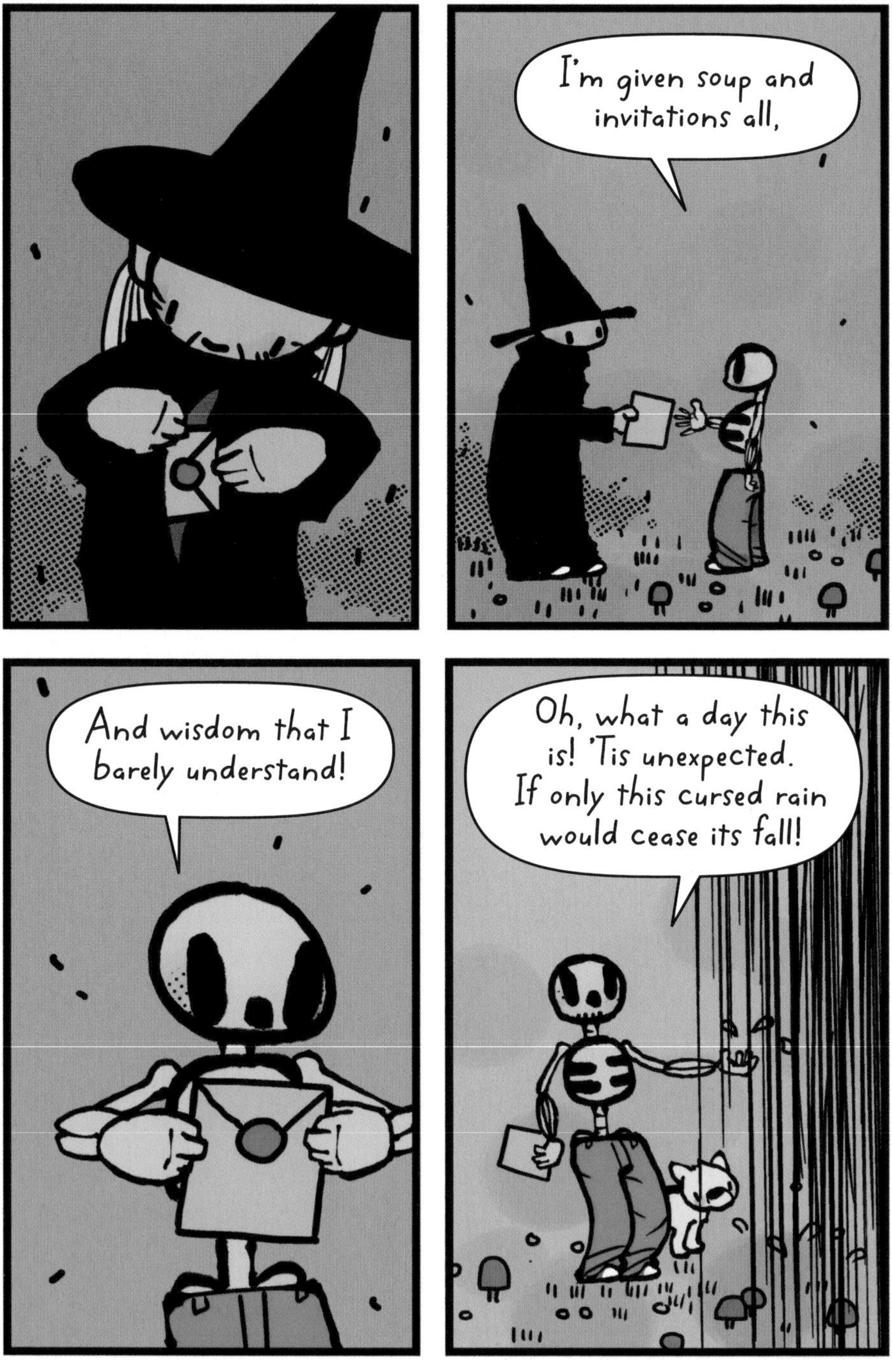
I'm given soup and invitations all,
And wisdom that I barely understand!
Oh, what a day this is! 'Tis unexpected. If only this cursed rain would cease its fall!

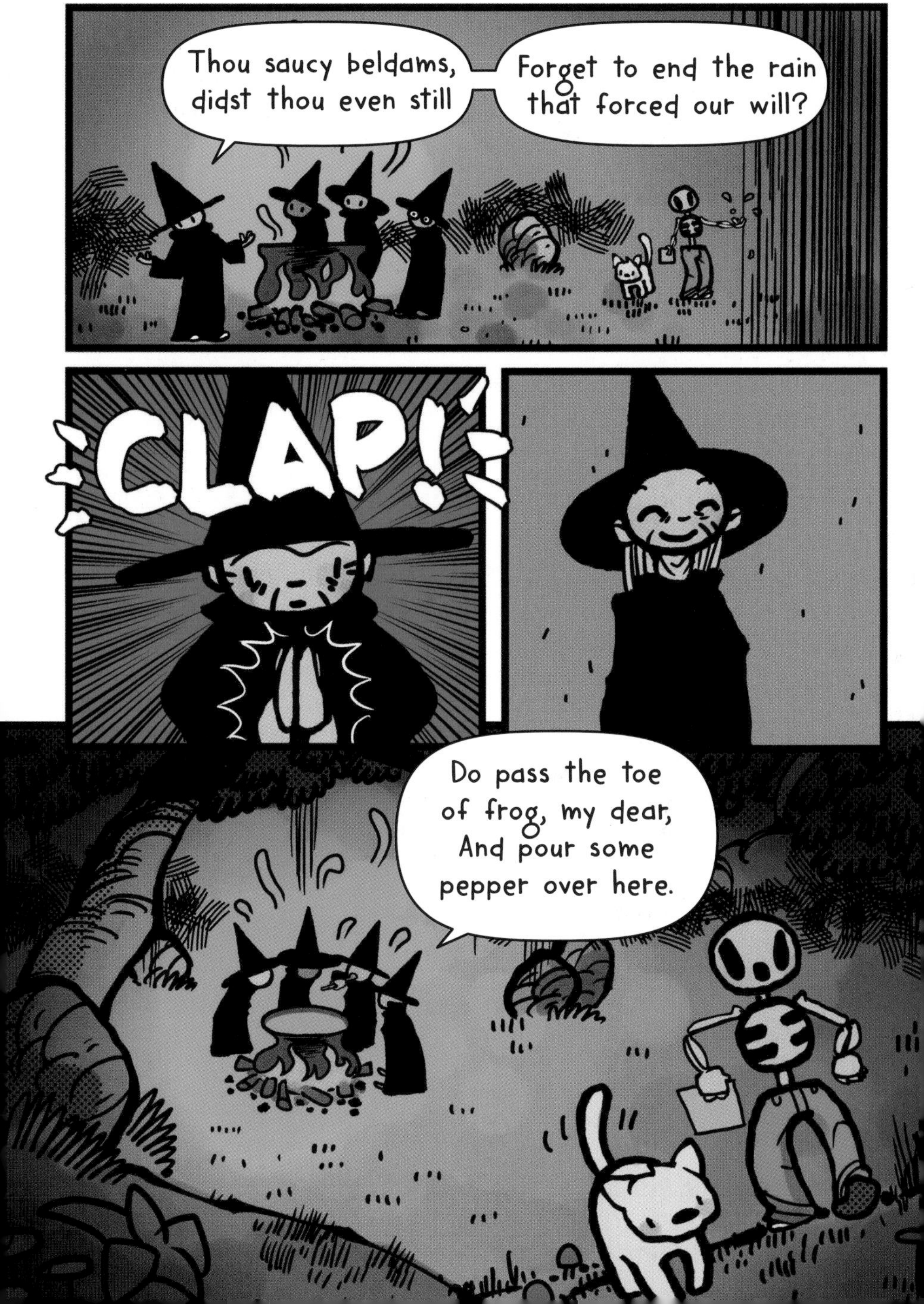

Thou saucy beldams, didst thou even still
Forget to end the rain that forced our will?
CLAP!
Do pass the toe of frog, my dear, And pour some pepper over here.

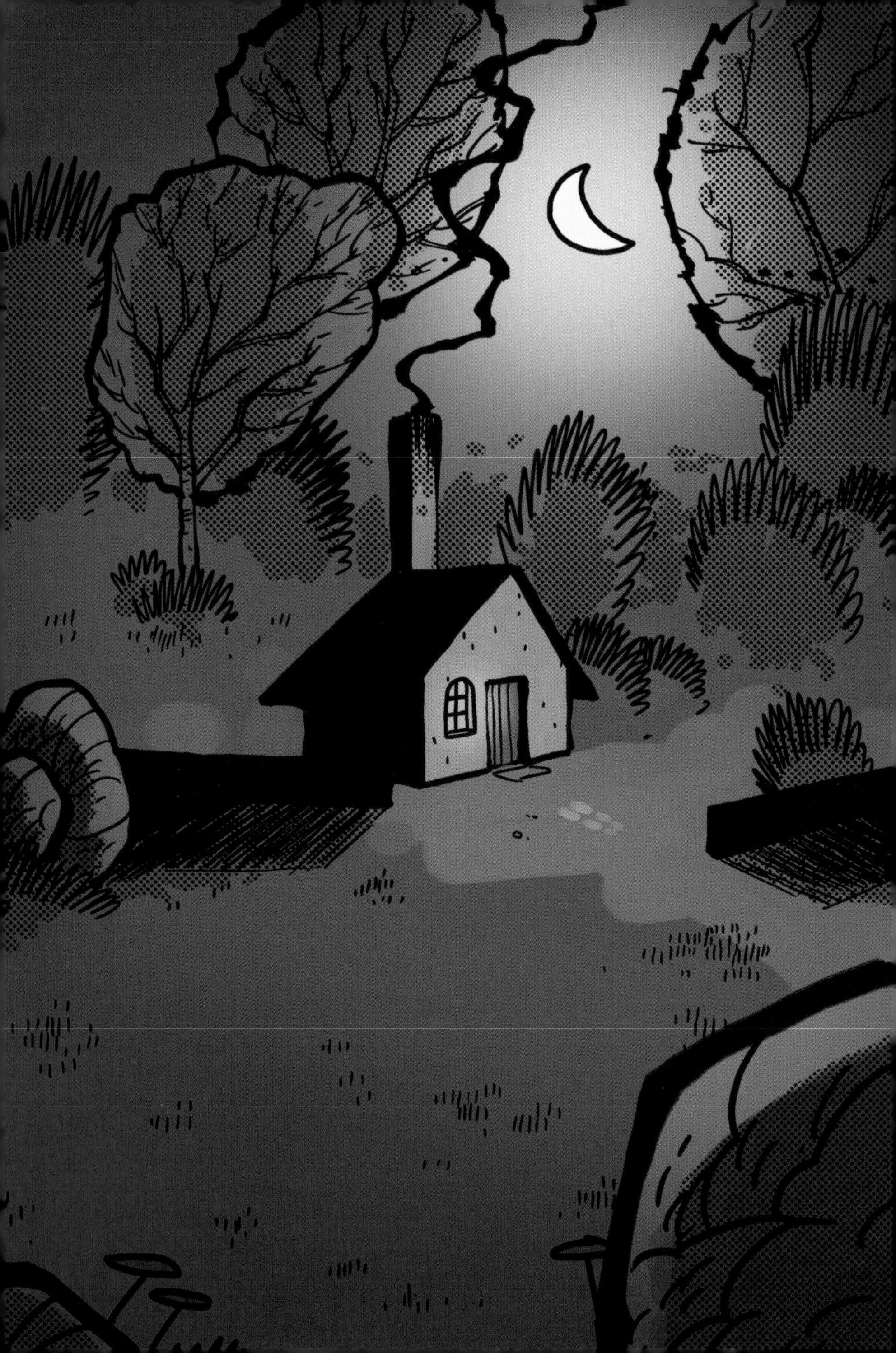

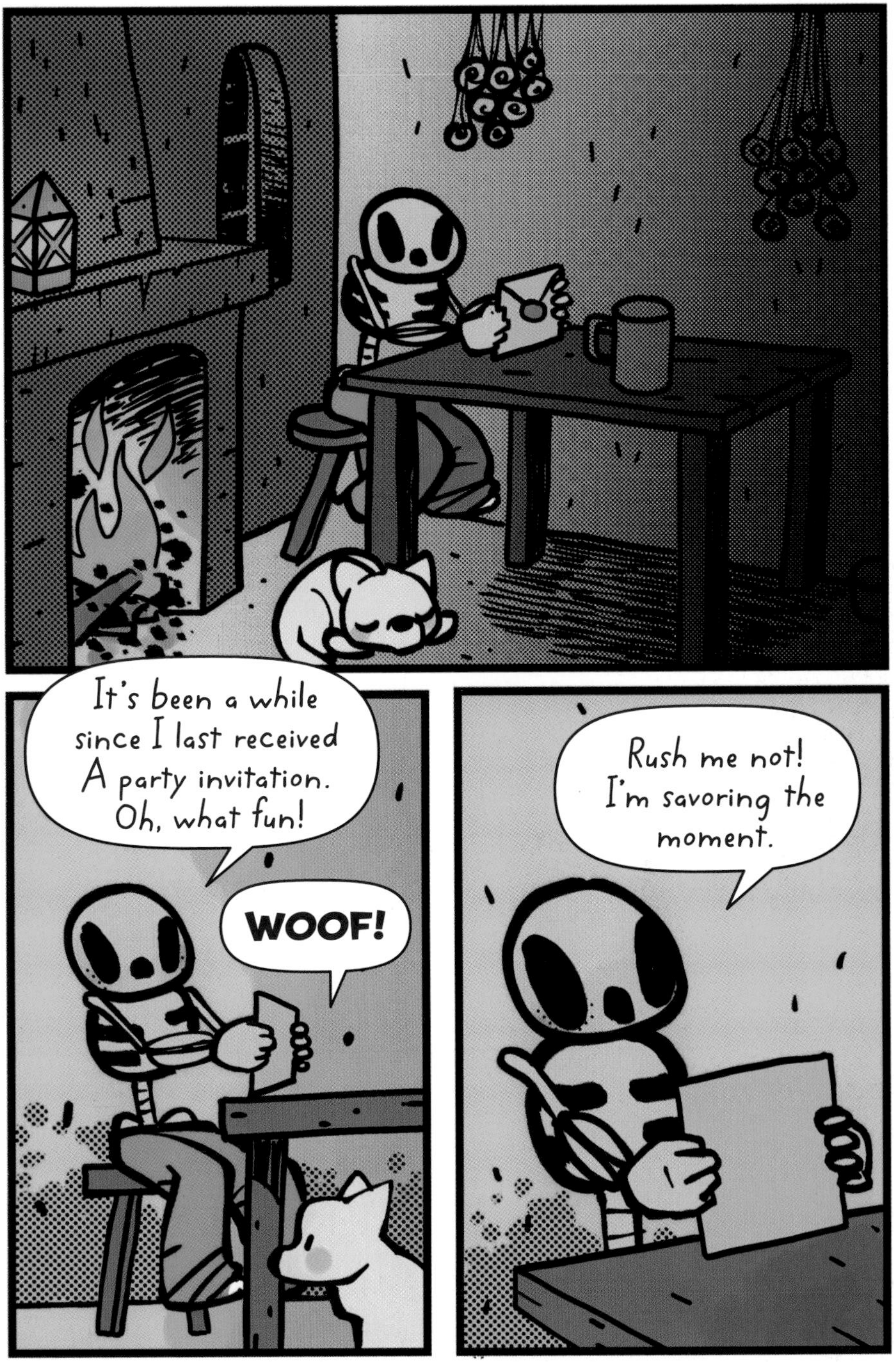
It's been a while since I last received A party invitation. Oh, what fun!
WOOF!
Rush me not! I'm savoring the moment.

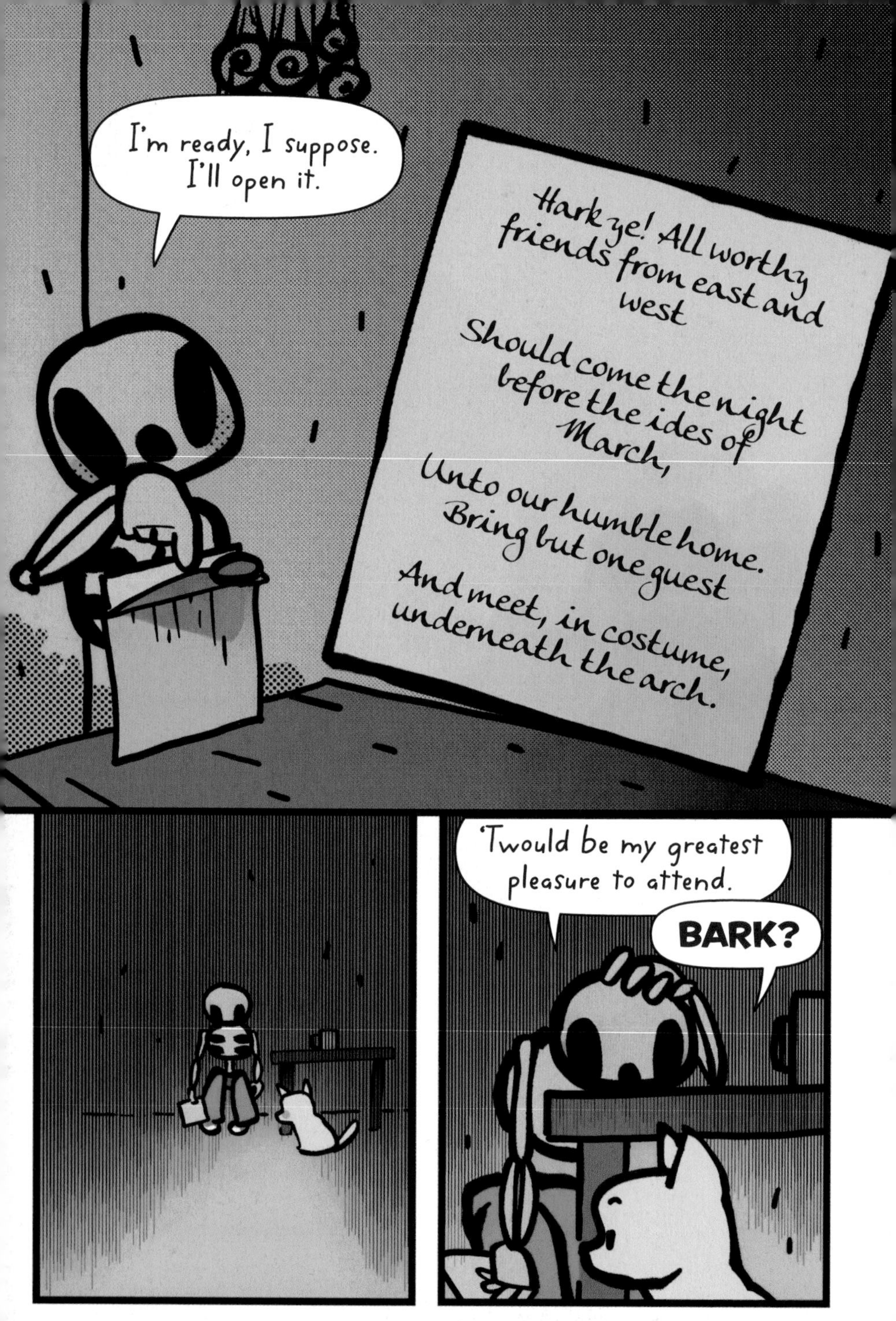
I'm ready, I suppose. I'll open it.
Hark ye! All worthy friends from east and west
Should come the night before the ides of March,
Unto our humble home. Bring but one guest
And meet, in costume, underneath the arch.
'Twould be my greatest pleasure to attend.
BARK?

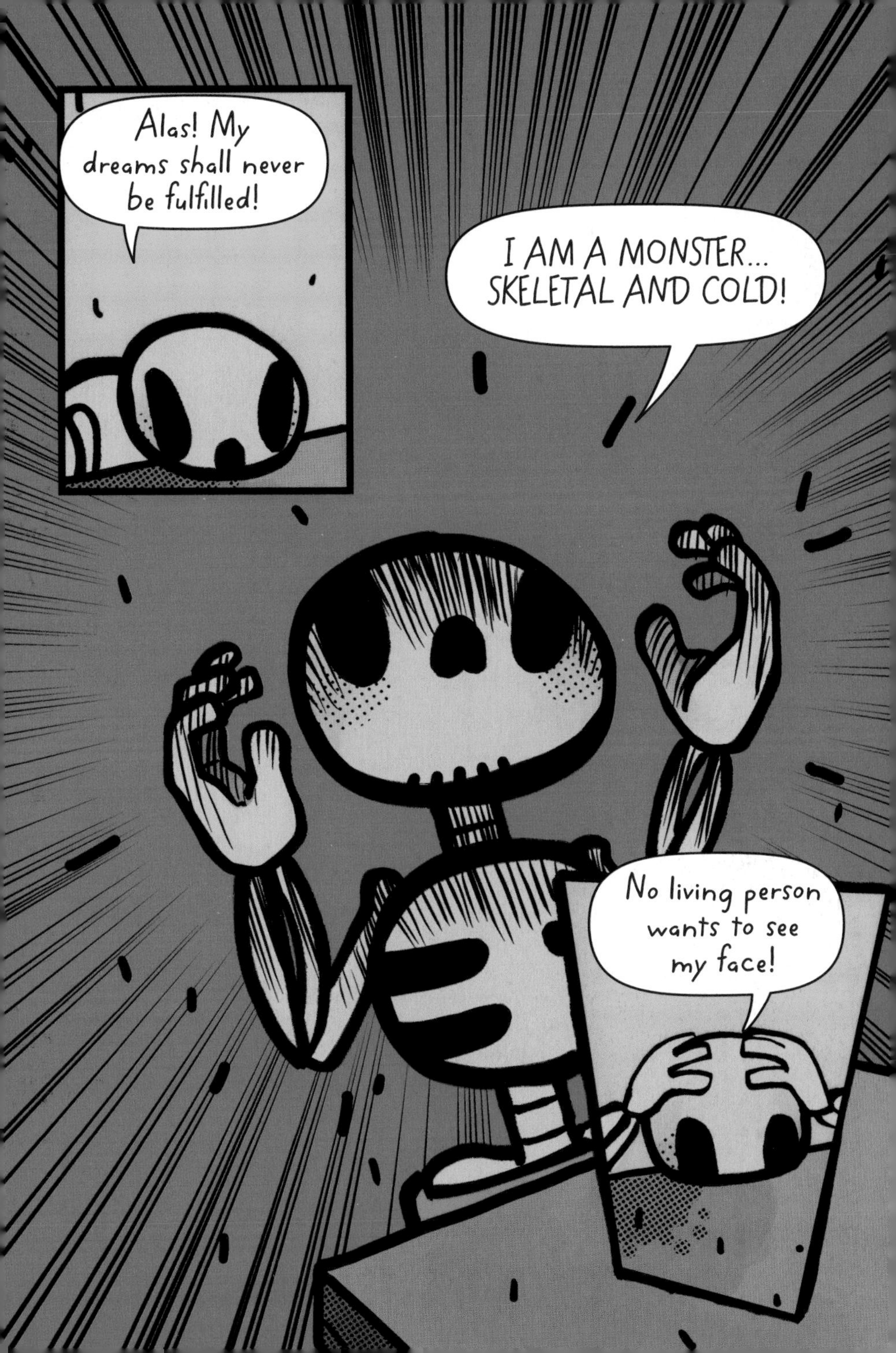
Alas! My dreams shall never be fulfilled!
I AM A MONSTER... SKELETAL AND COLD!
No living person wants to see my face!

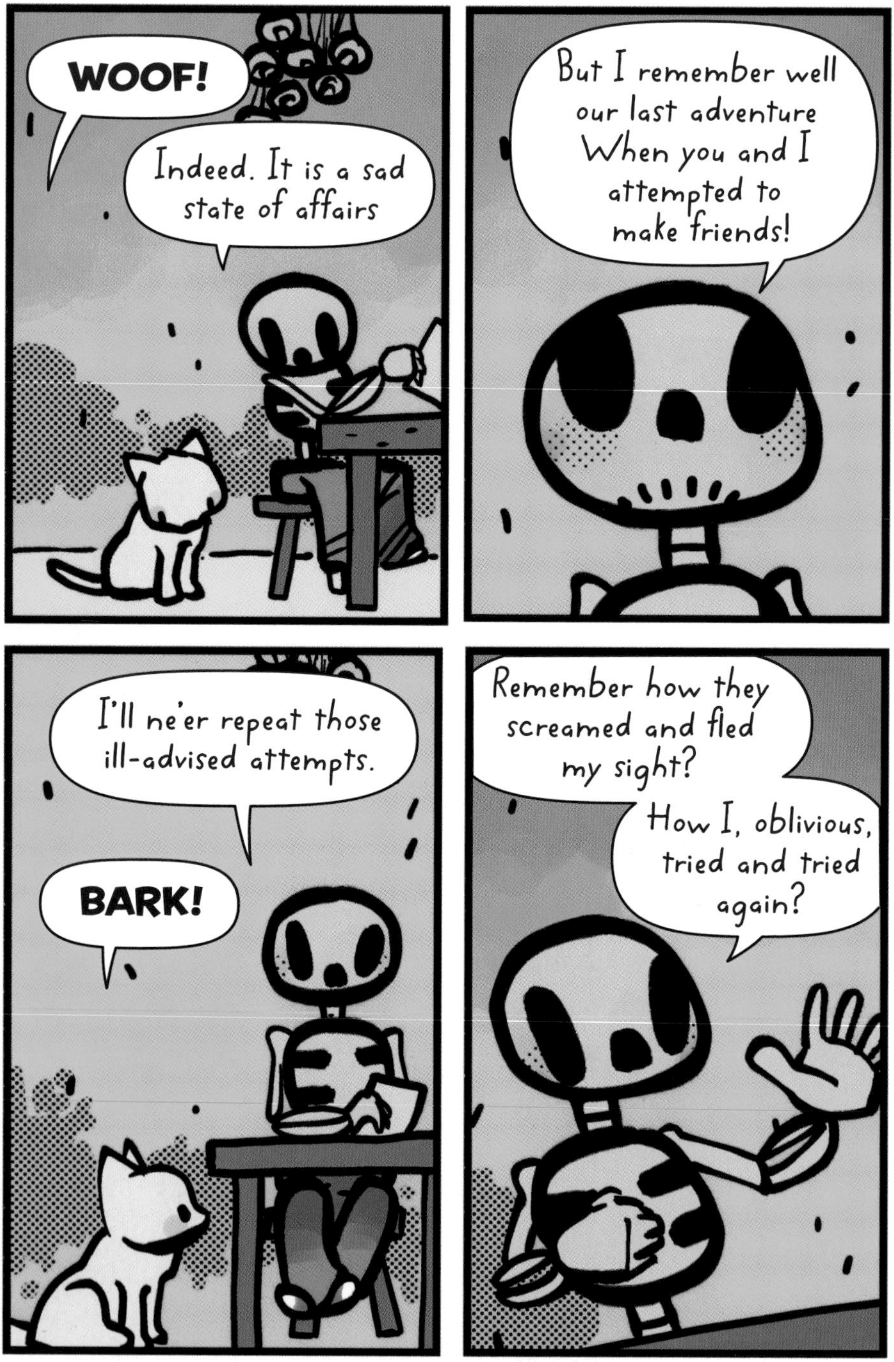
WOOF!
Indeed. It is a sad state of affairs
But I remember well our last adventure When you and I attempted to make friends!
I'll ne'er repeat those ill-advised attempts.
BARK!
Remember how they screamed and fled my sight?
How I, oblivious, tried and tried again?

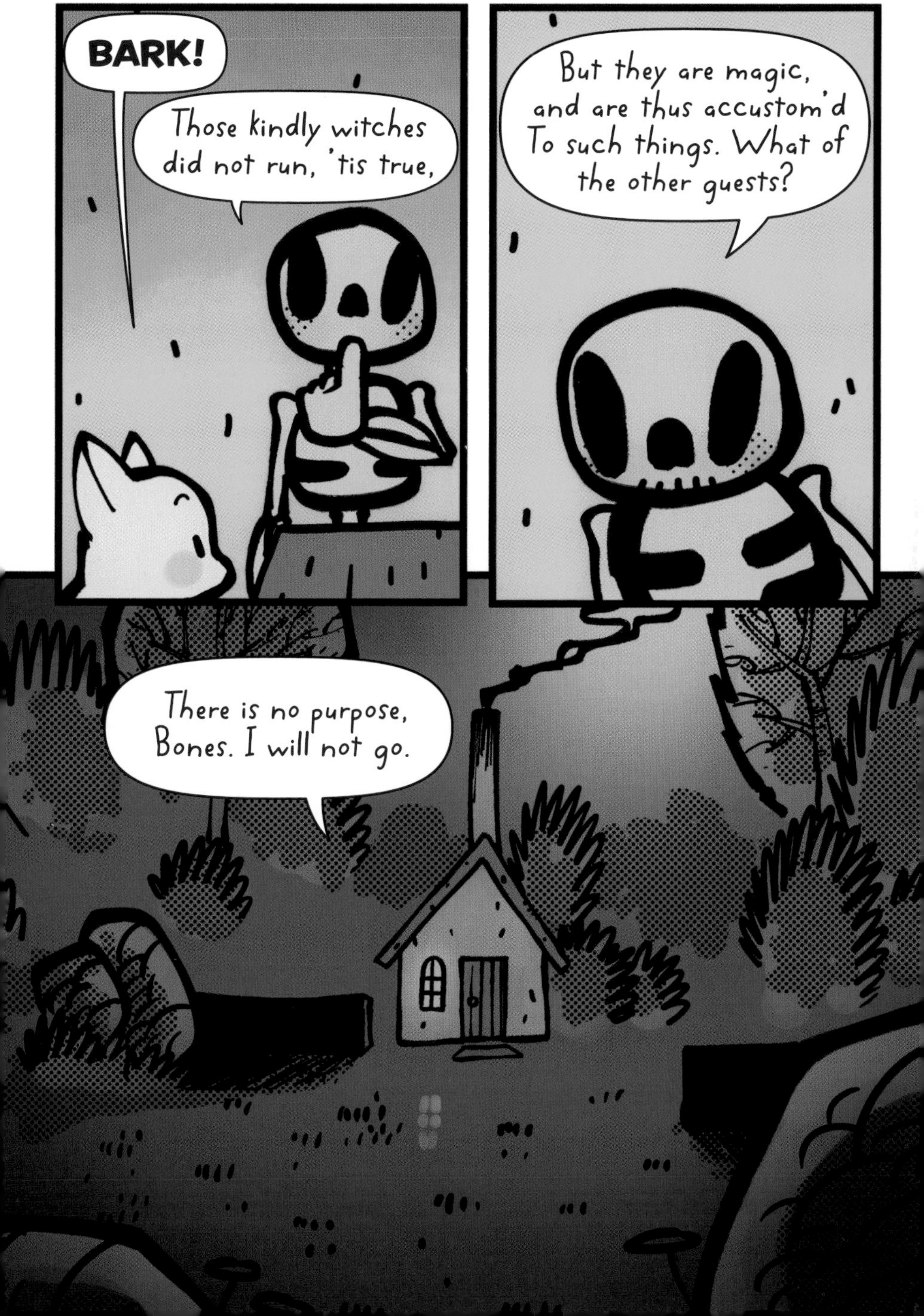
BARK!
Those kindly witches did not run, 'tis true,
But they are magic, and are thus accustom'd To such things. What of the other guests?
There is no purpose, Bones. I will not go.

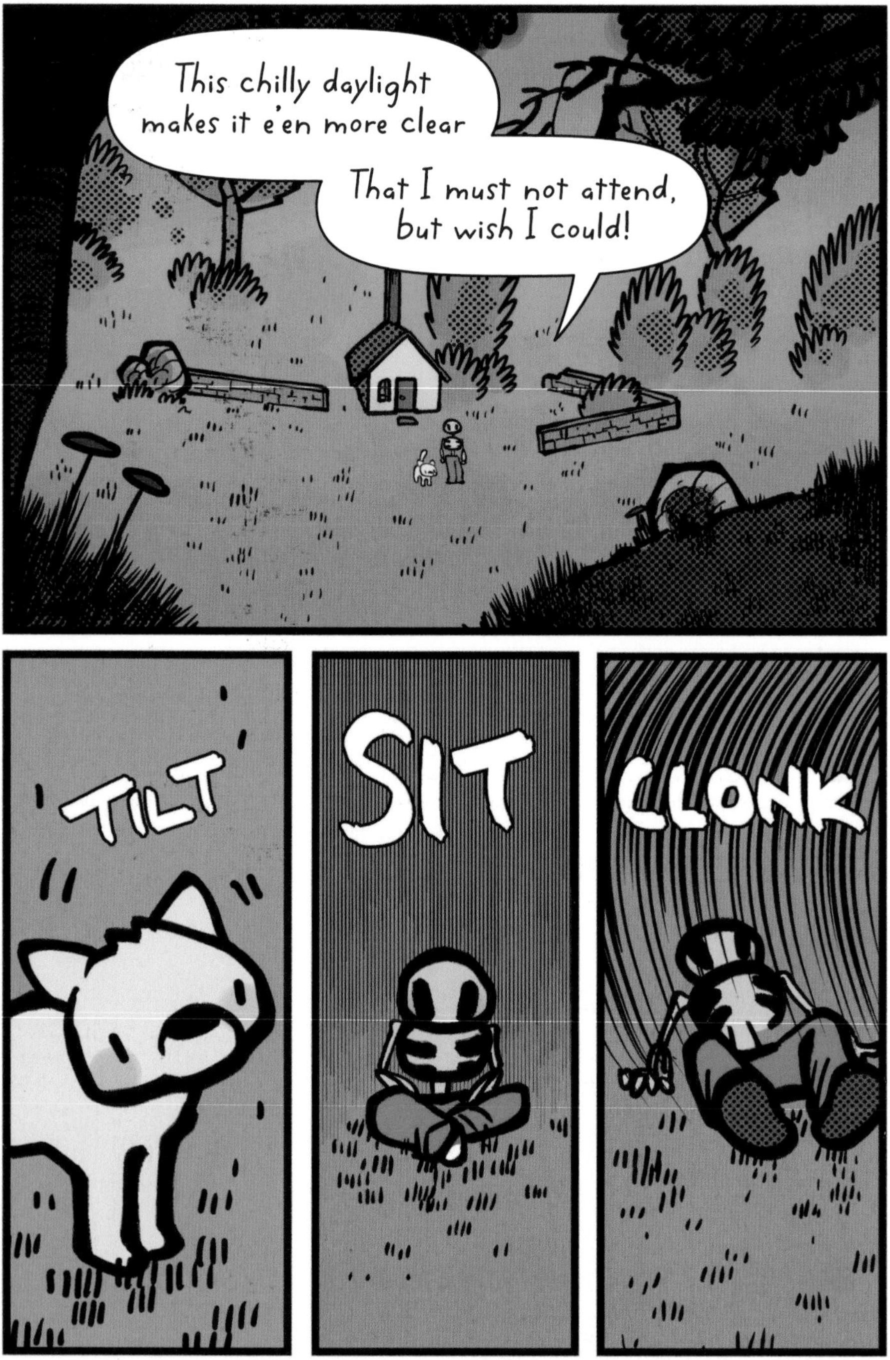
This chilly daylight makes it e'en more clear
That I must not attend, but wish I could!
TILT
SIT
CLONK

WHOOSH
drag drag drag
BARK! BARK! BARK!

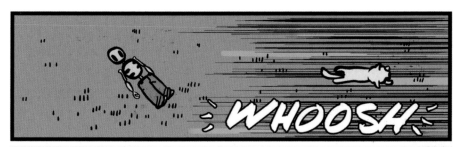

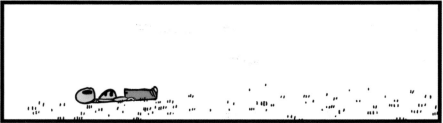

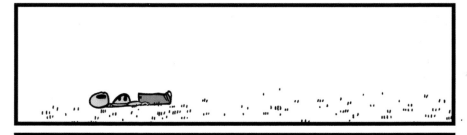

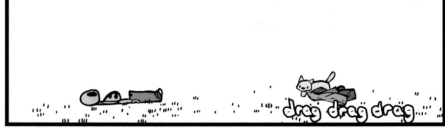

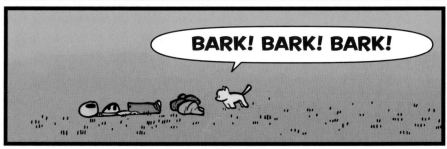

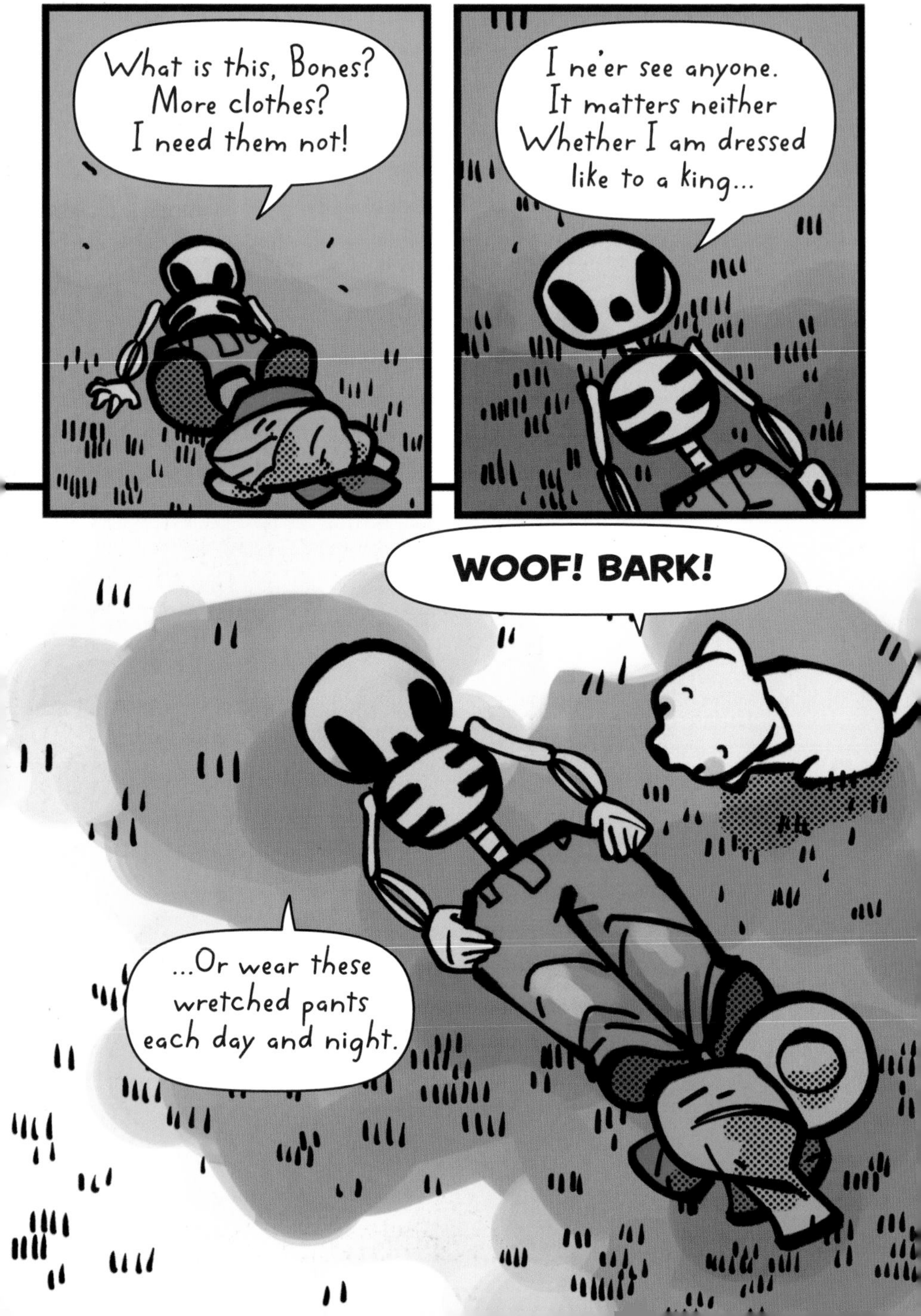
What is this, Bones? More clothes? I need them not!
I ne'er see anyone. It matters neither Whether I am dressed like to a king...
WOOF! BARK!
...Or wear these wretched pants each day and night.

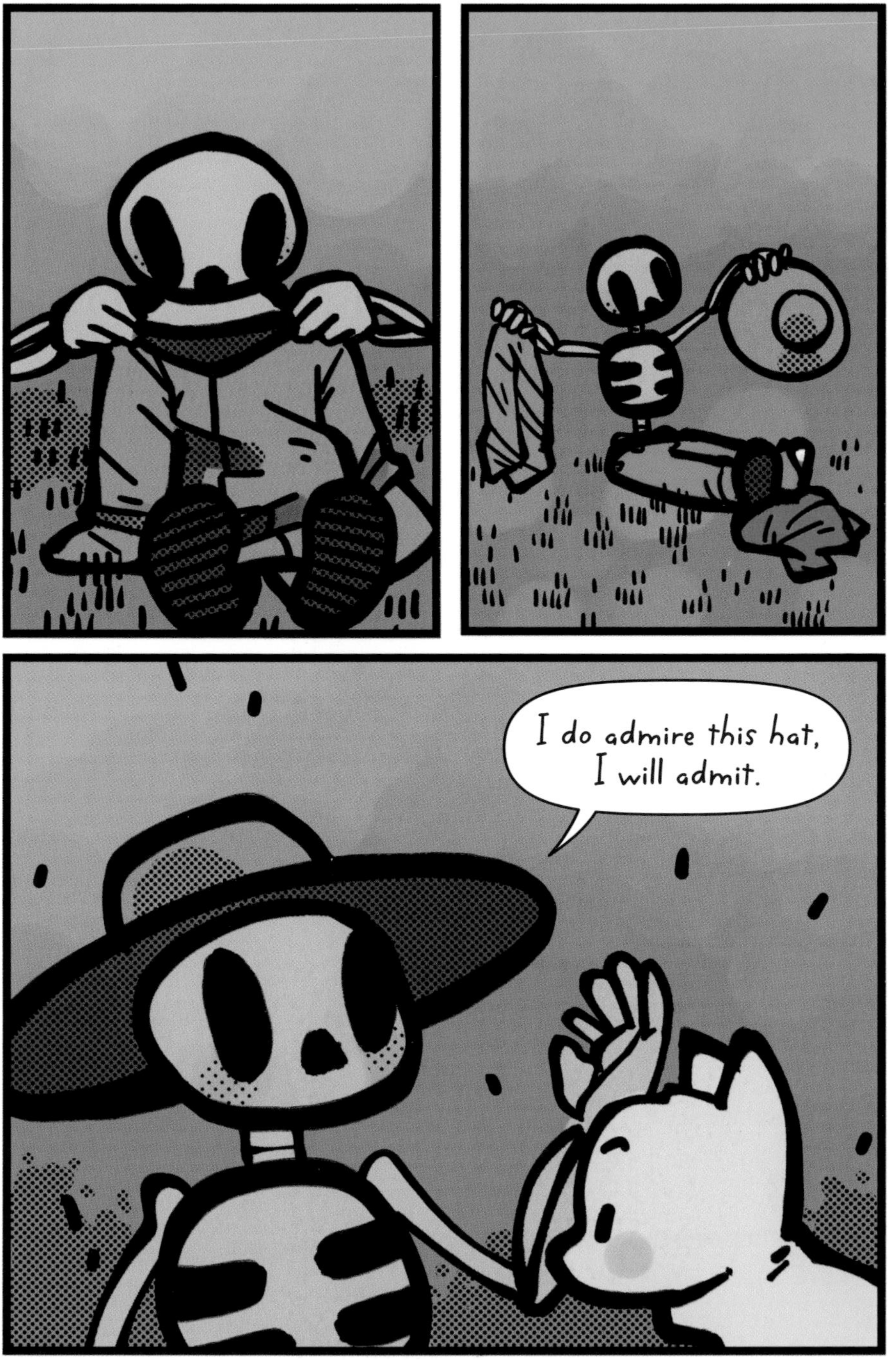
I do admire this hat, I will admit.

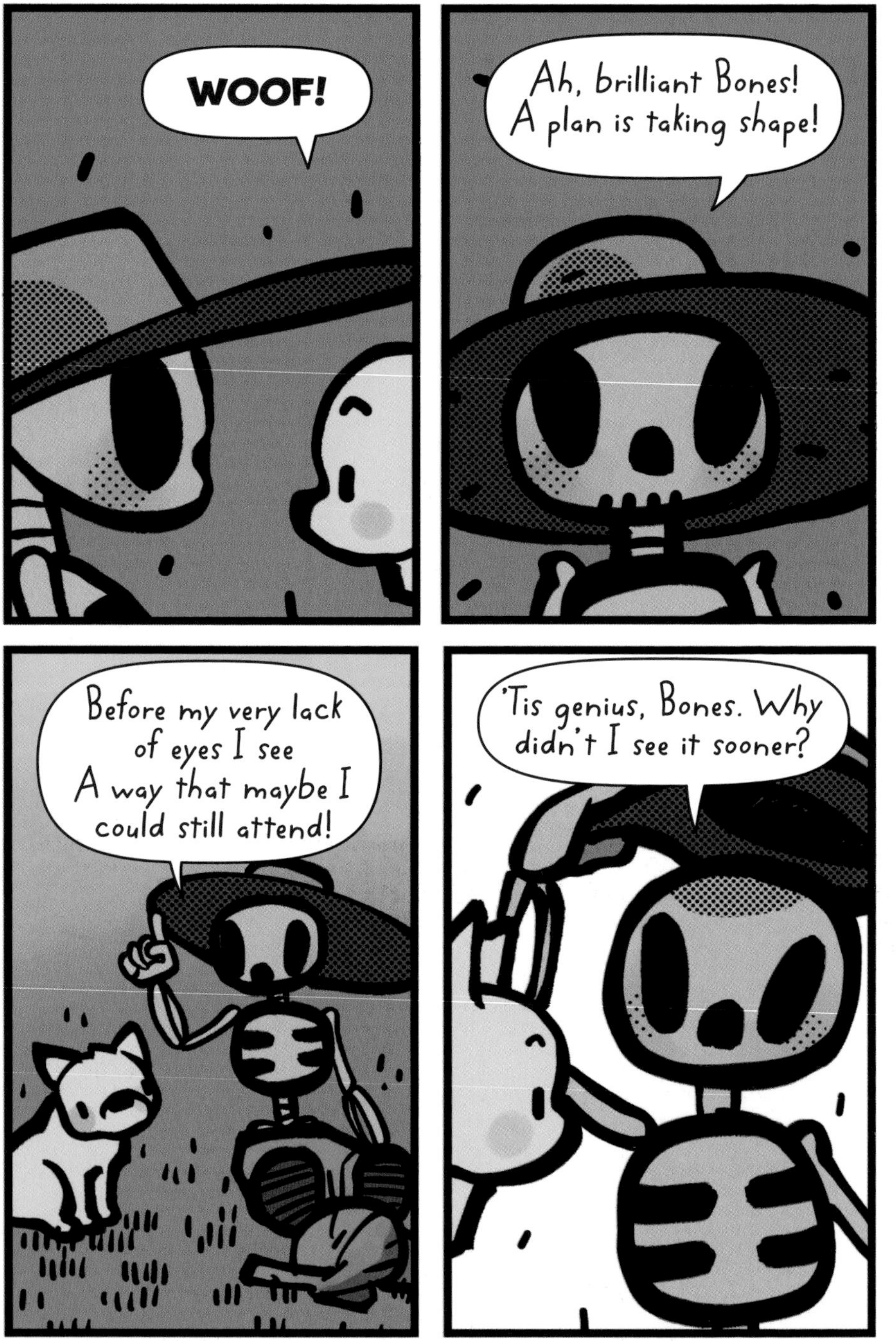
WOOF!
Ah, brilliant Bones! A plan is taking shape!
Before my very lack of eyes I see A way that maybe I could still attend!
'Tis genius, Bones. Why didn't I see it sooner?

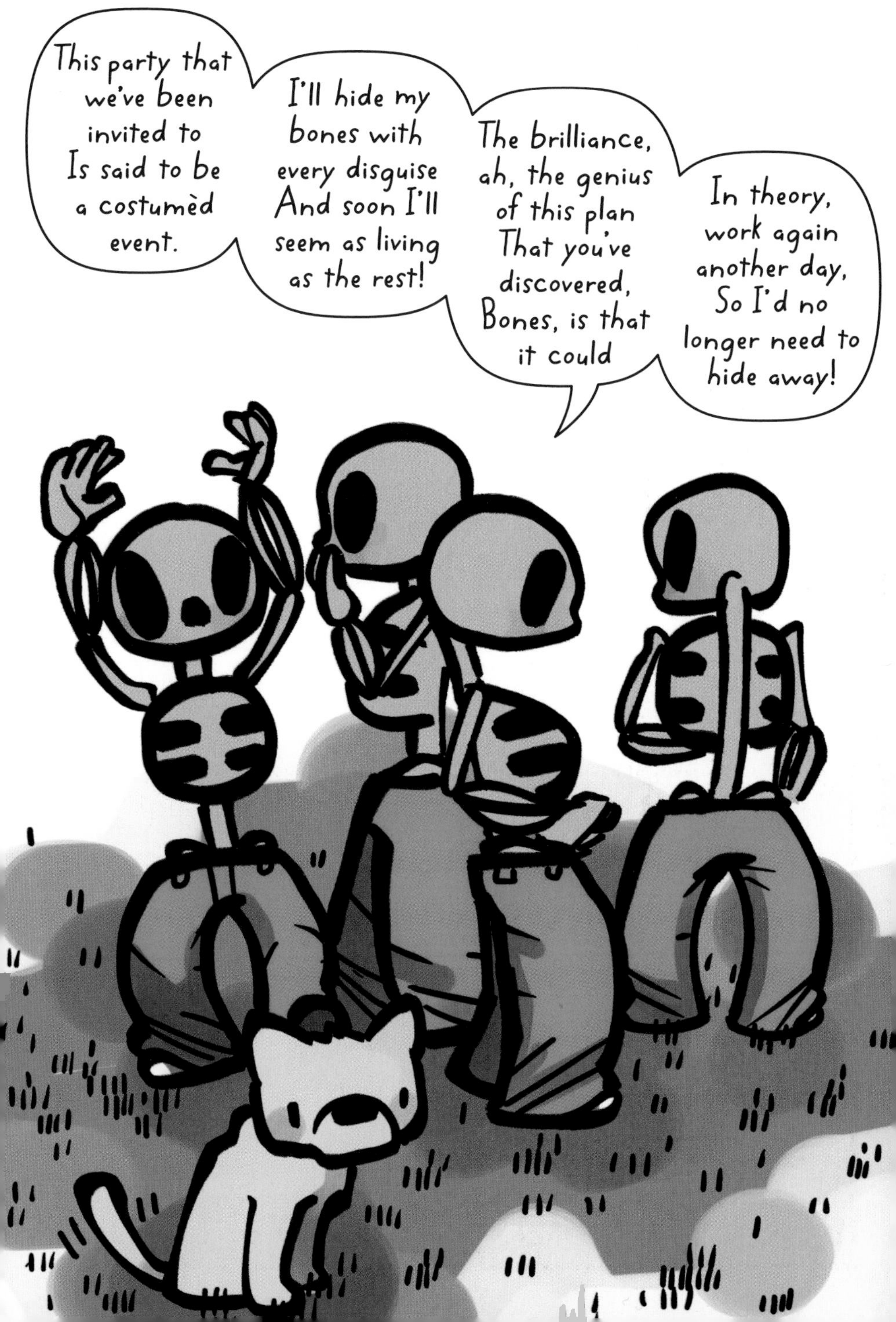
This party that we've been invited to Is said to be a costumèd event.
I'll hide my bones with every disguise And soon I'll seem as living as the rest!
The brilliance, ah, the genius of this plan That you've discovered, Bones, is that it could
In theory, work again another day, So I'd no longer need to hide away!

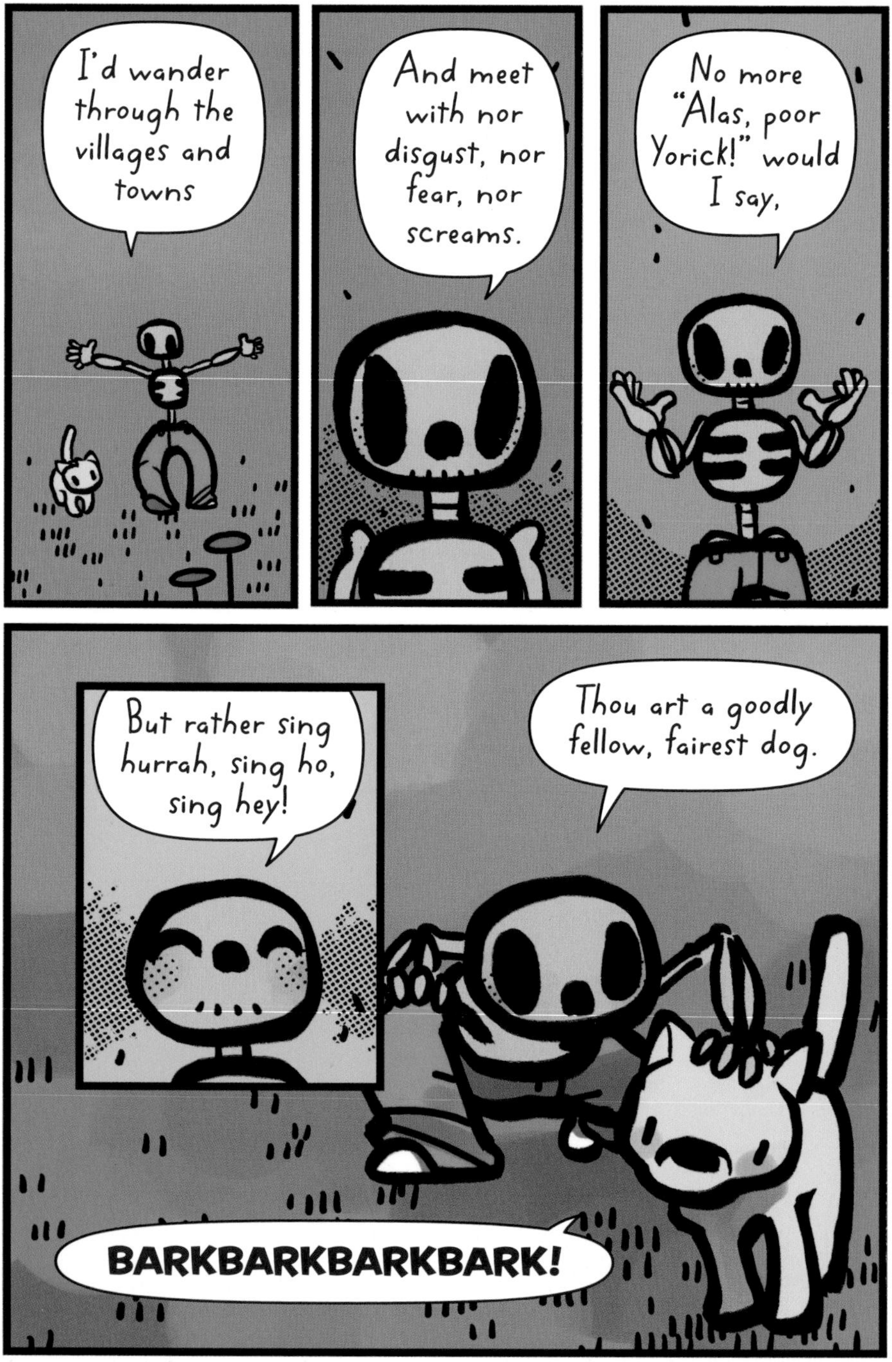
I'd wander through the villages and towns
And meet with nor disgust, nor fear, nor screams.
No more "Alas, poor Yorick!" would I say,
But rather sing hurrah, sing ho, sing hey!
Thou art a goodly fellow, fairest dog.
BARKBARKBARKBARK!

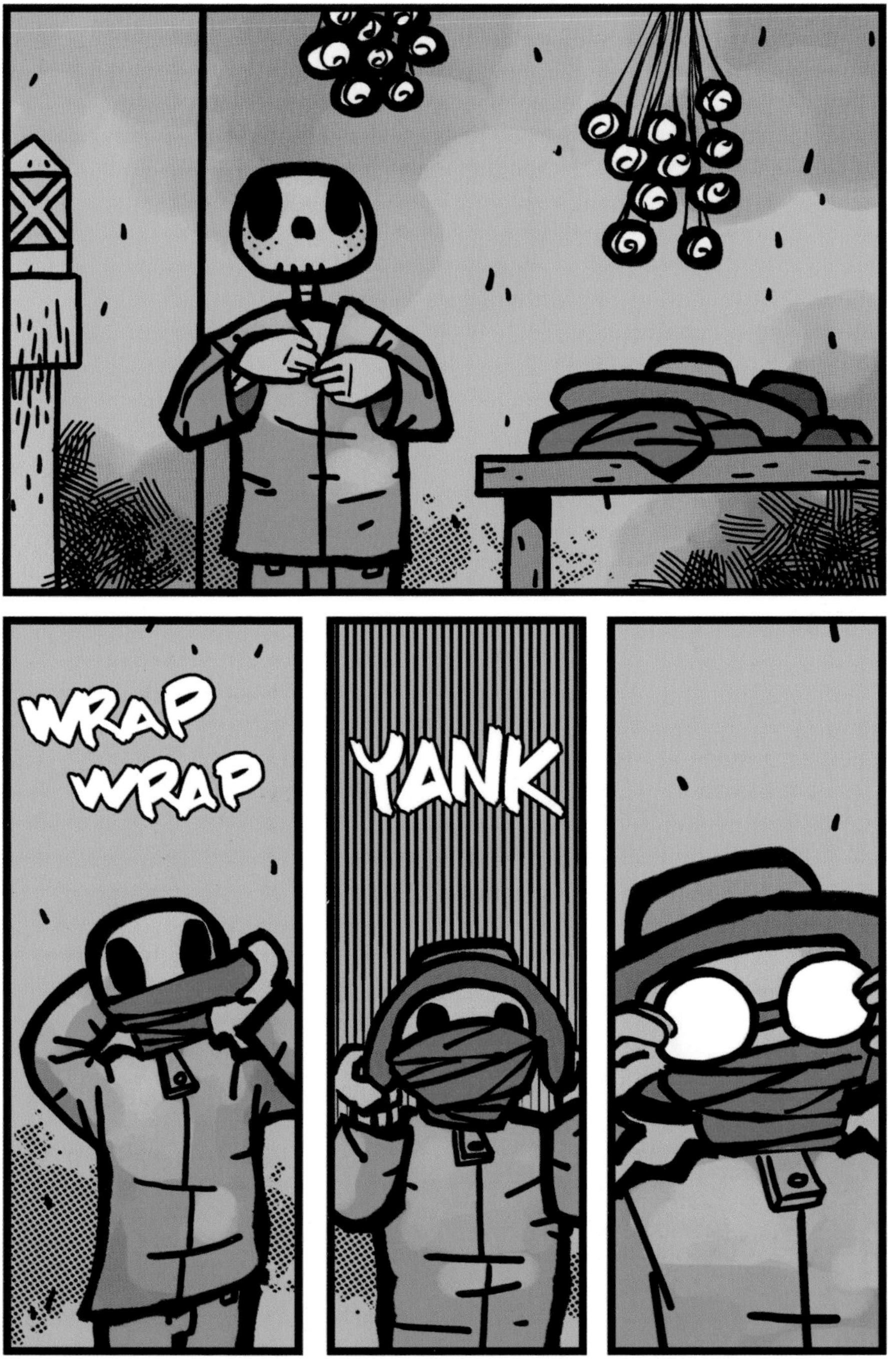
WRAP
WRAP
YANK

Oh gracious world!
Look, Bones,
you'd never know
By looking at me what
a thing I am!

But what to do
with thee, my dearest
friend?

To clothe thee
would not suit
thee well,
I'm sure.
What then
shalt thou
wear to be
disguised?

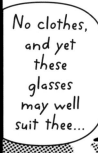

No clothes,
and yet
these
glasses
may well
suit thee...

WOOF!

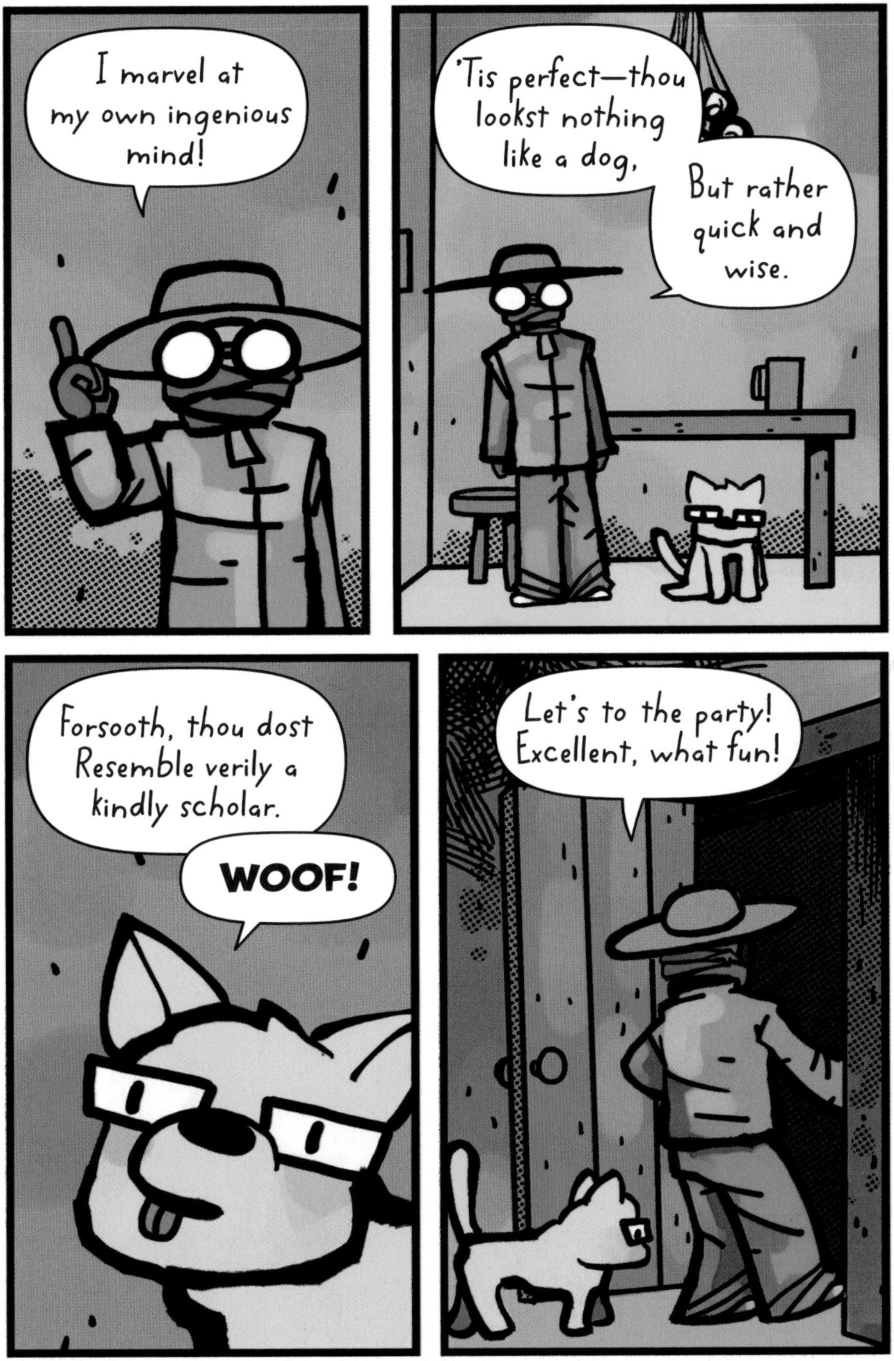
I marvel at my own ingenious mind!
'Tis perfect—thou lookst nothing like a dog,
But rather quick and wise.
Forsooth, thou dost Resemble verily a kindly scholar.
WOOF!
Let's to the party! Excellent, what fun!

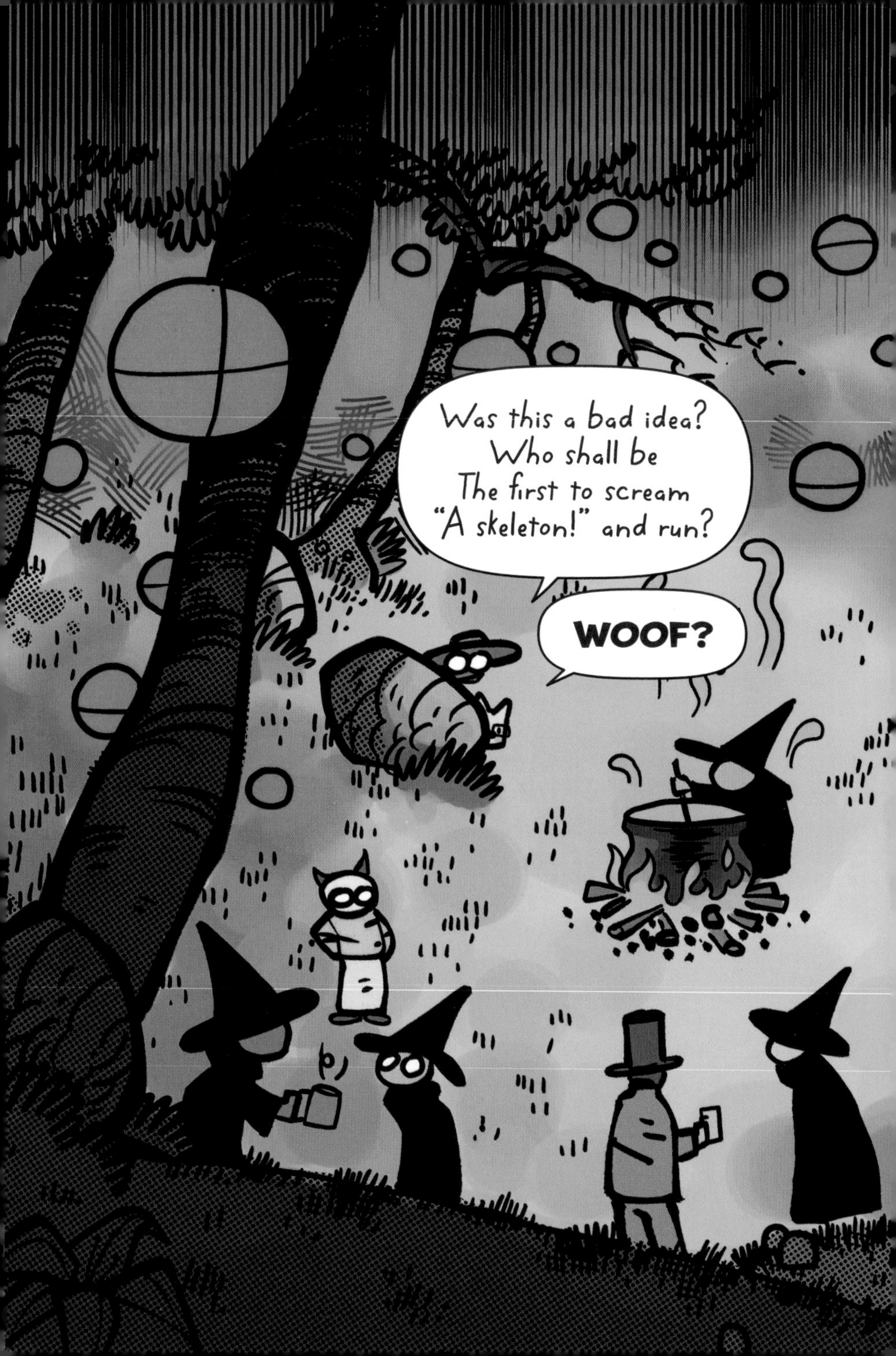
Was this a bad idea? Who shall be The first to scream "A skeleton!" and run?
WOOF?

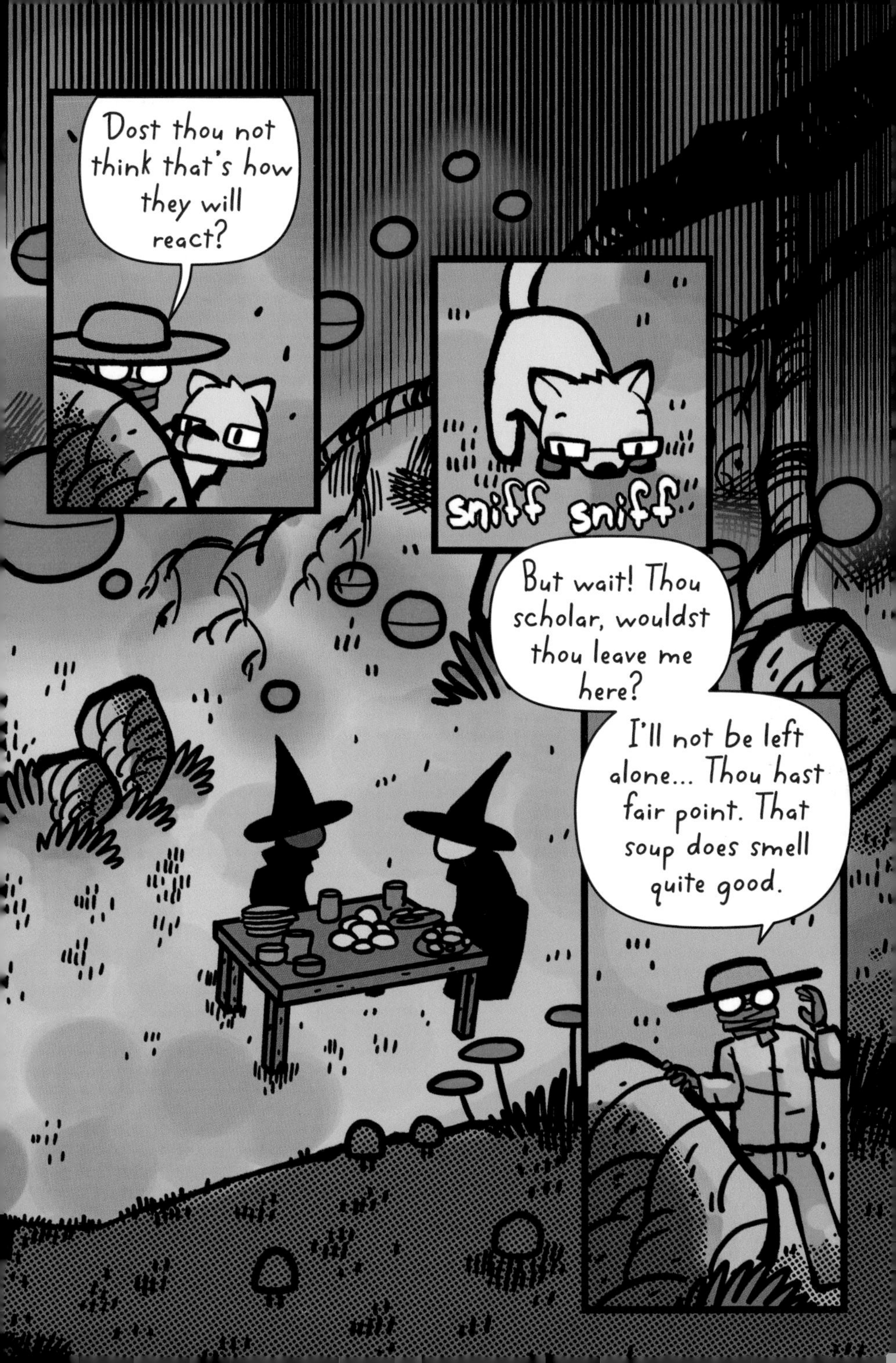
Dost thou not think that's how they will react?
sniff sniff
But wait! Thou scholar, wouldst thou leave me here?
I'll not be left alone... Thou hast fair point. That soup does smell quite good.

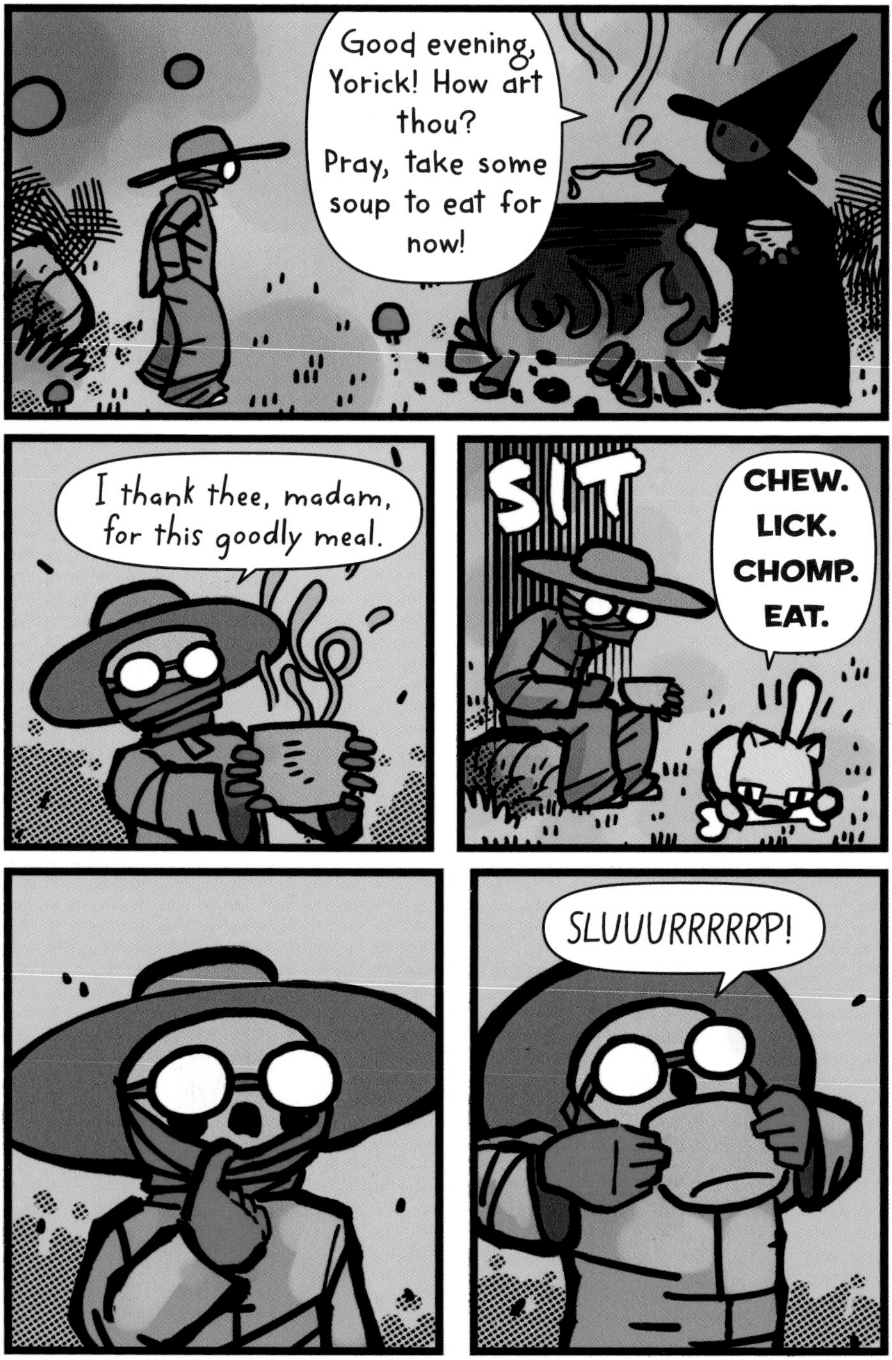
Good evening, Yorick! How art thou? Pray, take some soup to eat for now!
I thank thee, madam, for this goodly meal.
SIT
CHEW. LICK. CHOMP. EAT.
SLUUURRRRRP!

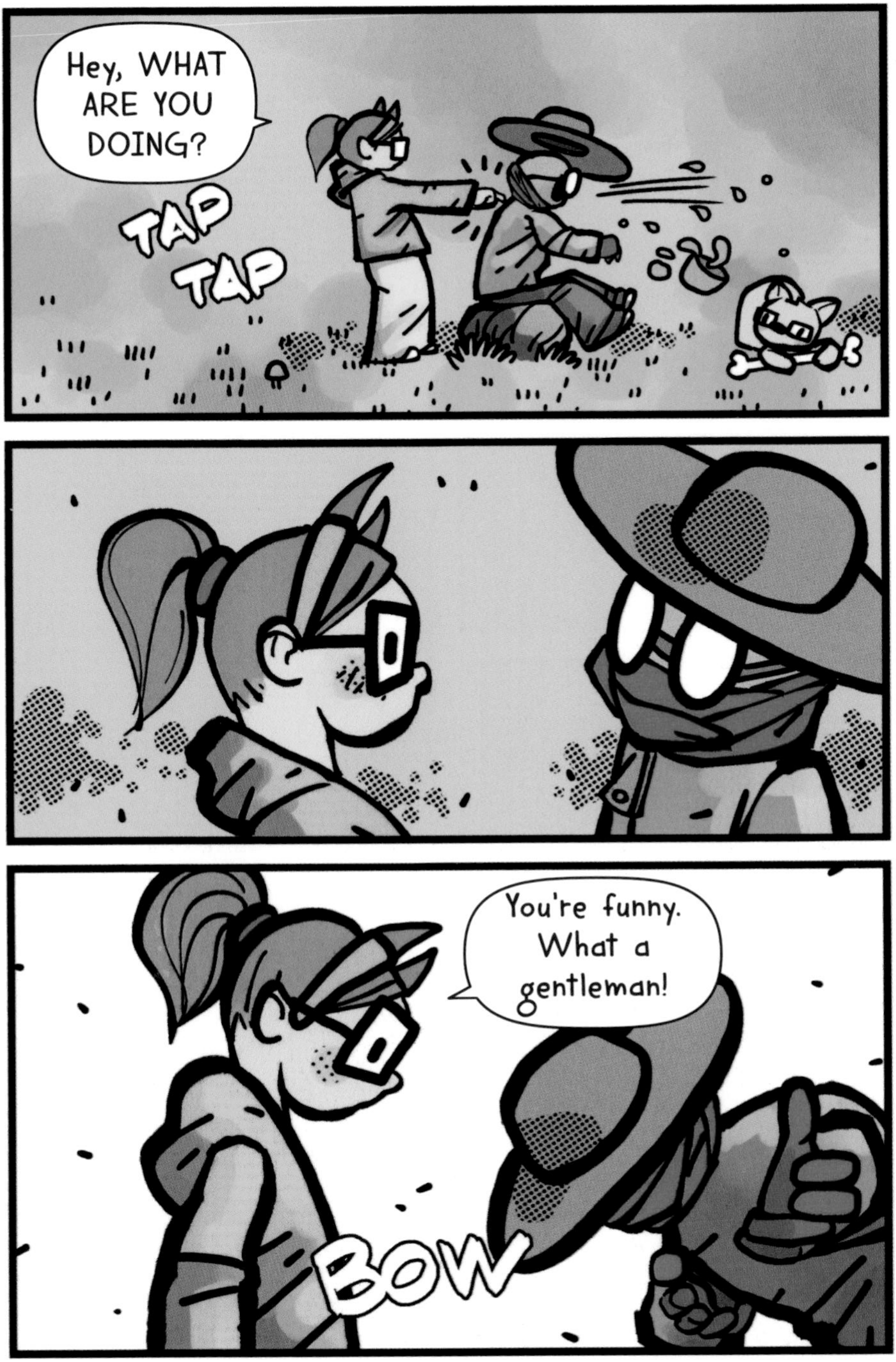
Hey, WHAT ARE YOU DOING?
TAP
TAP
You're funny. What a gentleman!
BOW

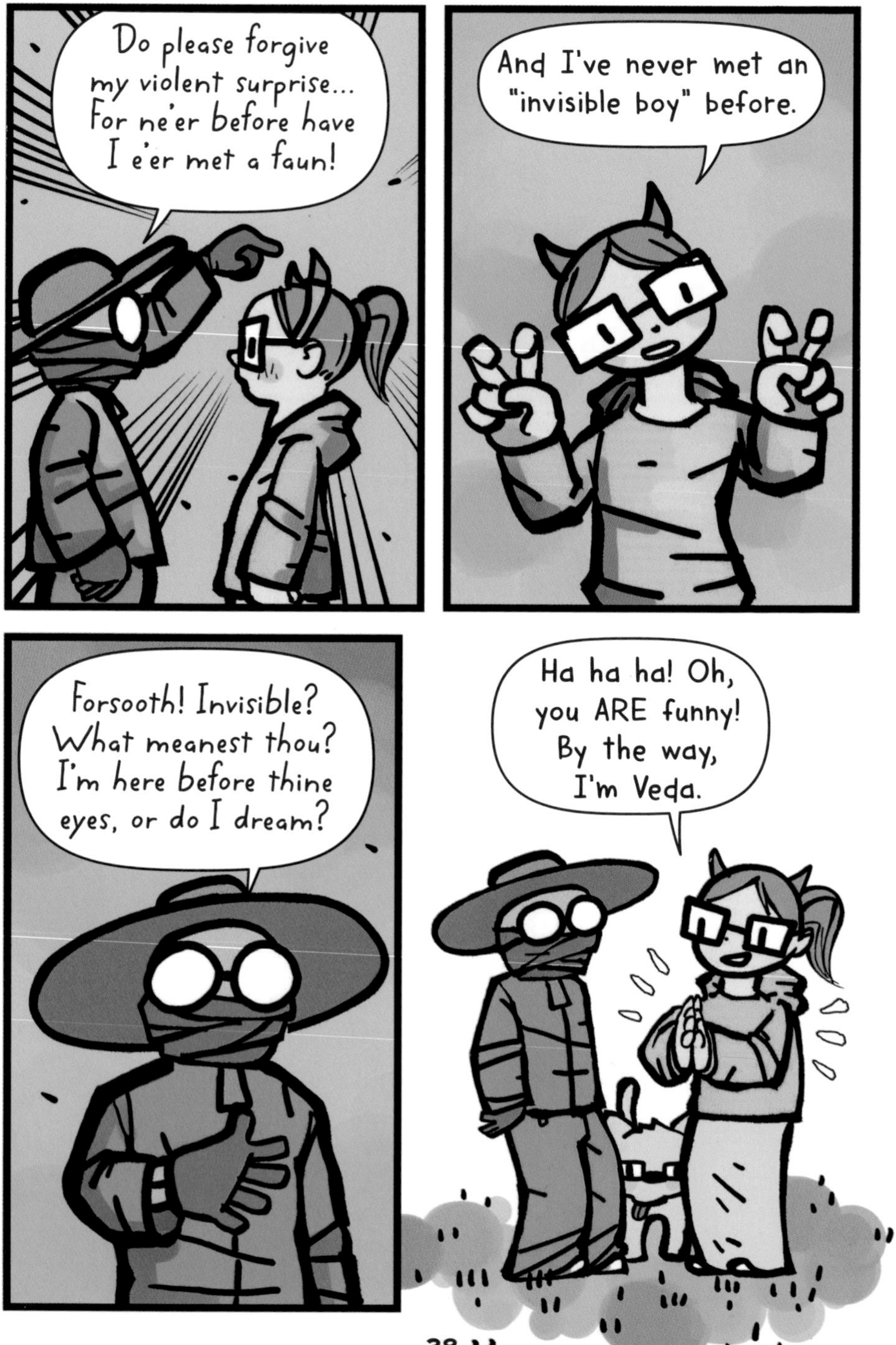
Do please forgive my violent surprise... For ne'er before have I e'er met a faun!
And I've never met an "invisible boy" before.
Forsooth! Invisible? What meanest thou? I'm here before thine eyes, or do I dream?
Ha ha ha! Oh, you ARE funny! By the way, I'm Veda.

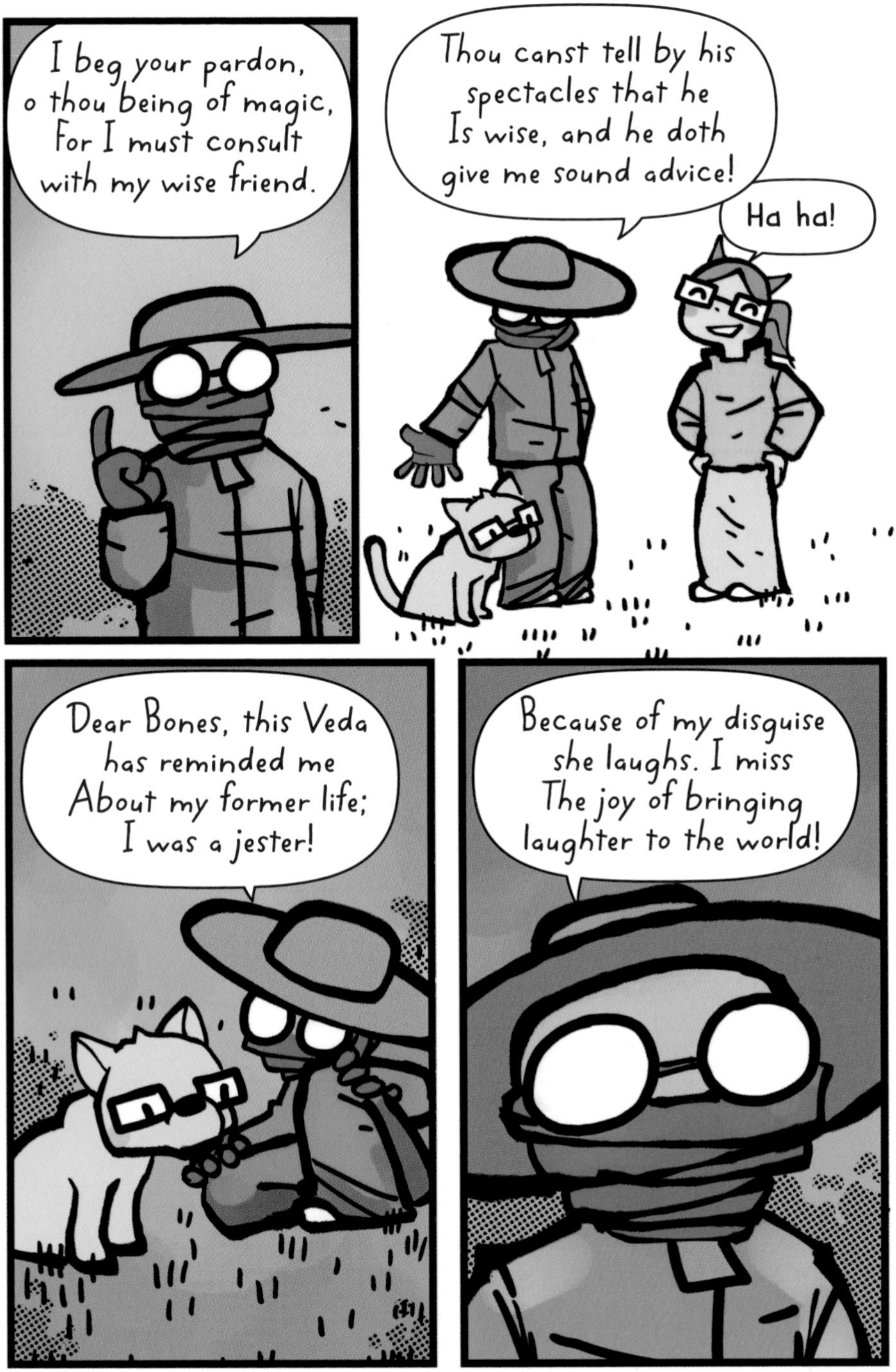
I beg your pardon, o thou being of magic, For I must consult with my wise friend.
Thou canst tell by his spectacles that he Is wise, and he doth give me sound advice!
Ha ha!
Dear Bones, this Veda has reminded me About my former life; I was a jester!
Because of my disguise she laughs. I miss The joy of bringing laughter to the world!

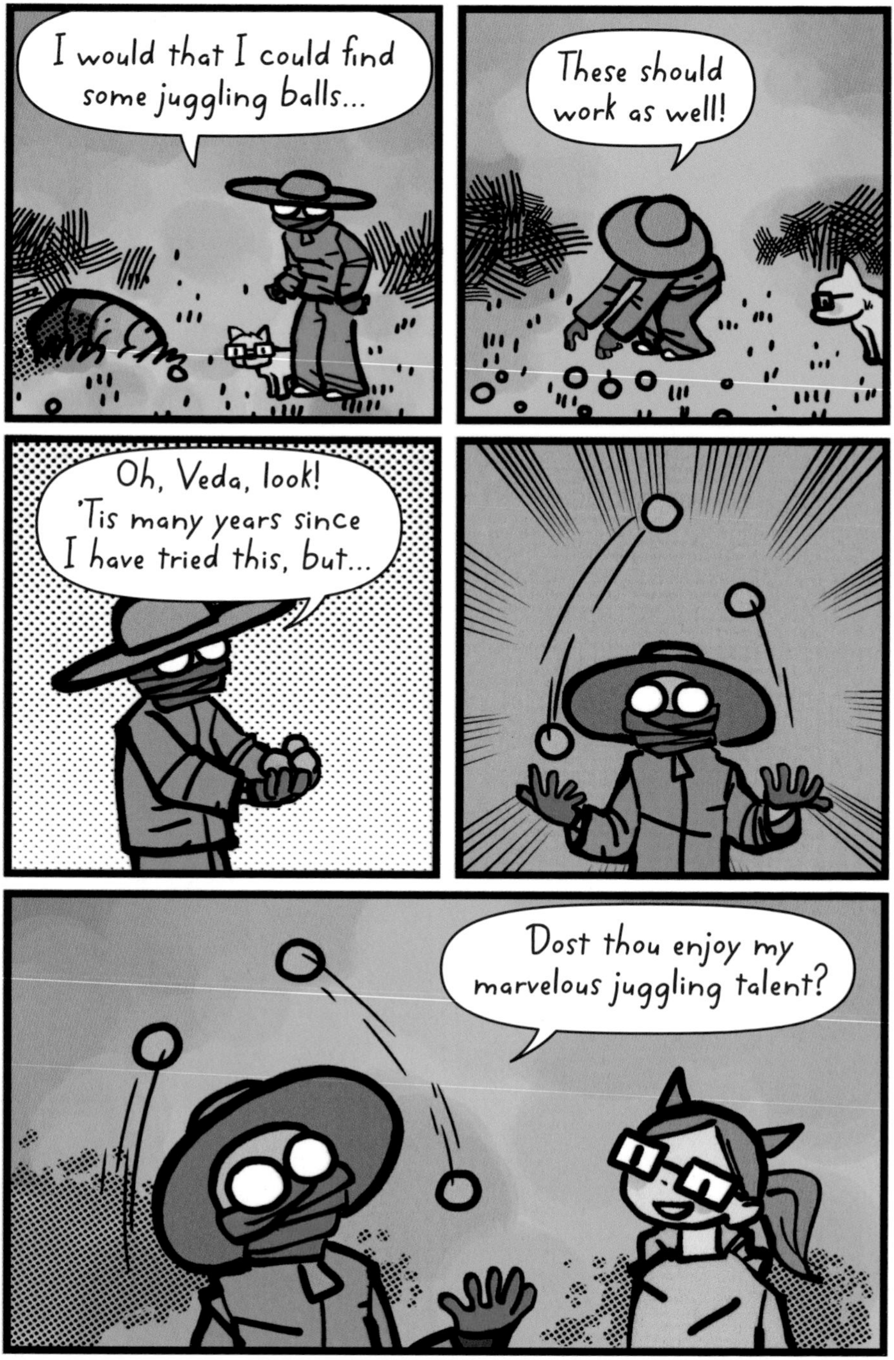
I would that I could find some juggling balls...
These should work as well!
Oh, Veda, look! 'Tis many years since I have tried this, but...
Dost thou enjoy my marvelous juggling talent?

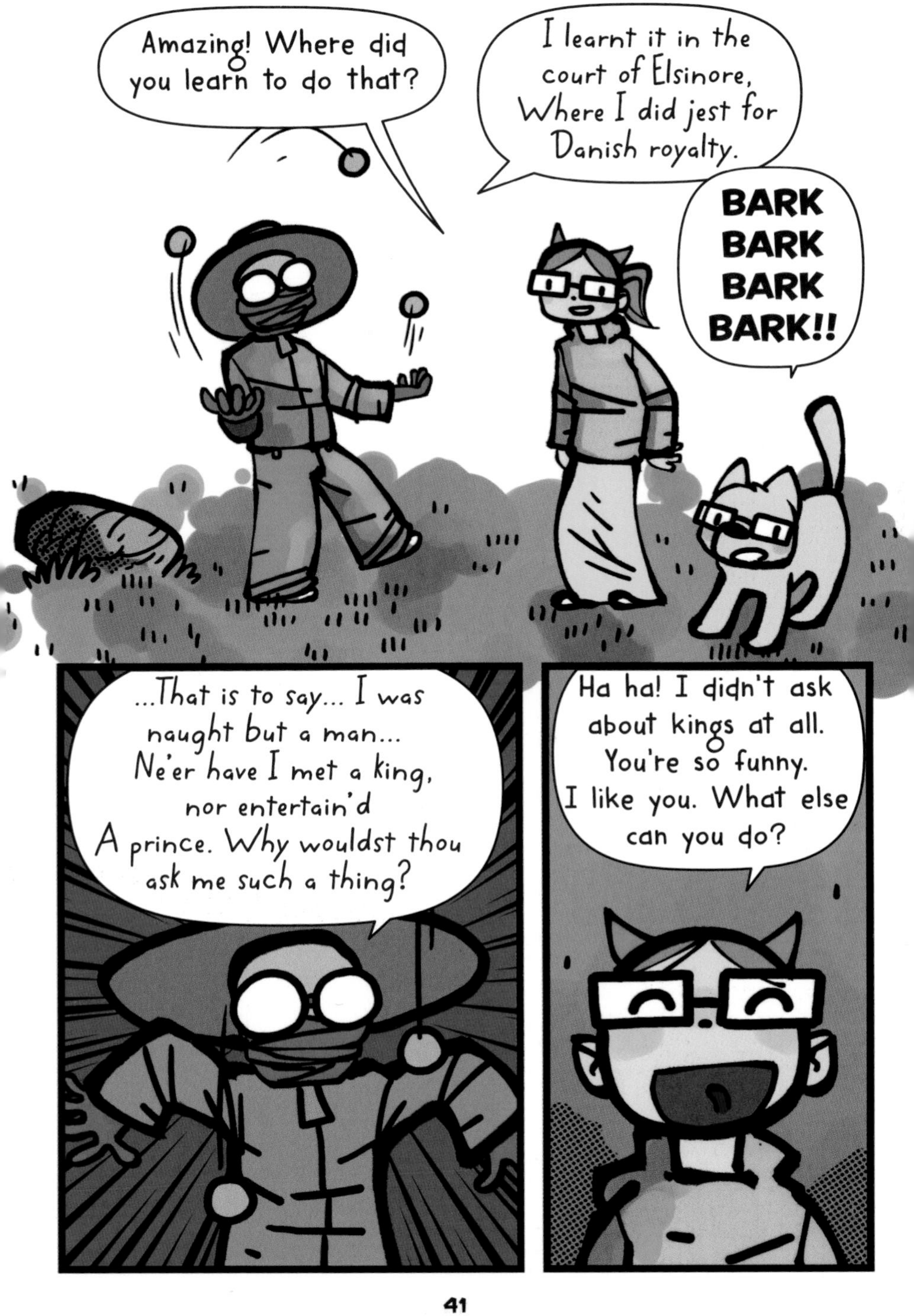
Amazing! Where did you learn to do that?
I learnt it in the court of Elsinore, Where I did jest for Danish royalty.
BARK BARK BARK BARK!!
...That is to say... I was naught but a man... Ne'er have I met a king, nor entertain'd A prince. Why wouldst thou ask me such a thing?
Ha ha! I didn't ask about kings at all. You're so funny. I like you. What else can you do?

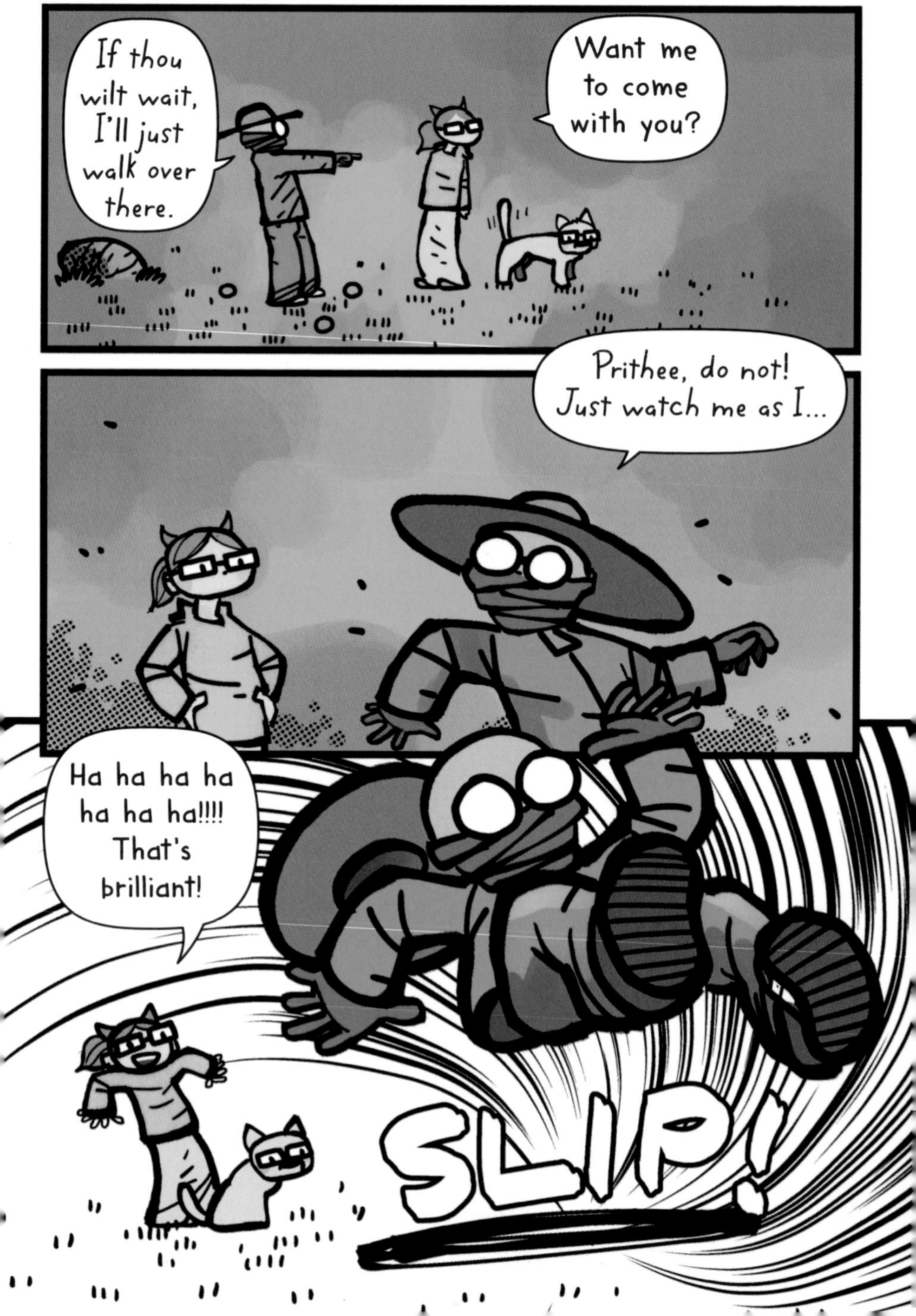
If thou wilt wait, I'll just walk over there.
Want me to come with you?
Prithee, do not! Just watch me as I...
Ha ha ha ha ha ha ha!!!! That's brilliant!
SLIP!

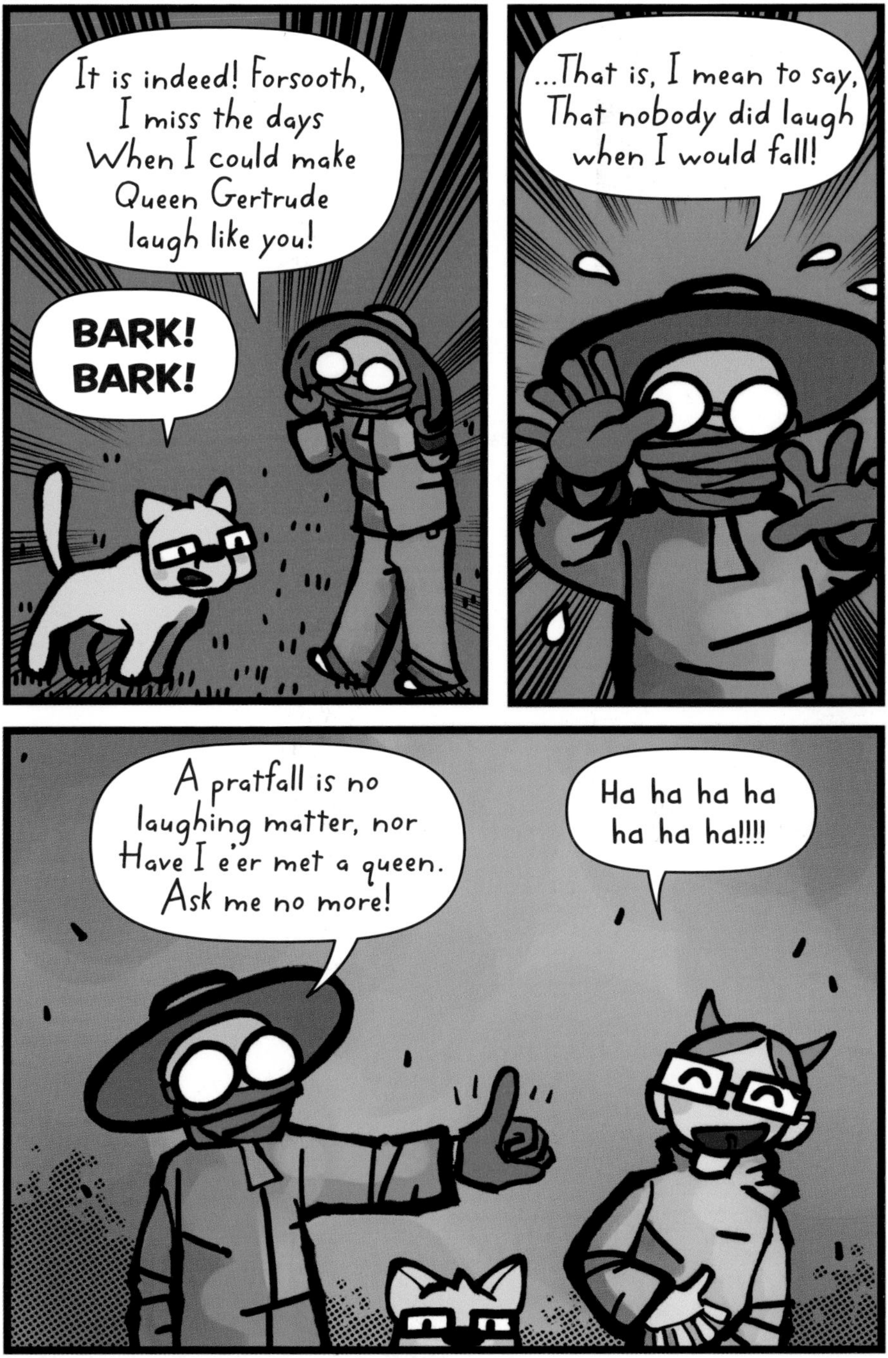
It is indeed! Forsooth, I miss the days When I could make Queen Gertrude laugh like you!
BARK! BARK!
...That is, I mean to say, That nobody did laugh when I would fall!
A pratfall is no laughing matter, nor Have I e'er met a queen. Ask me no more!
Ha ha ha ha ha ha ha!!!!

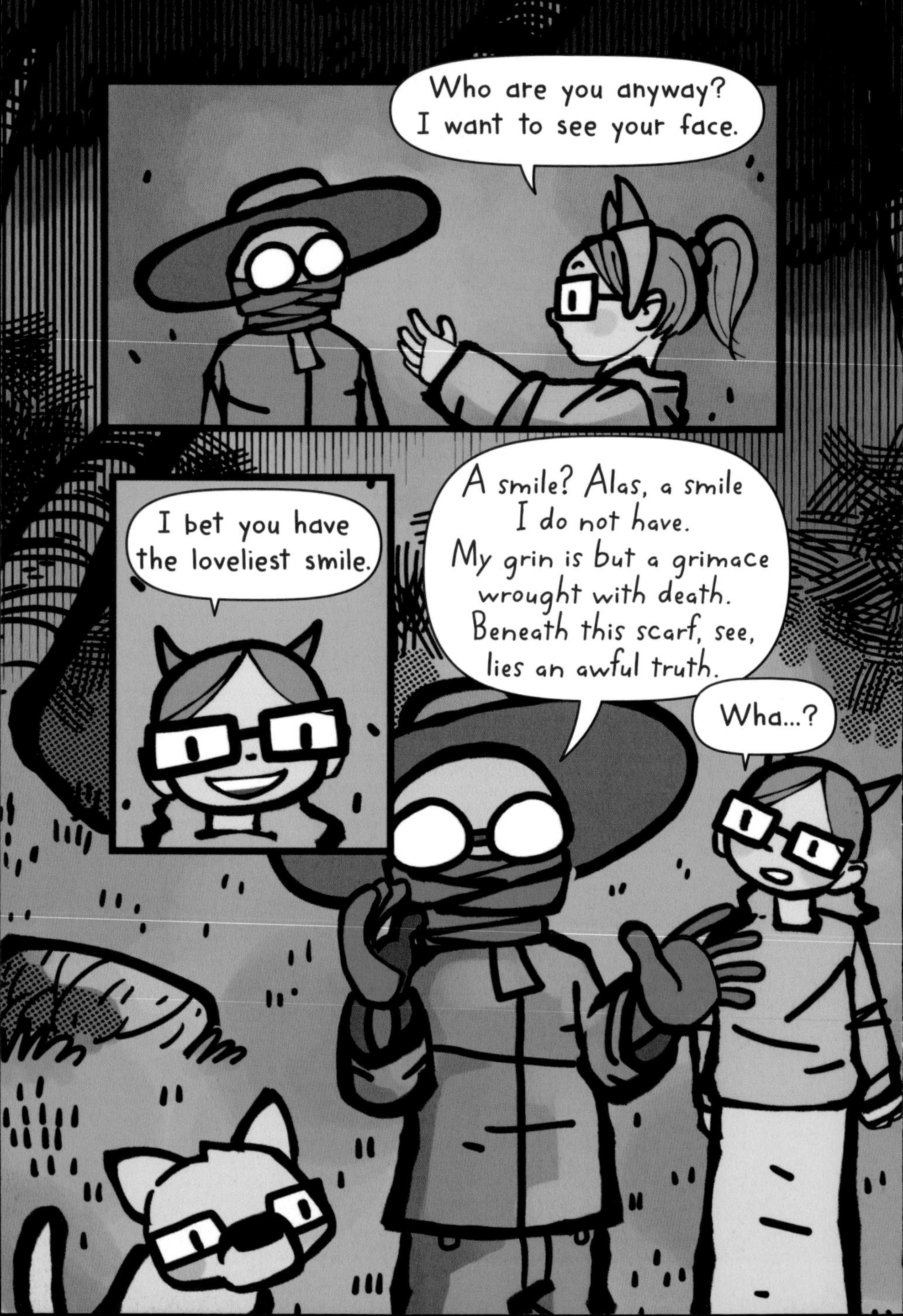
Who are you anyway? I want to see your face.
I bet you have the loveliest smile.
A smile? Alas, a smile I do not have. My grin is but a grimace wrought with death. Beneath this scarf, see, lies an awful truth.
Wha...?

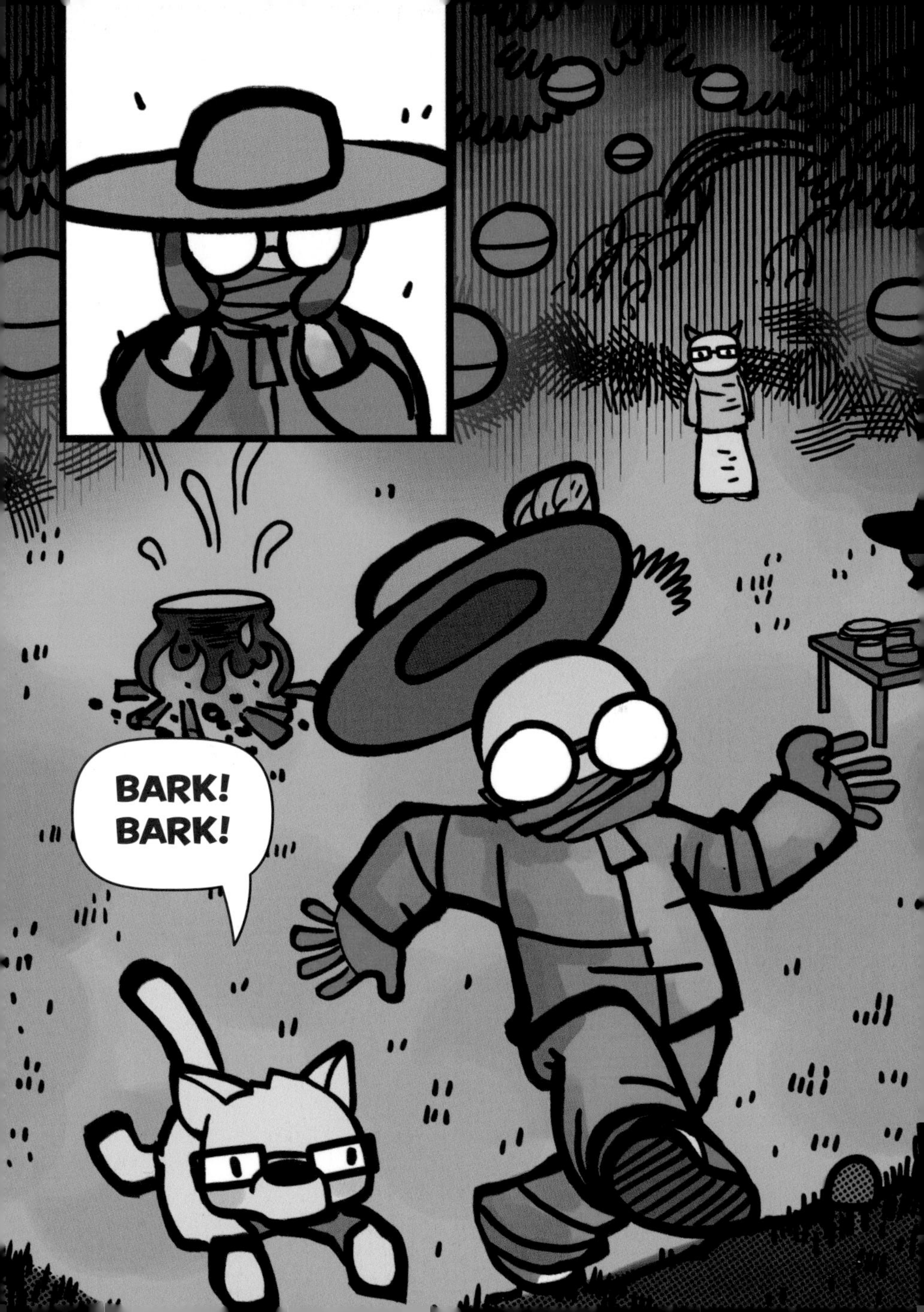
BARK! BARK!

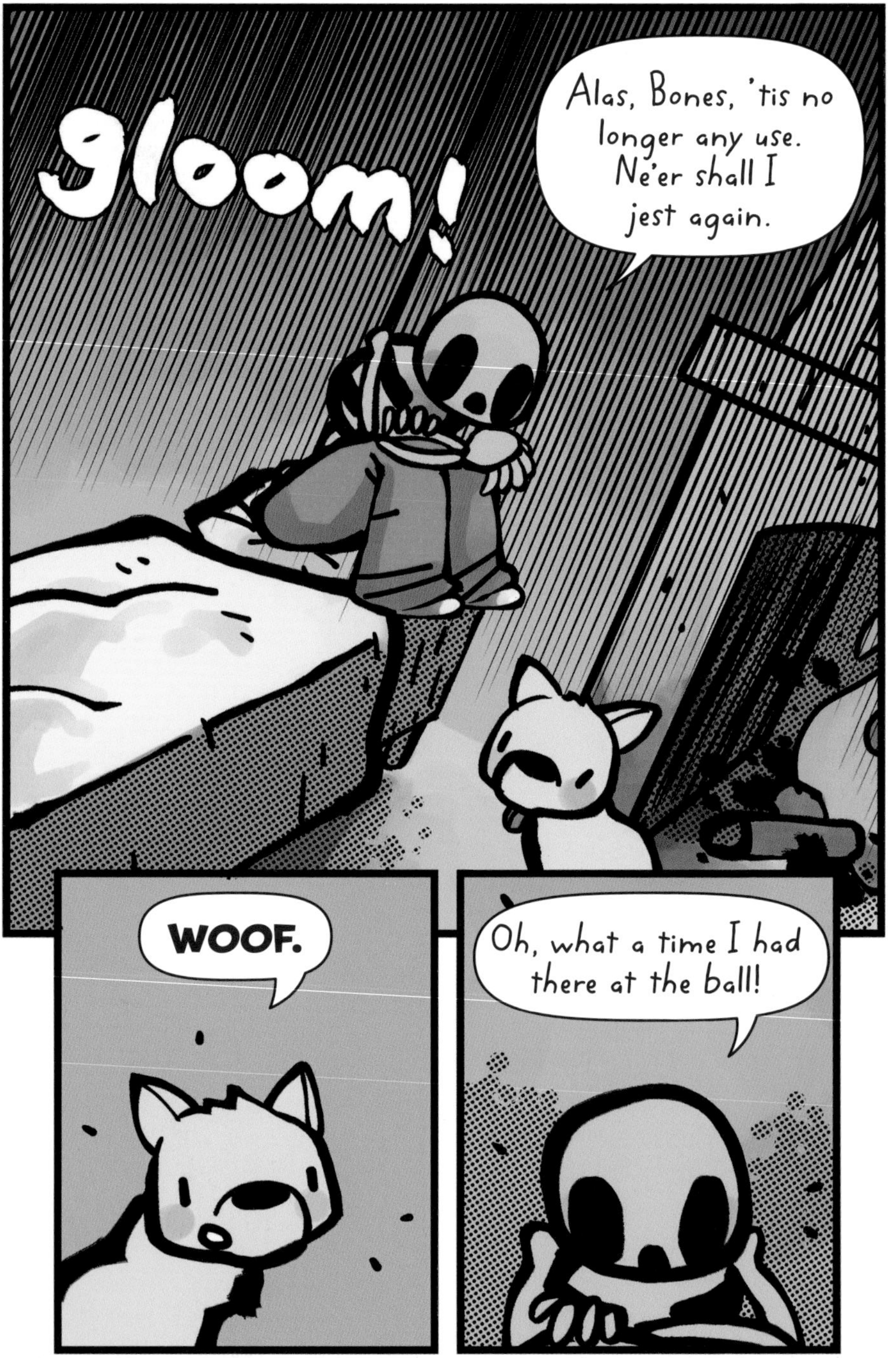
gloom!
Alas, Bones, 'tis no longer any use. Ne'er shall I jest again.
WOOF.
Oh, what a time I had there at the ball!

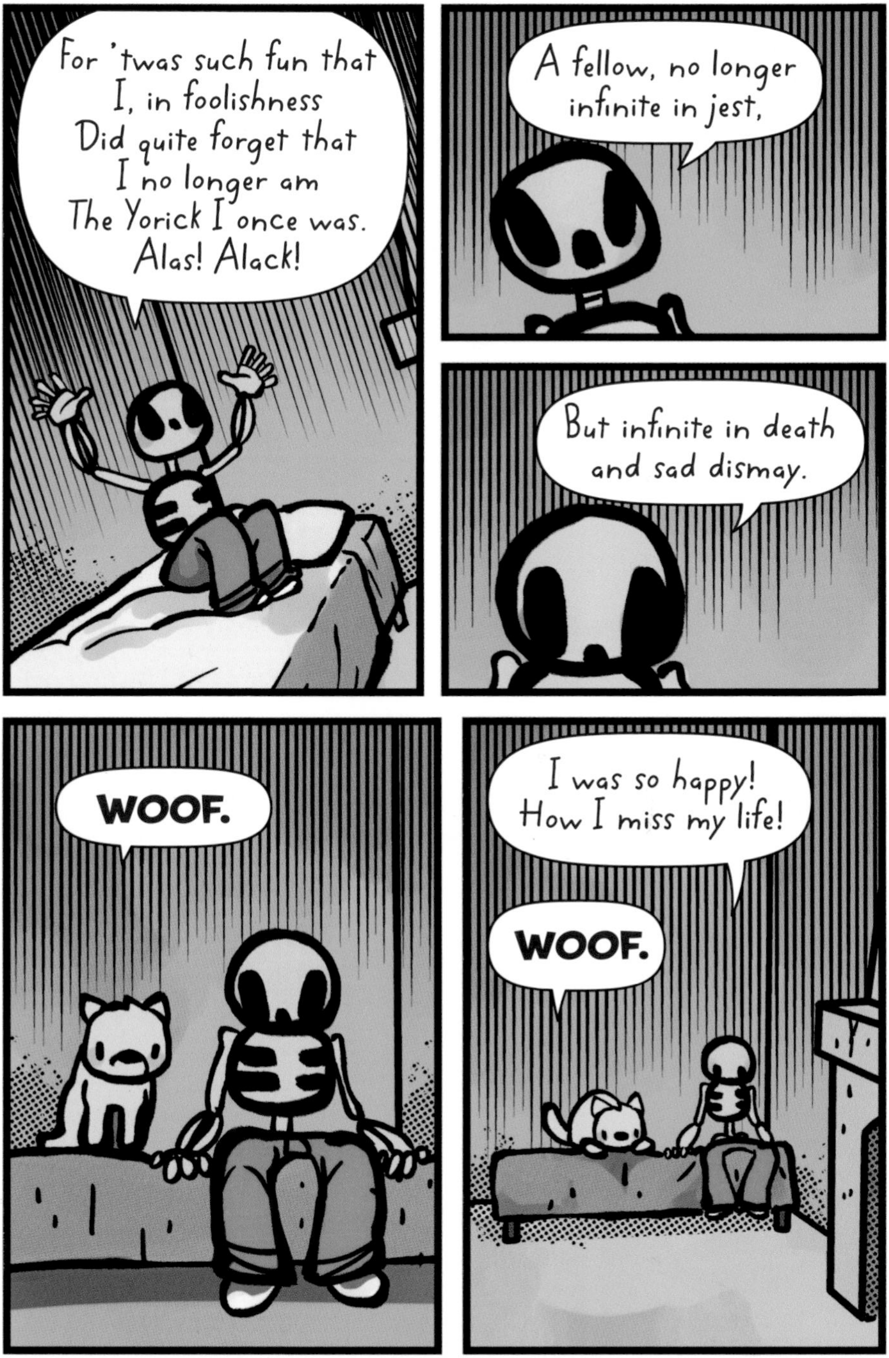
For 'twas such fun that I, in foolishness Did quite forget that I no longer am The Yorick I once was. Alas! Alack!
A fellow, no longer infinite in jest,
But infinite in death and sad dismay.
WOOF.
I was so happy! How I miss my life!
WOOF.

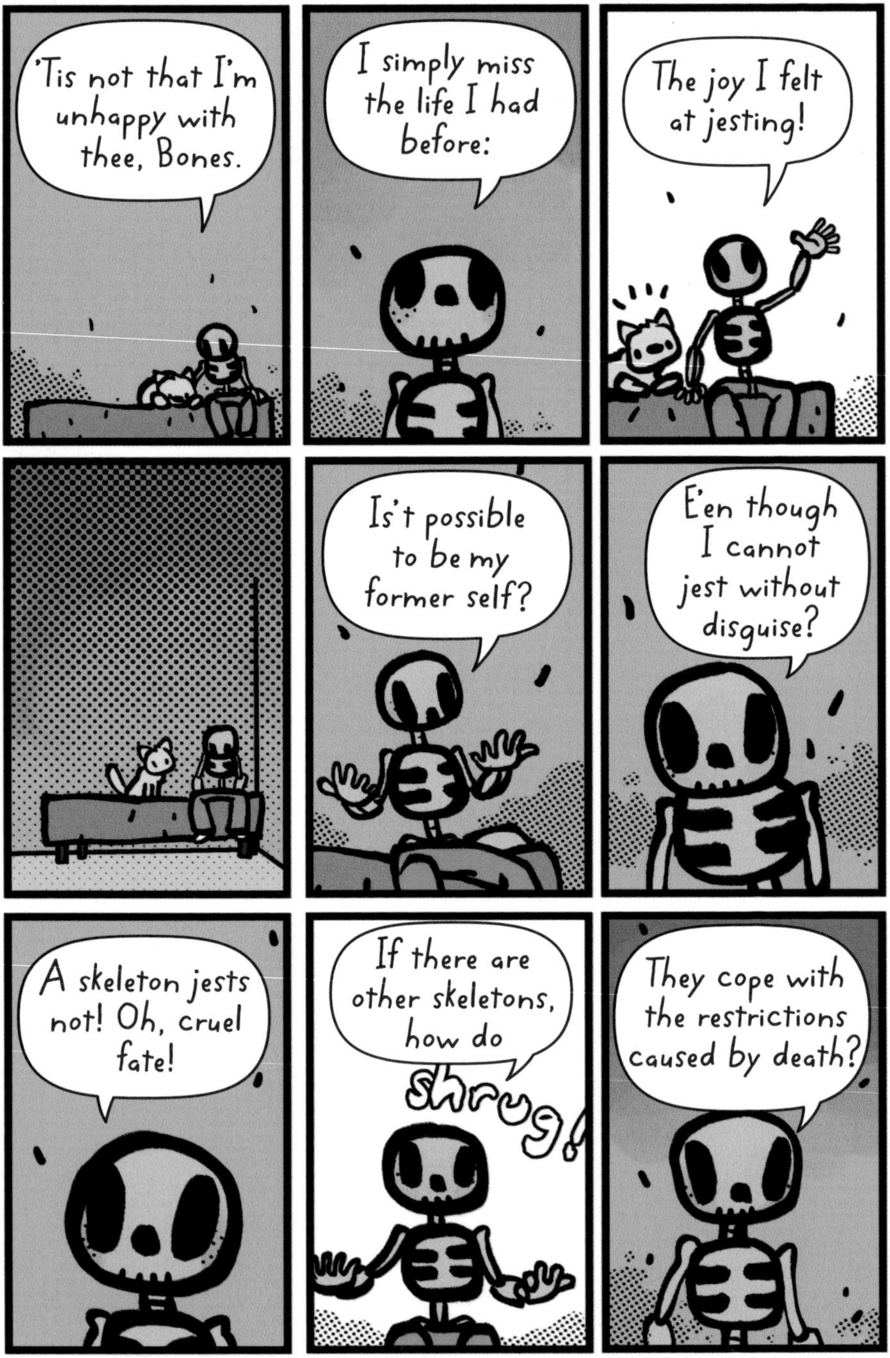
'Tis not that I'm unhappy with thee, Bones.
I simply miss the life I had before:
The joy I felt at jesting!
Is't possible to be my former self?
E'en though I cannot jest without disguise?
A skeleton jests not! Oh, cruel fate!
If there are other skeletons, how do
shrug!
They cope with the restrictions caused by death?

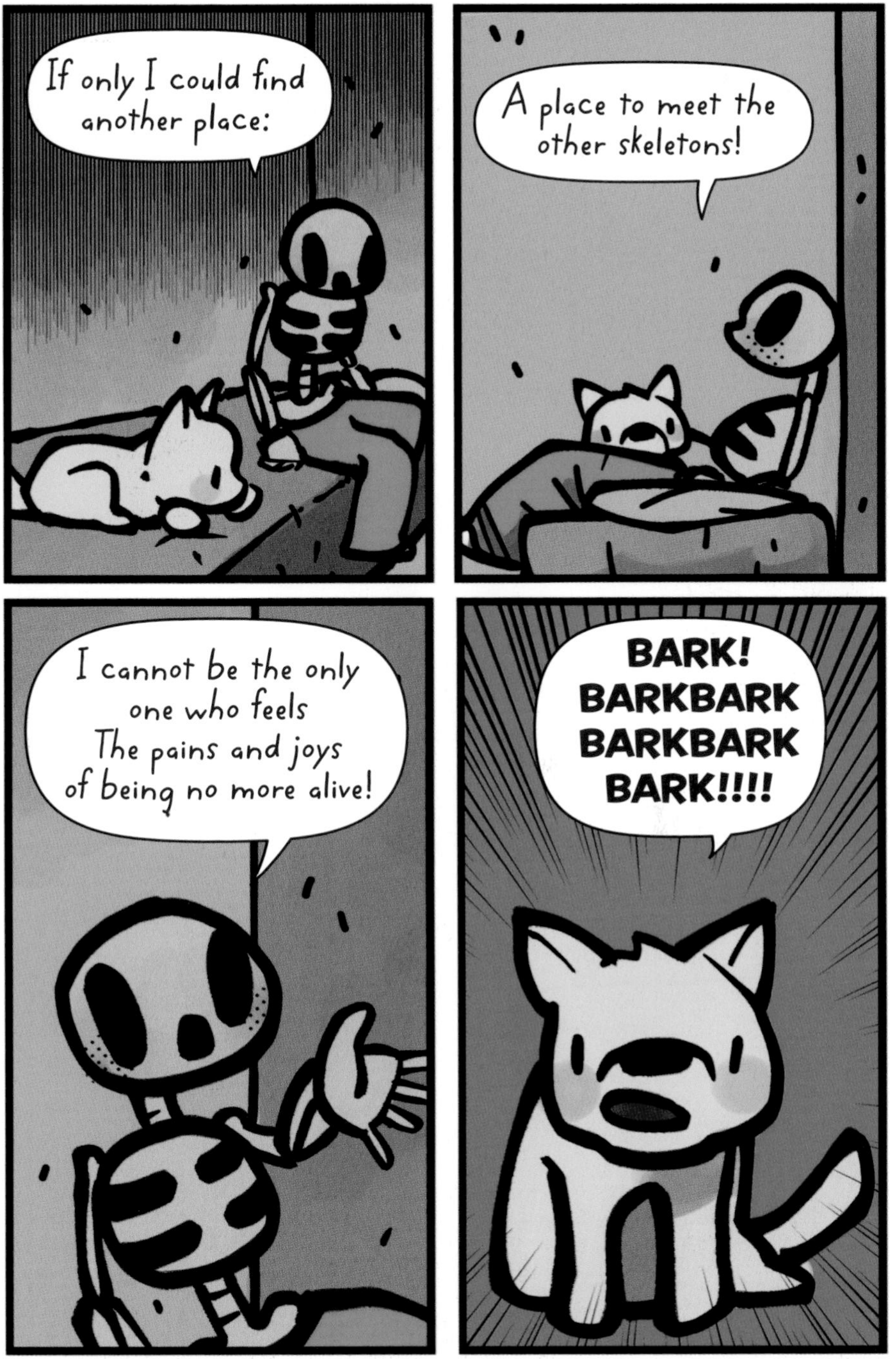
If only I could find another place:
A place to meet the other skeletons!
I cannot be the only one who feels The pains and joys of being no more alive!
BARK! BARKBARK BARKBARK BARK!!!!

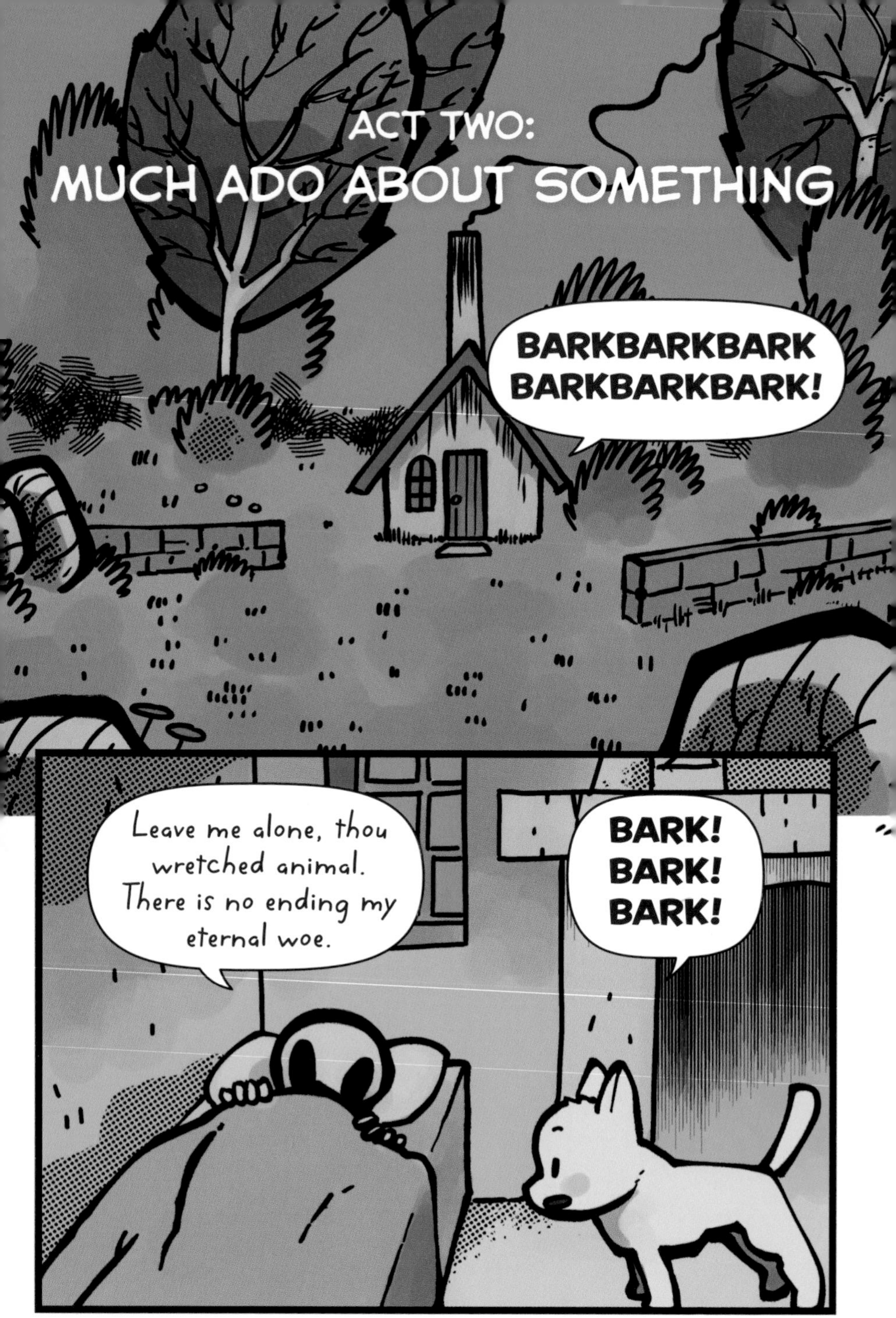
ACT TWO:
MUCH ADO ABOUT SOMETHING
BARKBARKBARK BARKBARKBARK!
Leave me alone, thou wretched animal. There is no ending my eternal woe.
BARK! BARK! BARK!

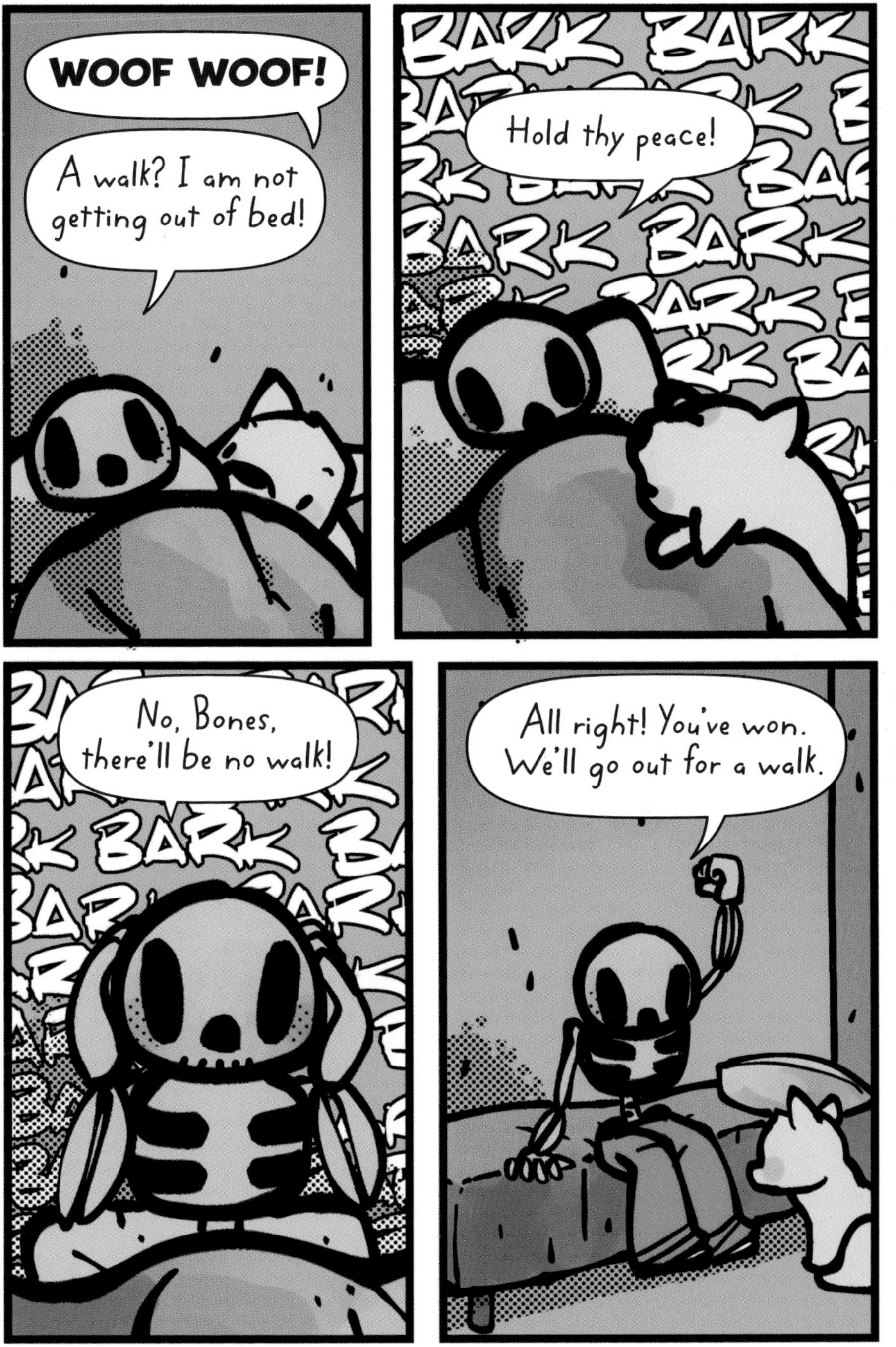
WOOF WOOF!
A walk? I am not getting out of bed!
BARK BARK
Hold thy peace!
No, Bones, there'll be no walk!
All right! You've won. We'll go out for a walk.

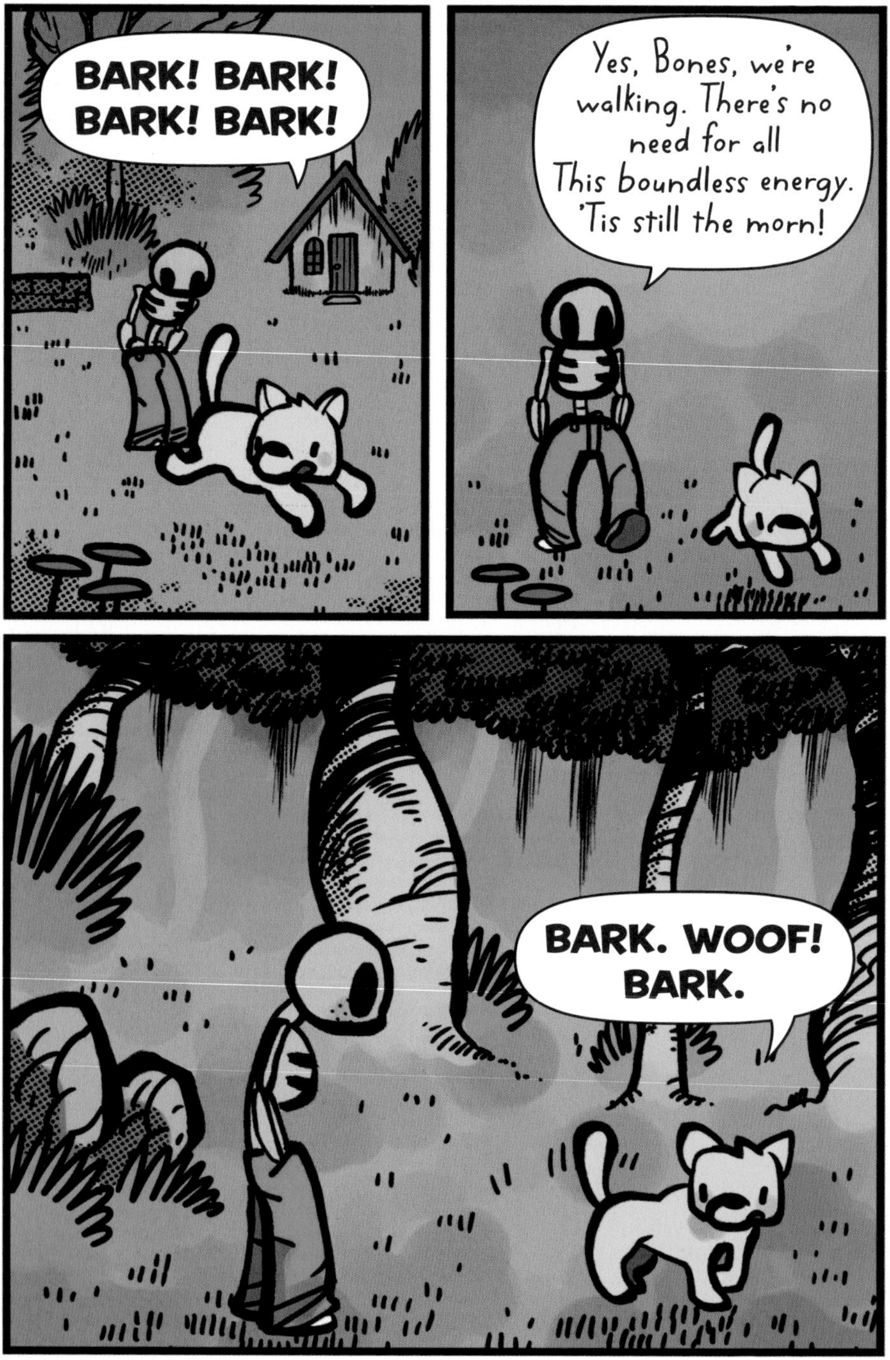
BARK! BARK! BARK! BARK!
Yes, Bones, we're walking. There's no need for all This boundless energy. 'Tis still the morn!
BARK. WOOF! BARK.

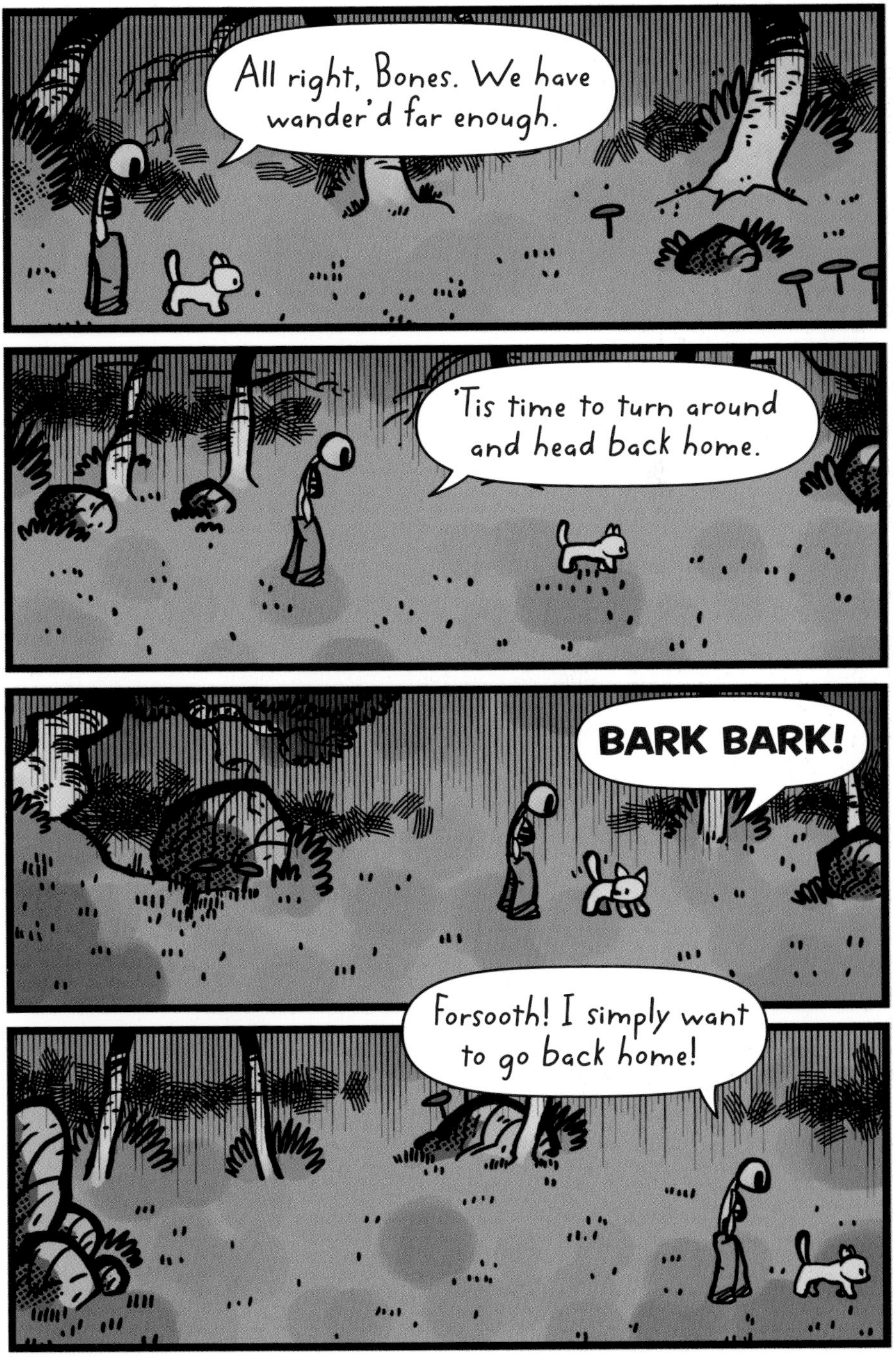
All right, Bones. We have wander'd far enough.
'Tis time to turn around and head back home.
BARK BARK!
Forsooth! I simply want to go back home!

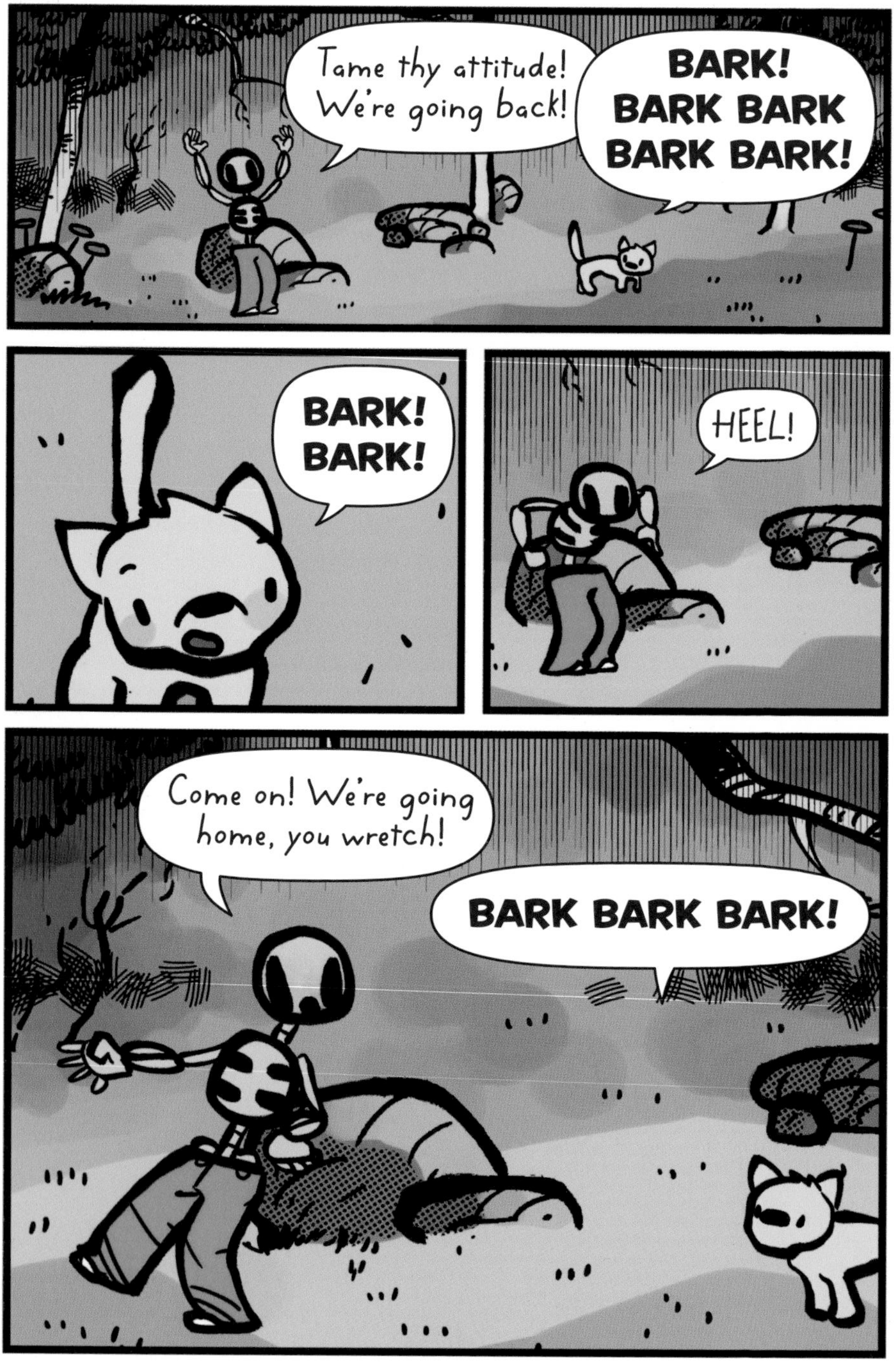

Tame thy attitude! We're going back!
BARK! BARK BARK BARK BARK!
BARK! BARK!
HEEL!
Come on! We're going home, you wretch!
BARK BARK BARK!

I promise thee I'll give thee bones at home.
Well, one, but 'twill be nice and juicy still!
Come!

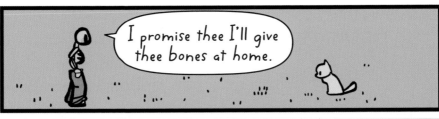

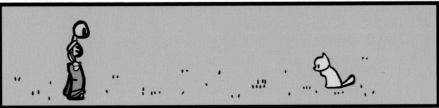

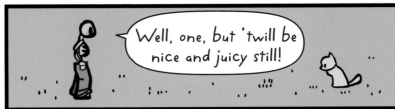

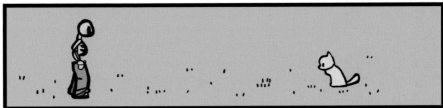

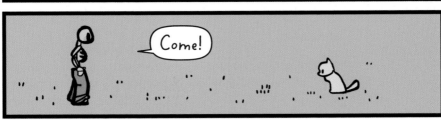

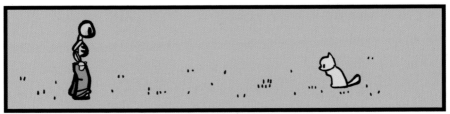

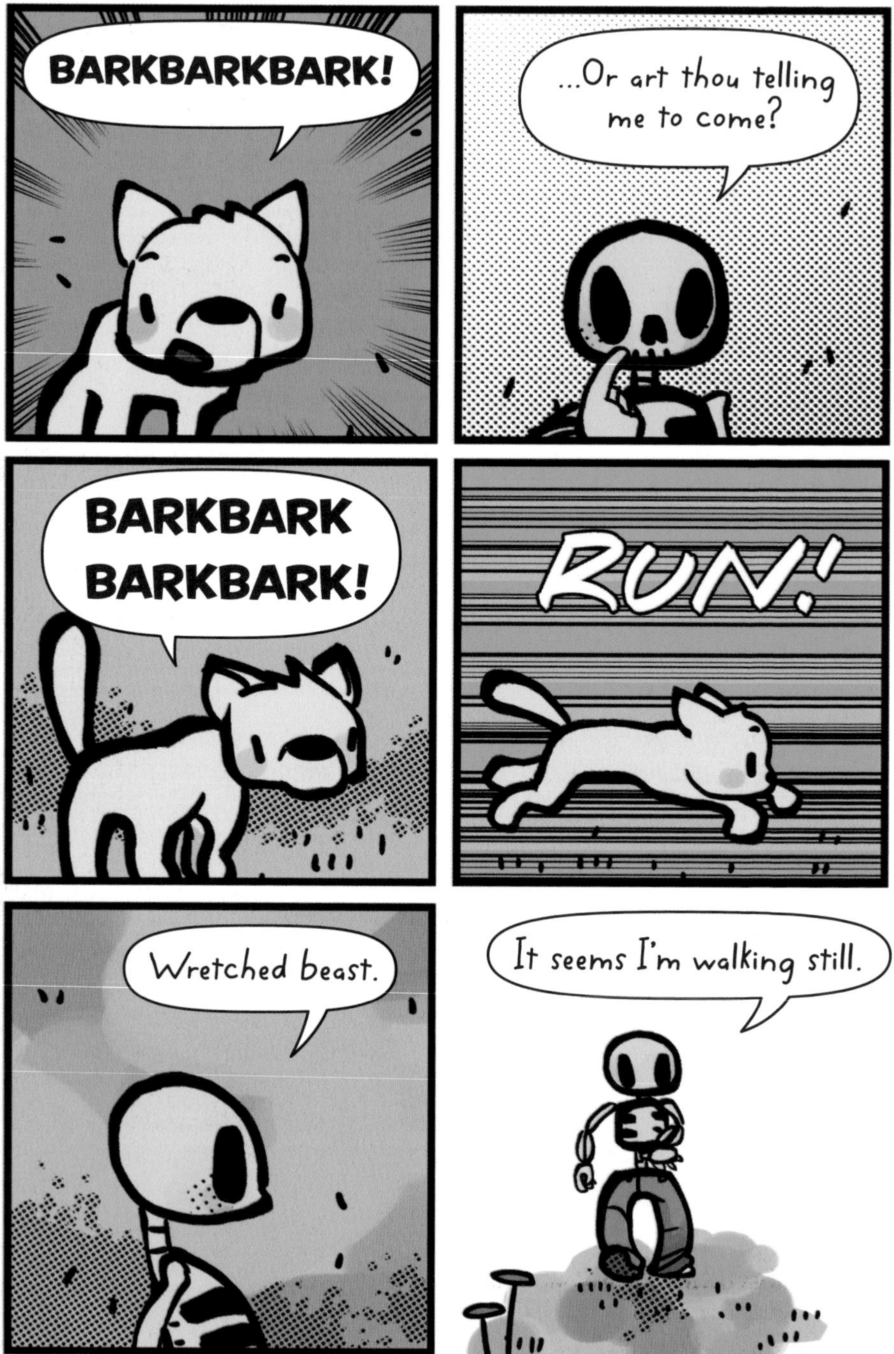
BARKBARKBARK!
...Or art thou telling me to come?
BARKBARK BARKBARK!
RUN!
Wretched beast.
It seems I'm walking still.

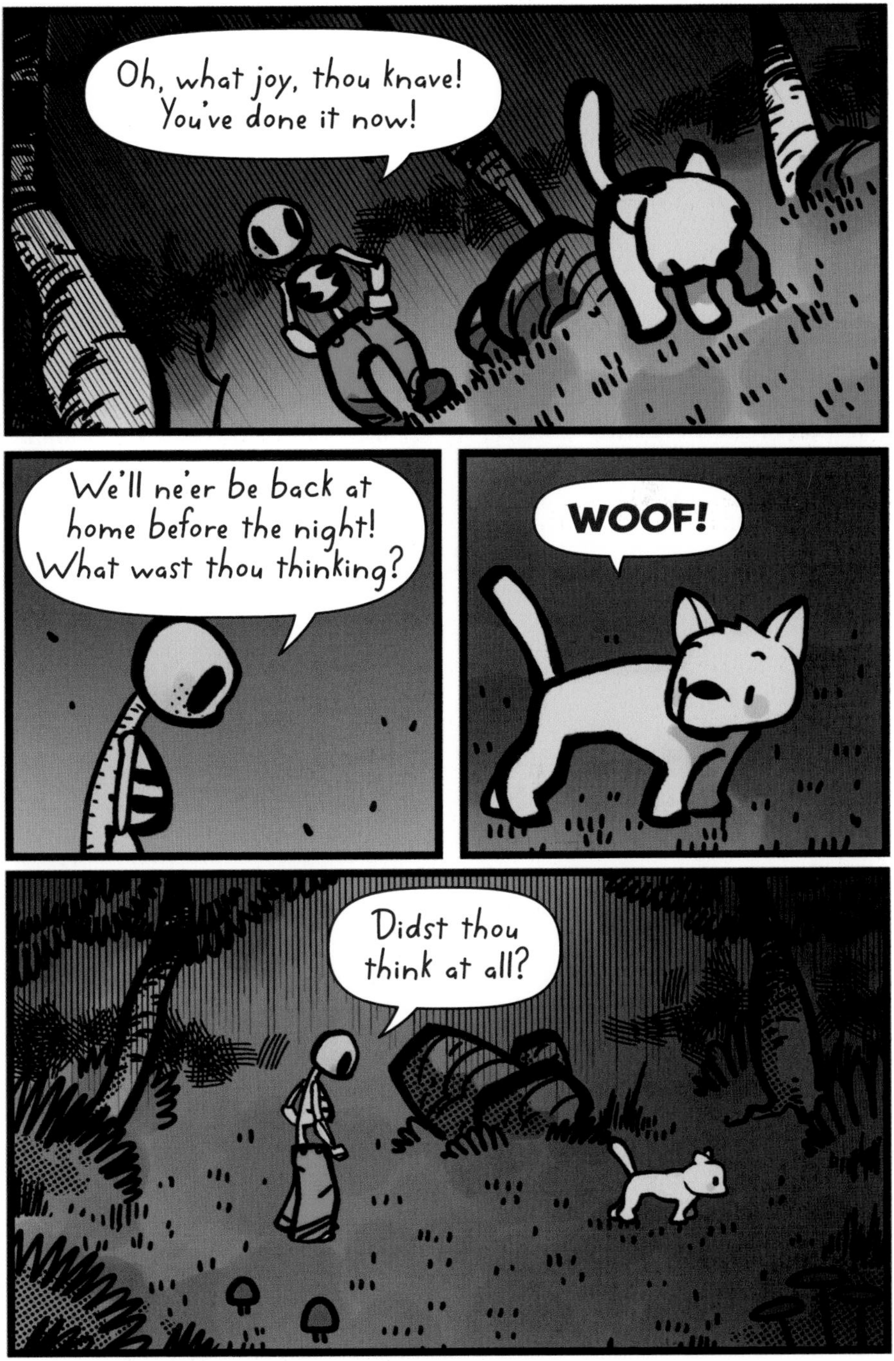
Oh, what joy, thou knave! You've done it now!
We'll ne'er be back at home before the night! What wast thou thinking?
WOOF!
Didst thou think at all?

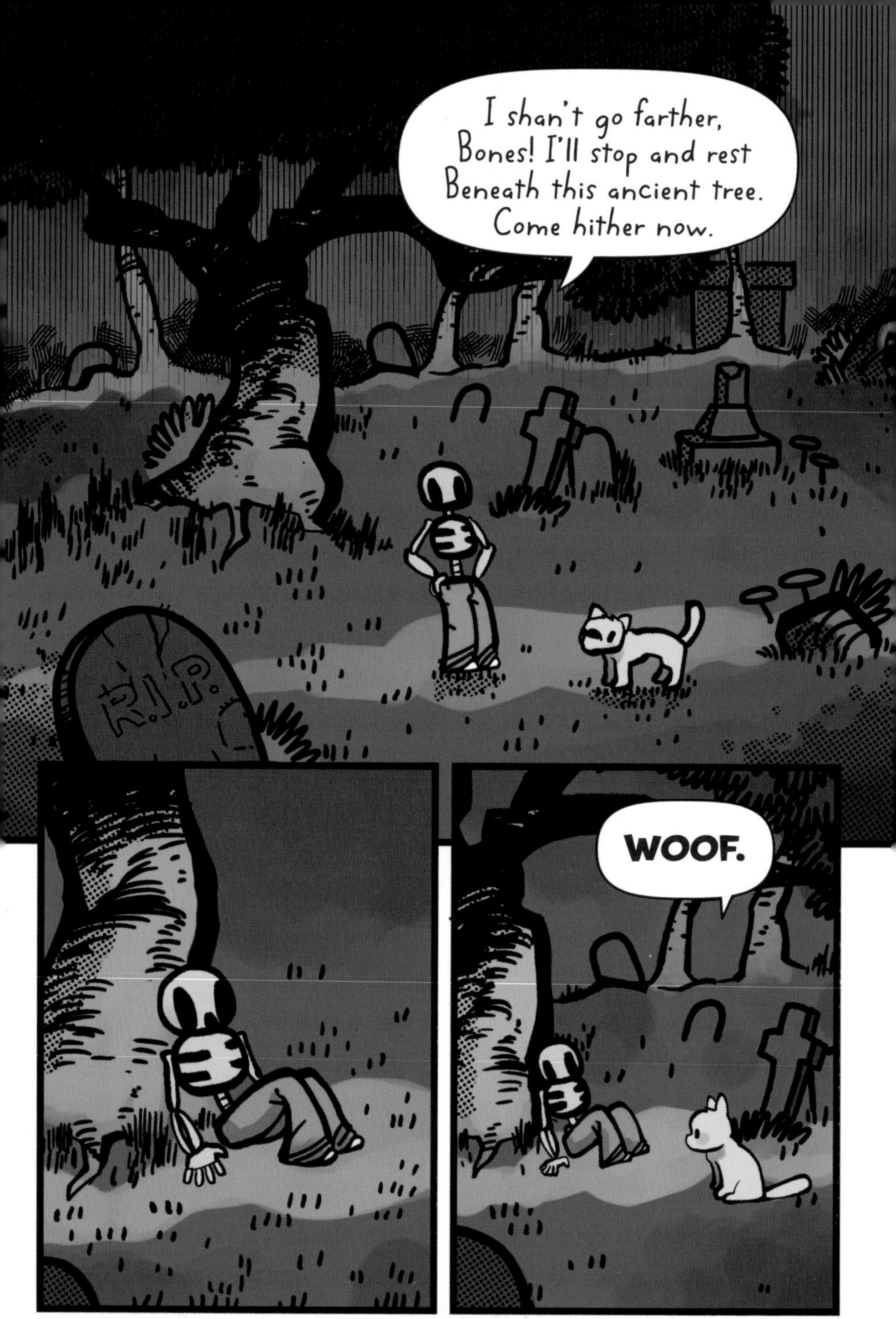
I shan't go farther, Bones! I'll stop and rest Beneath this ancient tree. Come hither now.
R.I.P.
WOOF.

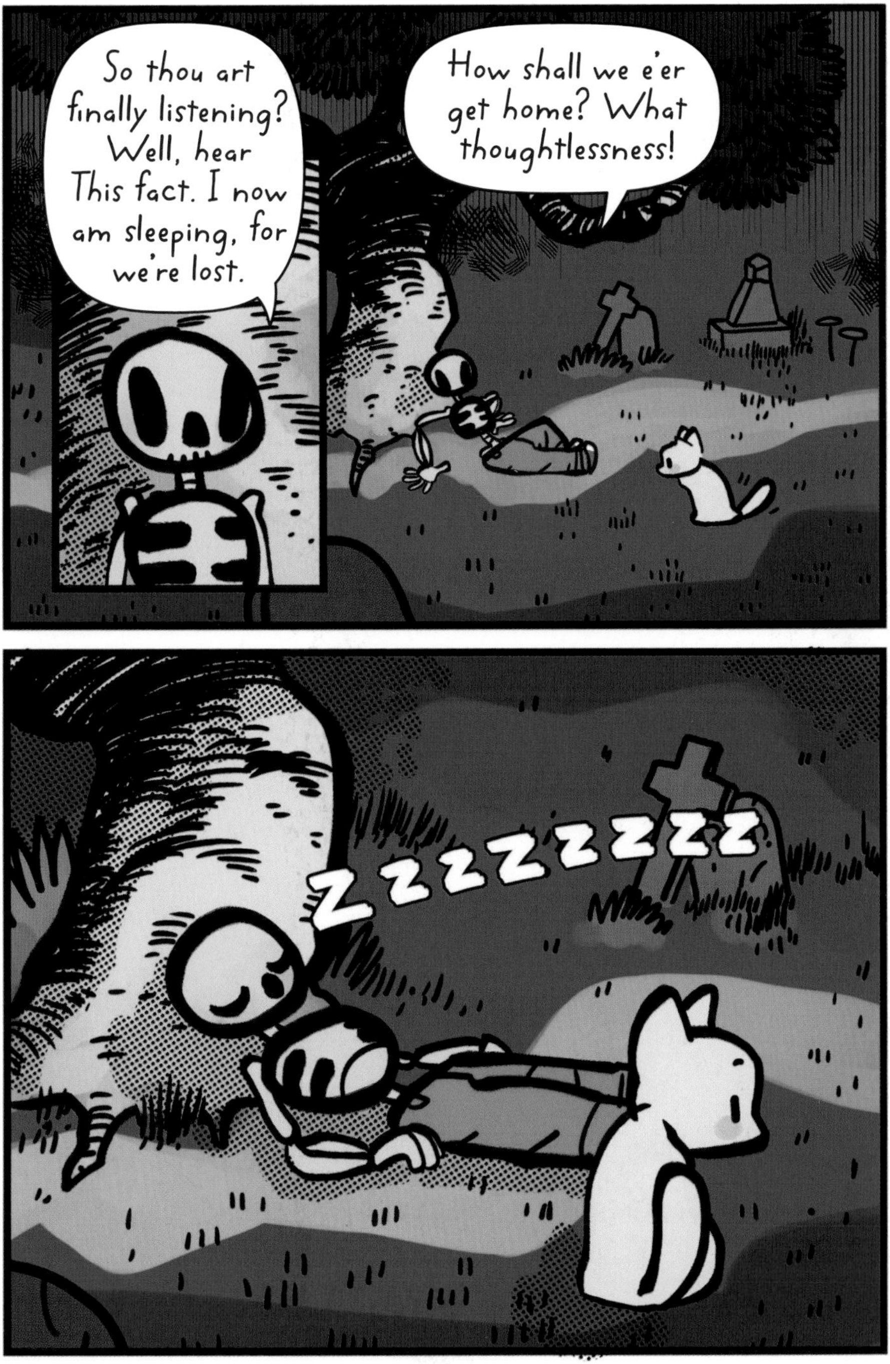
So thou art finally listening? Well, hear This fact. I now am sleeping, for we're lost.
How shall we e'er get home? What thoughtlessness!
ZZZZZZZZZ

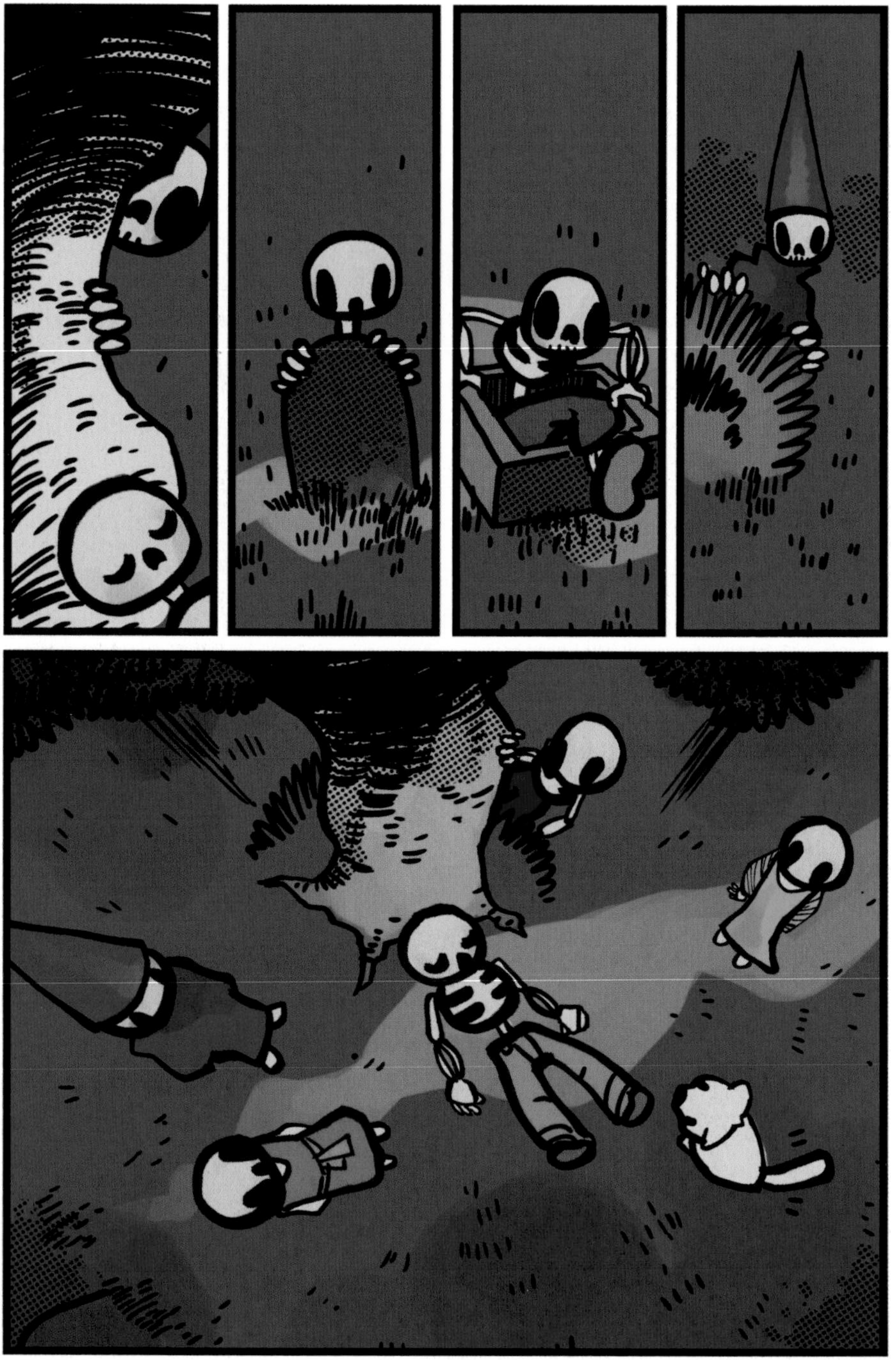

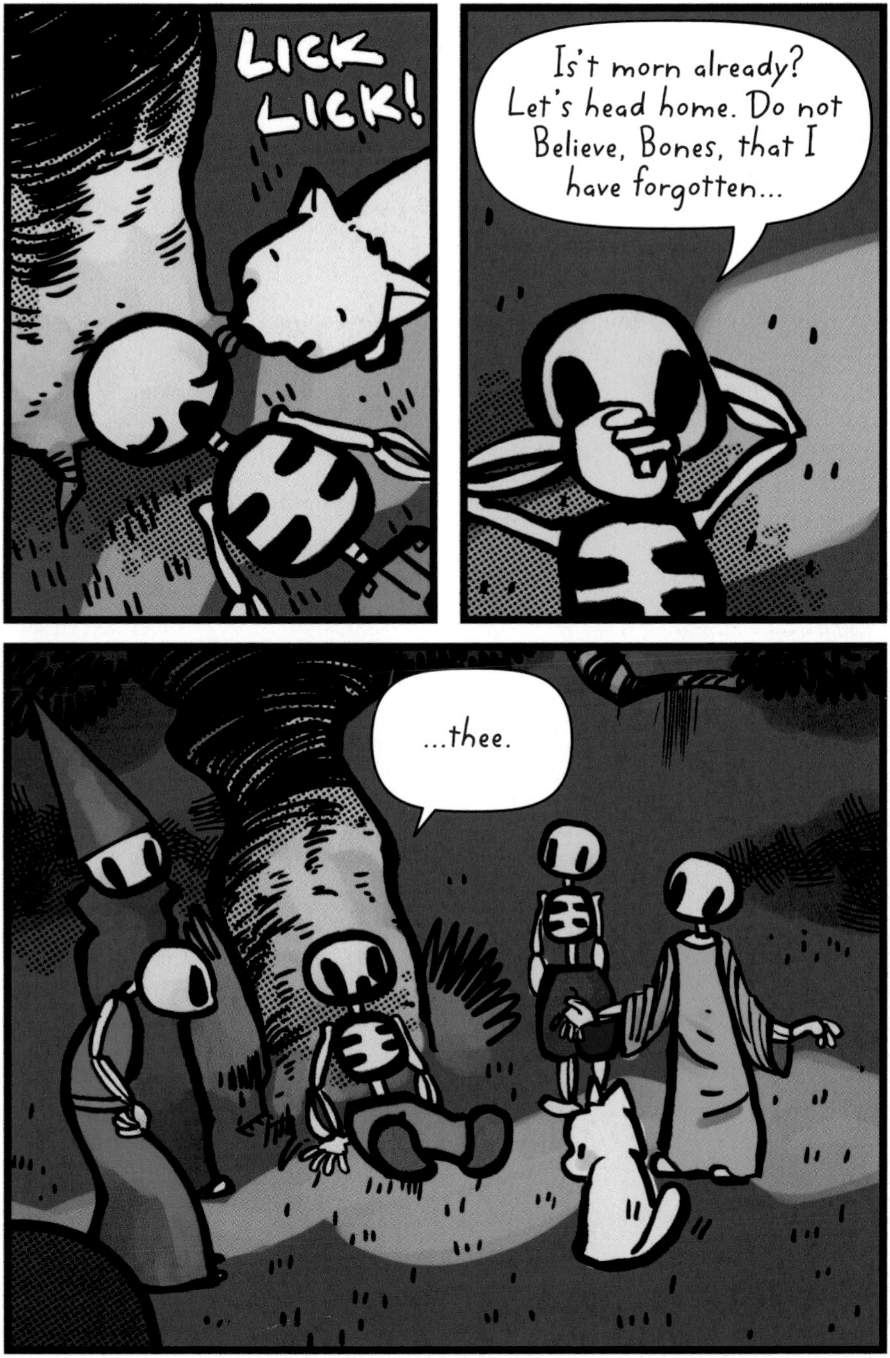
LICK LICK!
Is't morn already? Let's head home. Do not Believe, Bones, that I have forgotten...
...thee.

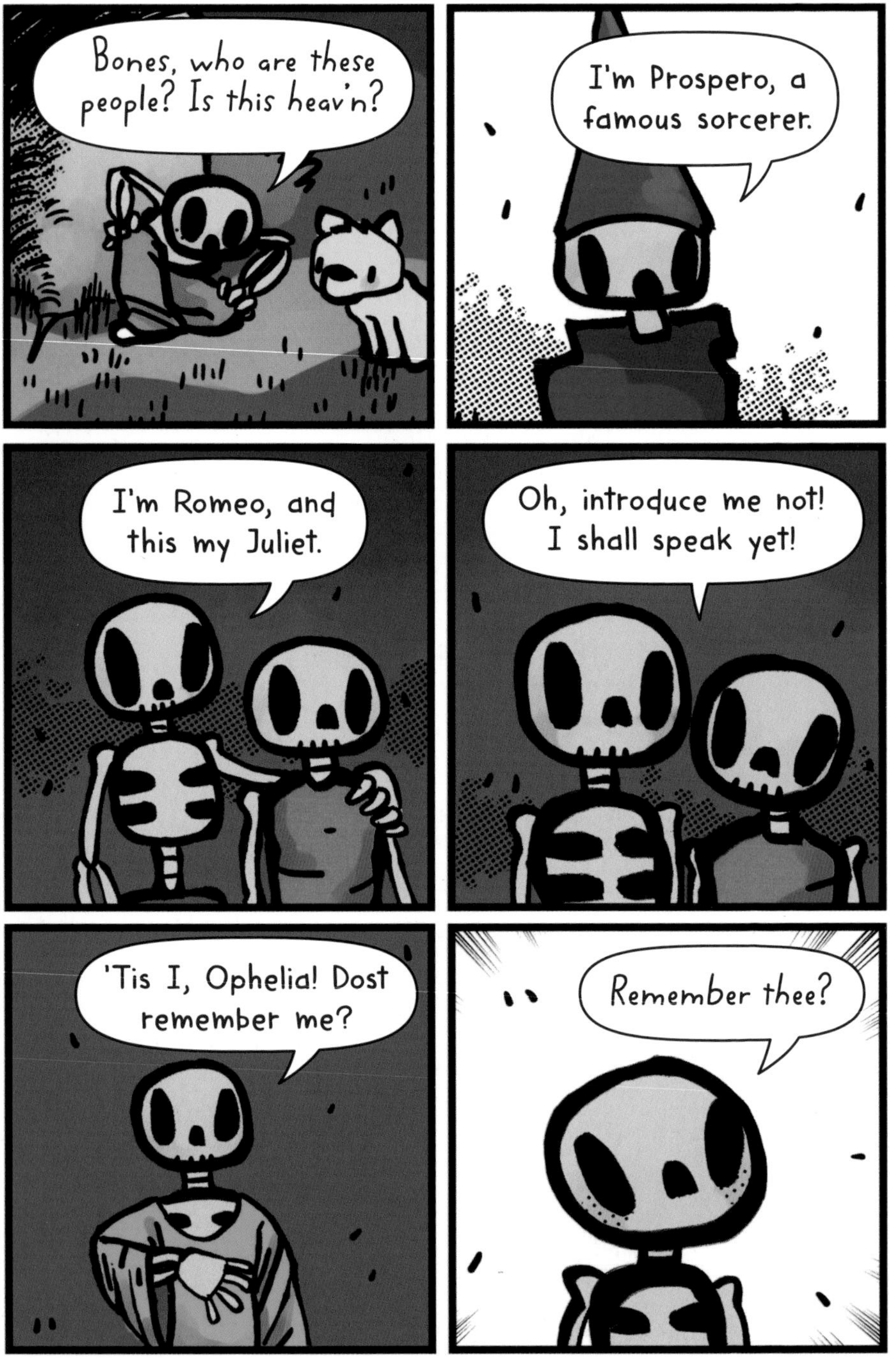
Bones, who are these people? Is this heav'n?
I'm Prospero, a famous sorcerer.
I'm Romeo, and this my Juliet.
Oh, introduce me not! I shall speak yet!
'Tis I, Ophelia! Dost remember me?
Remember thee?

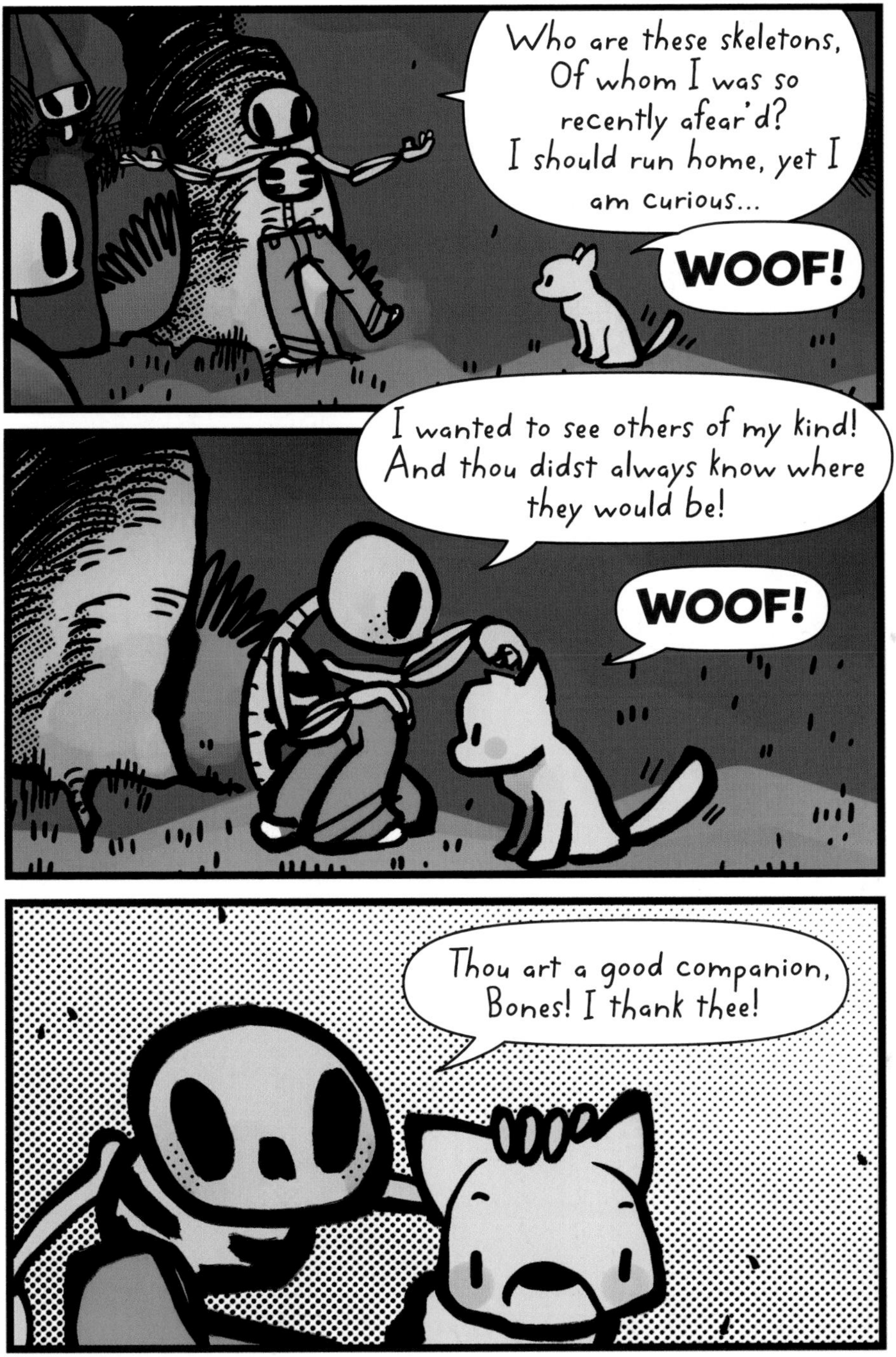
Who are these skeletons,
Of whom I was so
recently afear'd?
I should run home, yet I
am curious...
WOOF!
I wanted to see others of my kind!
And thou didst always know where
they would be!
WOOF!
Thou art a good companion,
Bones! I thank thee!

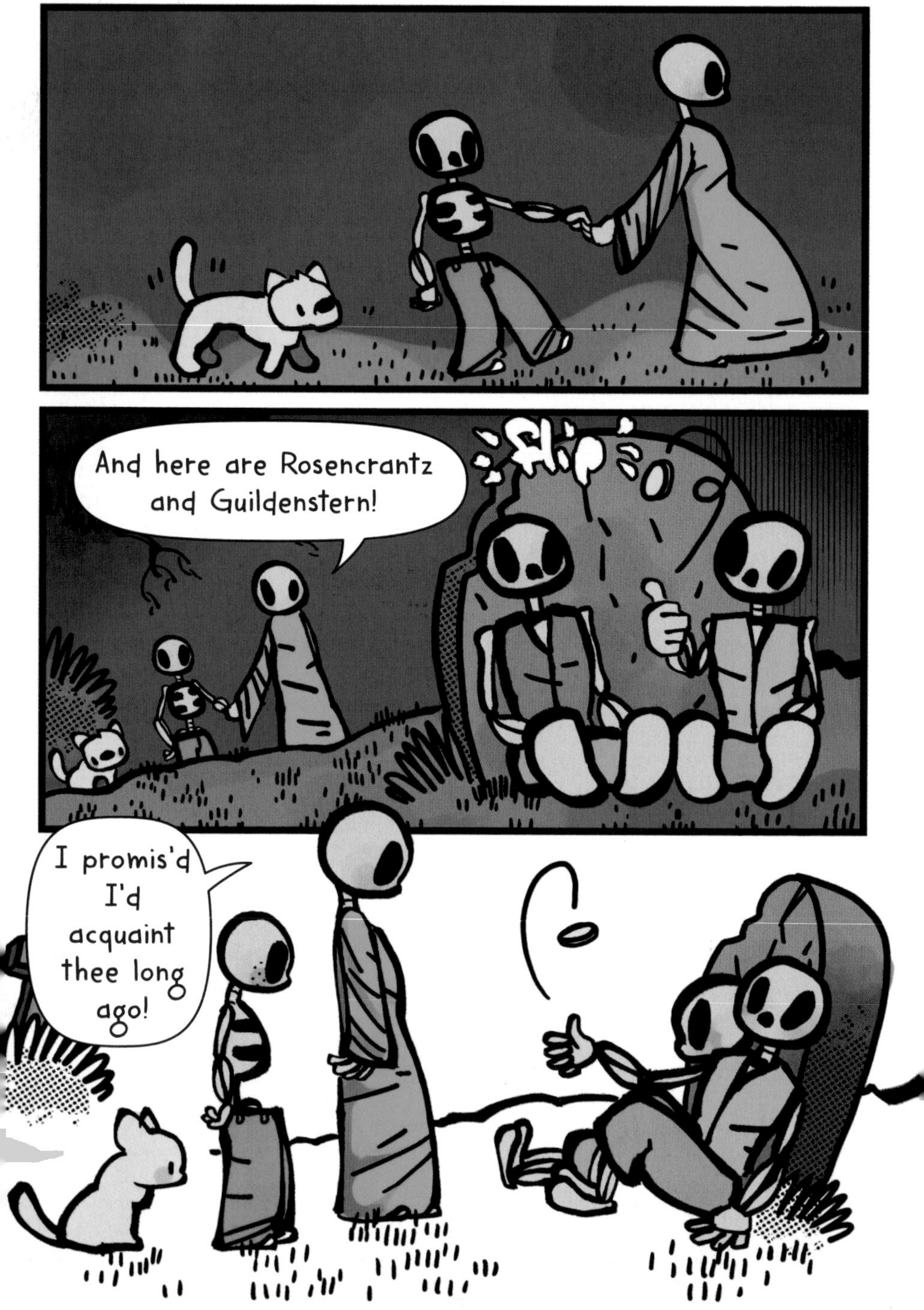
And here are Rosencrantz and Guildenstern!
I promis'd I'd acquaint thee long ago!

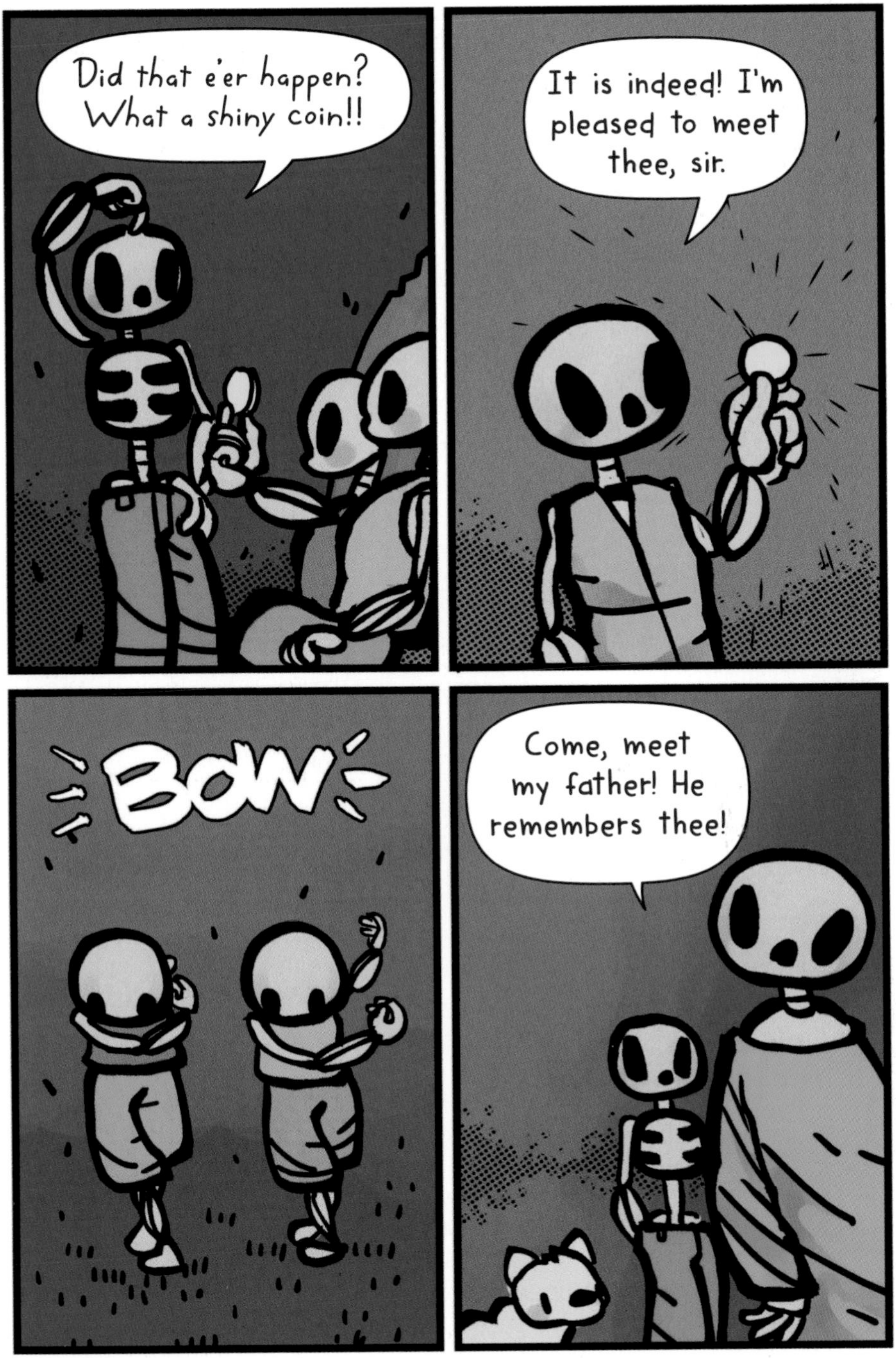
Did that e'er happen? What a shiny coin!!
It is indeed! I'm pleased to meet thee, sir.
BOW
Come, meet my father! He remembers thee!

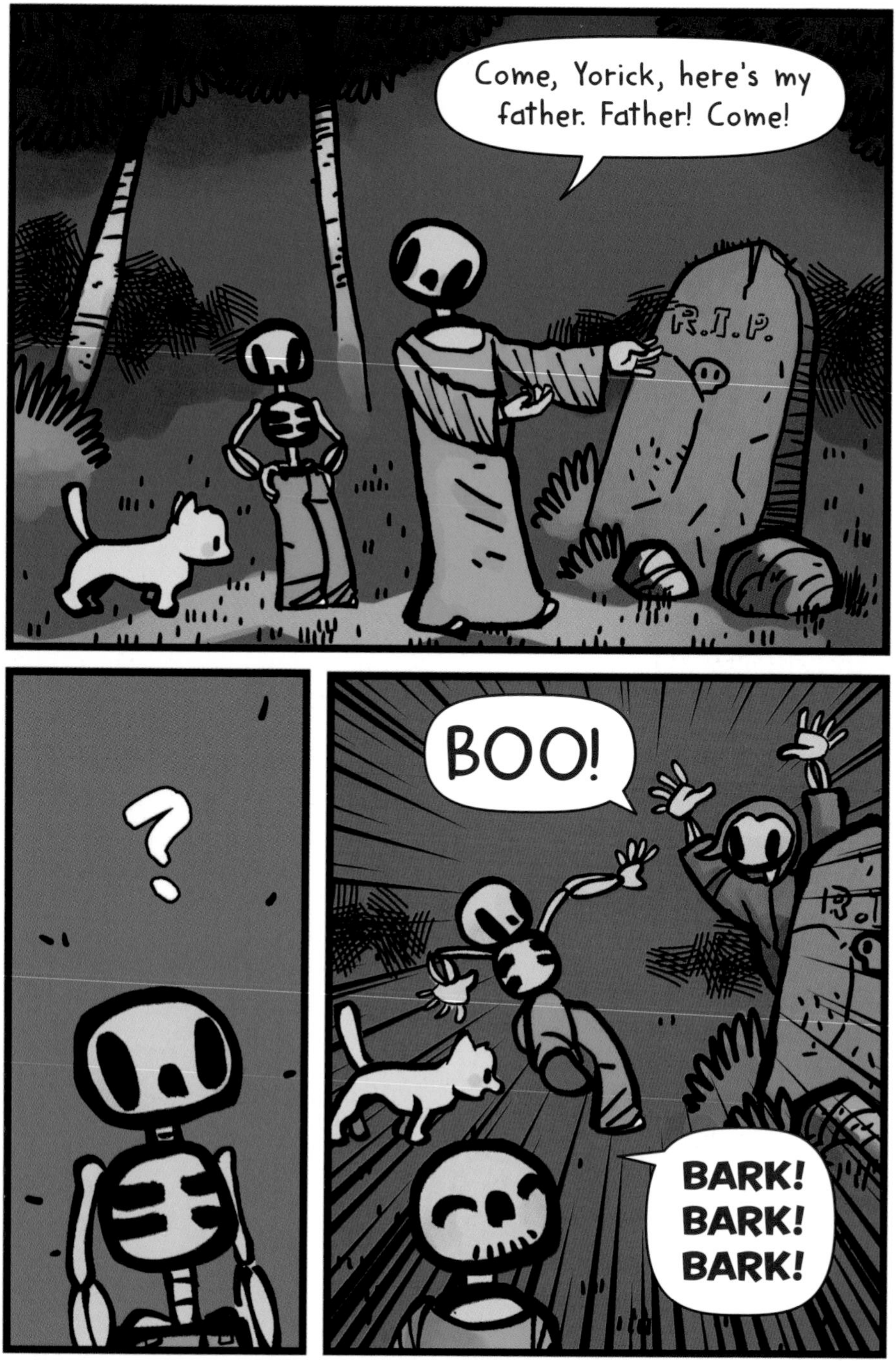
Come, Yorick, here's my father. Father! Come!
R.I.P.
?
BOO!
BARK! BARK! BARK!

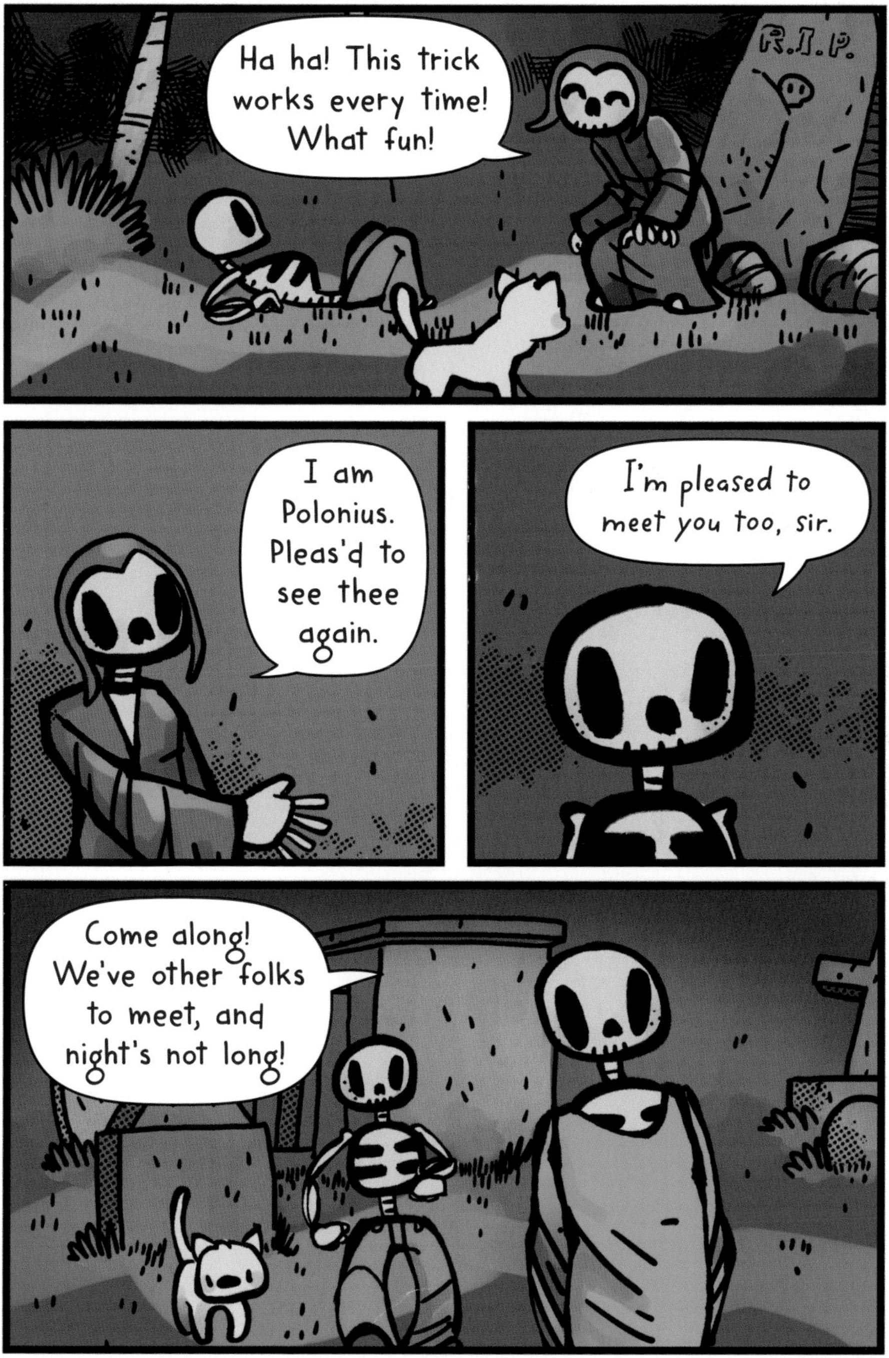
R.I.P.
Ha ha! This trick works every time! What fun!
I am Polonius. Pleas'd to see thee again.
I'm pleased to meet you too, sir.
Come along! We've other folks to meet, and night's not long!

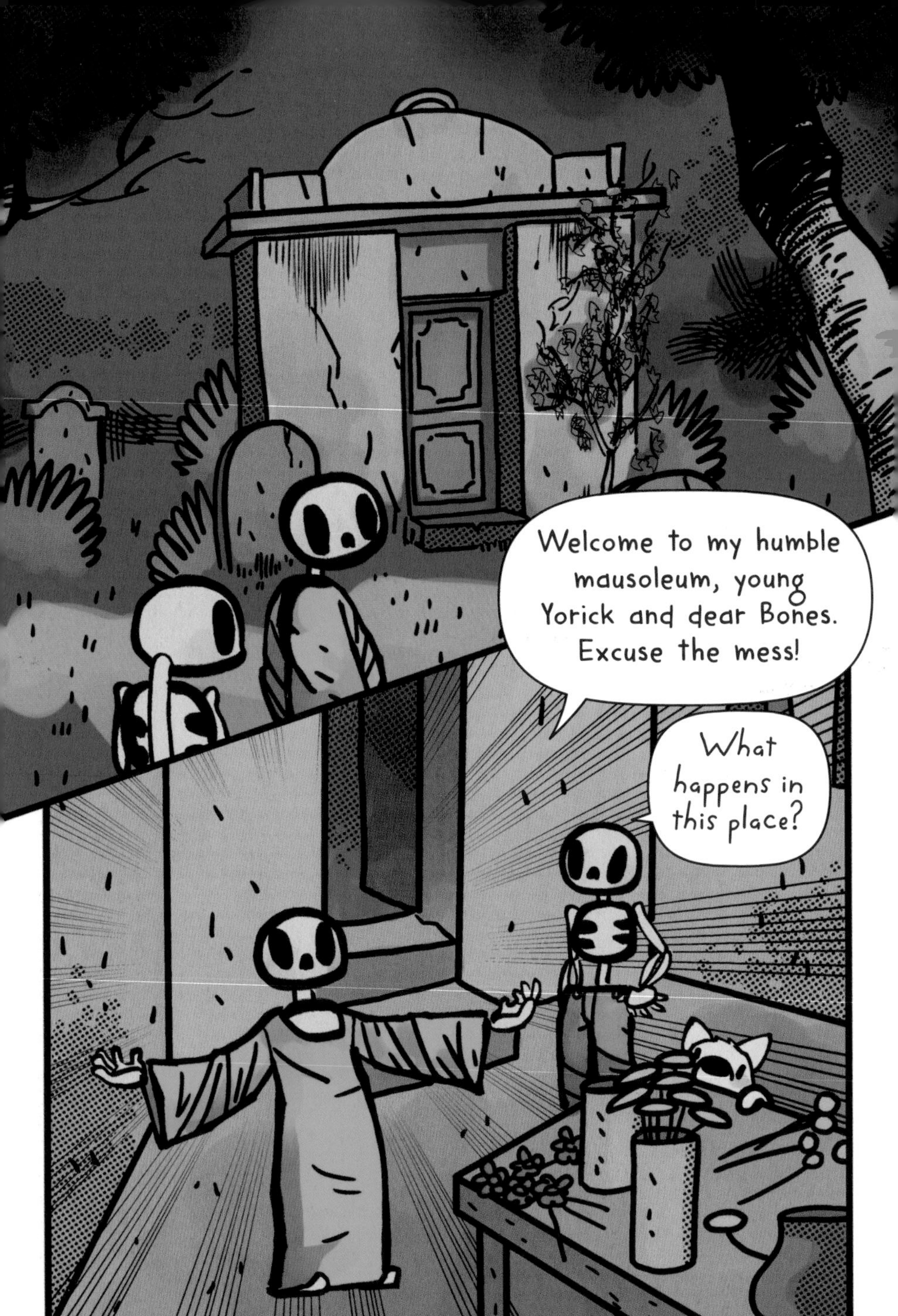
Welcome to my humble mausoleum, young Yorick and dear Bones. Excuse the mess!
What happens in this place?

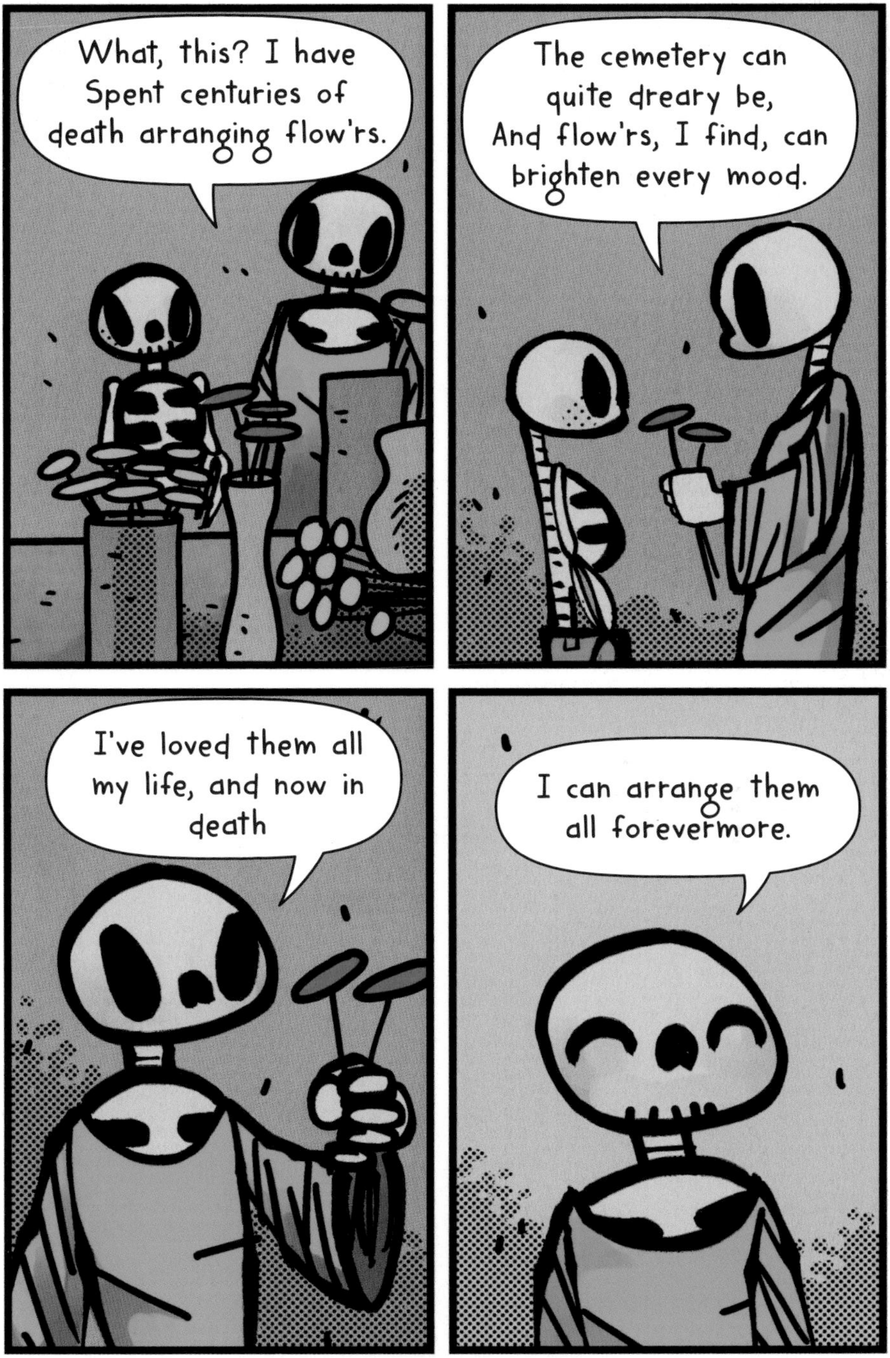
What, this? I have Spent centuries of death arranging flow'rs.
The cemetery can quite dreary be, And flow'rs, I find, can brighten every mood.
I've loved them all my life, and now in death
I can arrange them all forevermore.

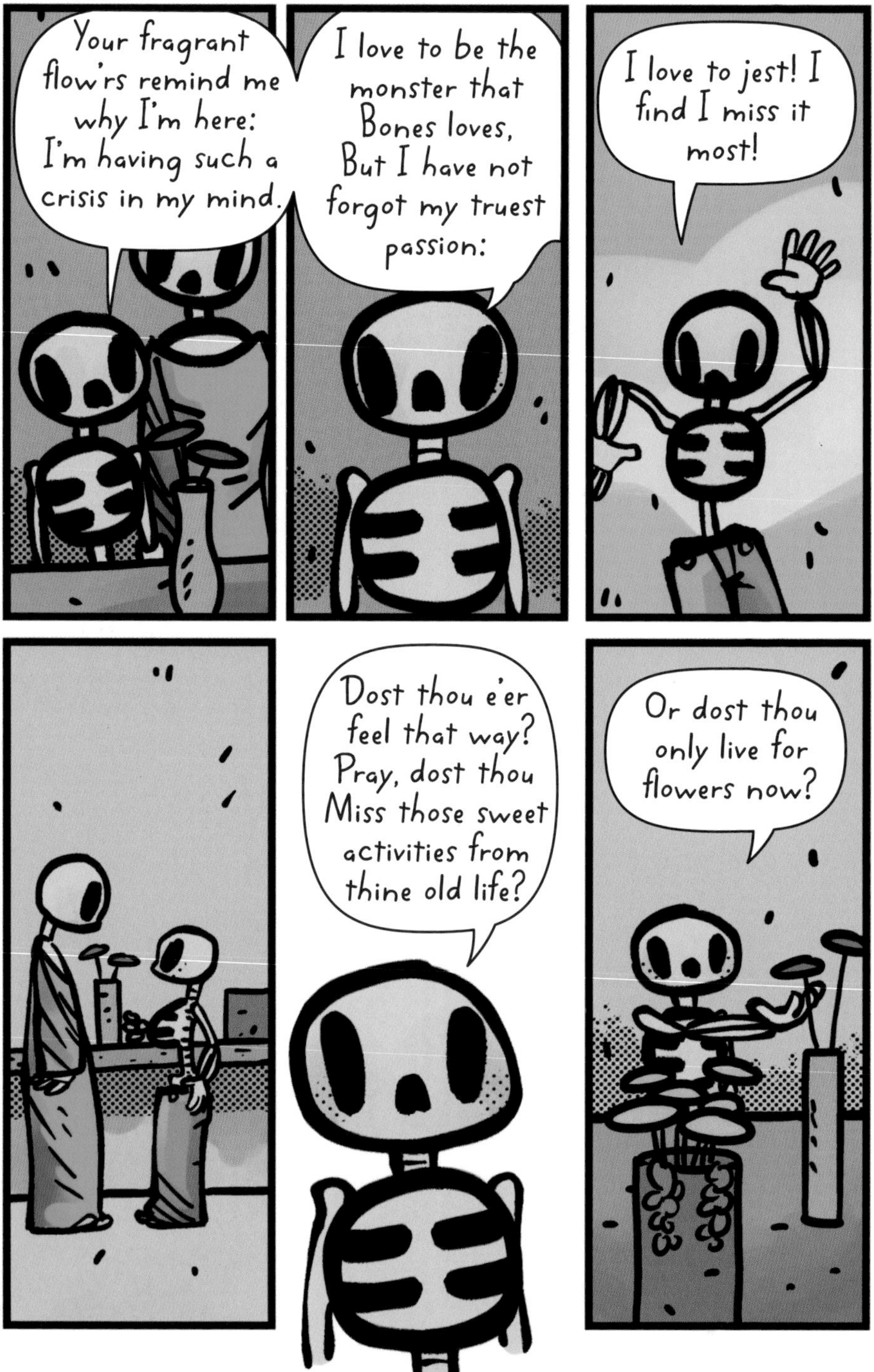
Your fragrant flow'rs remind me why I'm here: I'm having such a crisis in my mind.
I love to be the monster that Bones loves, But I have not forgot my truest passion:
I love to jest! I find I miss it most!
Dost thou e'er feel that way? Pray, dost thou Miss those sweet activities from thine old life?
Or dost thou only live for flowers now?

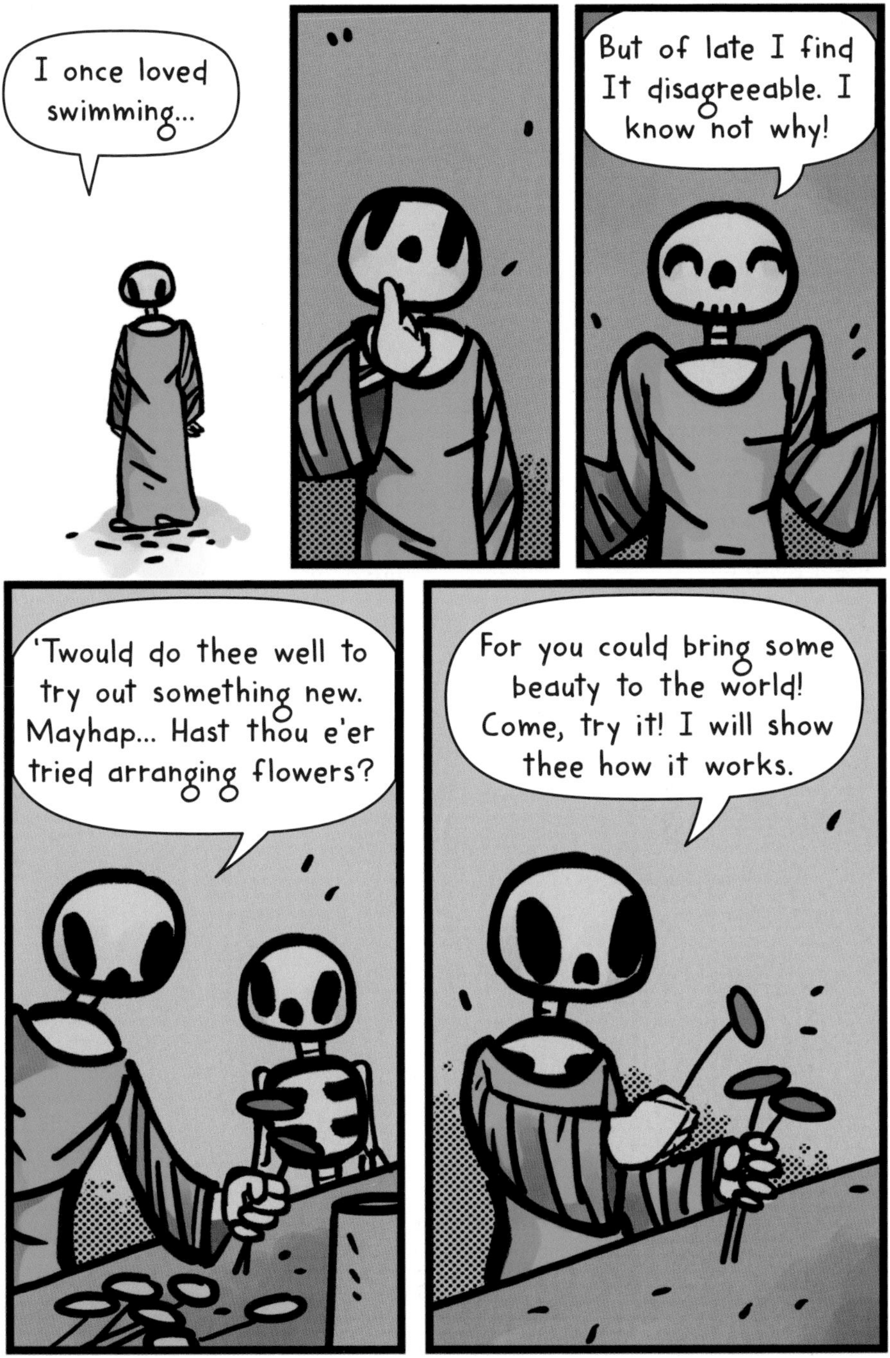
I once loved swimming...
But of late I find It disagreeable. I know not why!
'Twould do thee well to try out something new. Mayhap... Hast thou e'er tried arranging flowers?
For you could bring some beauty to the world! Come, try it! I will show thee how it works.

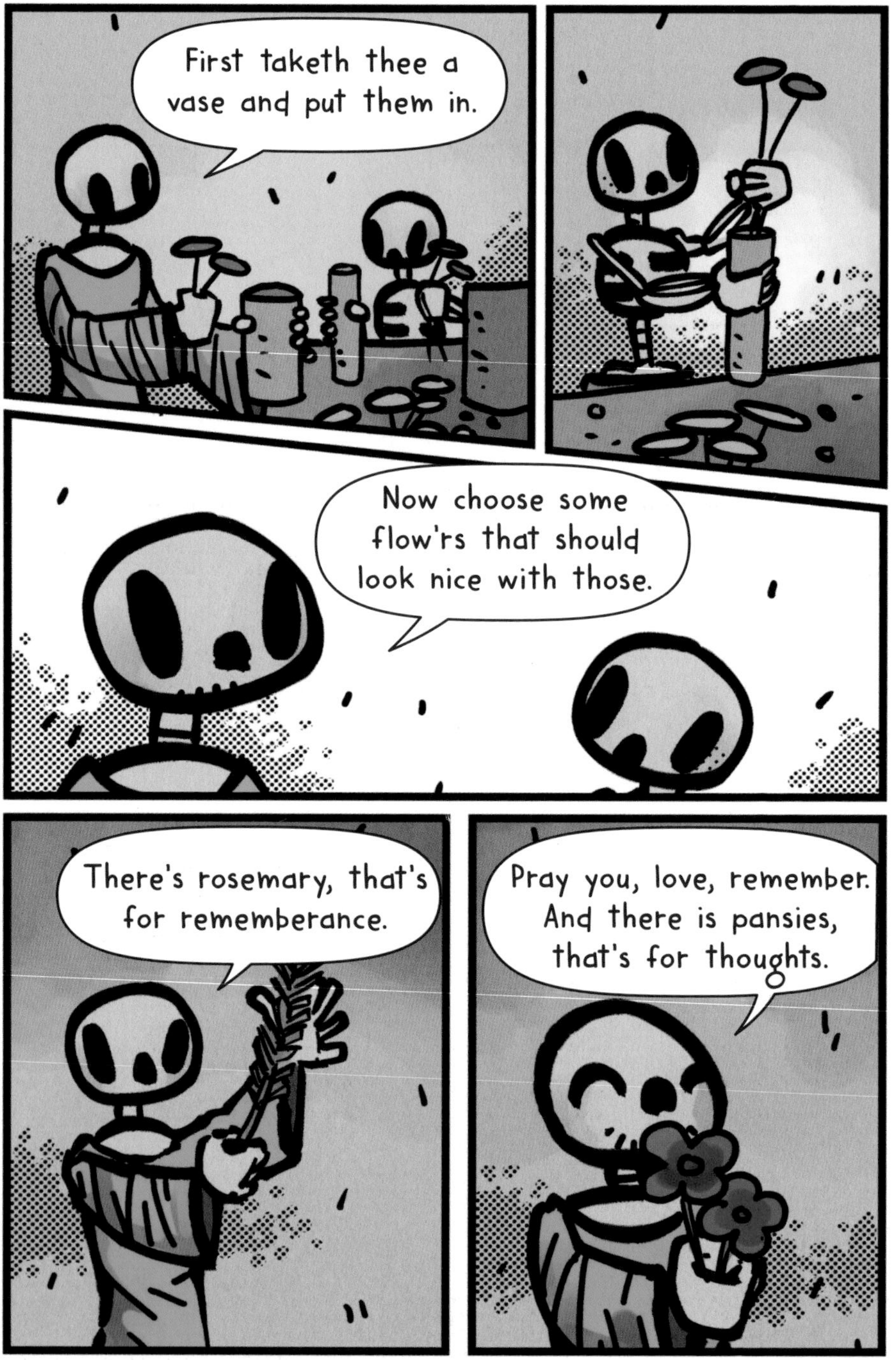
First taketh thee a vase and put them in.
Now choose some flow'rs that should look nice with those.
There's rosemary, that's for rememberance.
Pray you, love, remember. And there is pansies, that's for thoughts.

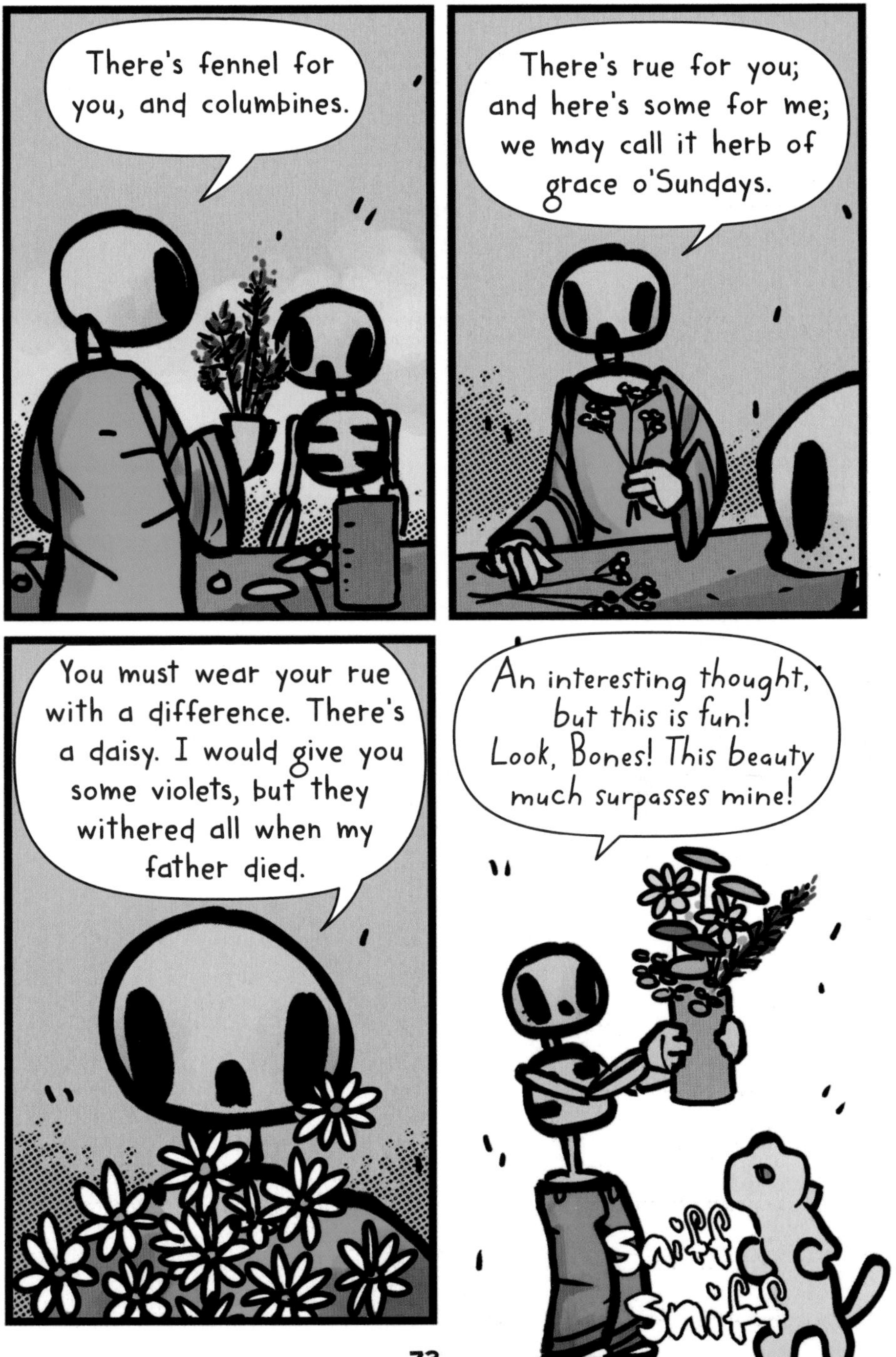
There's fennel for you, and columbines.
There's rue for you; and here's some for me; we may call it herb of grace o'Sundays.
You must wear your rue with a difference. There's a daisy. I would give you some violets, but they withered all when my father died.
An interesting thought, but this is fun! Look, Bones! This beauty much surpasses mine!
Sniff Sniff

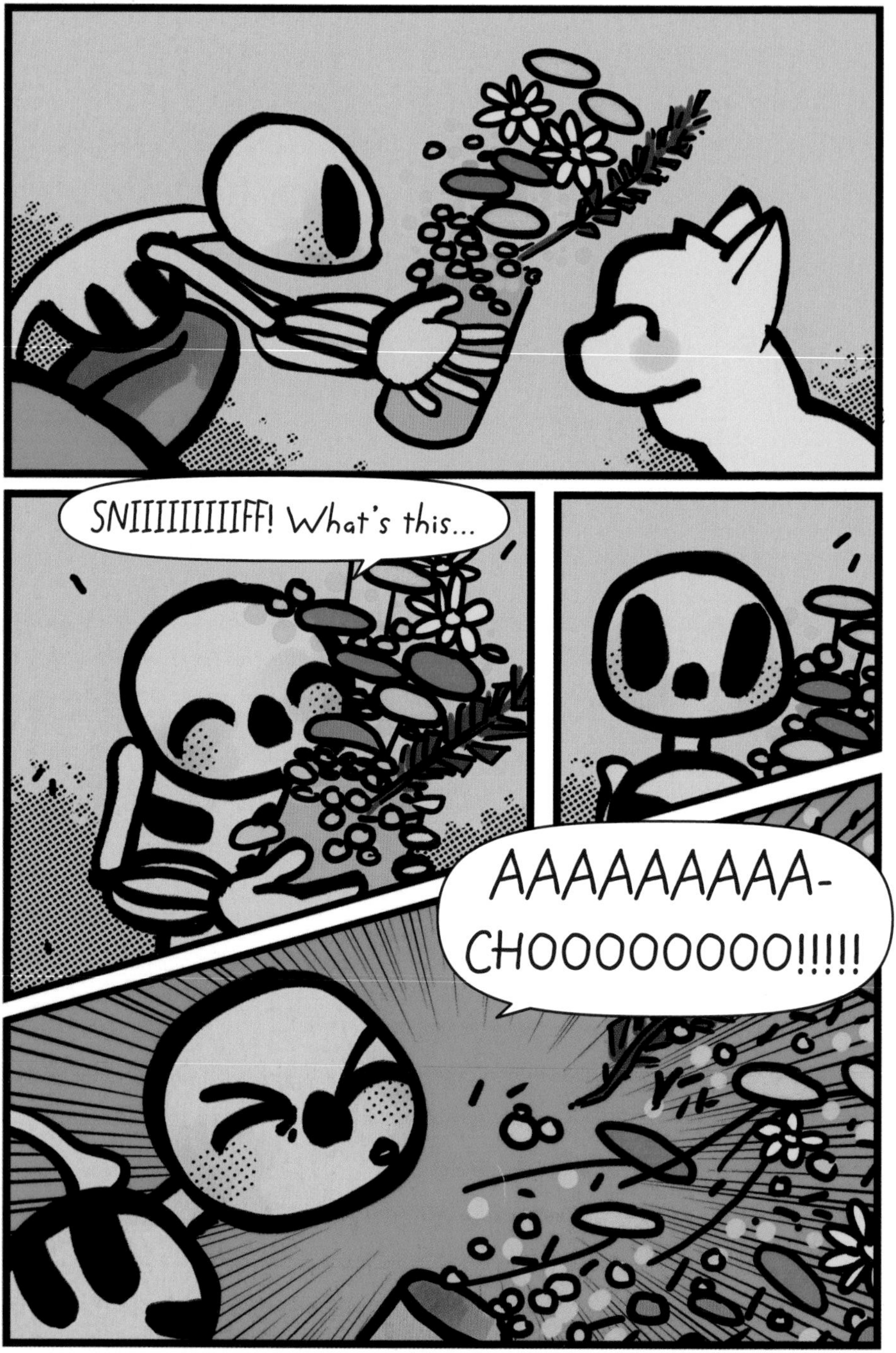
SNIIIIIIIIIFF! What's this...
AAAAAAAAA-CHOOOOOOOO!!!!!

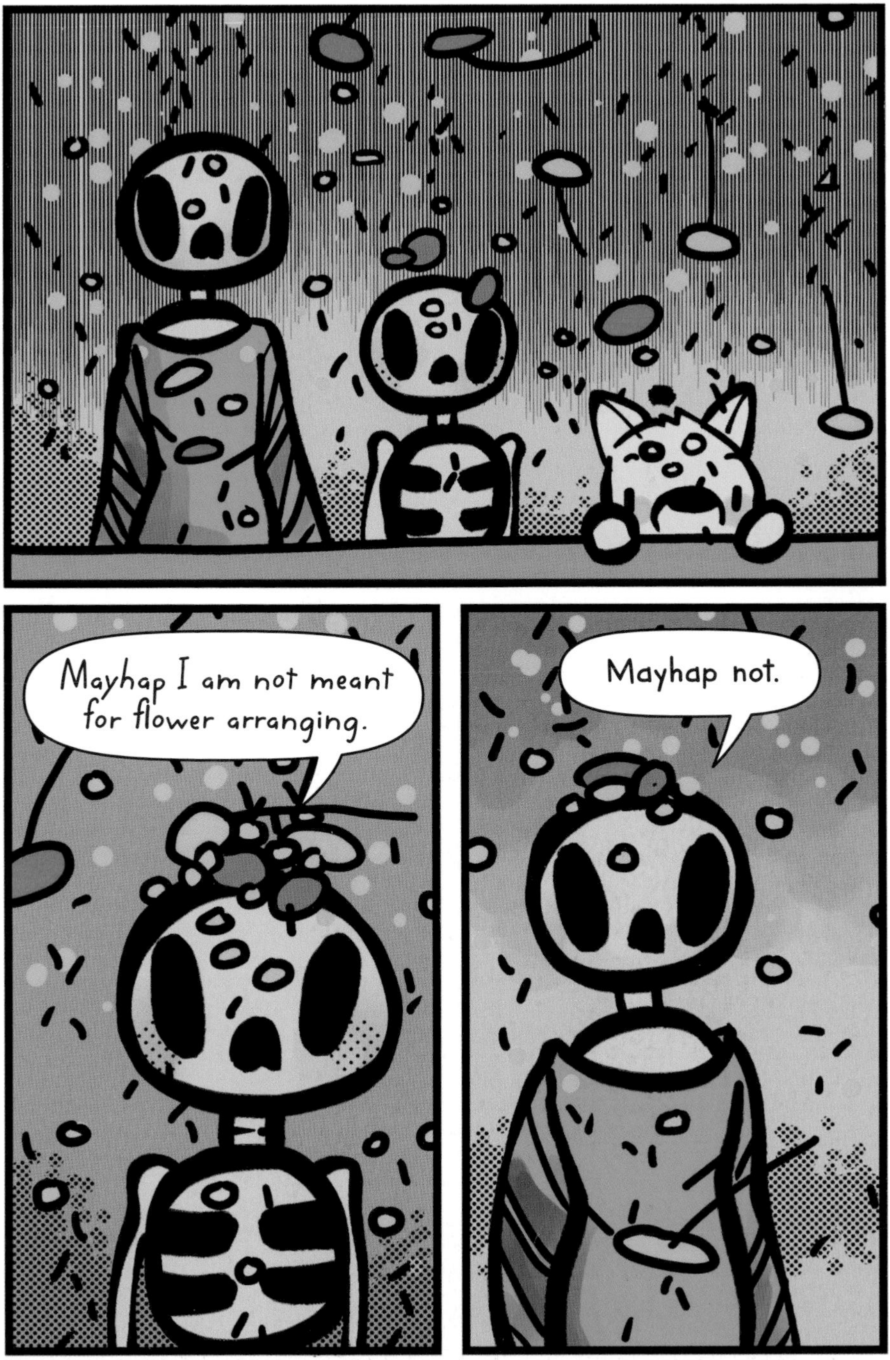
Mayhap I am not meant for flower arranging.
Mayhap not.

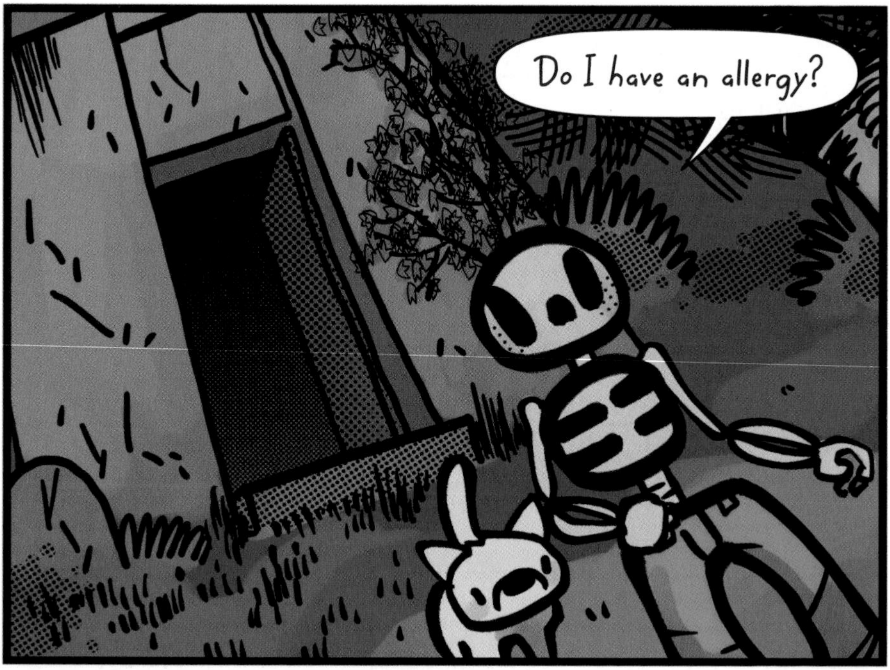
Do I have an allergy?

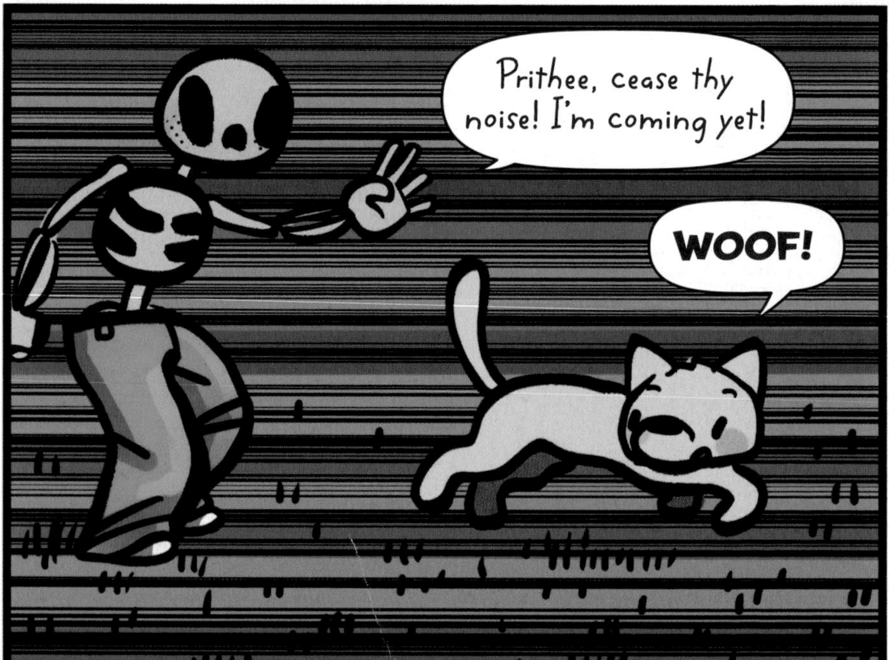
Prithee, cease thy noise! I'm coming yet!
WOOF!

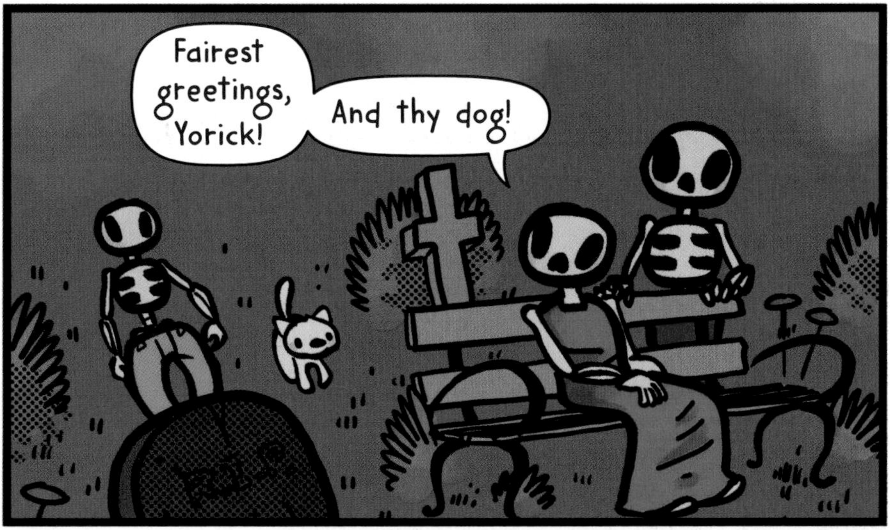
Fairest greetings, Yorick!
And thy dog!

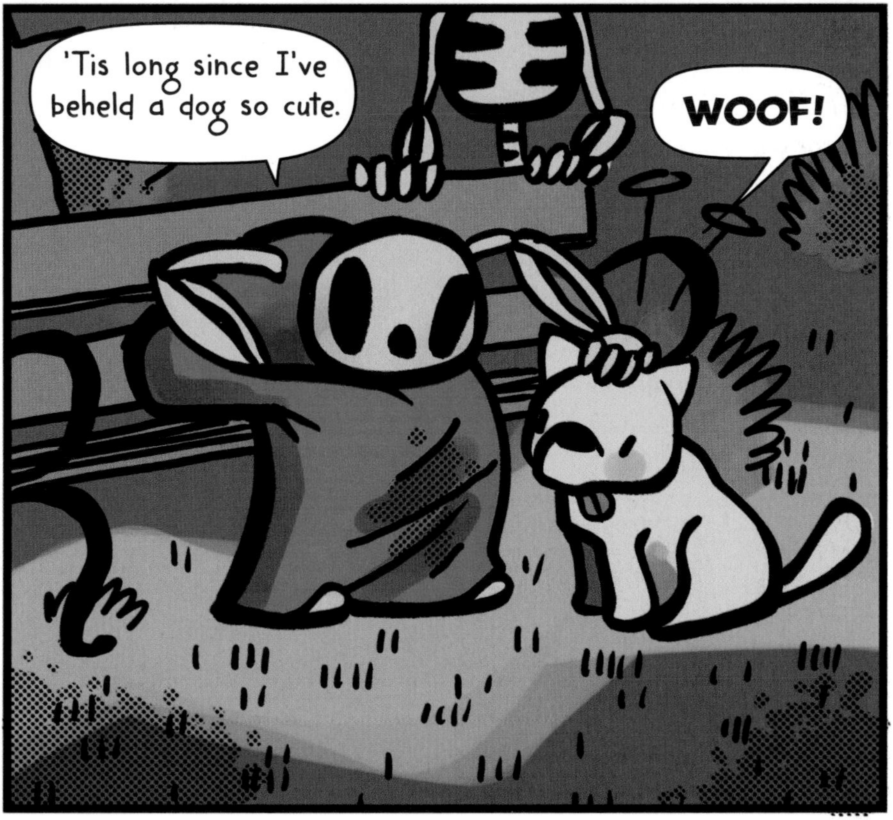
'Tis long since I've beheld a dog so cute.
WOOF!

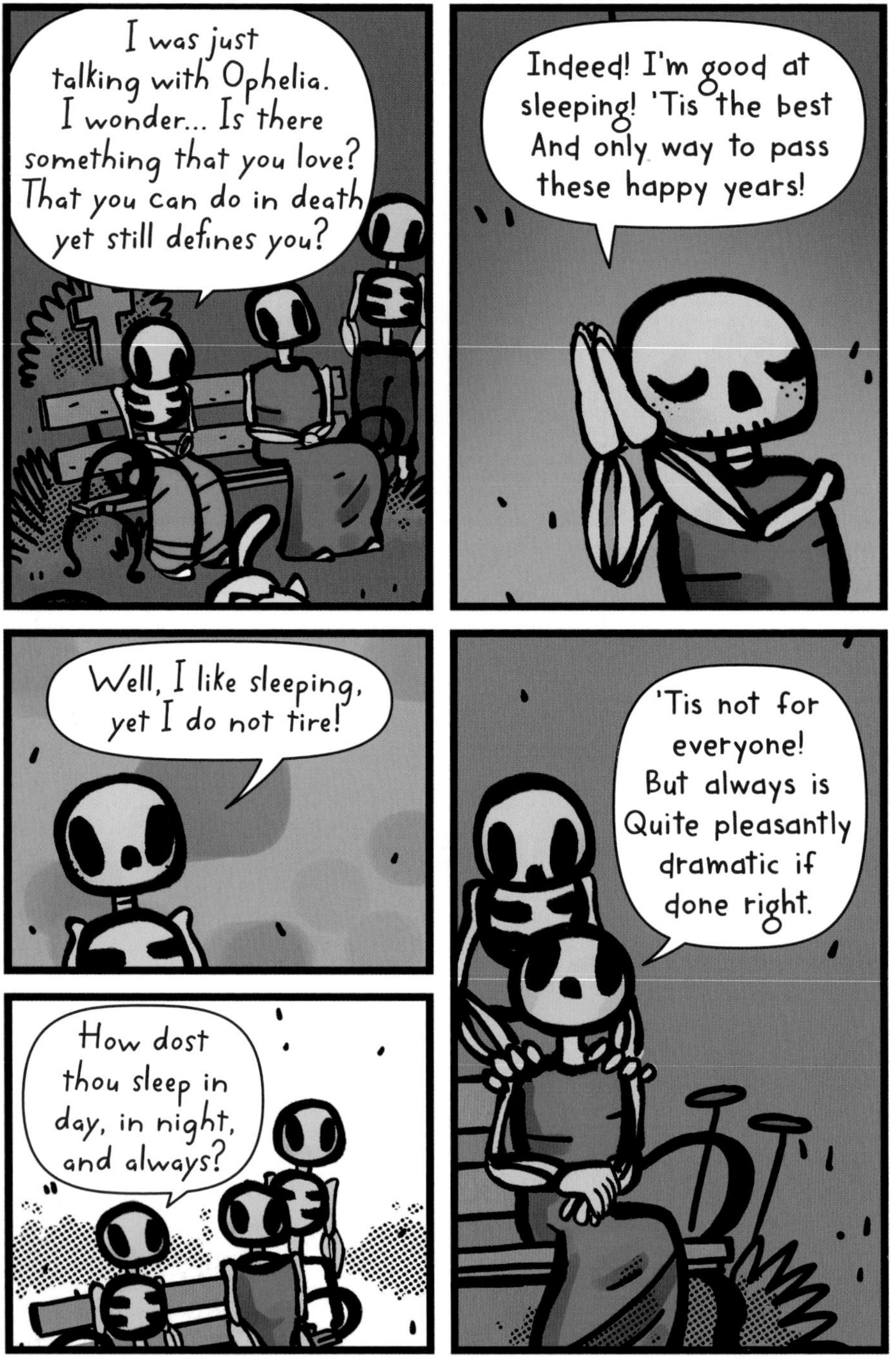
I was just talking with Ophelia. I wonder... Is there something that you love? That you can do in death yet still defines you?
Indeed! I'm good at sleeping! 'Tis the best And only way to pass these happy years!
Well, I like sleeping, yet I do not tire!
How dost thou sleep in day, in night, and always?
'Tis not for everyone! But always is Quite pleasantly dramatic if done right.

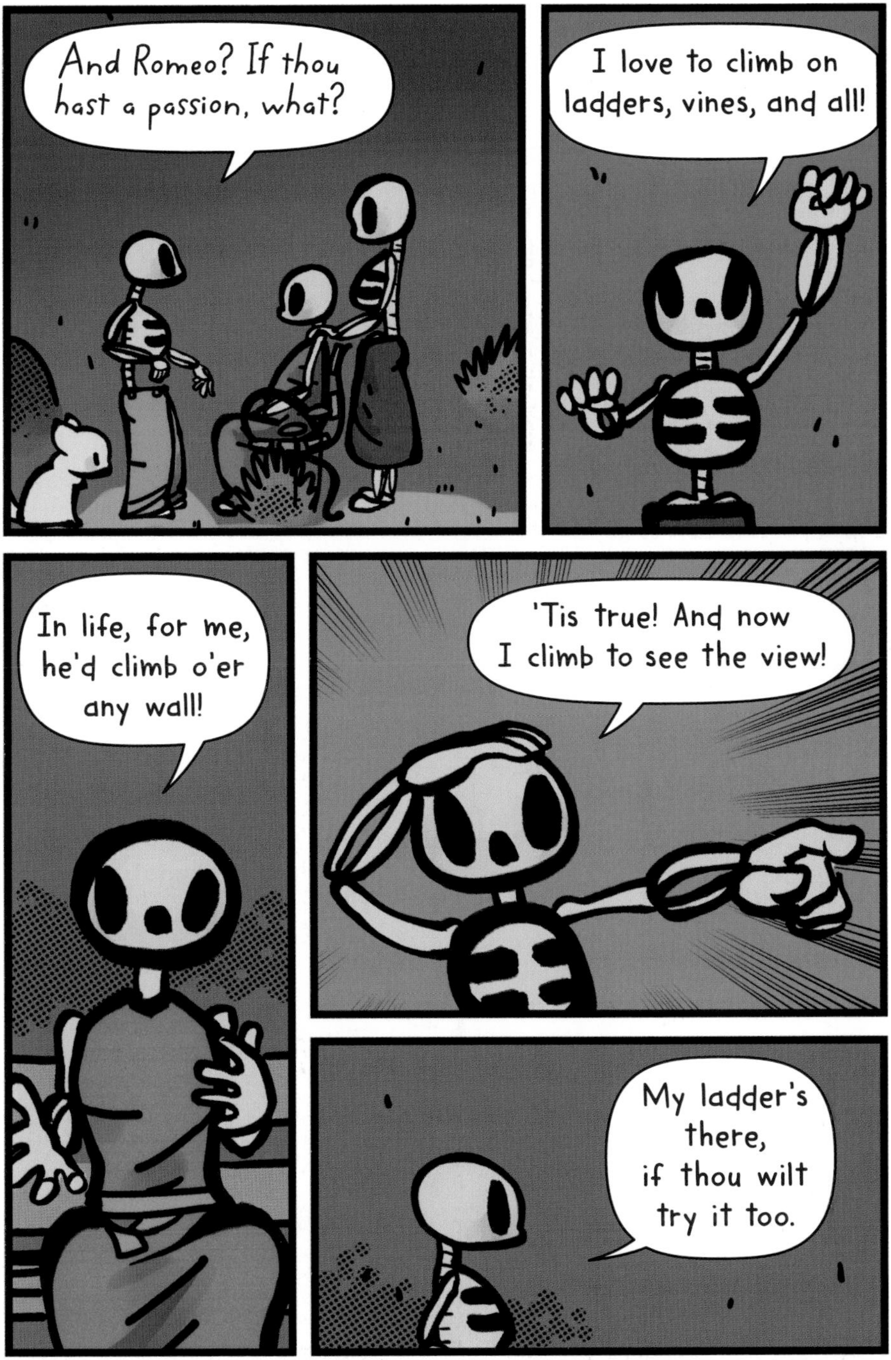

And Romeo? If thou hast a passion, what?
I love to climb on ladders, vines, and all!
In life, for me, he'd climb o'er any wall!
'Tis true! And now I climb to see the view!
My ladder's there, if thou wilt try it too.

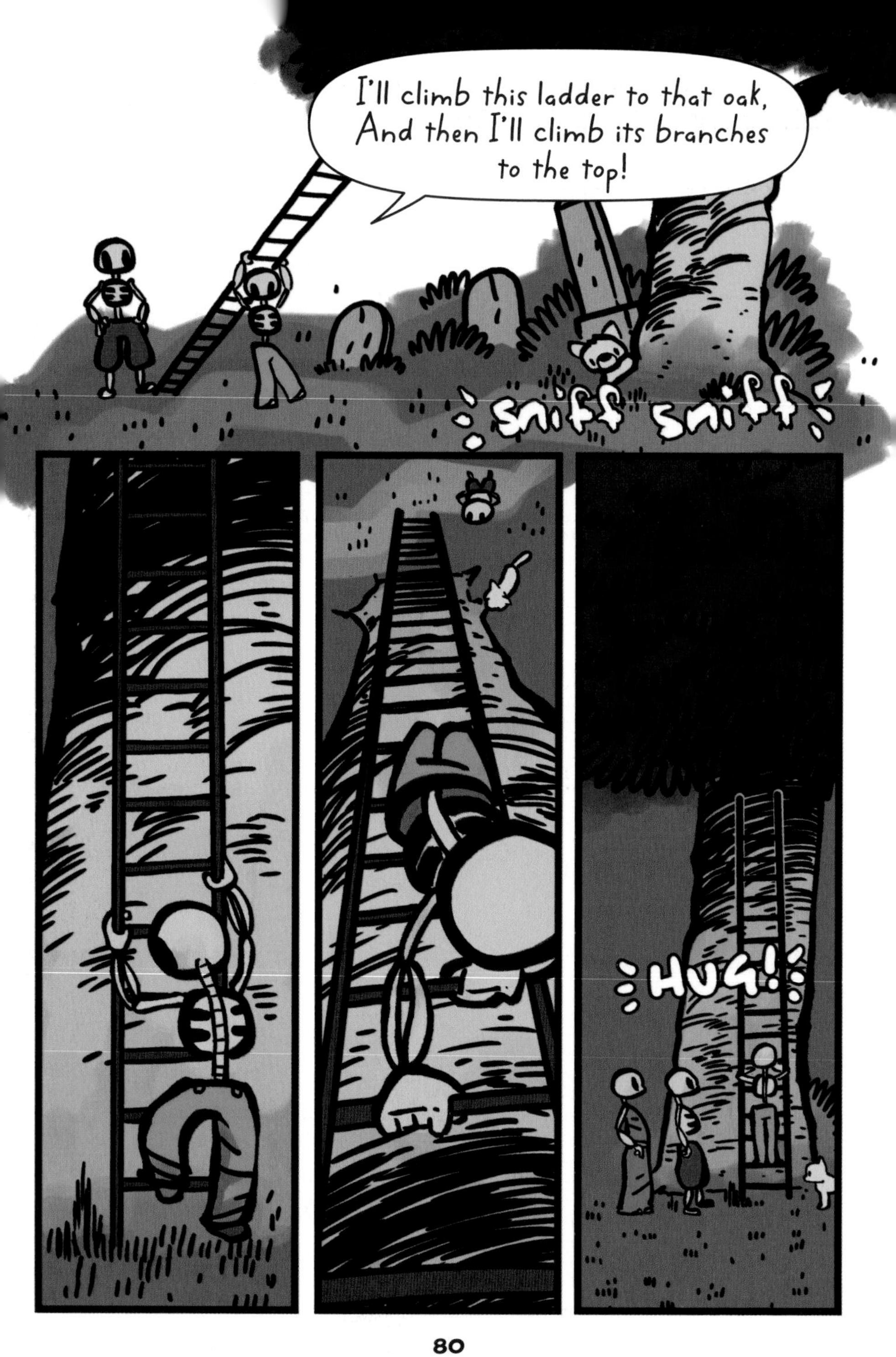
I'll climb this ladder to that oak, And then I'll climb its branches to the top!
sniff sniff
HUG!

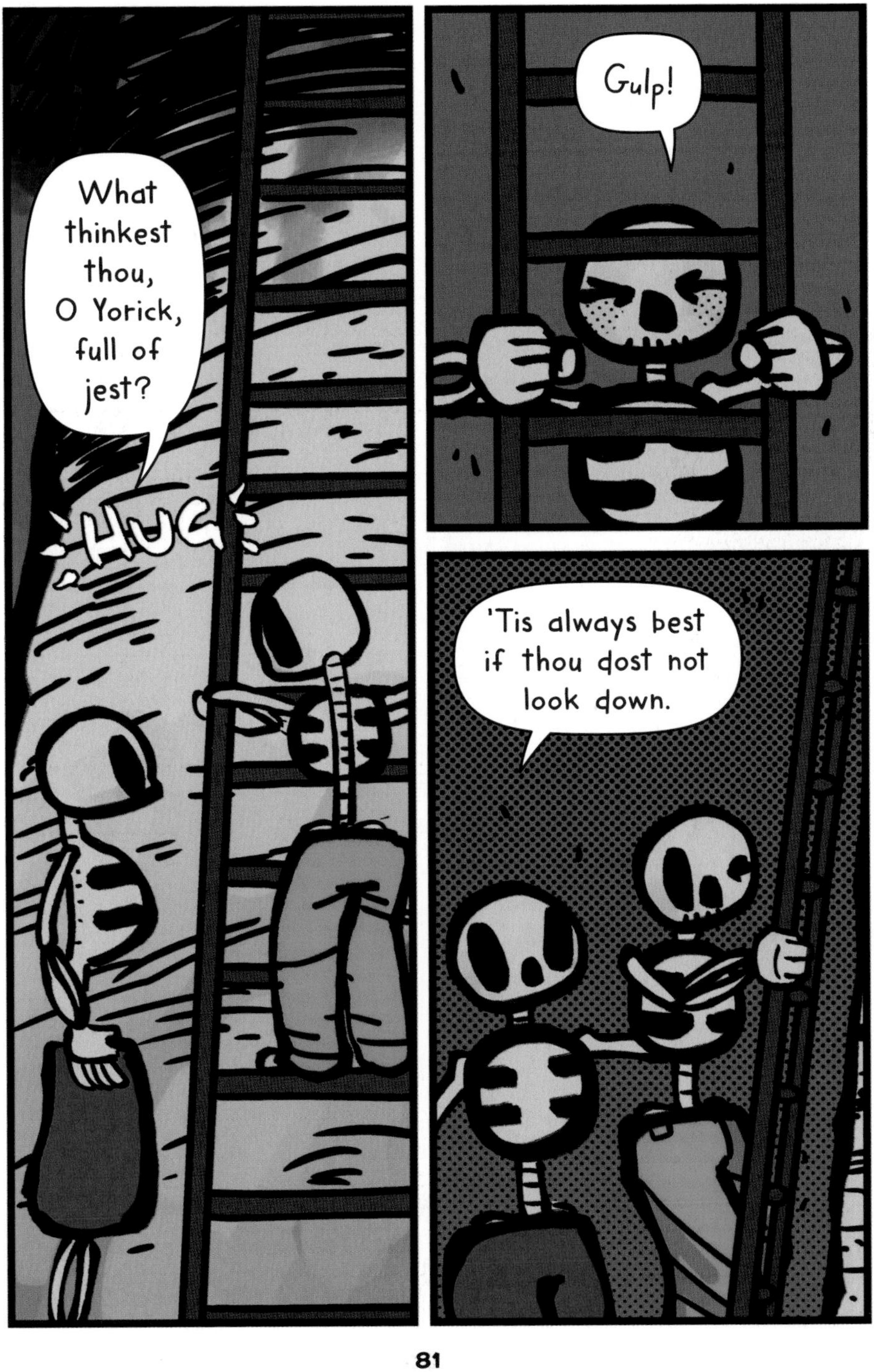
What thinkest thou, O Yorick, full of jest?
HUG
Gulp!
'Tis always best if thou dost not look down.

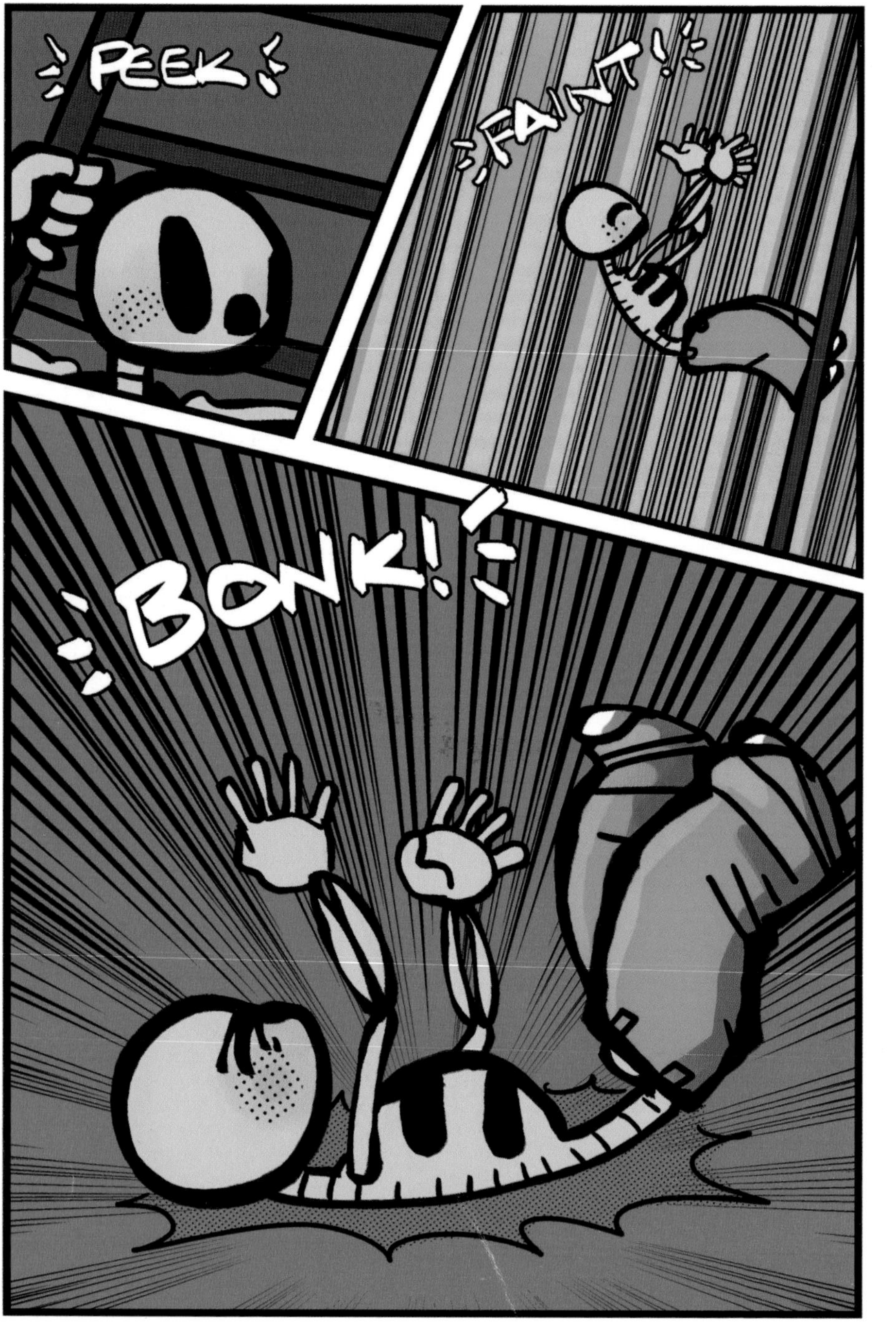
PEEK
FAINT!
BONK!

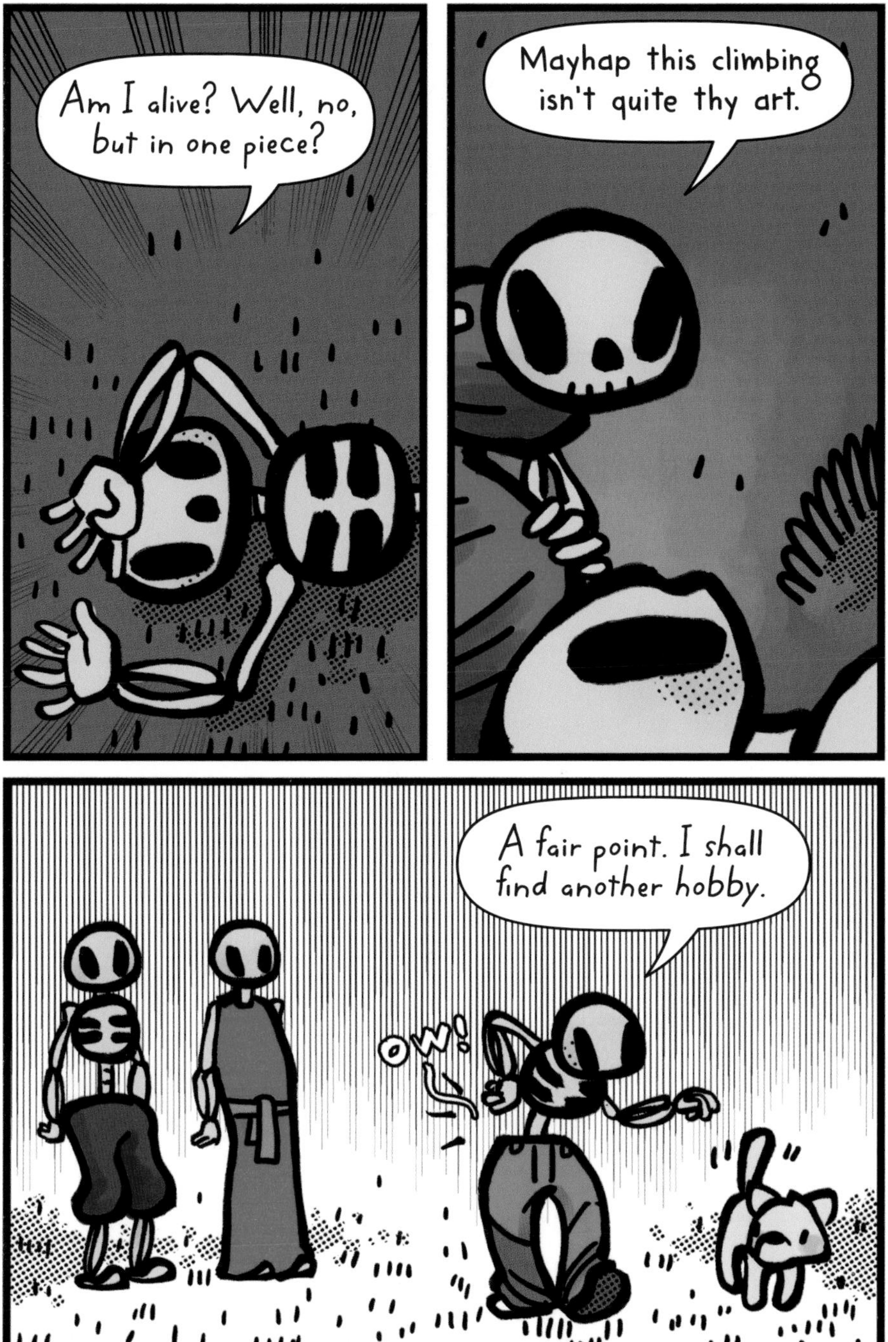
Am I alive? Well, no, but in one piece?
Mayhap this climbing isn't quite thy art.
A fair point. I shall find another hobby.
OW!

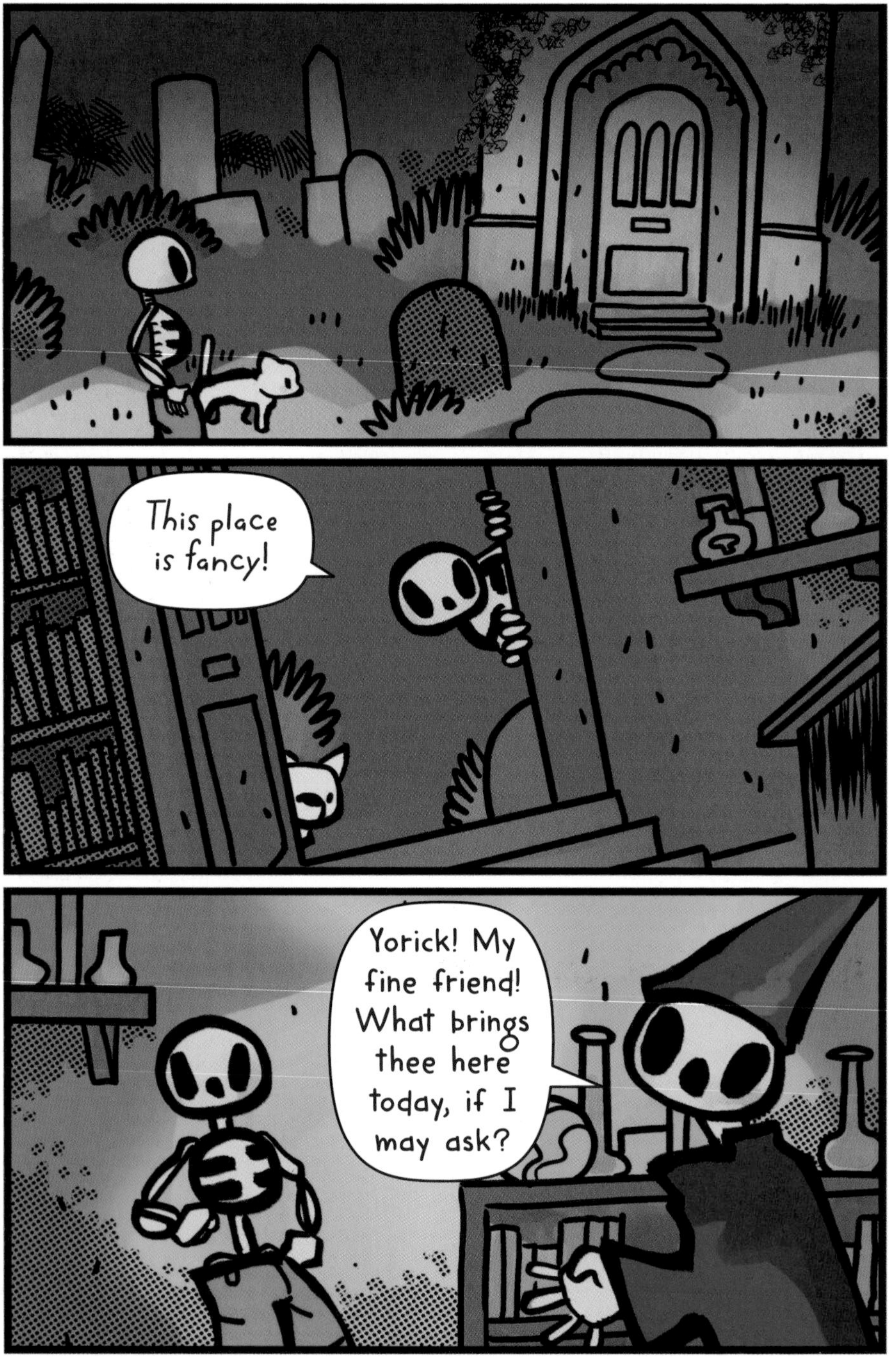
This place is fancy!
Yorick! My fine friend! What brings thee here today, if I may ask?

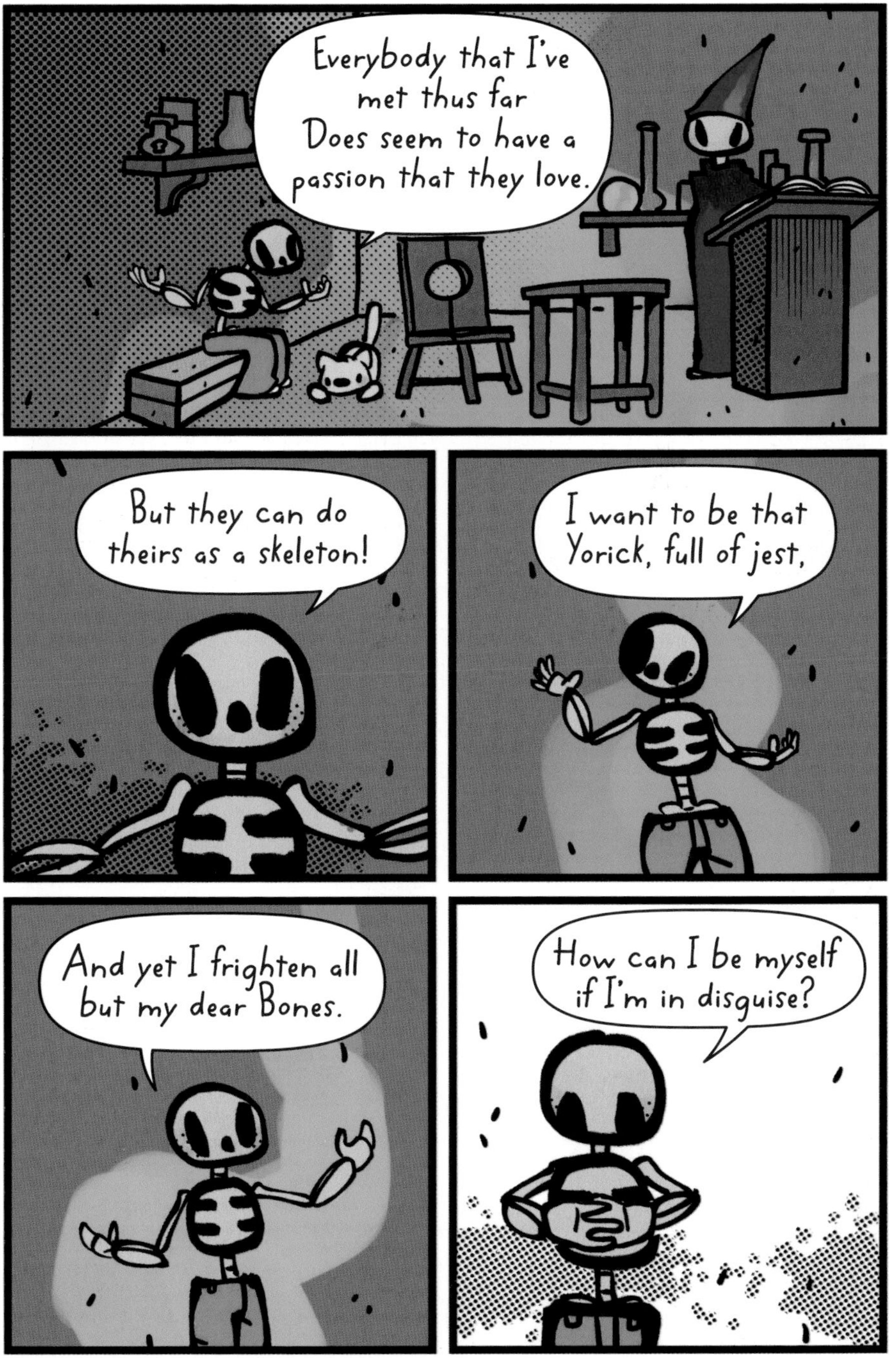
Everybody that I've met thus far Does seem to have a passion that they love.
But they can do theirs as a skeleton!
I want to be that Yorick, full of jest,
And yet I frighten all but my dear Bones.
How can I be myself if I'm in disguise?

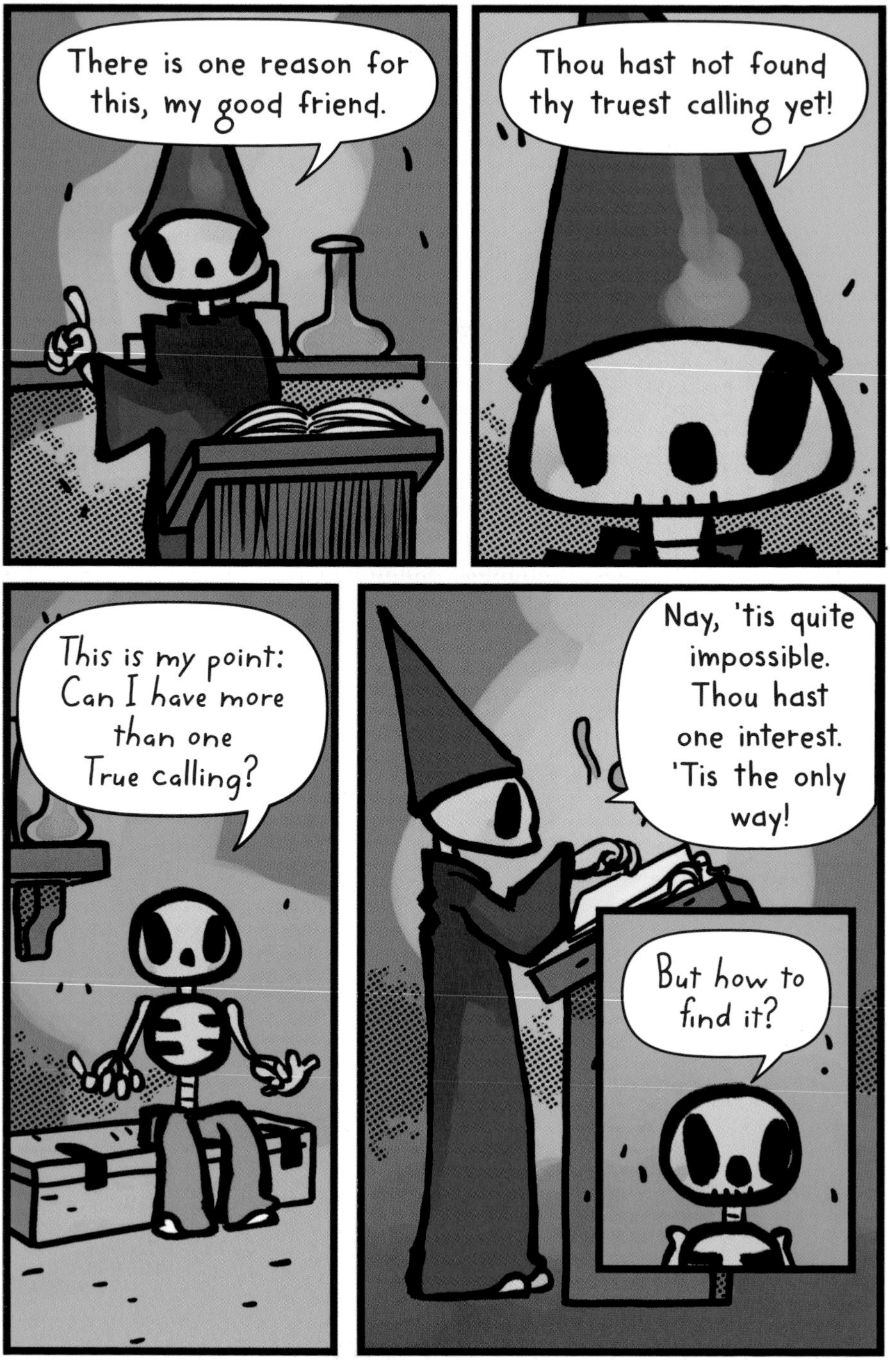
There is one reason for this, my good friend.
Thou hast not found thy truest calling yet!
This is my point: Can I have more than one True calling?
Nay, 'tis quite impossible. Thou hast one interest. 'Tis the only way!
But how to find it?

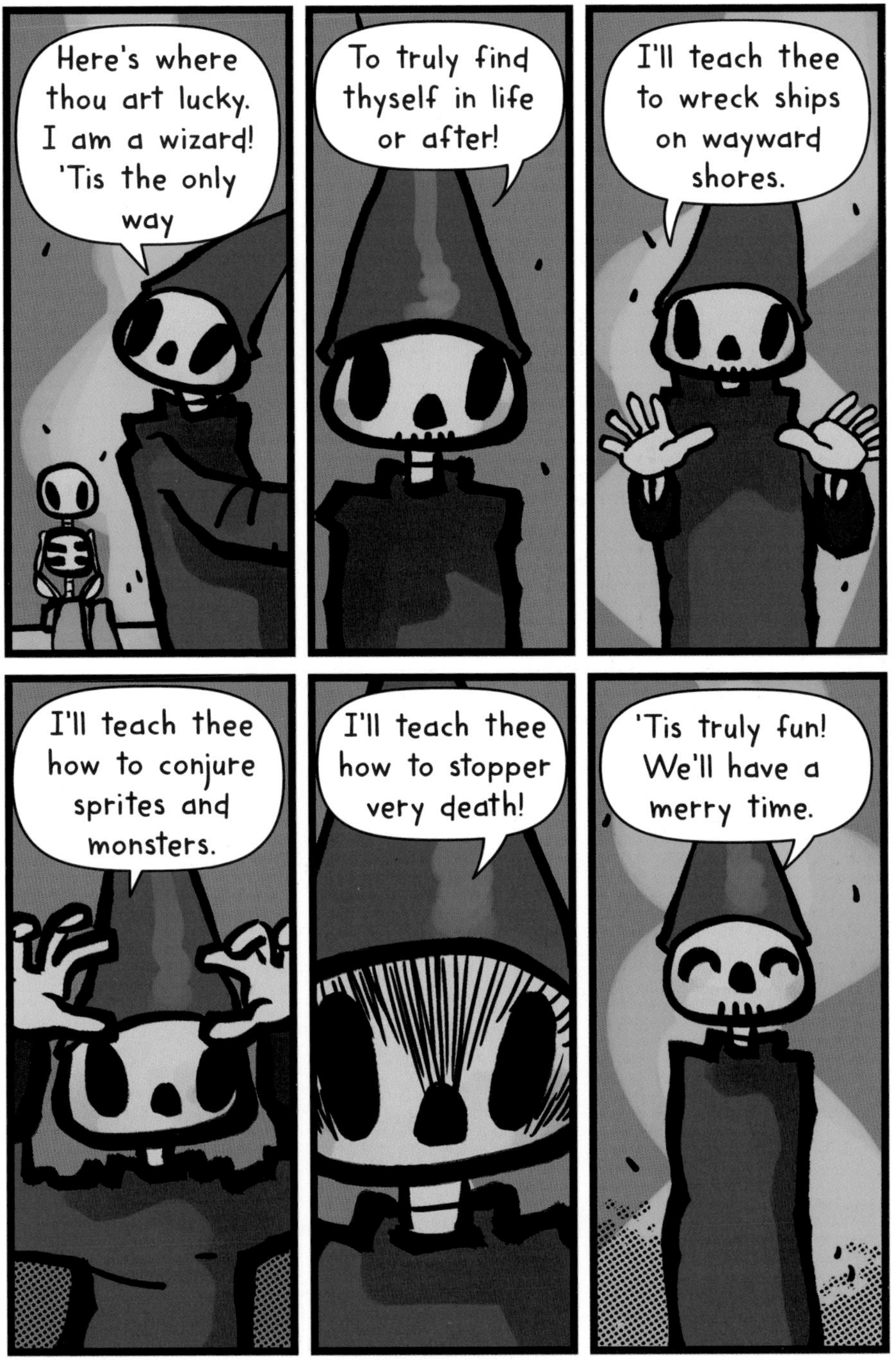
Here's where thou art lucky. I am a wizard! 'Tis the only way
To truly find thyself in life or after!
I'll teach thee to wreck ships on wayward shores.
I'll teach thee how to conjure sprites and monsters.
I'll teach thee how to stopper very death!
'Tis truly fun! We'll have a merry time.

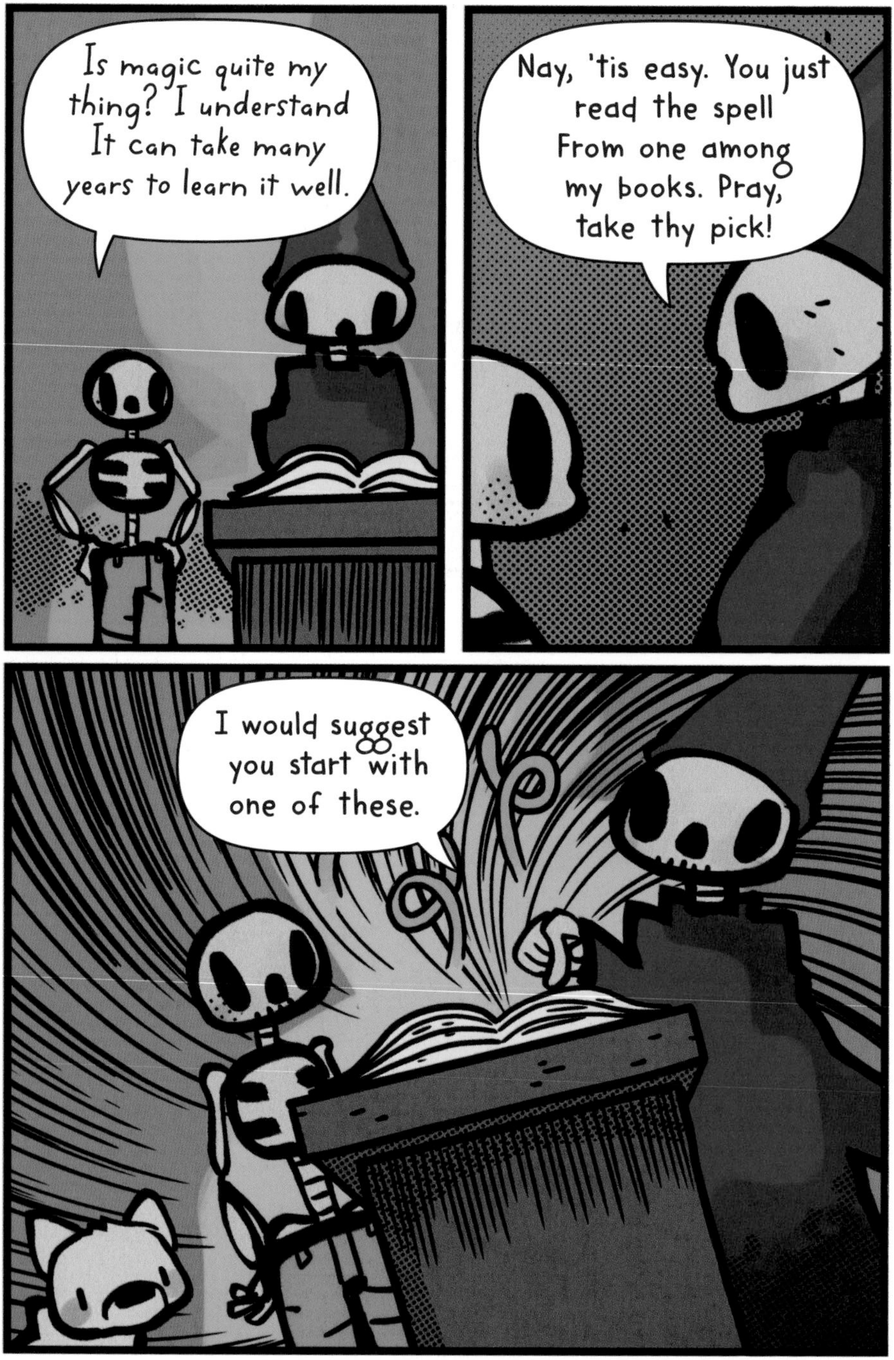
Is magic quite my thing? I understand It can take many years to learn it well.
Nay, 'tis easy. You just read the spell From one among my books. Pray, take thy pick!
I would suggest you start with one of these.

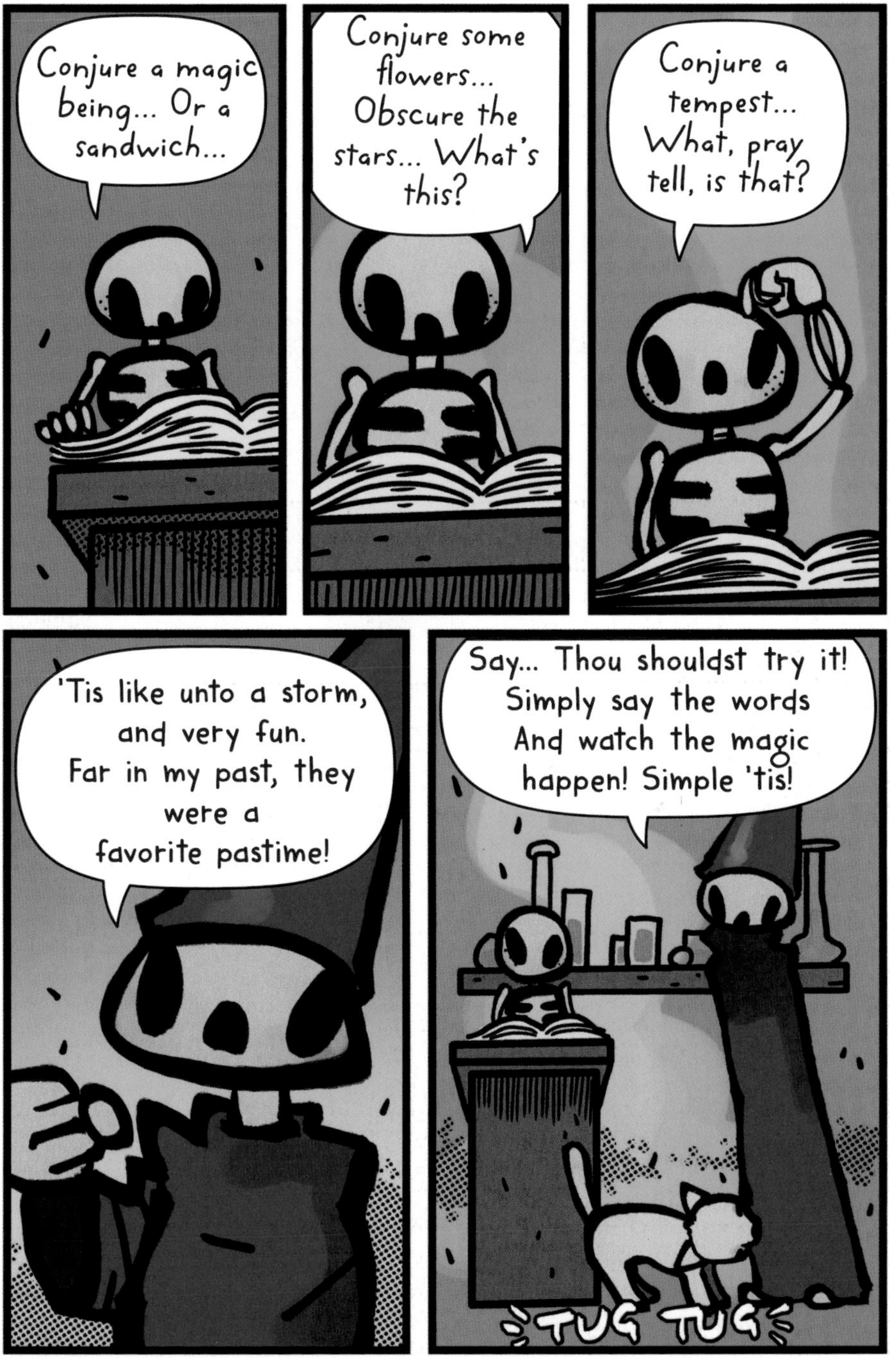
Conjure a magic being... Or a sandwich...
Conjure some flowers... Obscure the stars... What's this?
Conjure a tempest... What, pray tell, is that?
'Tis like unto a storm, and very fun. Far in my past, they were a favorite pastime!
Say... Thou shouldst try it! Simply say the words And watch the magic happen! Simple 'tis!
TUG TUG

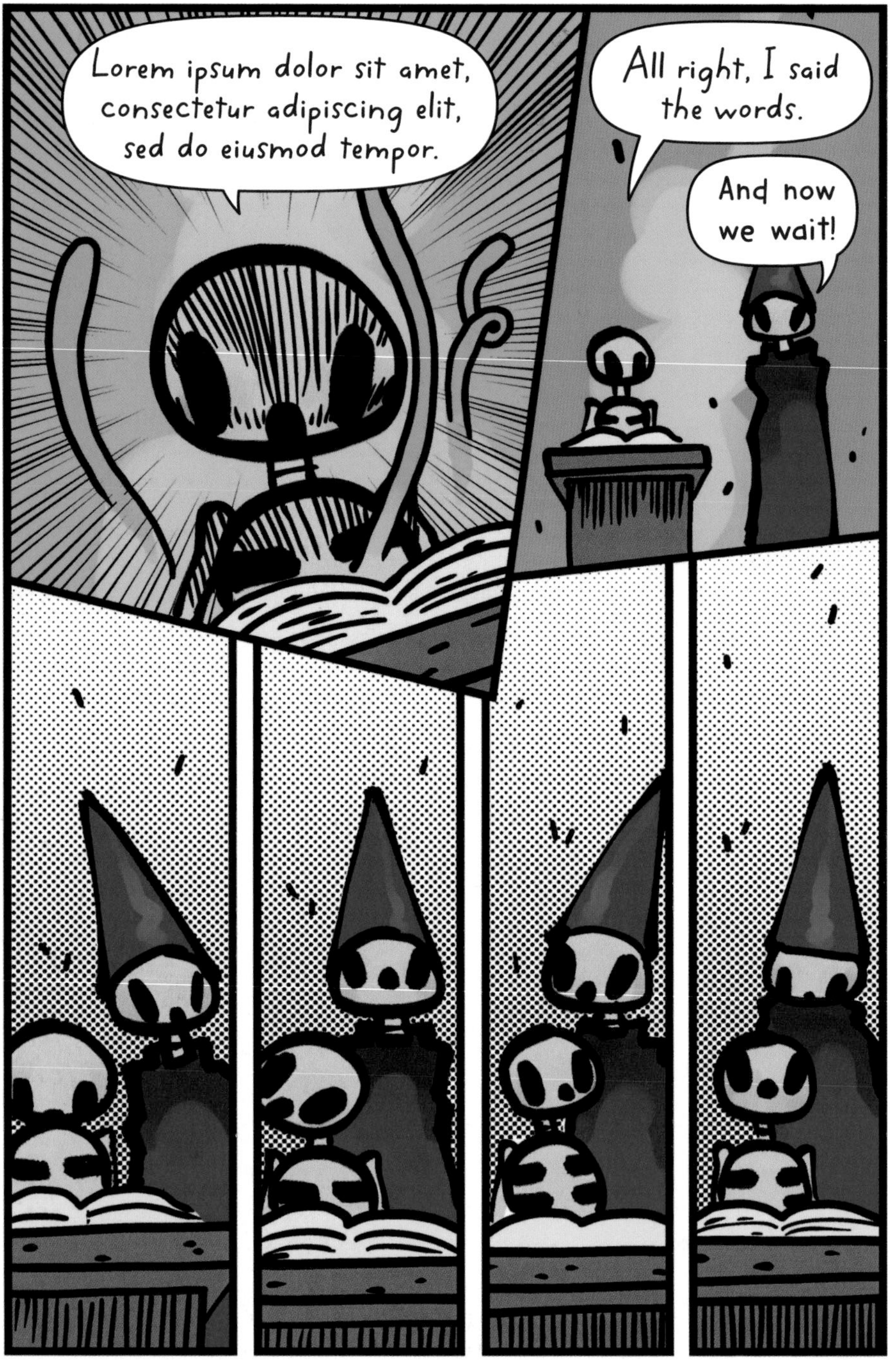
Lorem ipsum dolor sit amet, consectetur adipiscing elit, sed do eiusmod tempor.
All right, I said the words.
And now we wait!

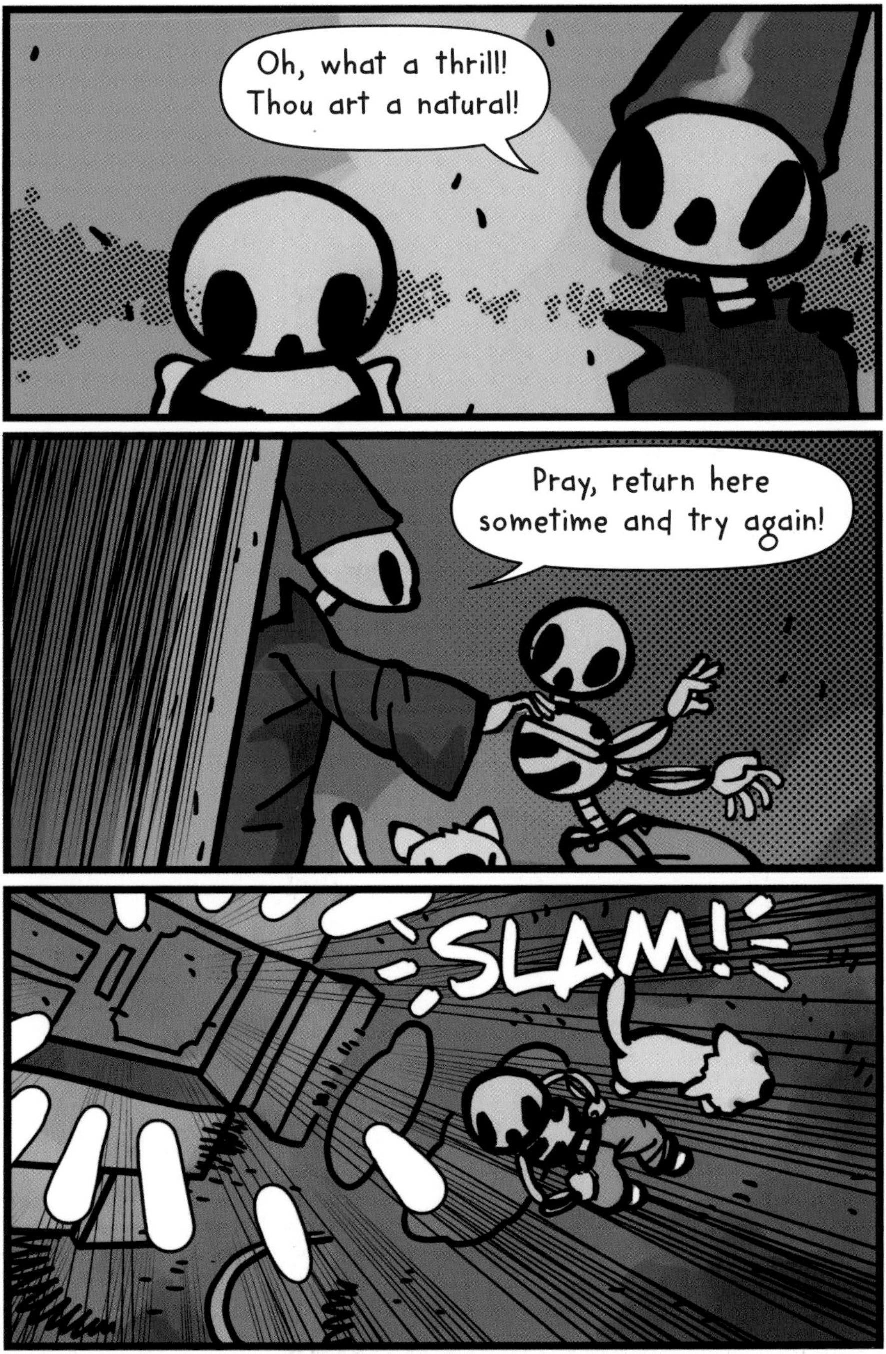
Oh, what a thrill! Thou art a natural!
Pray, return here sometime and try again!
SLAM!

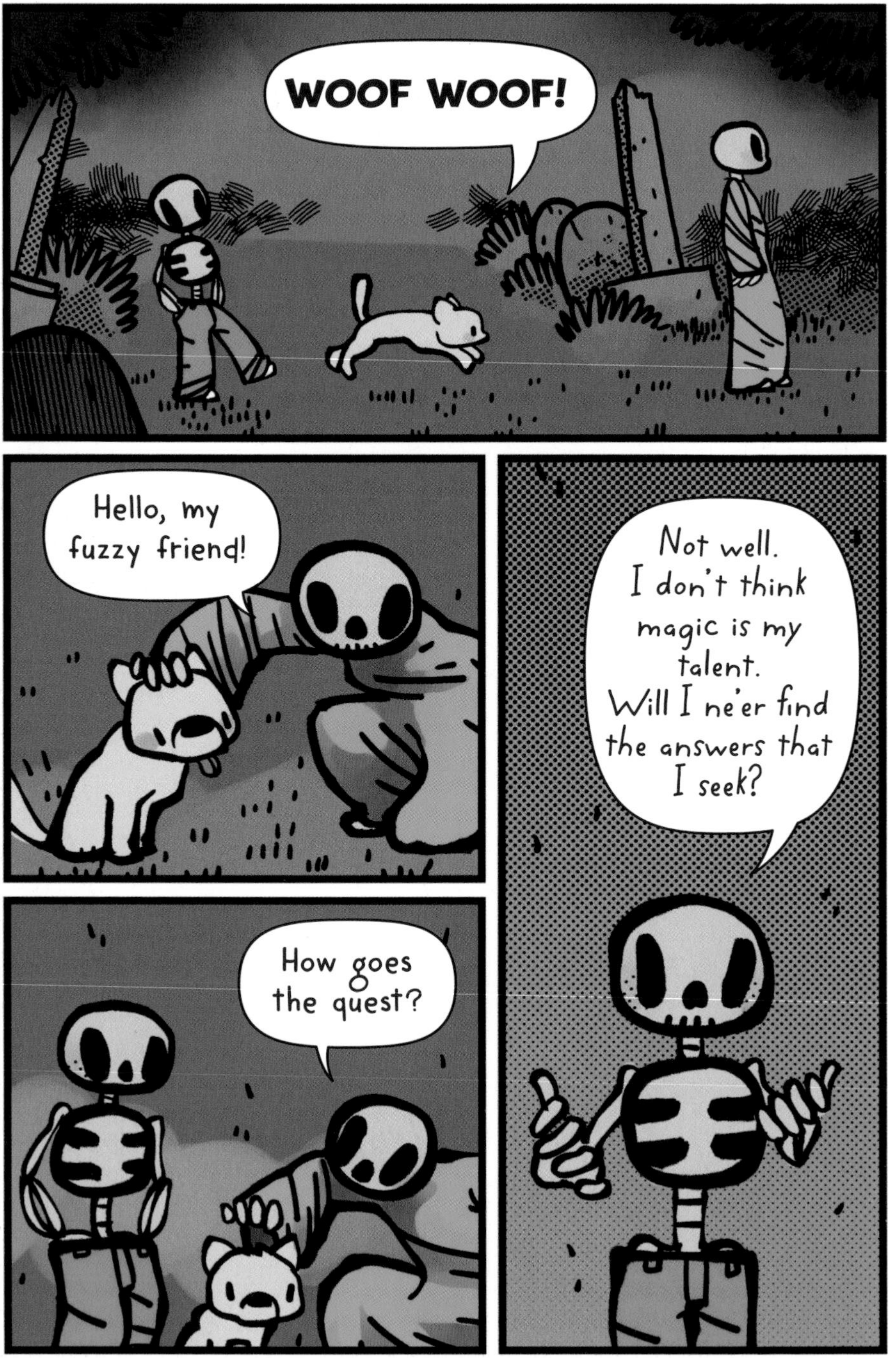
WOOF WOOF!
Hello, my fuzzy friend!
How goes the quest?
Not well. I don't think magic is my talent. Will I ne'er find the answers that I seek?

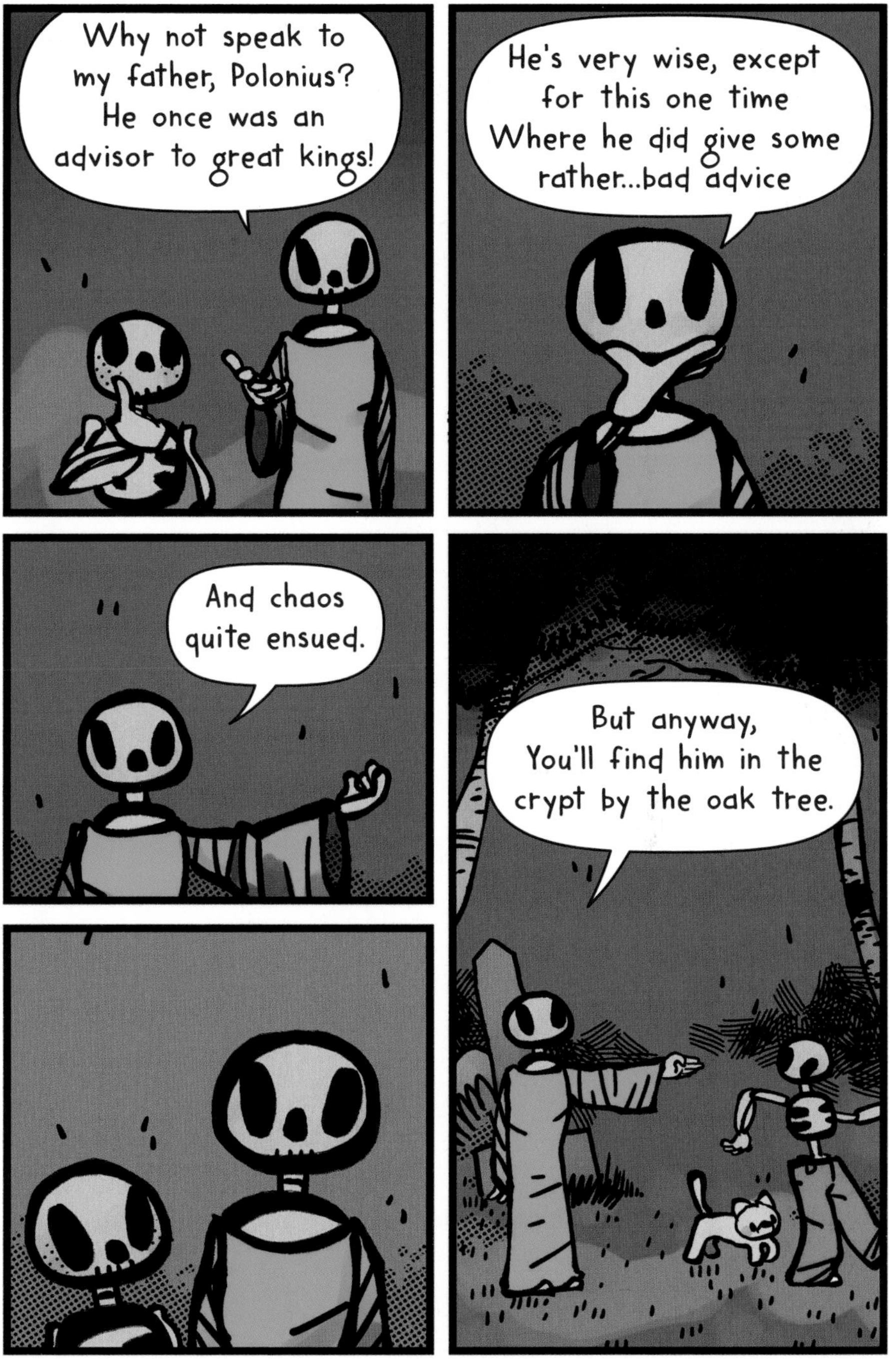
Why not speak to my father, Polonius? He once was an advisor to great kings!
He's very wise, except for this one time Where he did give some rather...bad advice
And chaos quite ensued.
But anyway, You'll find him in the crypt by the oak tree.

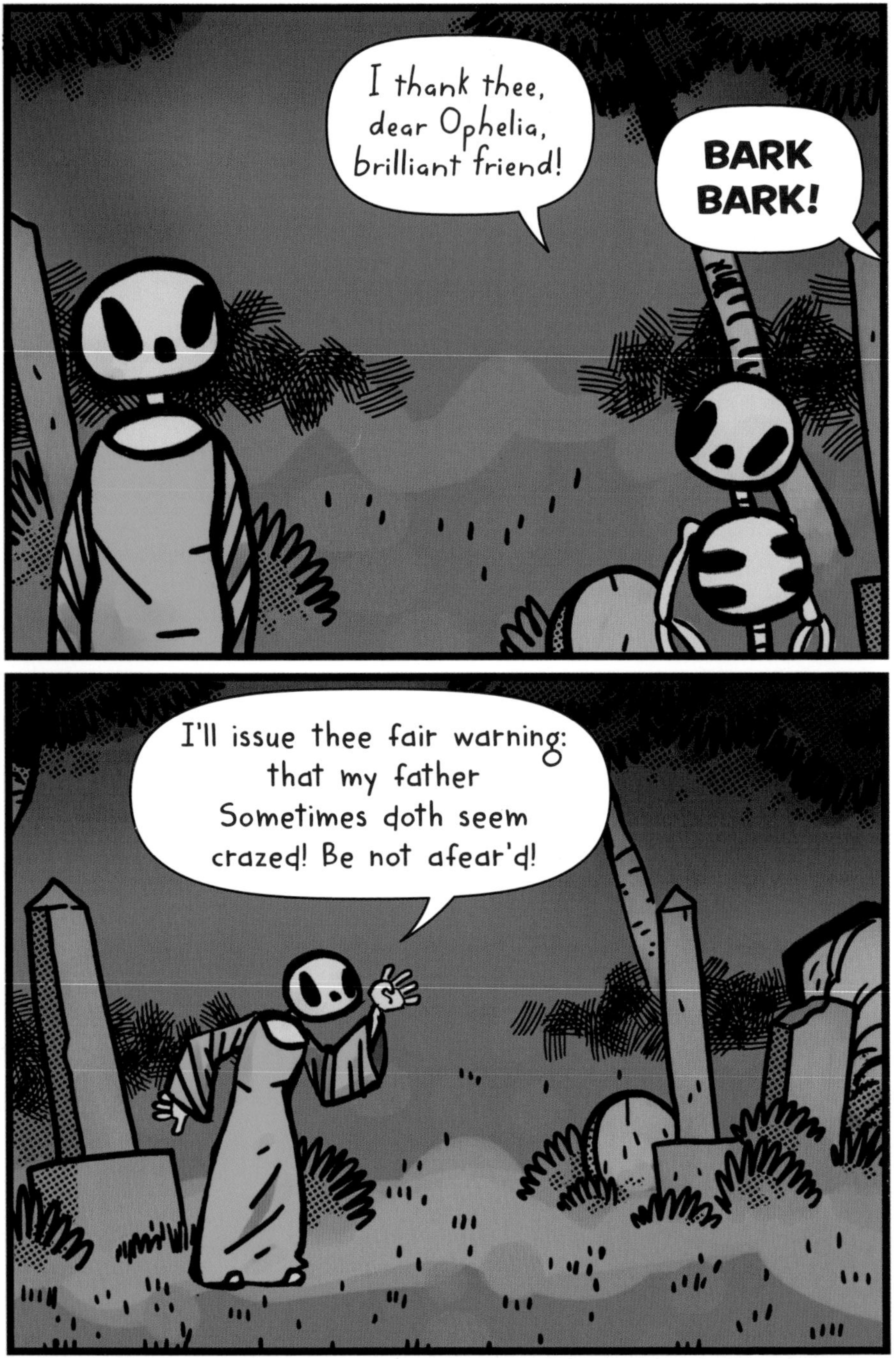
I thank thee, dear Ophelia, brilliant friend!
BARK BARK!
I'll issue thee fair warning: that my father Sometimes doth seem crazed! Be not afear'd!

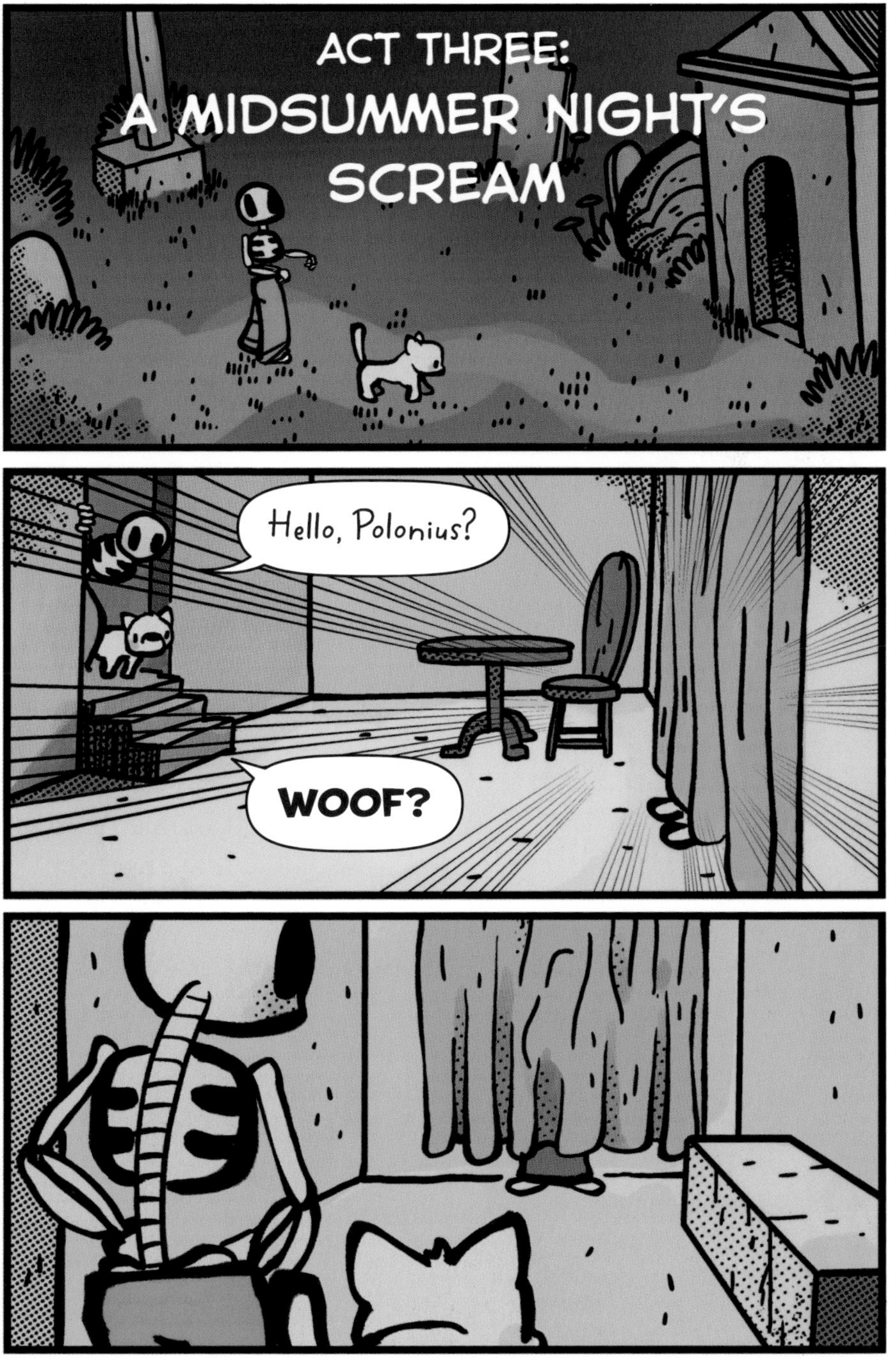
ACT THREE:
A MIDSUMMER NIGHT'S SCREAM
Hello, Polonius?
WOOF?

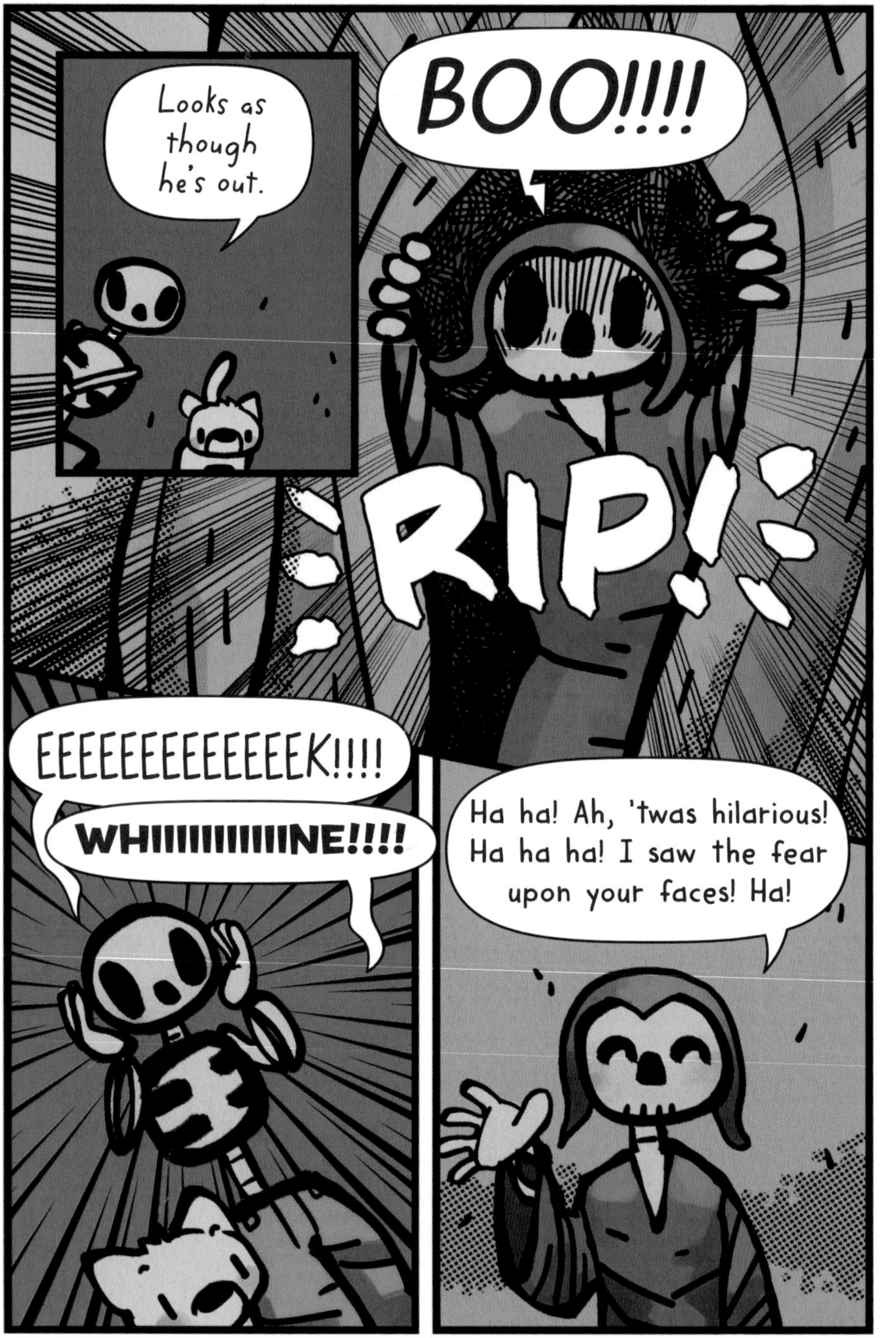
Looks as though he's out.
BOO!!!!
RIP!
EEEEEEEEEEEEEK!!!!
WHIIIIIIIIIIINE!!!!
Ha ha! Ah, 'twas hilarious! Ha ha ha! I saw the fear upon your faces! Ha!

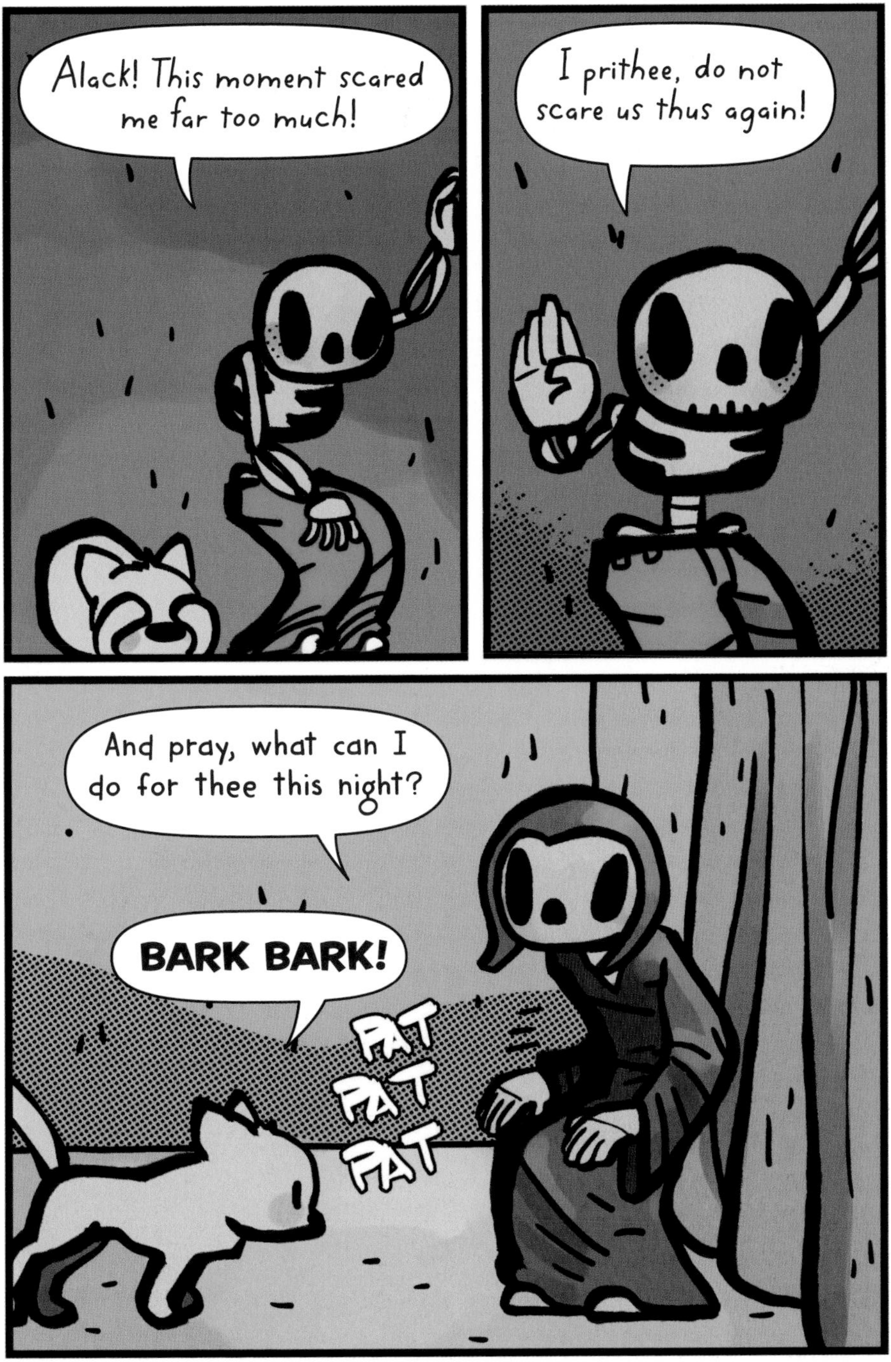
Alack! This moment scared me far too much!
I prithee, do not scare us thus again!
And pray, what can I do for thee this night?
BARK BARK!
PAT PAT PAT

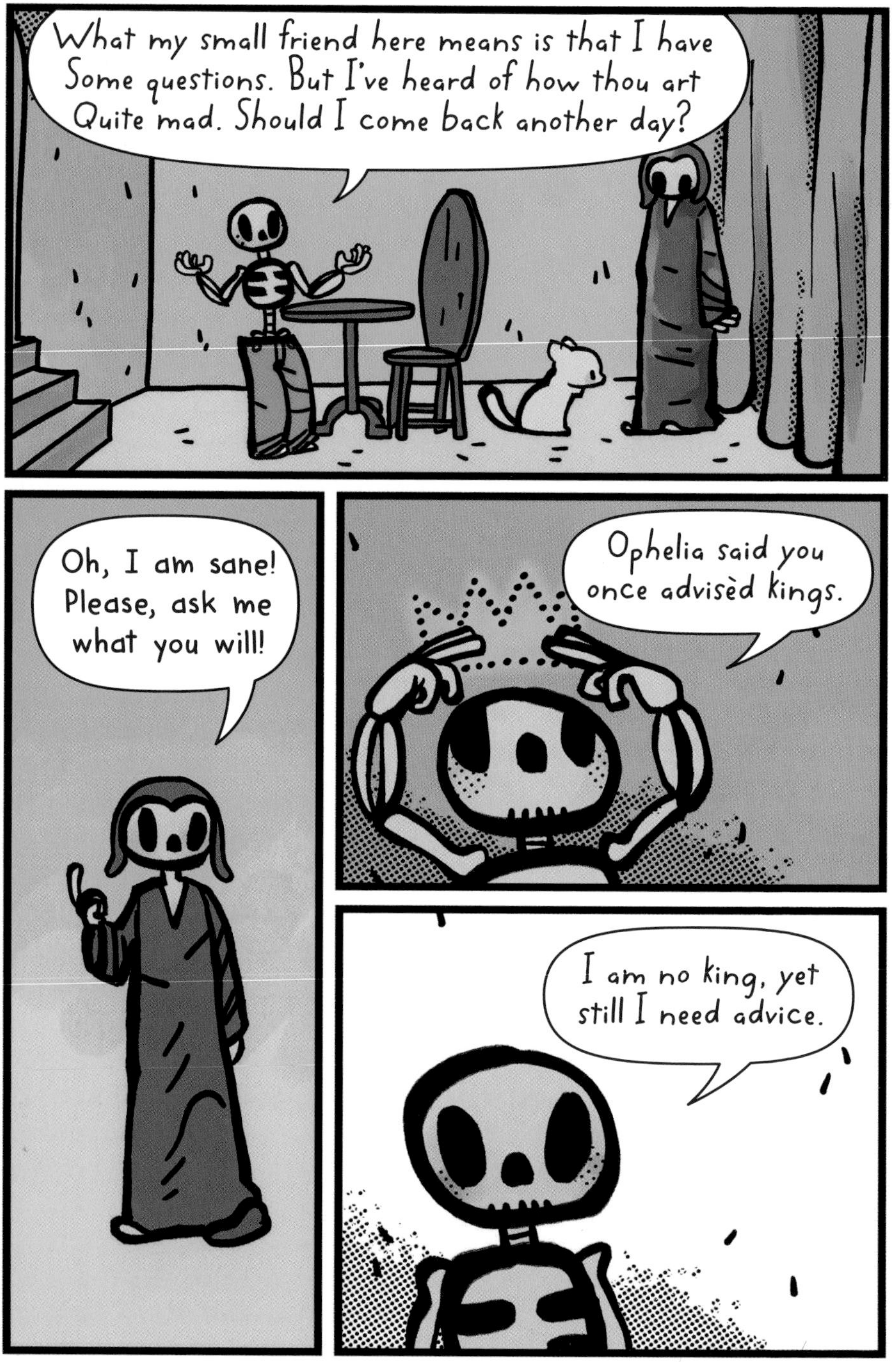
What my small friend here means is that I have Some questions. But I've heard of how thou art Quite mad. Should I come back another day?
Oh, I am sane! Please, ask me what you will!
Ophelia said you once advisèd kings.
I am no king, yet still I need advice.

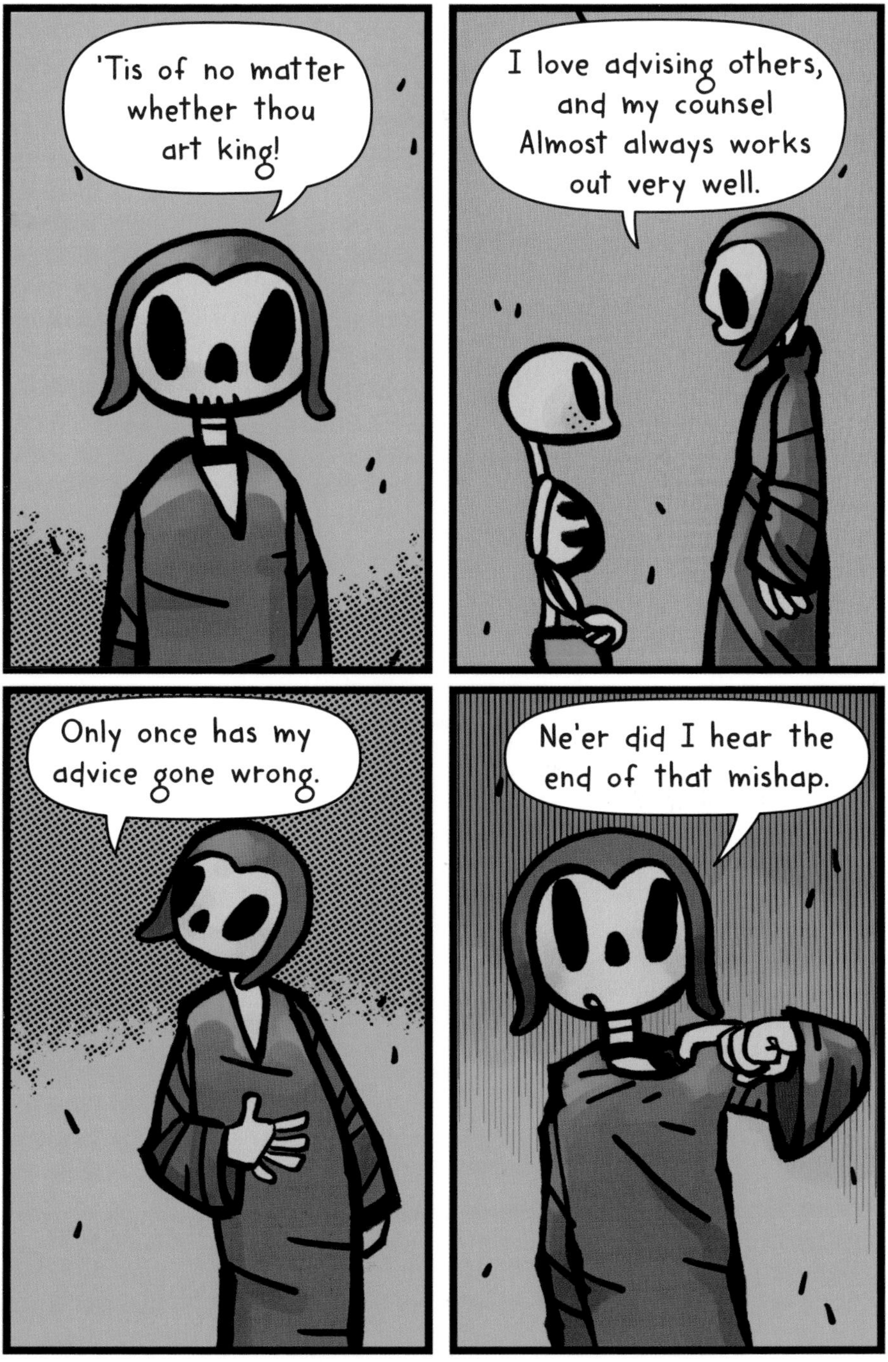
'Tis of no matter whether thou art king!
I love advising others, and my counsel Almost always works out very well.
Only once has my advice gone wrong.
Ne'er did I hear the end of that mishap.

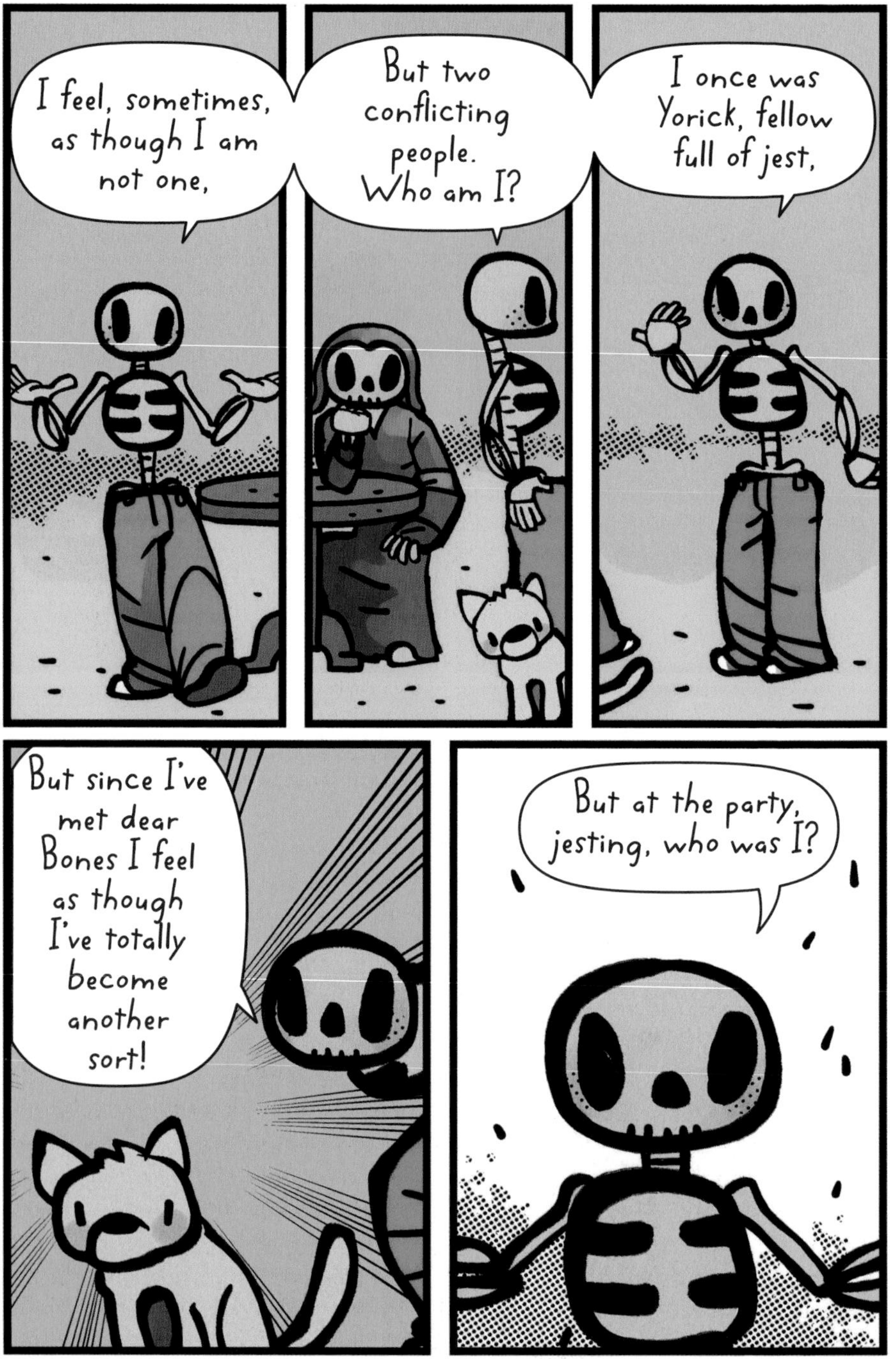
I feel, sometimes, as though I am not one,
But two conflicting people. Who am I?
I once was Yorick, fellow full of jest,
But since I've met dear Bones I feel as though I've totally become another sort!
But at the party, jesting, who was I?

I love to be myself, at home, with Bones,

But, though I had to hide my face, I loved To laugh and jest again.

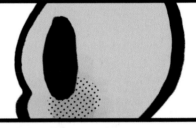

Those who I met Today seemed not to have this sad conflict.

Can I not be two people? Must I choose

Between these two essential parts of me?

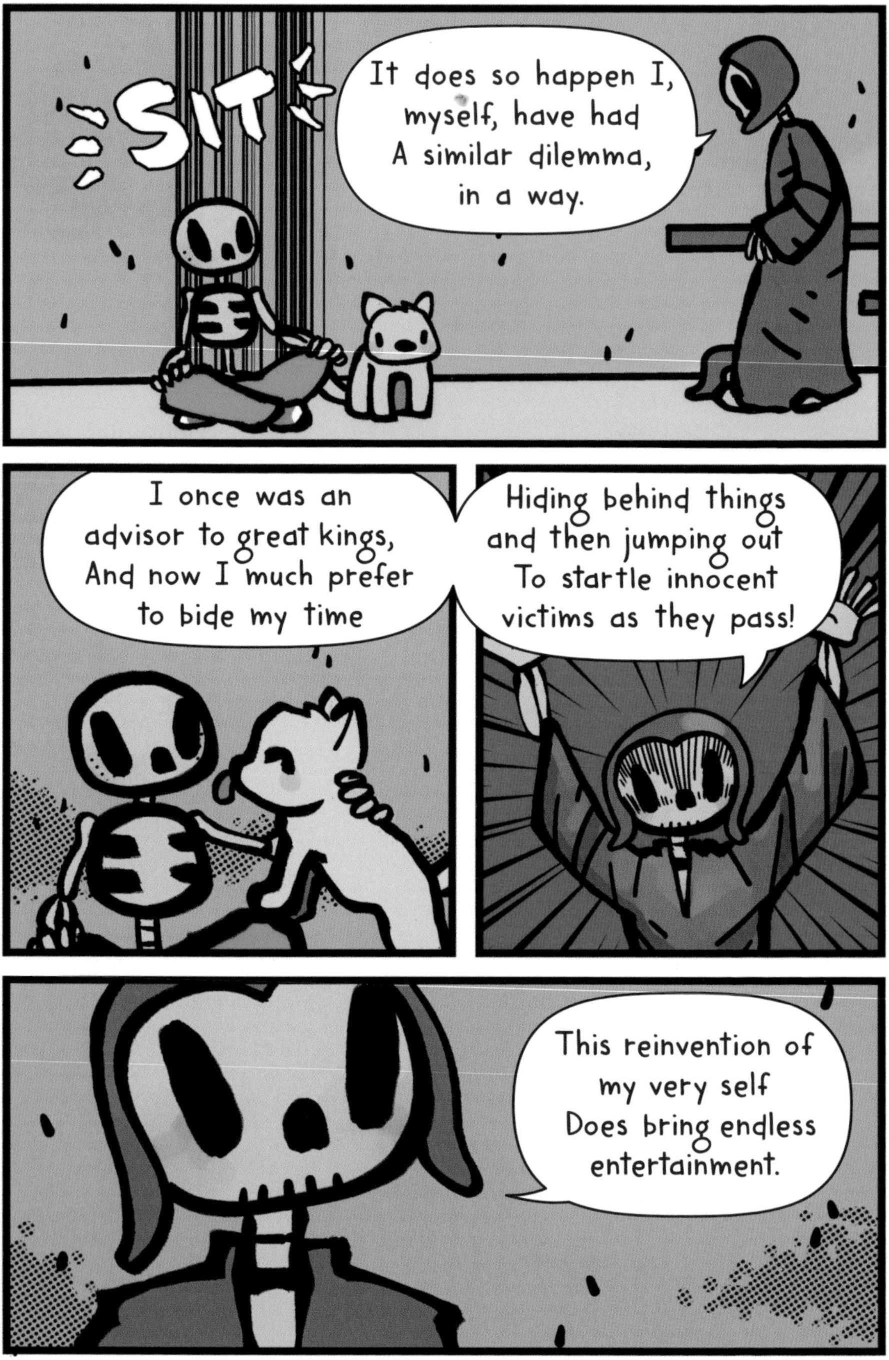
SIT
It does so happen I, myself, have had A similar dilemma, in a way.
I once was an advisor to great kings, And now I much prefer to bide my time
Hiding behind things and then jumping out To startle innocent victims as they pass!
This reinvention of my very self Does bring endless entertainment.

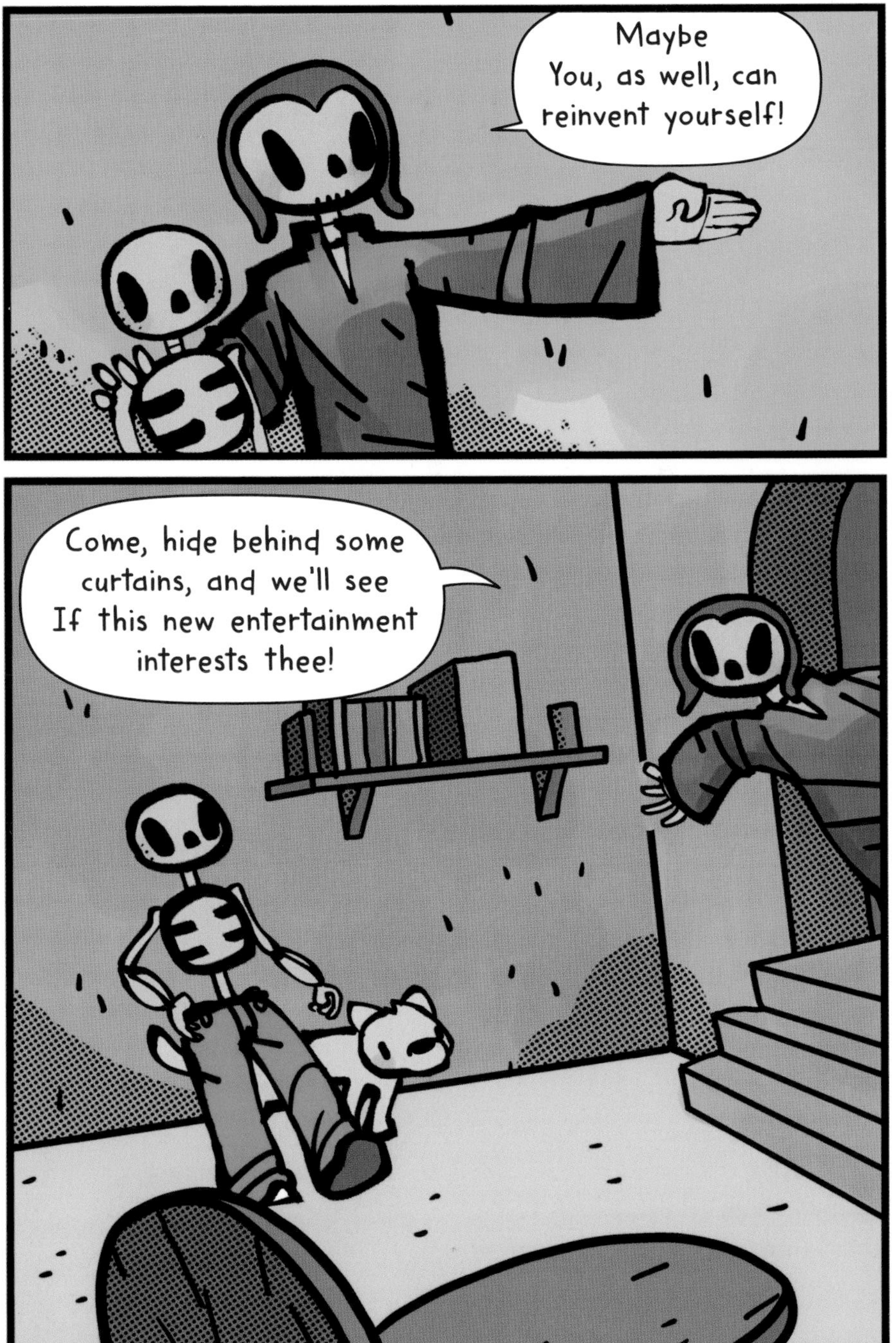
Maybe
You, as well, can
reinvent yourself!
Come, hide behind some
curtains, and we'll see
If this new entertainment
interests thee!

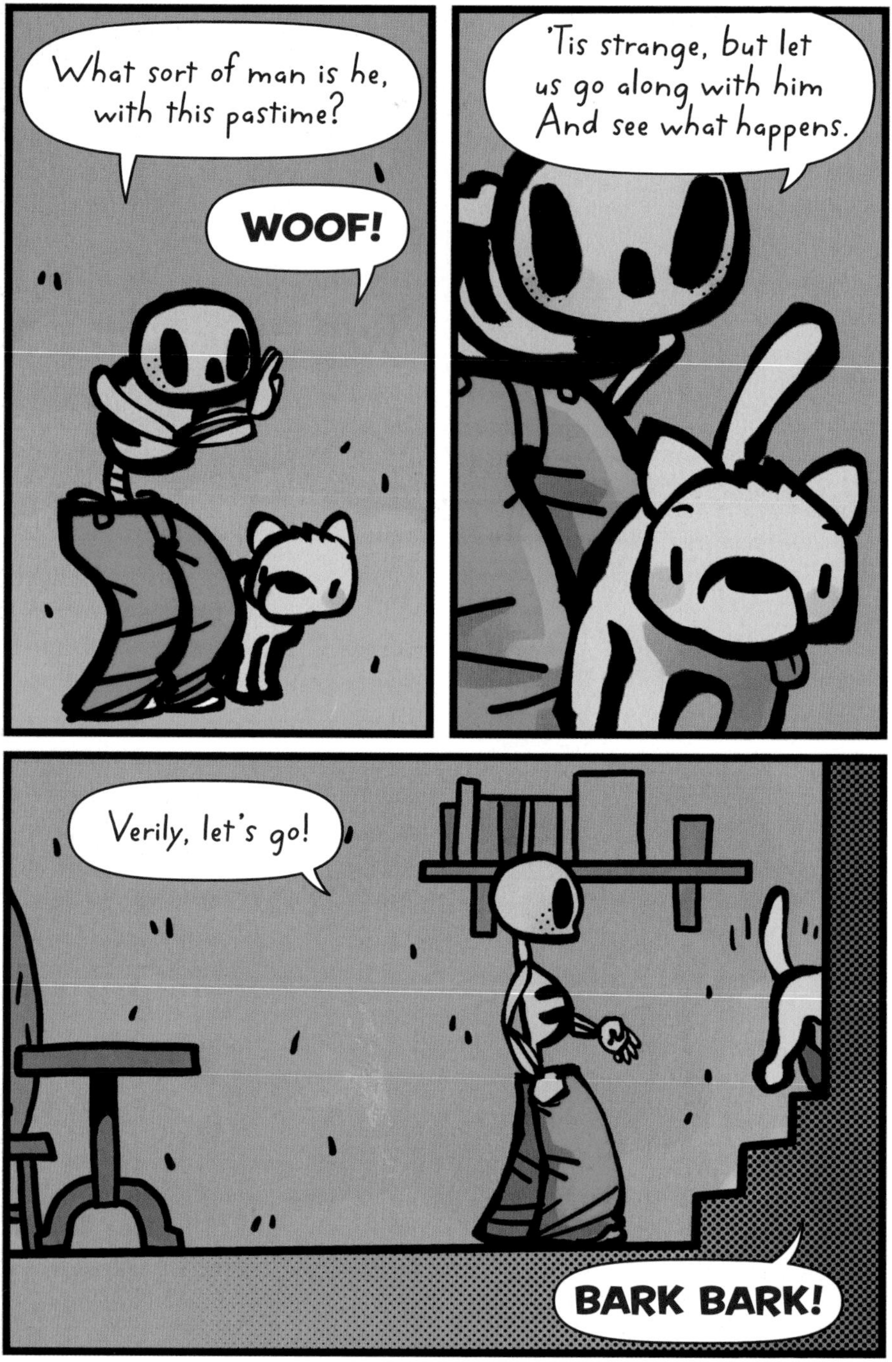
What sort of man is he, with this pastime?
WOOF!
'Tis strange, but let us go along with him And see what happens.
Verily, let's go!
BARK BARK!

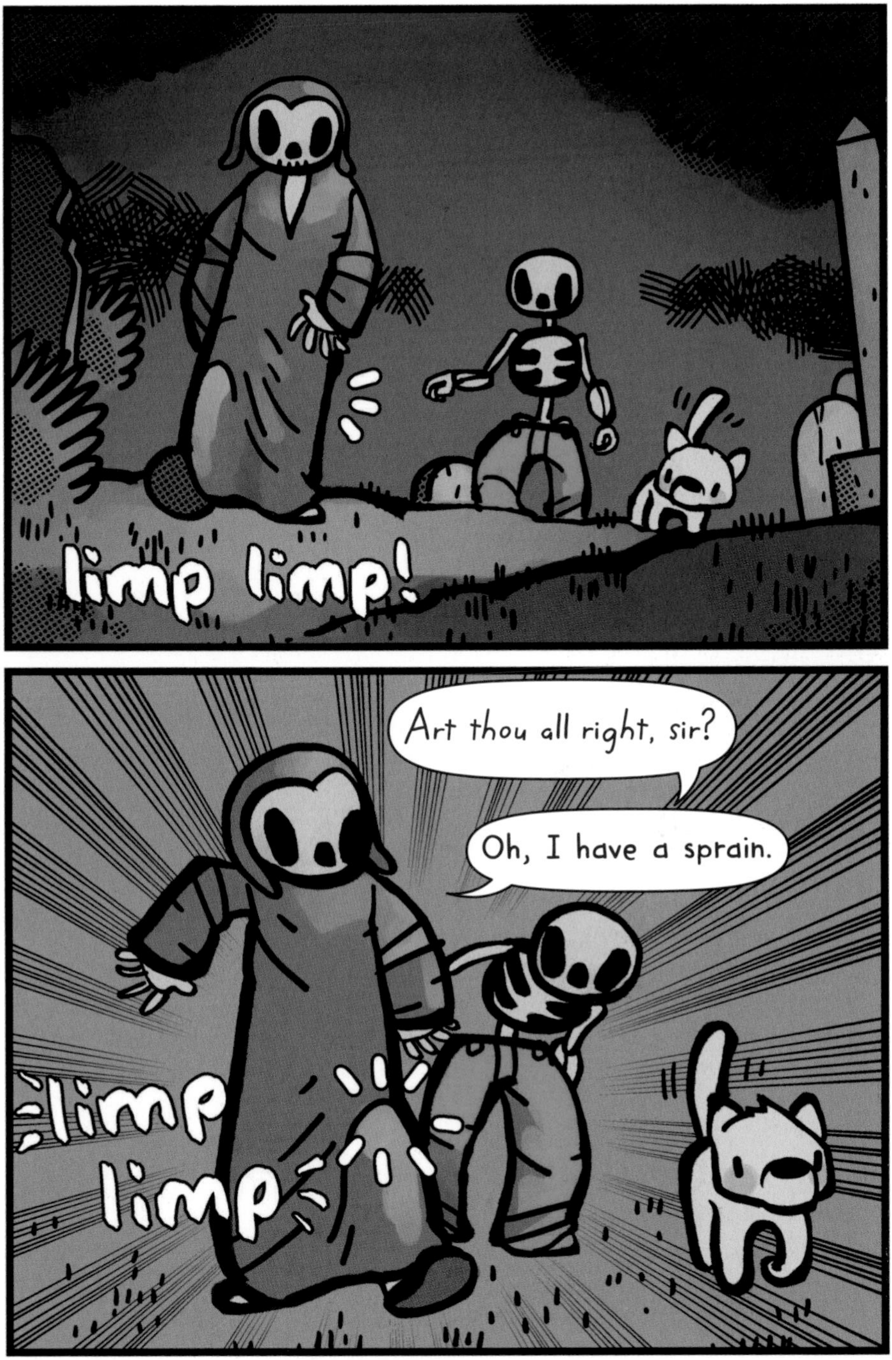
limp limp!
Art thou all right, sir?
Oh, I have a sprain.
limp
limp

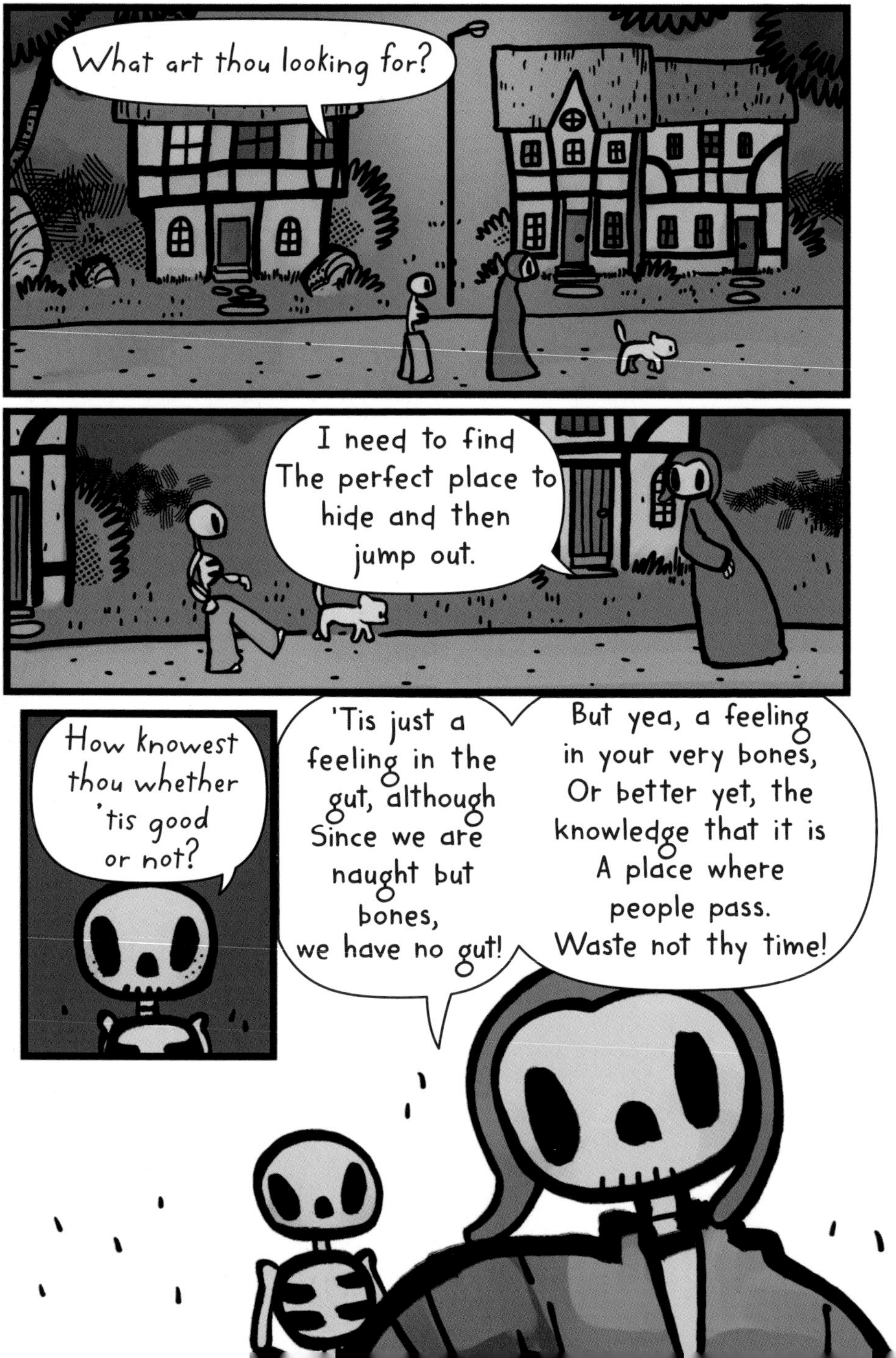
What art thou looking for?
I need to find The perfect place to hide and then jump out.
How knowest thou whether 'tis good or not?
'Tis just a feeling in the gut, although Since we are naught but bones, we have no gut!
But yea, a feeling in your very bones, Or better yet, the knowledge that it is A place where people pass. Waste not thy time!

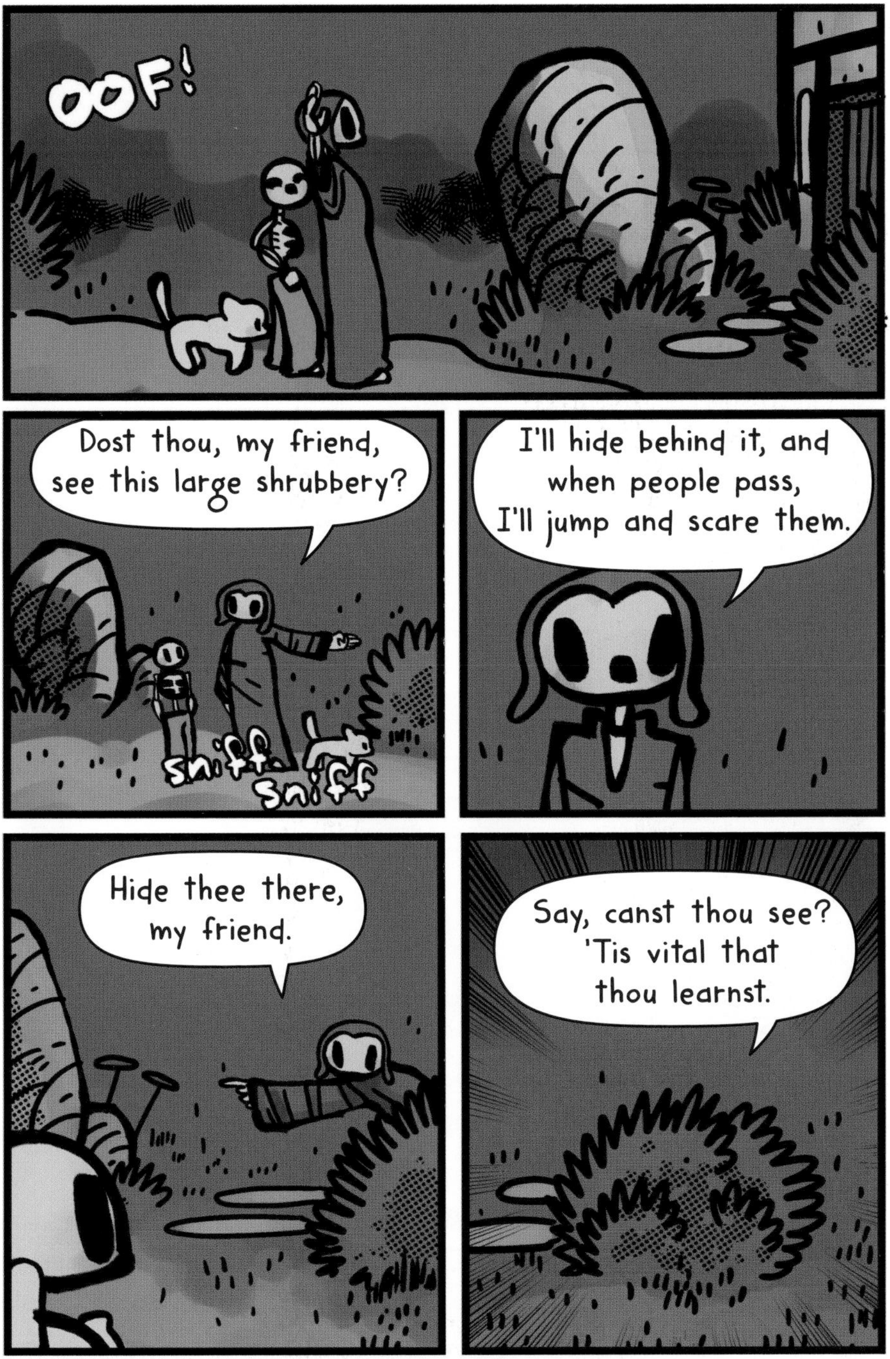
OOF!
Dost thou, my friend, see this large shrubbery?
sniff sniff
I'll hide behind it, and when people pass, I'll jump and scare them.
Hide thee there, my friend.
Say, canst thou see? 'Tis vital that thou learnst.

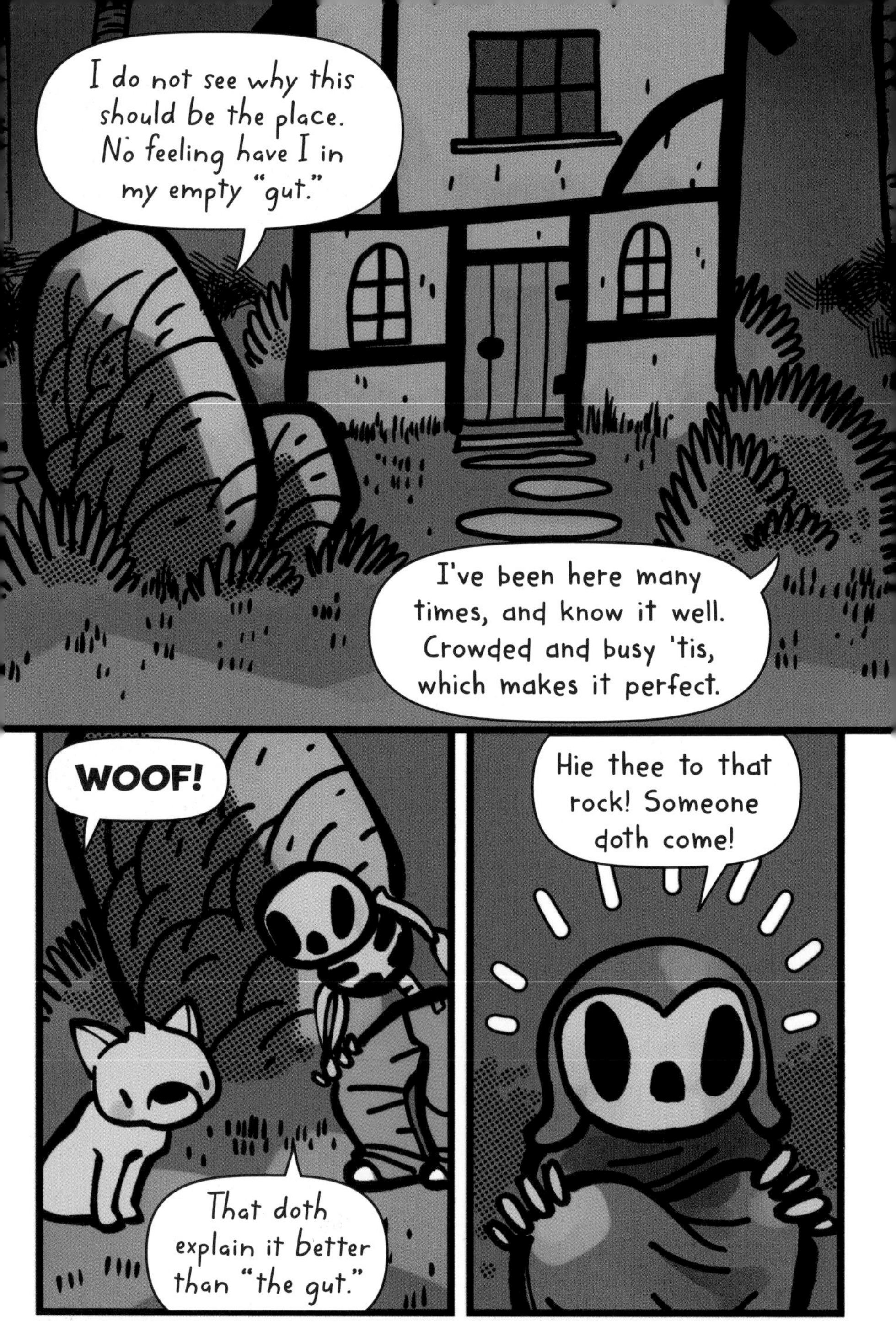
I do not see why this should be the place. No feeling have I in my empty "gut."
I've been here many times, and know it well. Crowded and busy 'tis, which makes it perfect.
WOOF!
That doth explain it better than "the gut."
Hie thee to that rock! Someone doth come!

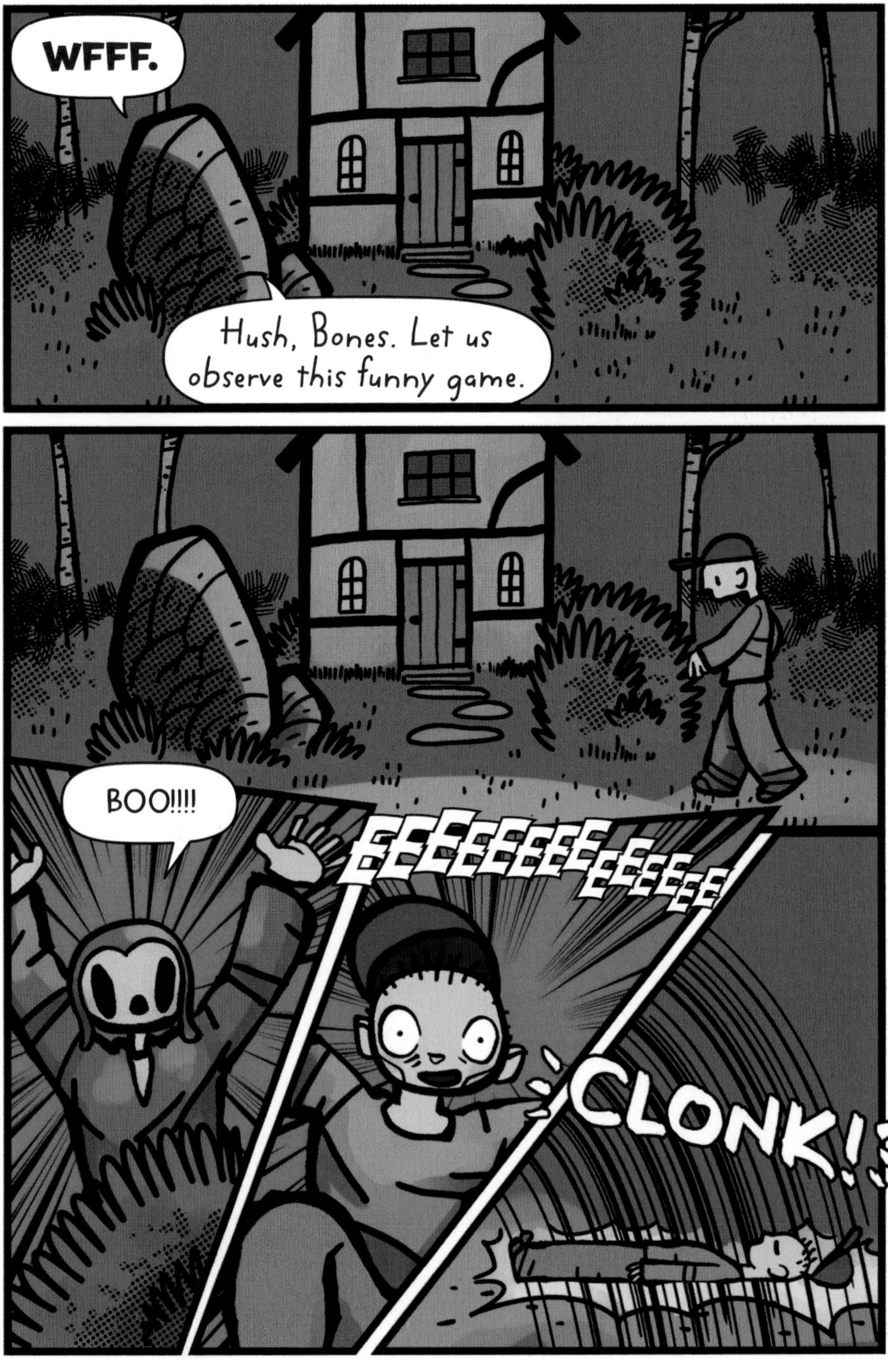
WFFF.
Hush, Bones. Let us observe this funny game.
BOO!!!!
EEEEEEEEEEEEEE
CLONK!

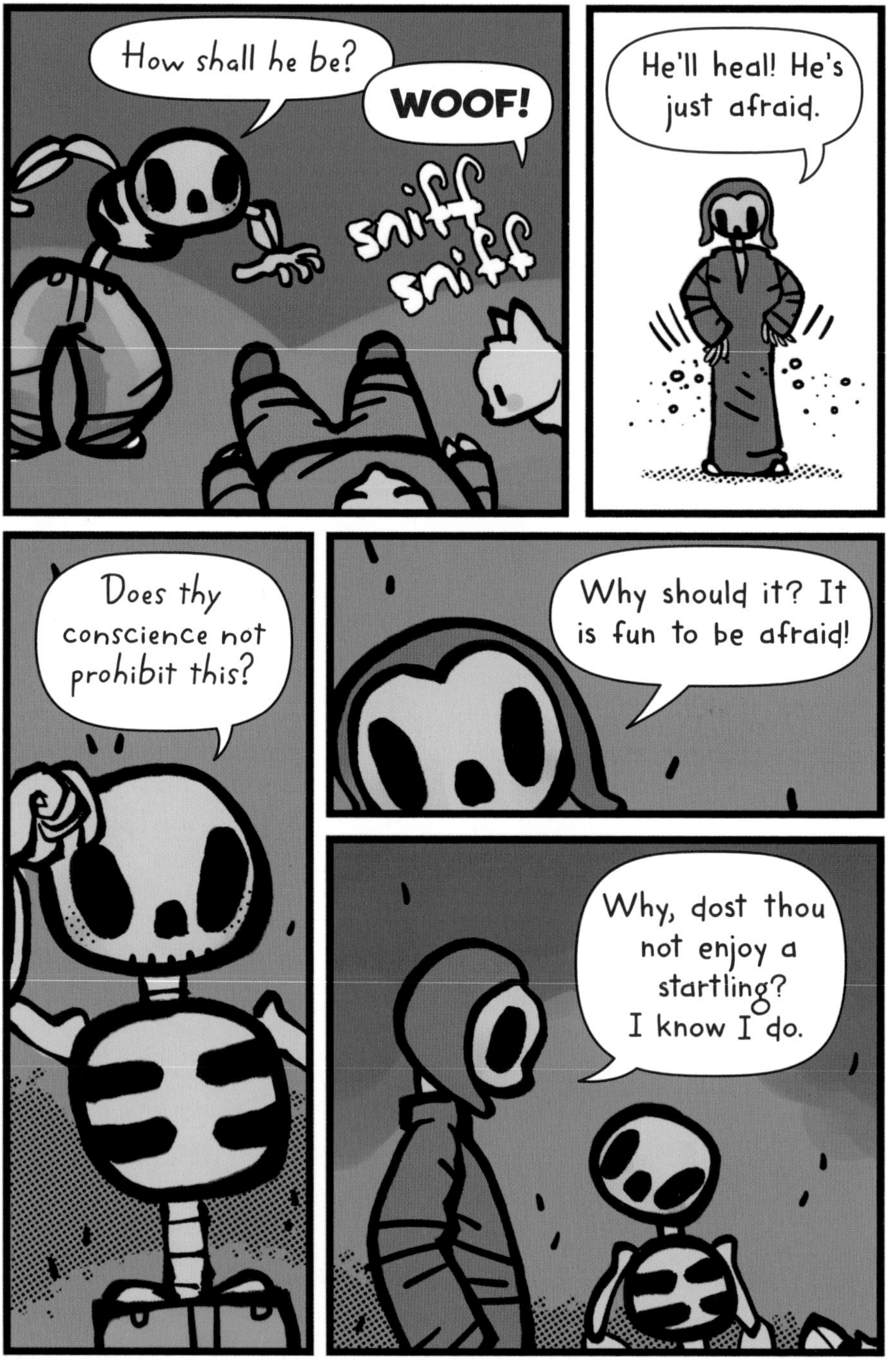
How shall he be?
WOOF!
sniff sniff
He'll heal! He's just afraid.
Does thy conscience not prohibit this?
Why should it? It is fun to be afraid!
Why, dost thou not enjoy a startling? I know I do.

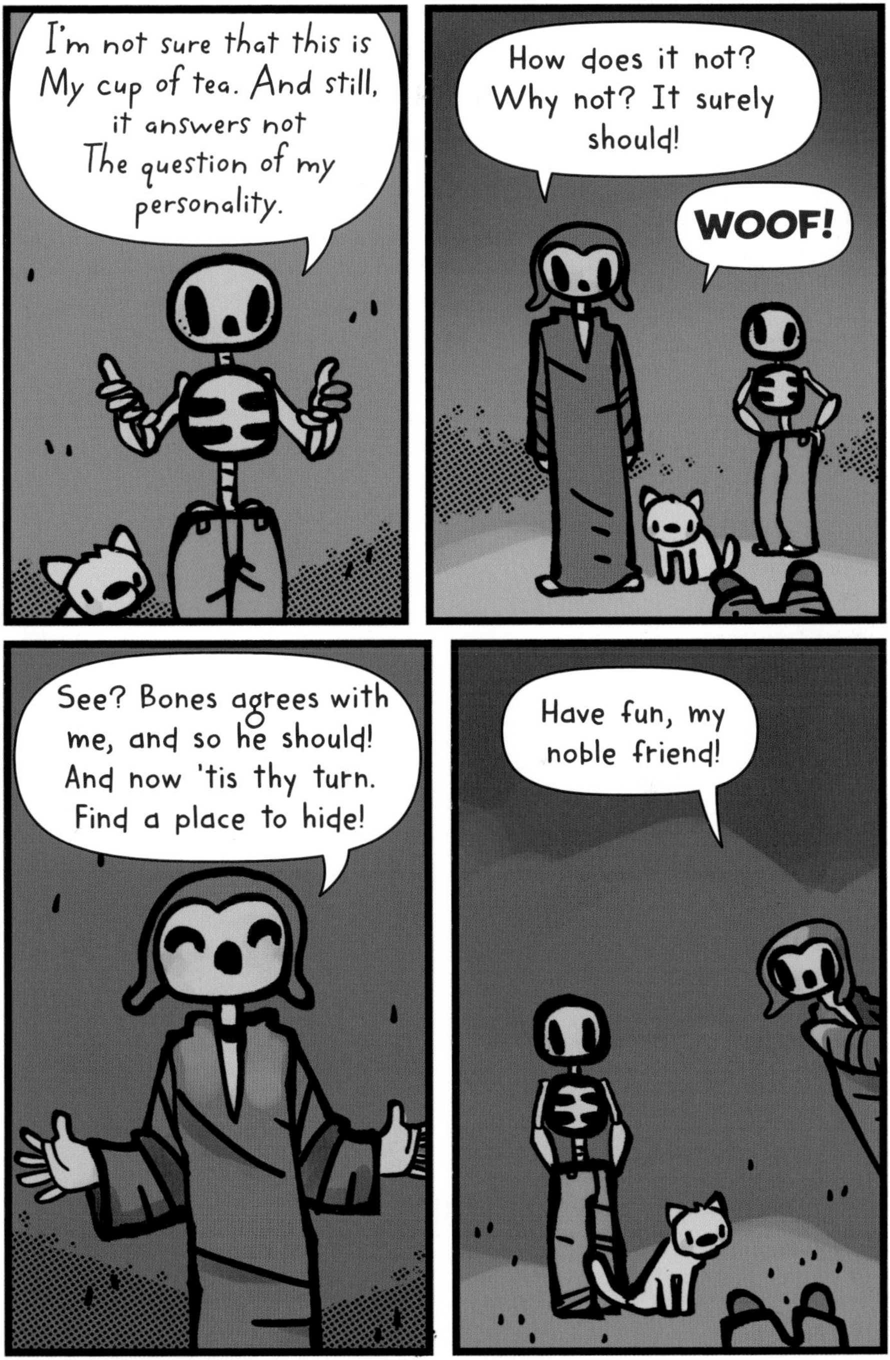
I'm not sure that this is My cup of tea. And still, it answers not The question of my personality.
How does it not? Why not? It surely should!
WOOF!
See? Bones agrees with me, and so he should! And now 'tis thy turn. Find a place to hide!
Have fun, my noble friend!

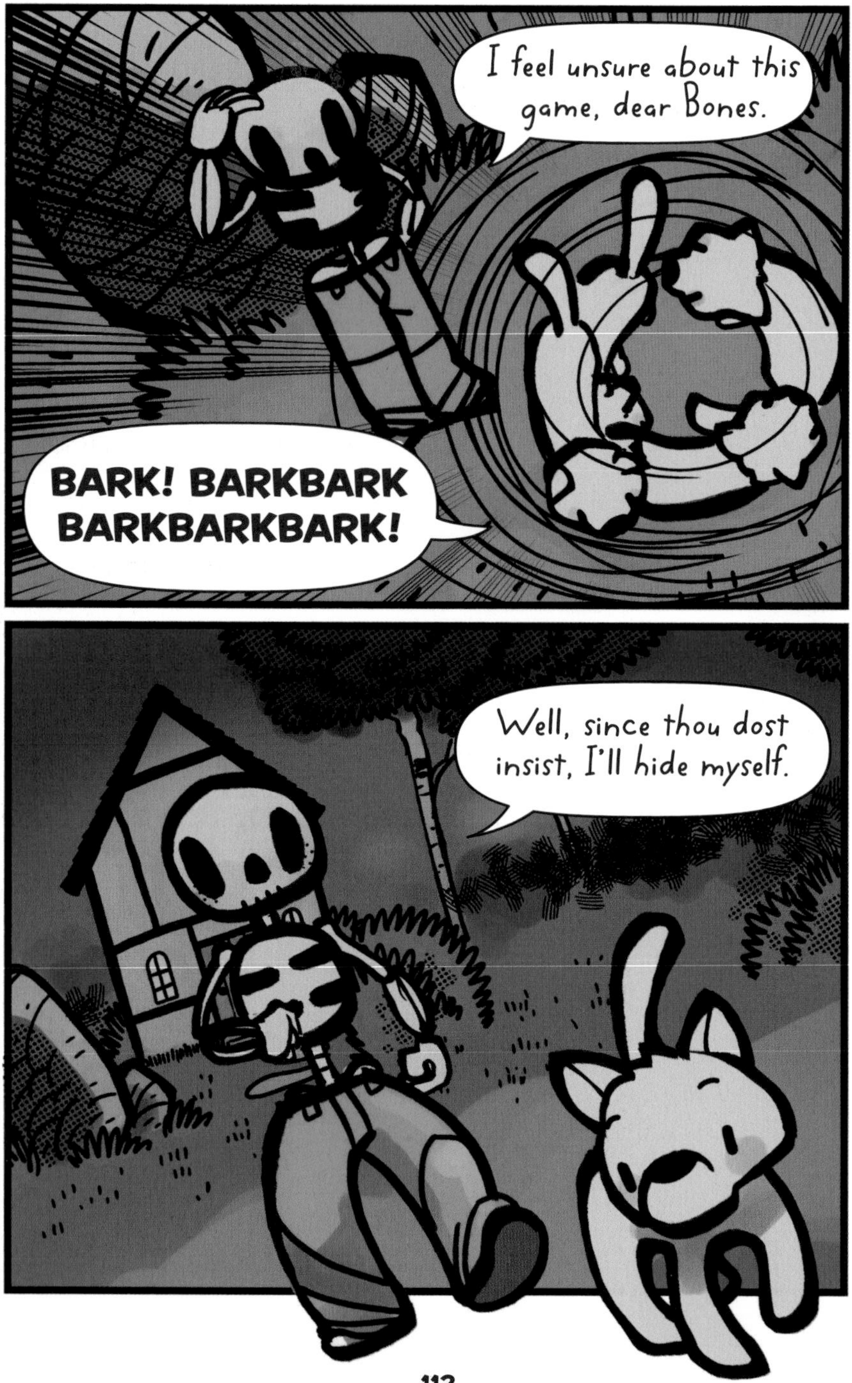
I feel unsure about this game, dear Bones.
BARK! BARKBARK BARKBARKBARK!
Well, since thou dost insist, I'll hide myself.

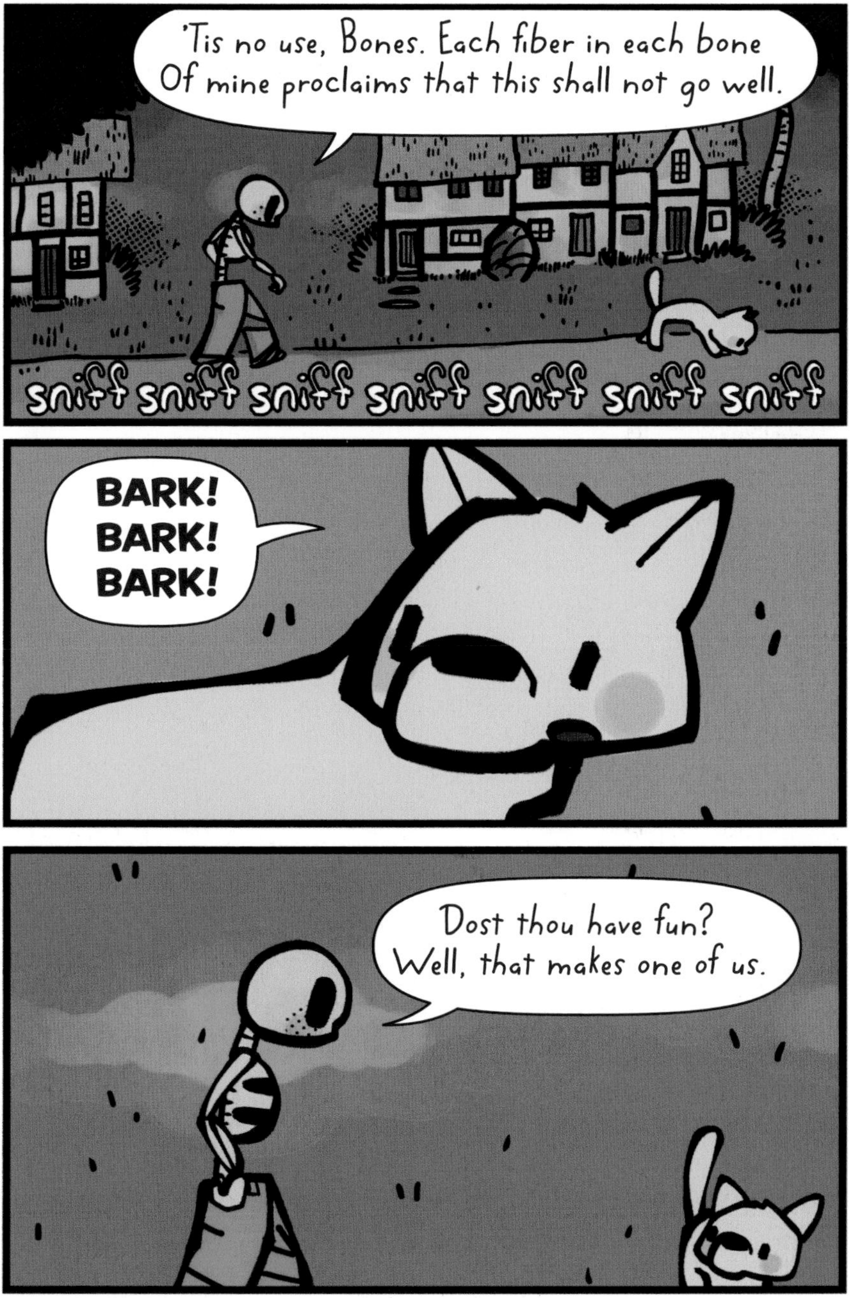
'Tis no use, Bones. Each fiber in each bone Of mine proclaims that this shall not go well.
sniff sniff sniff sniff sniff sniff sniff
BARK! BARK! BARK!
Dost thou have fun? Well, that makes one of us.

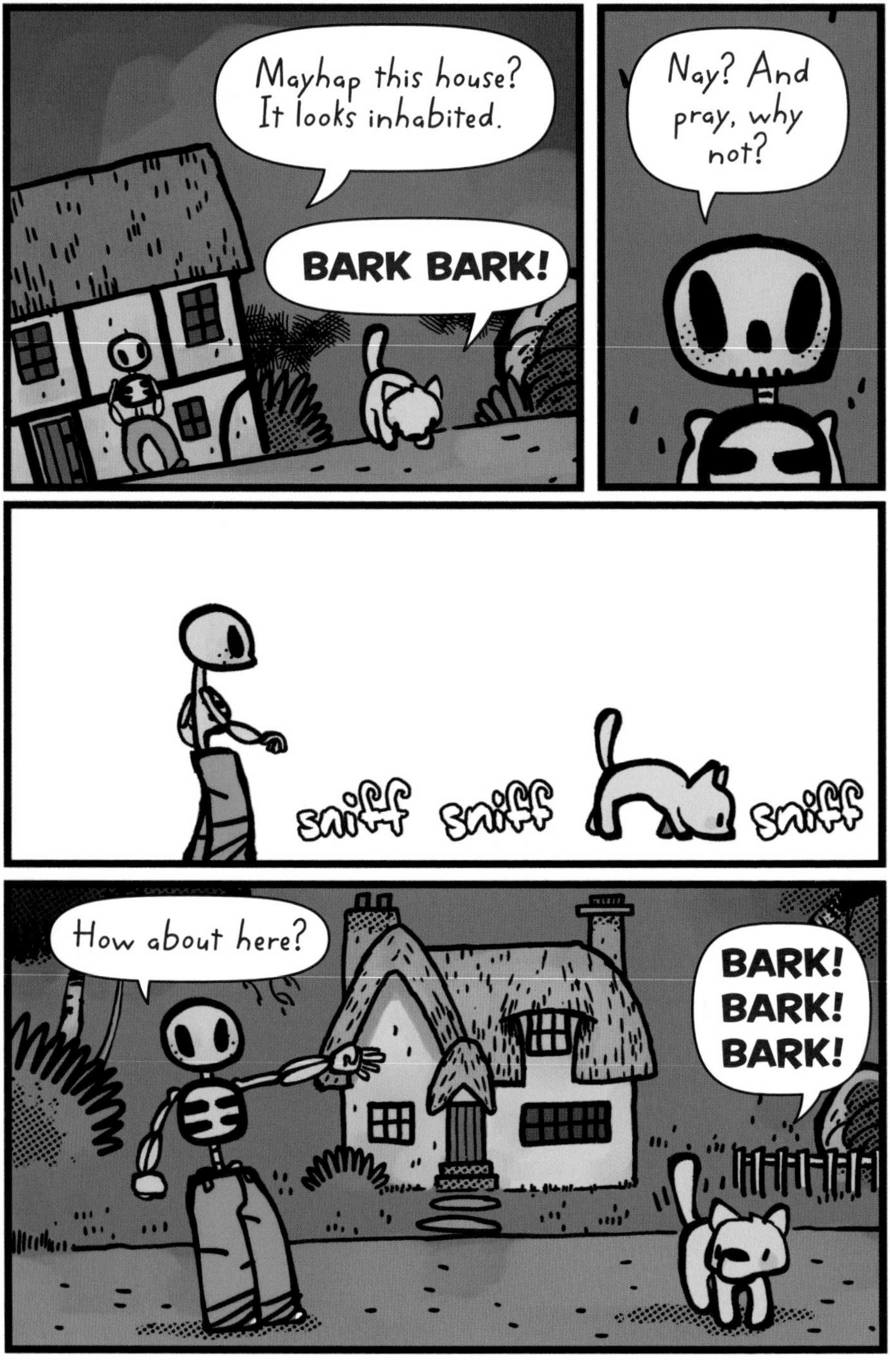
Mayhap this house? It looks inhabited.
BARK BARK!
Nay? And pray, why not?
sniff sniff sniff
How about here?
BARK! BARK! BARK!

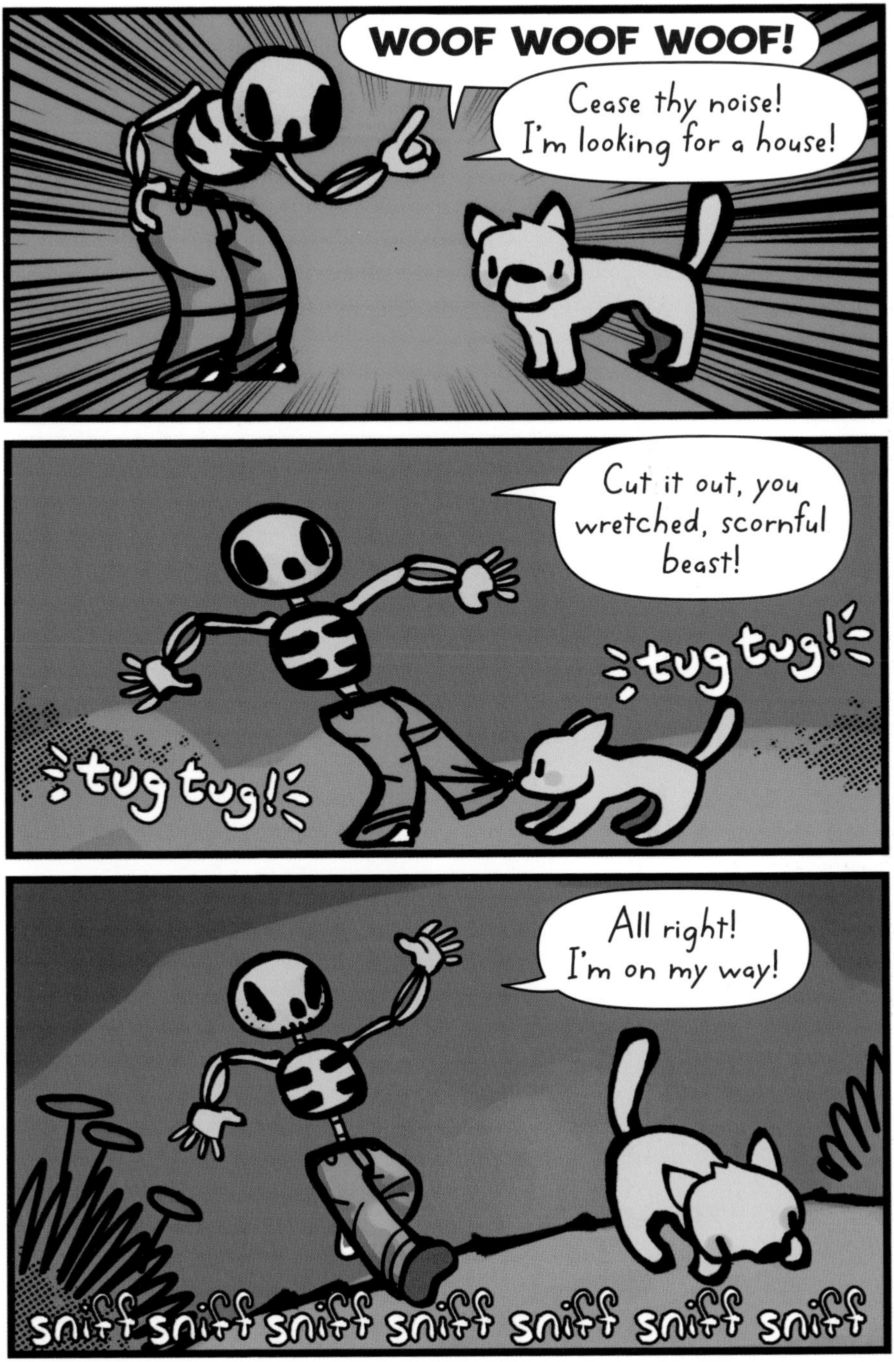
WOOF WOOF WOOF!
Cease thy noise! I'm looking for a house!
Cut it out, you wretched, scornful beast!
tug tug!
tug tug!
All right! I'm on my way!
sniff sniff sniff sniff sniff sniff sniff

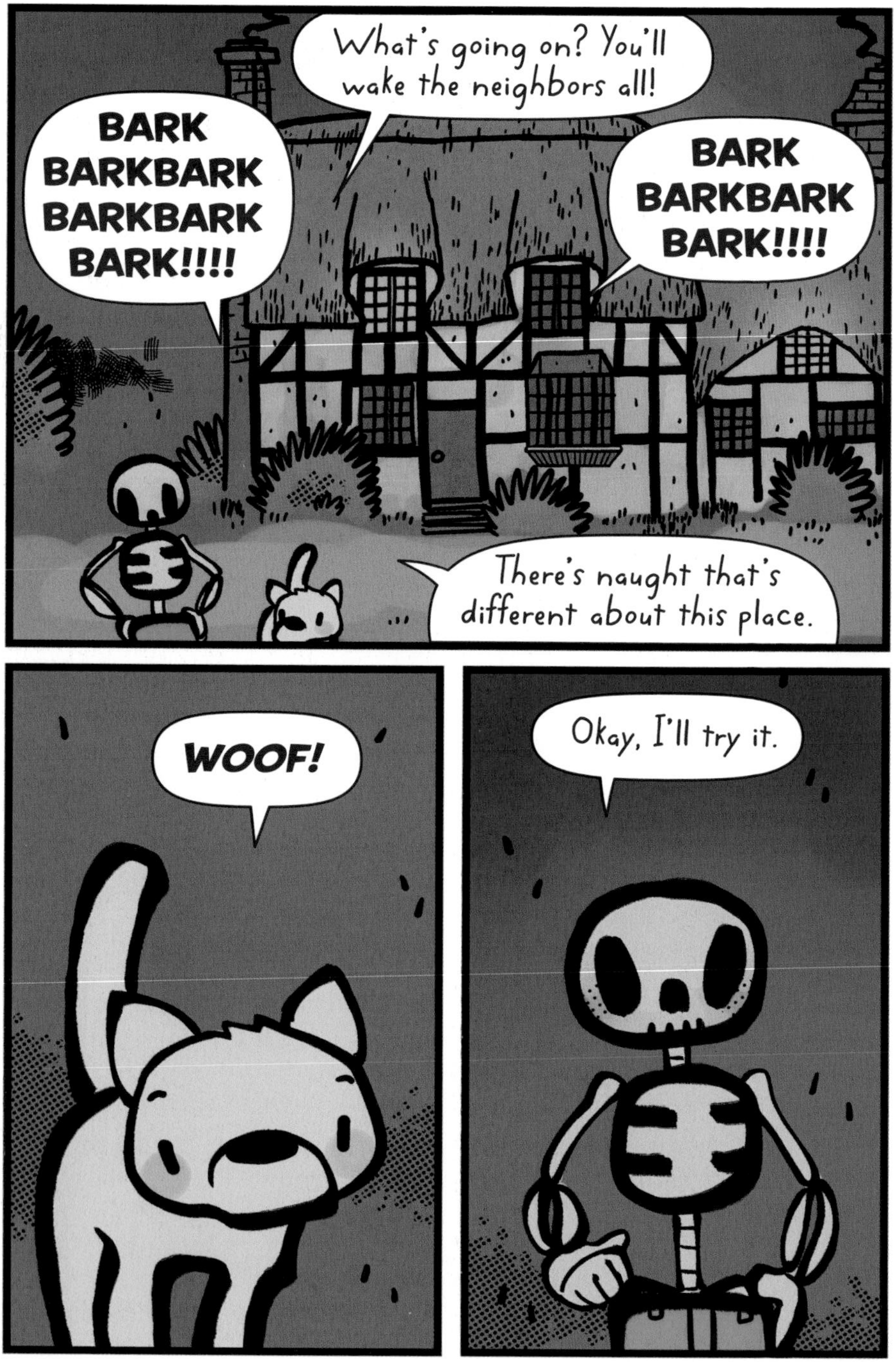
BARK BARKBARK BARKBARK BARK!!!!
What's going on? You'll wake the neighbors all!
BARK BARKBARK BARK!!!!
...
There's naught that's different about this place.
WOOF!
Okay, I'll try it.

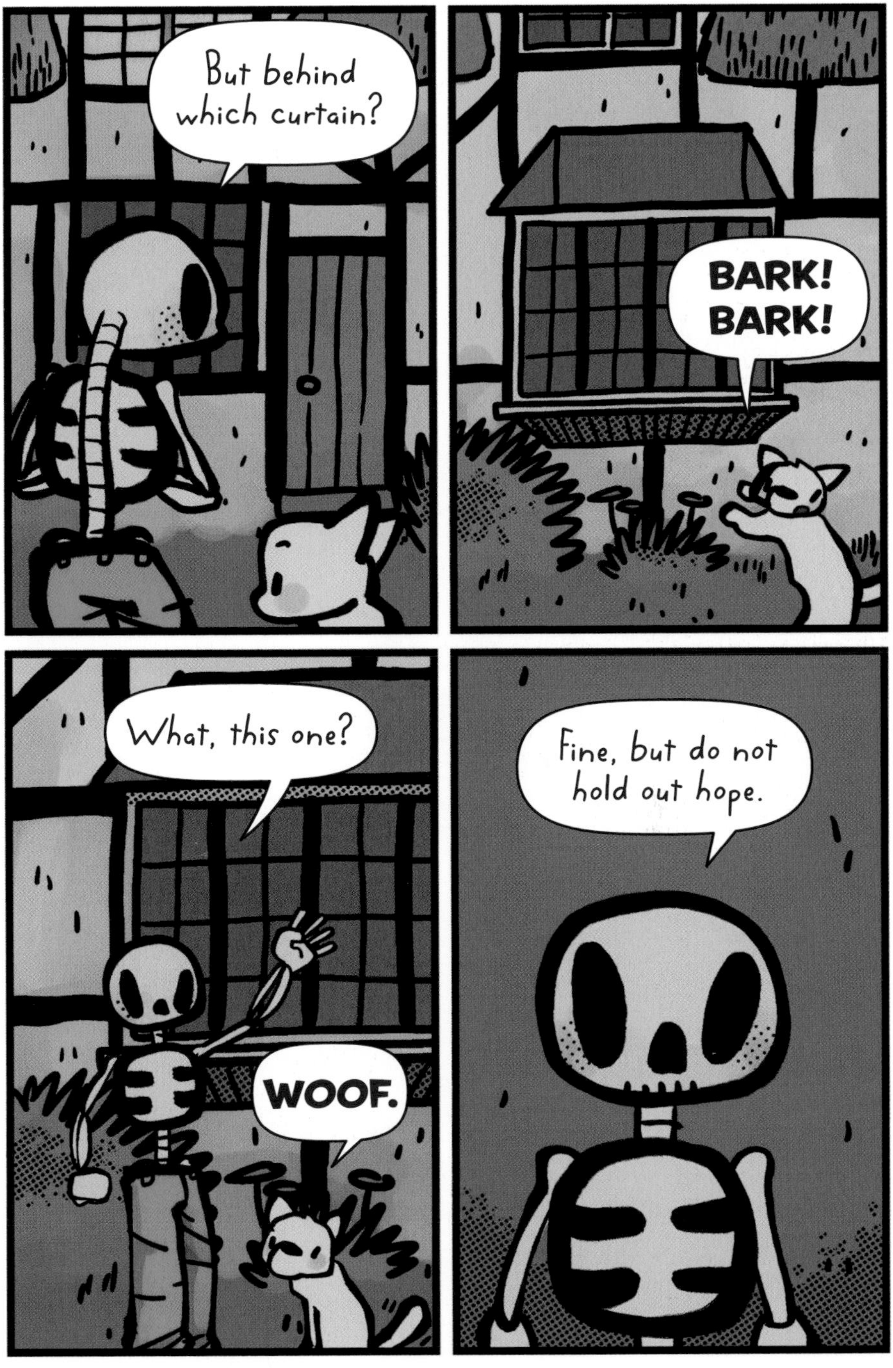
But behind which curtain?
BARK! BARK!
What, this one?
WOOF.
Fine, but do not hold out hope.

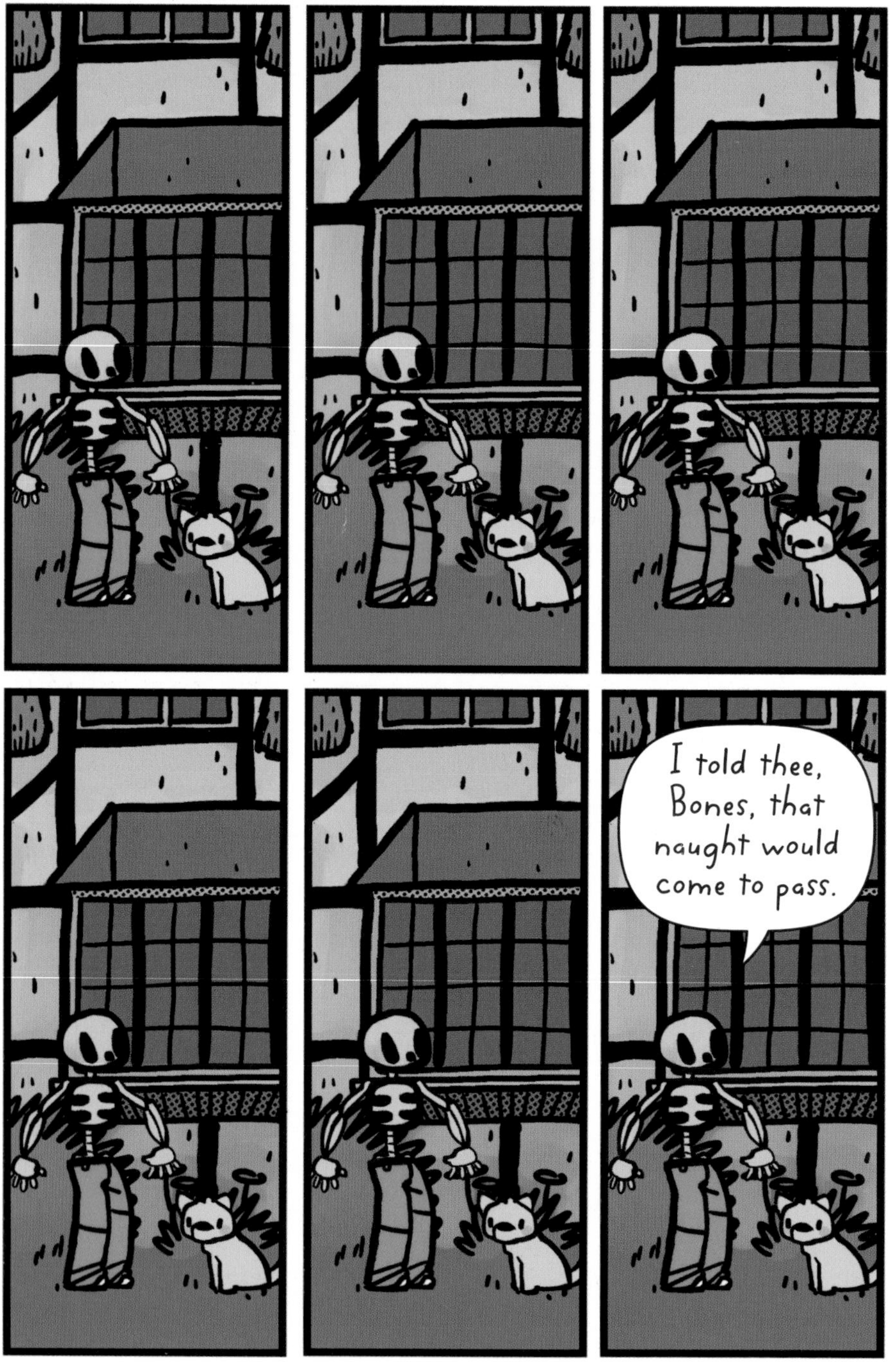
I told thee, Bones, that naught would come to pass.

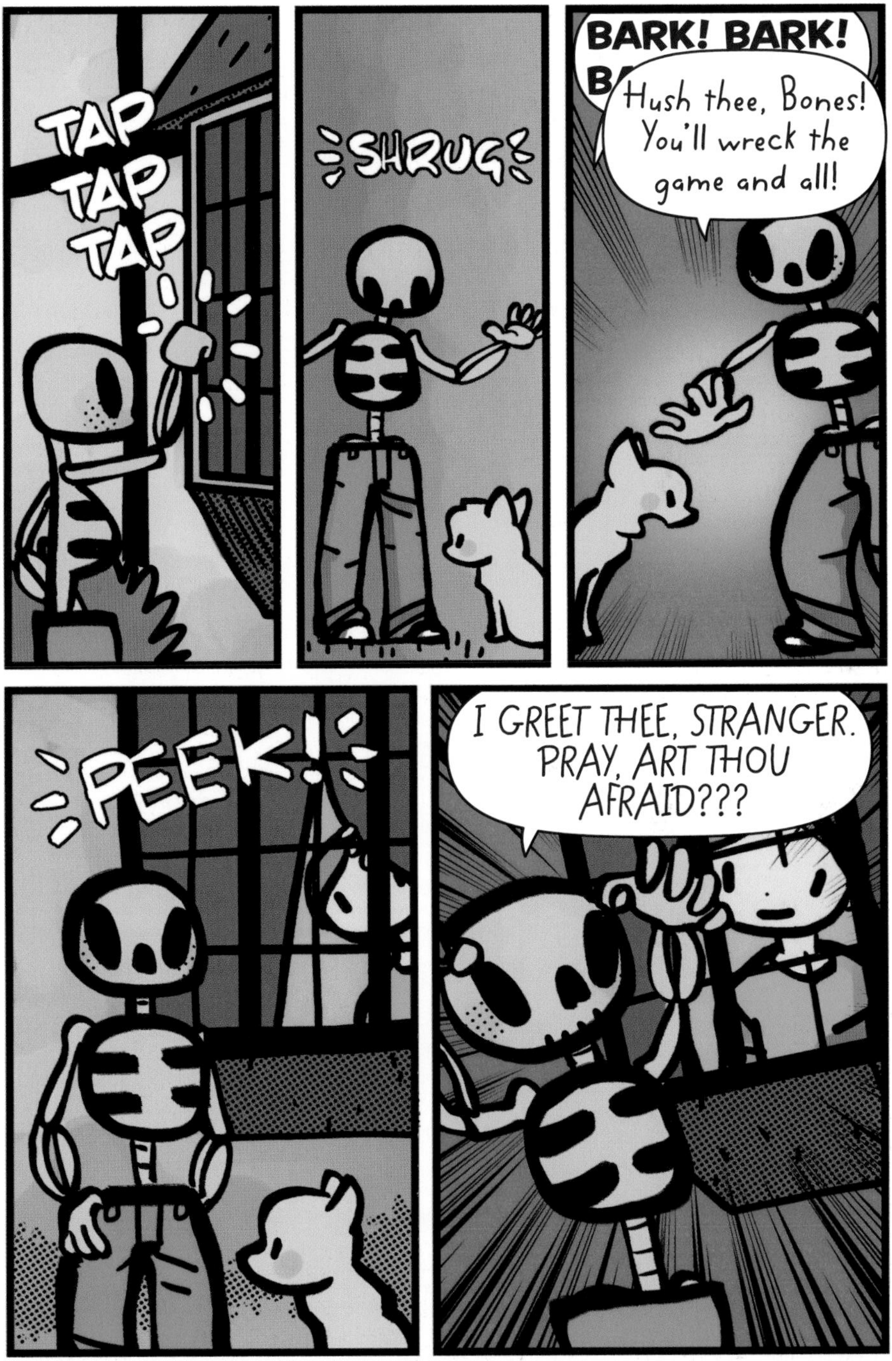
TAP
TAP
TAP
SHRUG
BARK! BARK!
BA
Hush thee, Bones! You'll wreck the game and all!
PEEK!
I GREET THEE, STRANGER. PRAY, ART THOU AFRAID???

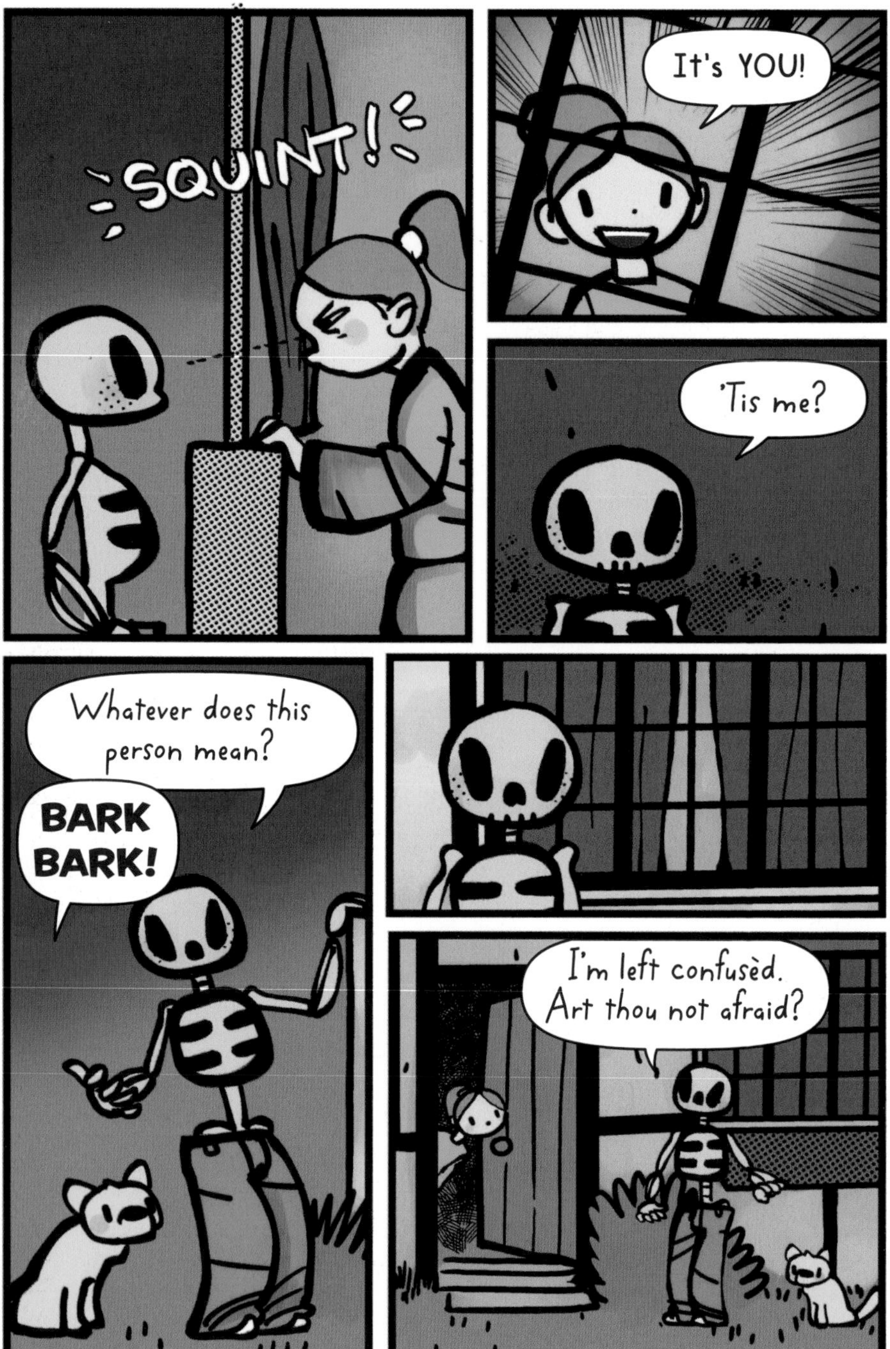
SQUINT!
It's YOU!
'Tis me?
Whatever does this person mean?
BARK BARK!
I'm left confusèd. Art thou not afraid?

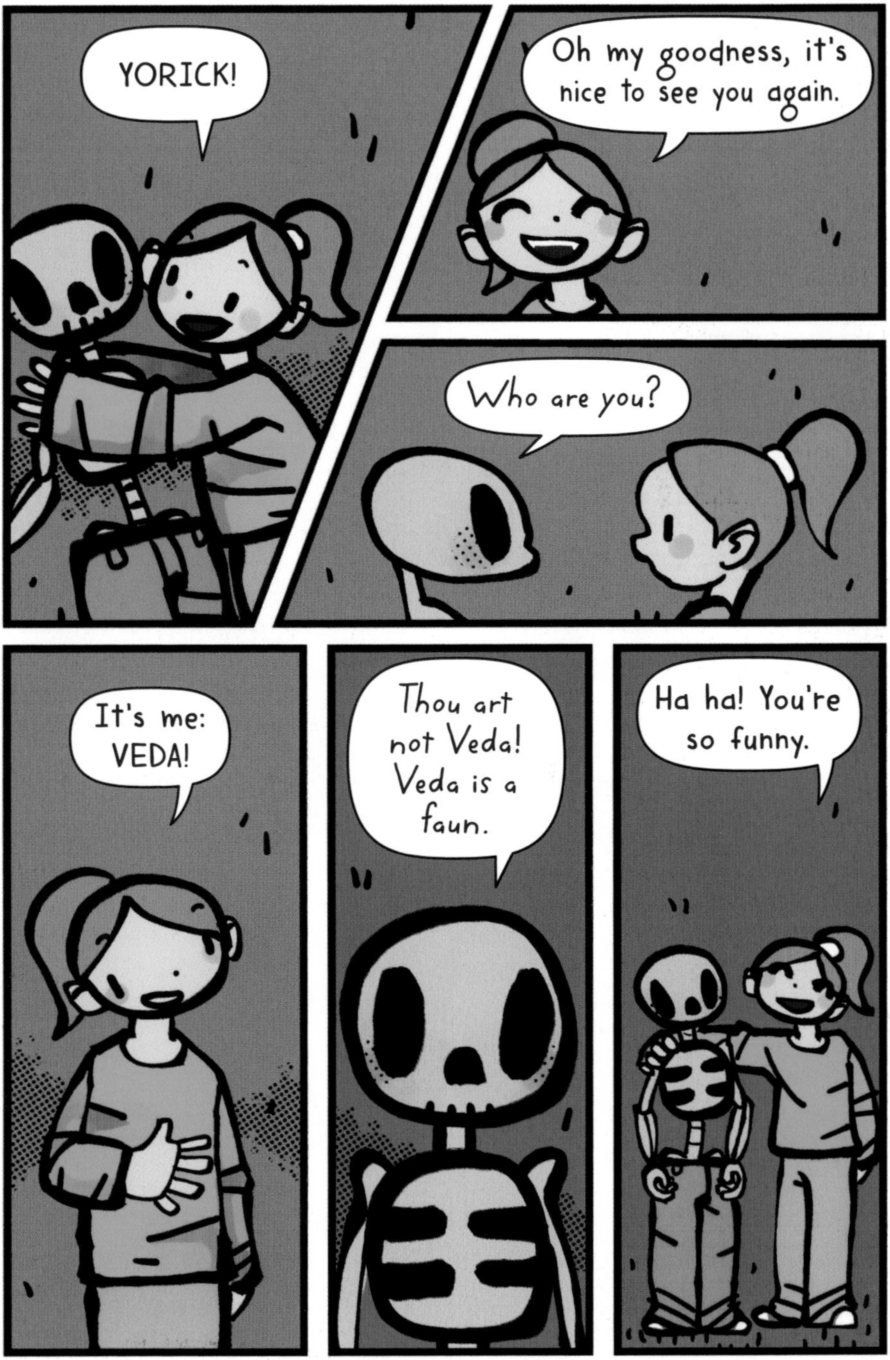
YORICK!
Oh my goodness, it's nice to see you again.
Who are you?
It's me: VEDA!
Thou art not Veda! Veda is a faun.
Ha ha! You're so funny.

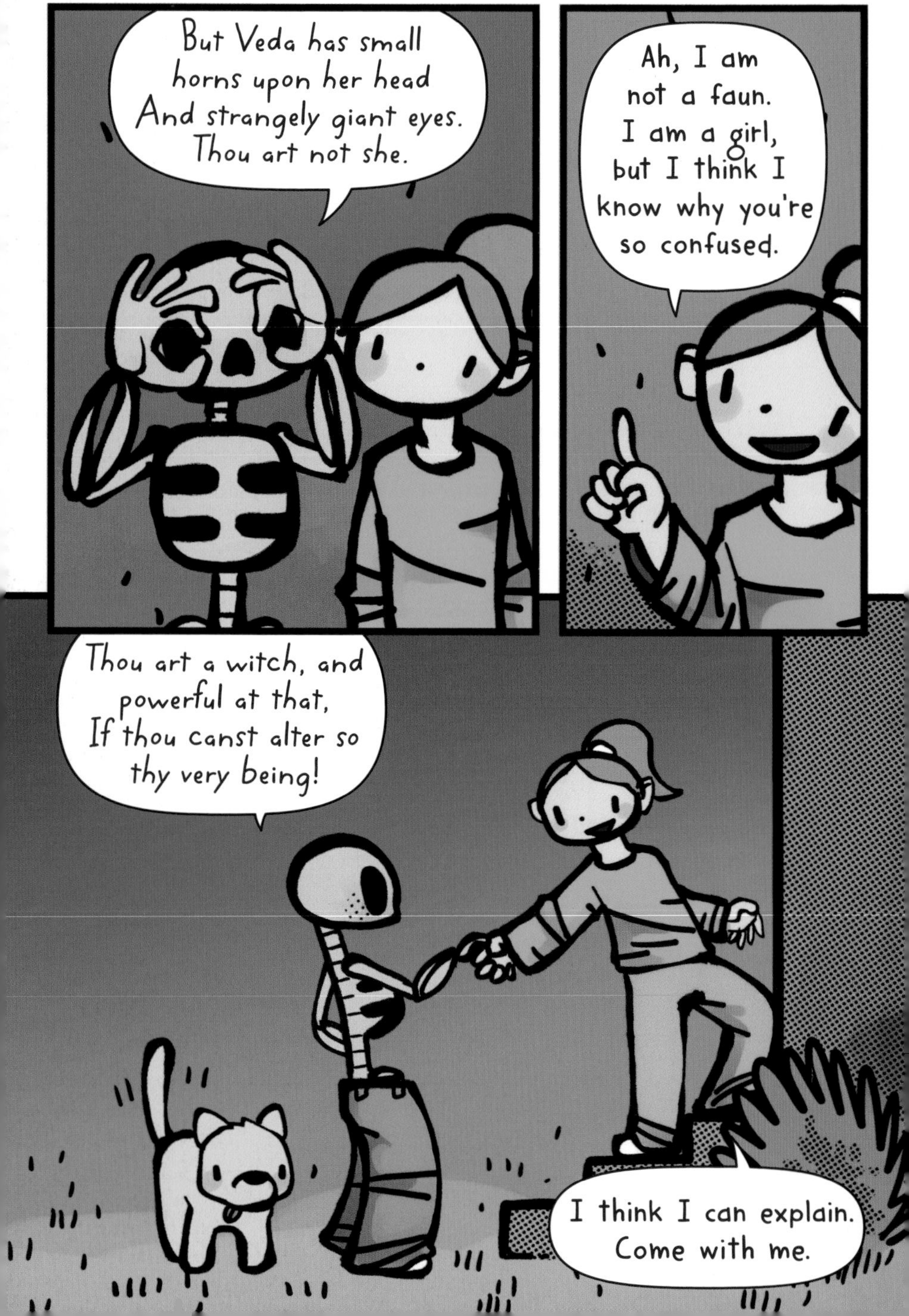
But Veda has small horns upon her head And strangely giant eyes. Thou art not she.
Ah, I am not a faun. I am a girl, but I think I know why you're so confused.
Thou art a witch, and powerful at that, If thou canst alter so thy very being!
I think I can explain. Come with me.

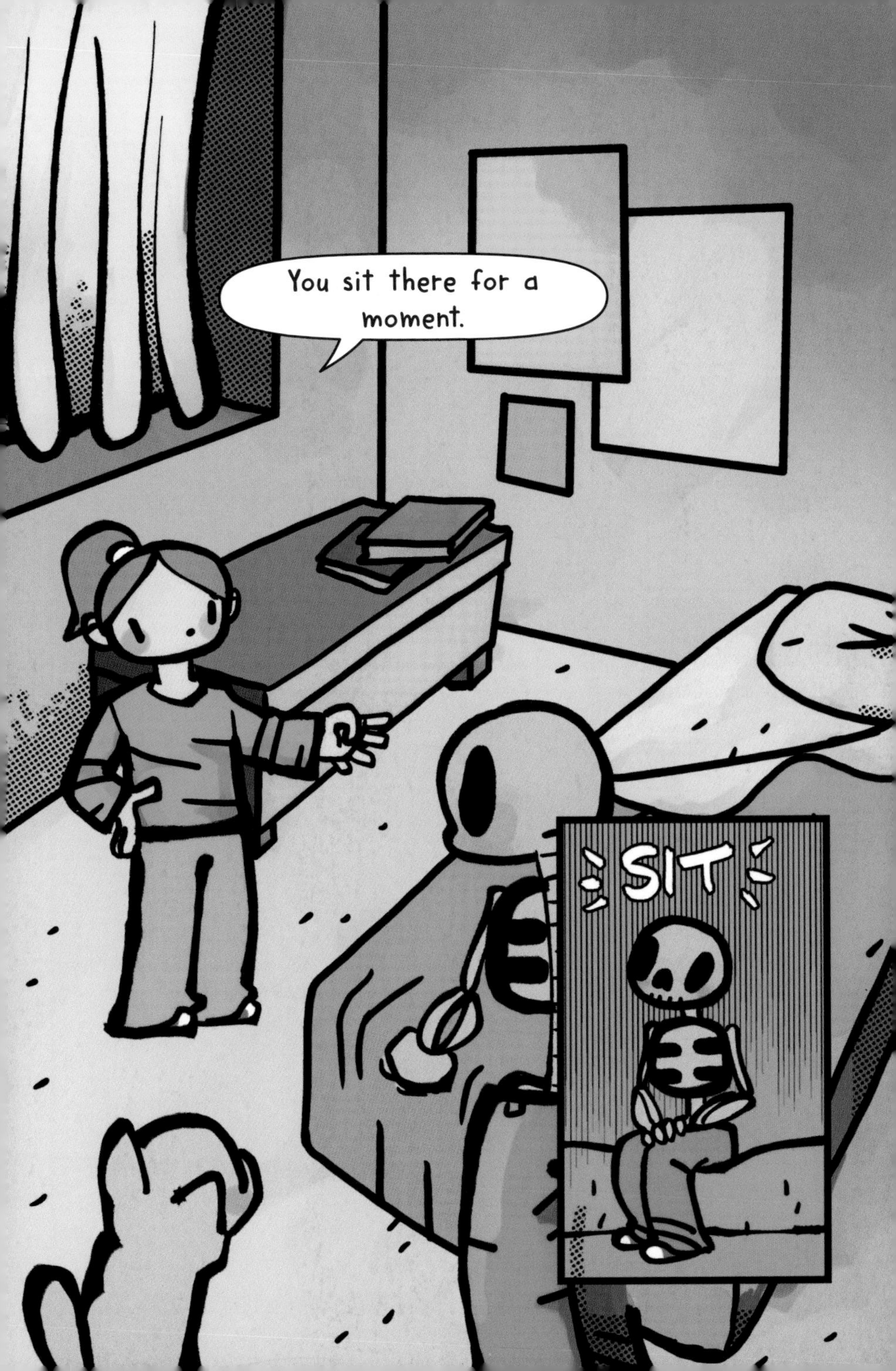
You sit there for a moment.
SIT

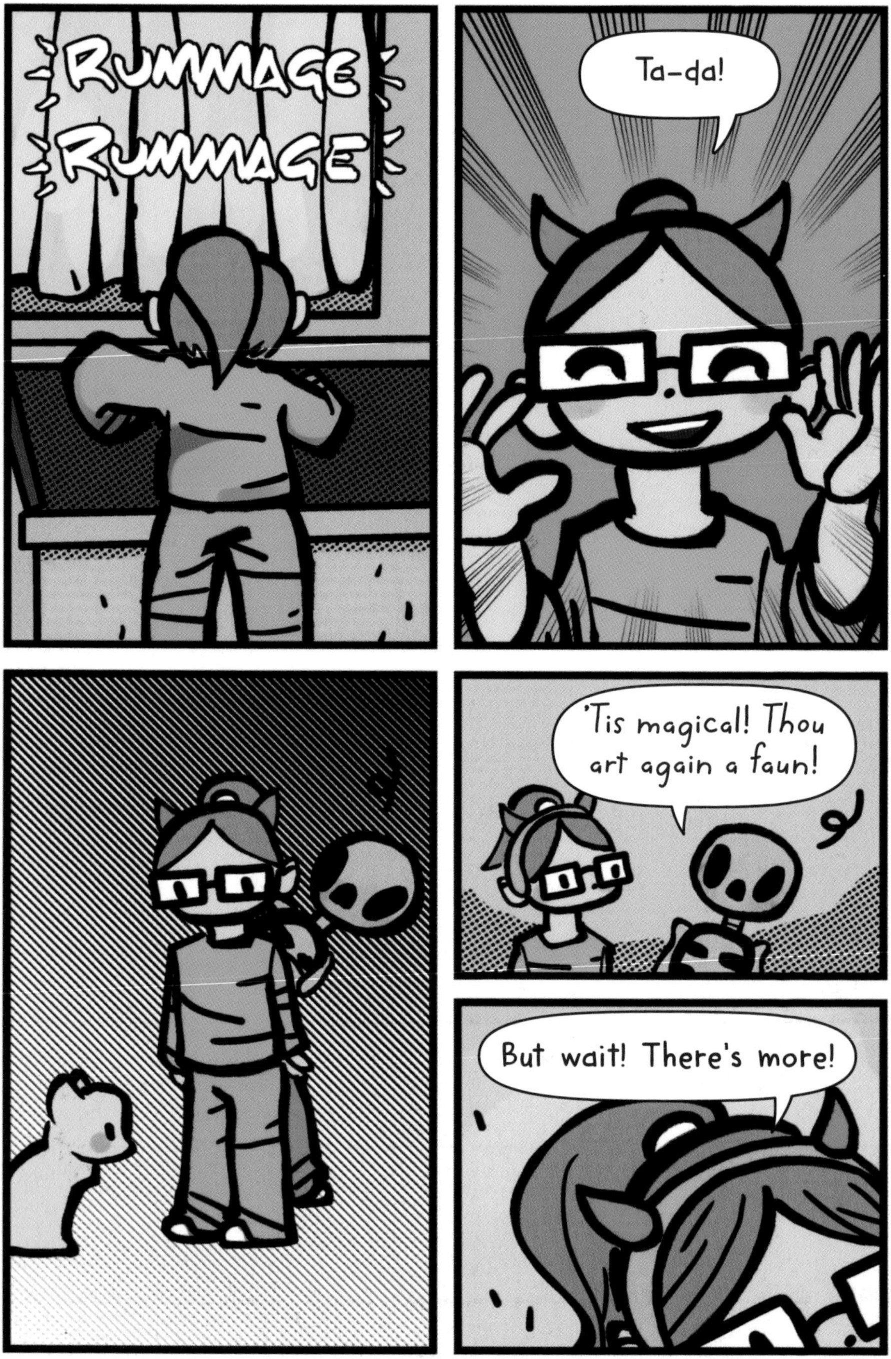
RUMMAGE
RUMMAGE
Ta-da!
'Tis magical! Thou art again a faun!
But wait! There's more!

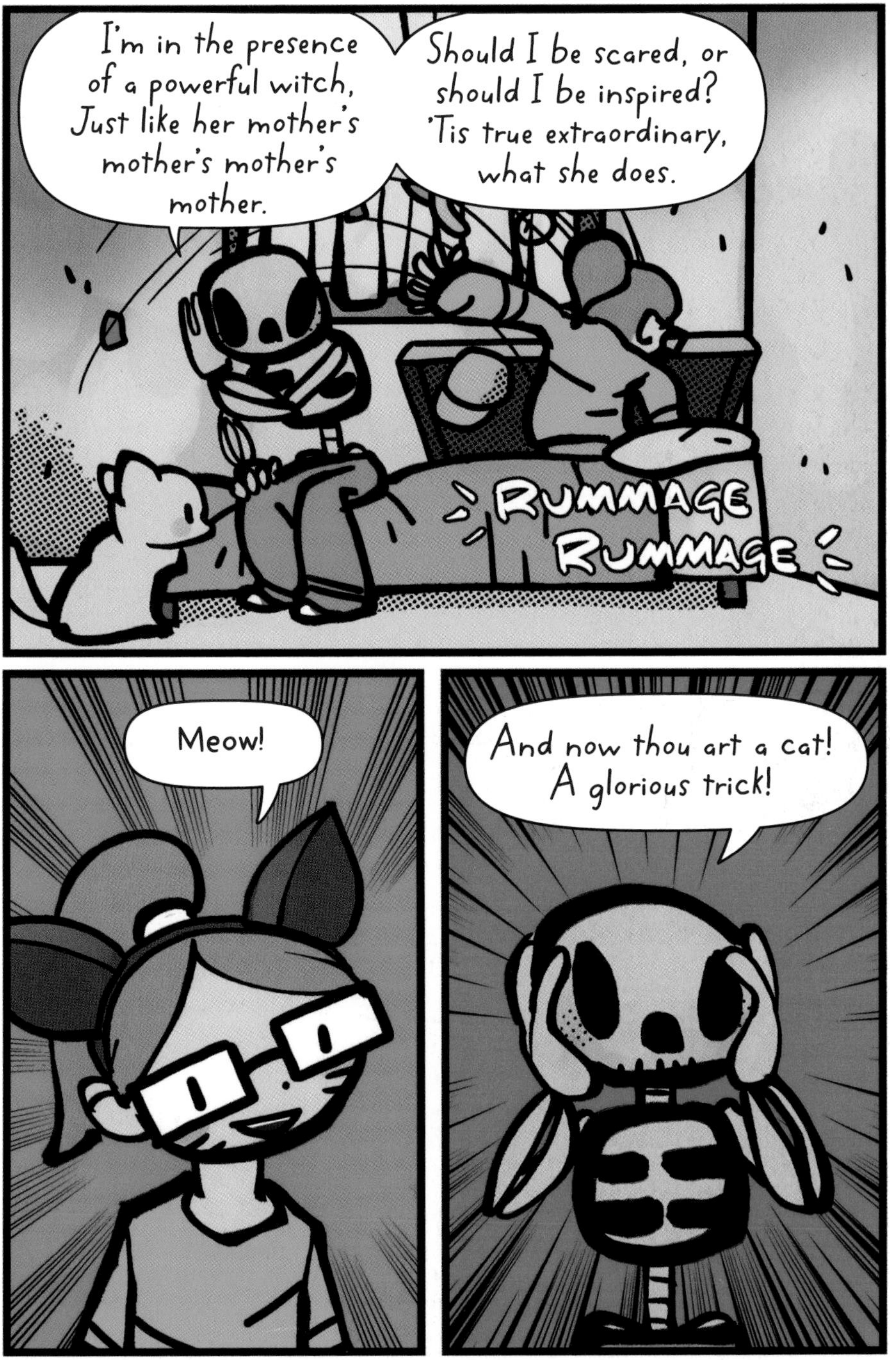
I'm in the presence of a powerful witch, Just like her mother's mother's mother's mother.
Should I be scared, or should I be inspired? 'Tis true extraordinary, what she does.
RUMMAGE RUMMAGE
Meow!
And now thou art a cat! A glorious trick!

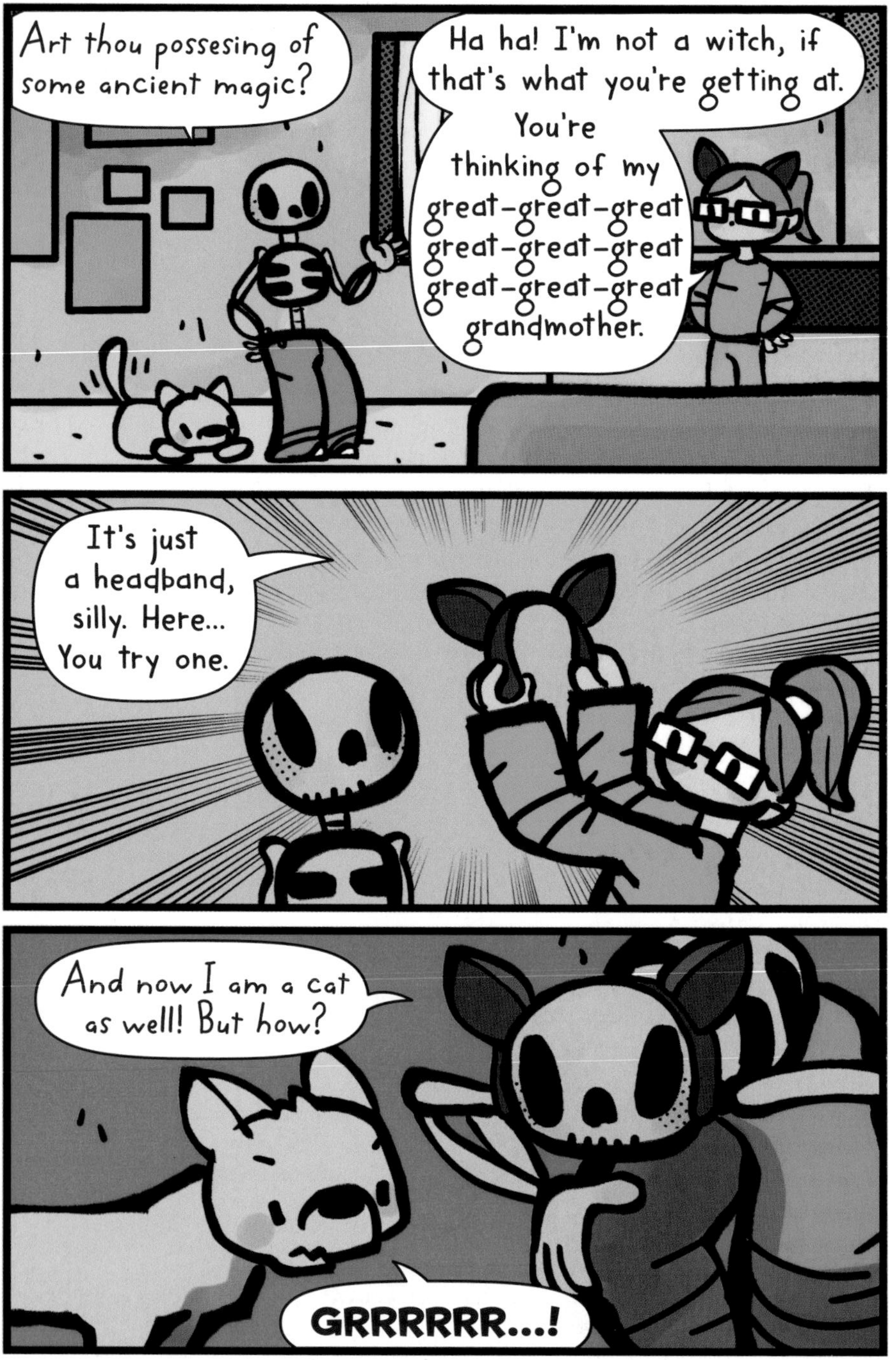
Art thou possesing of some ancient magic?
Ha ha! I'm not a witch, if that's what you're getting at. You're thinking of my great-great-great great-great-great great-great-great grandmother.
It's just a headband, silly. Here... You try one.
And now I am a cat as well! But how?
GRRRRRR...!

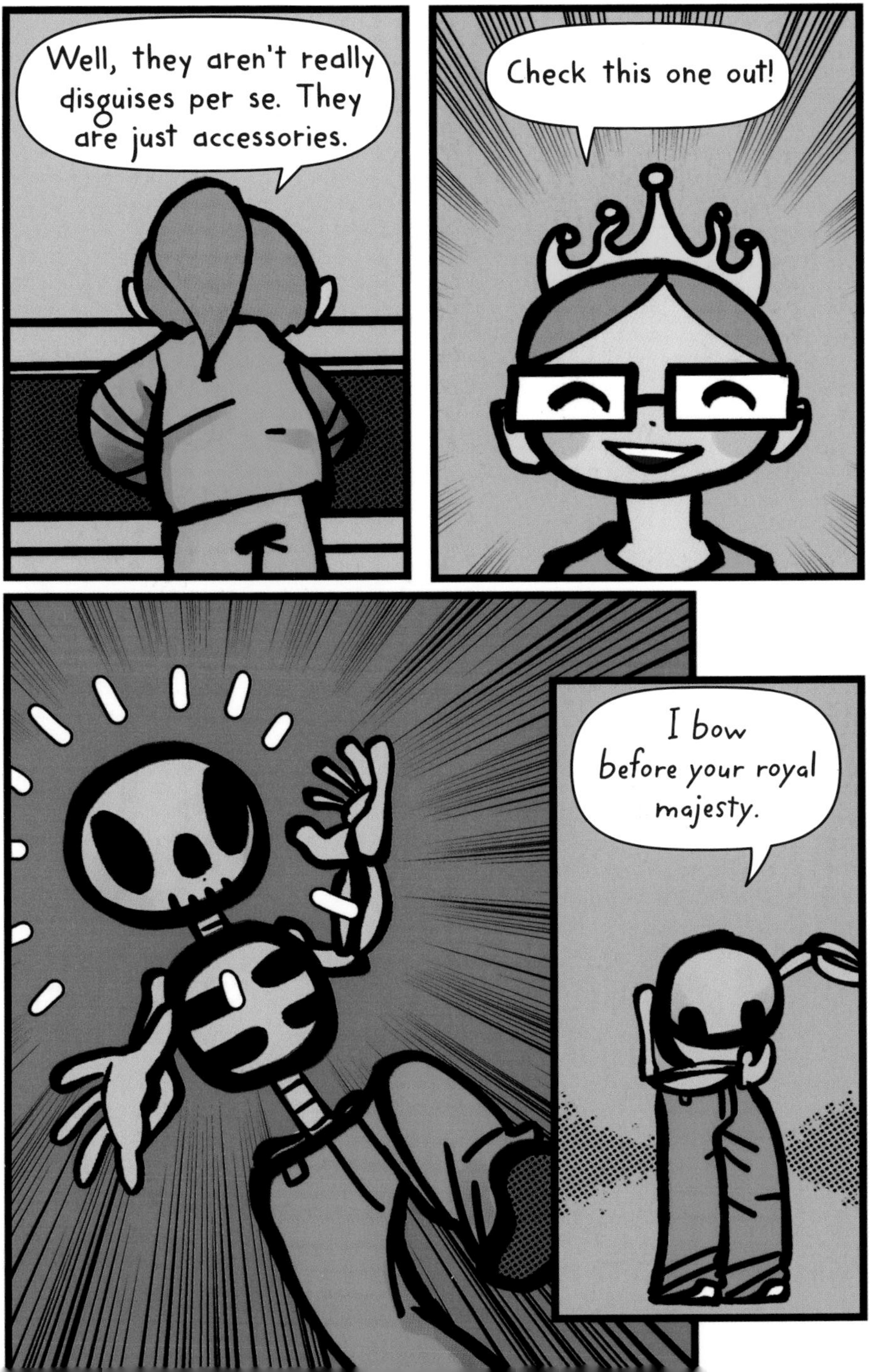
Well, they aren't really disguises per se. They are just accessories.
Check this one out!
I bow before your royal majesty.

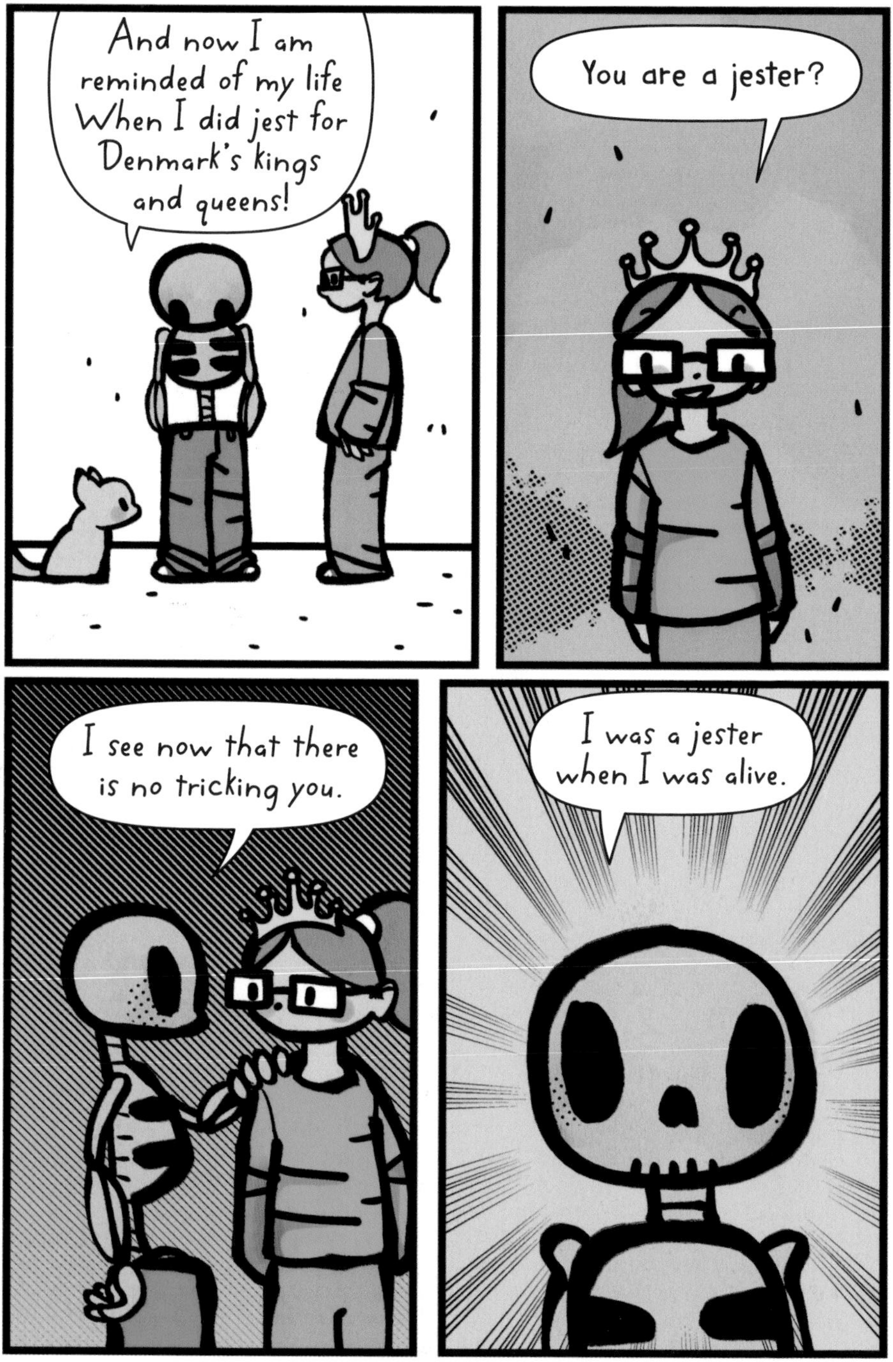
And now I am reminded of my life When I did jest for Denmark's kings and queens!
You are a jester?
I see now that there is no tricking you.
I was a jester when I was alive.

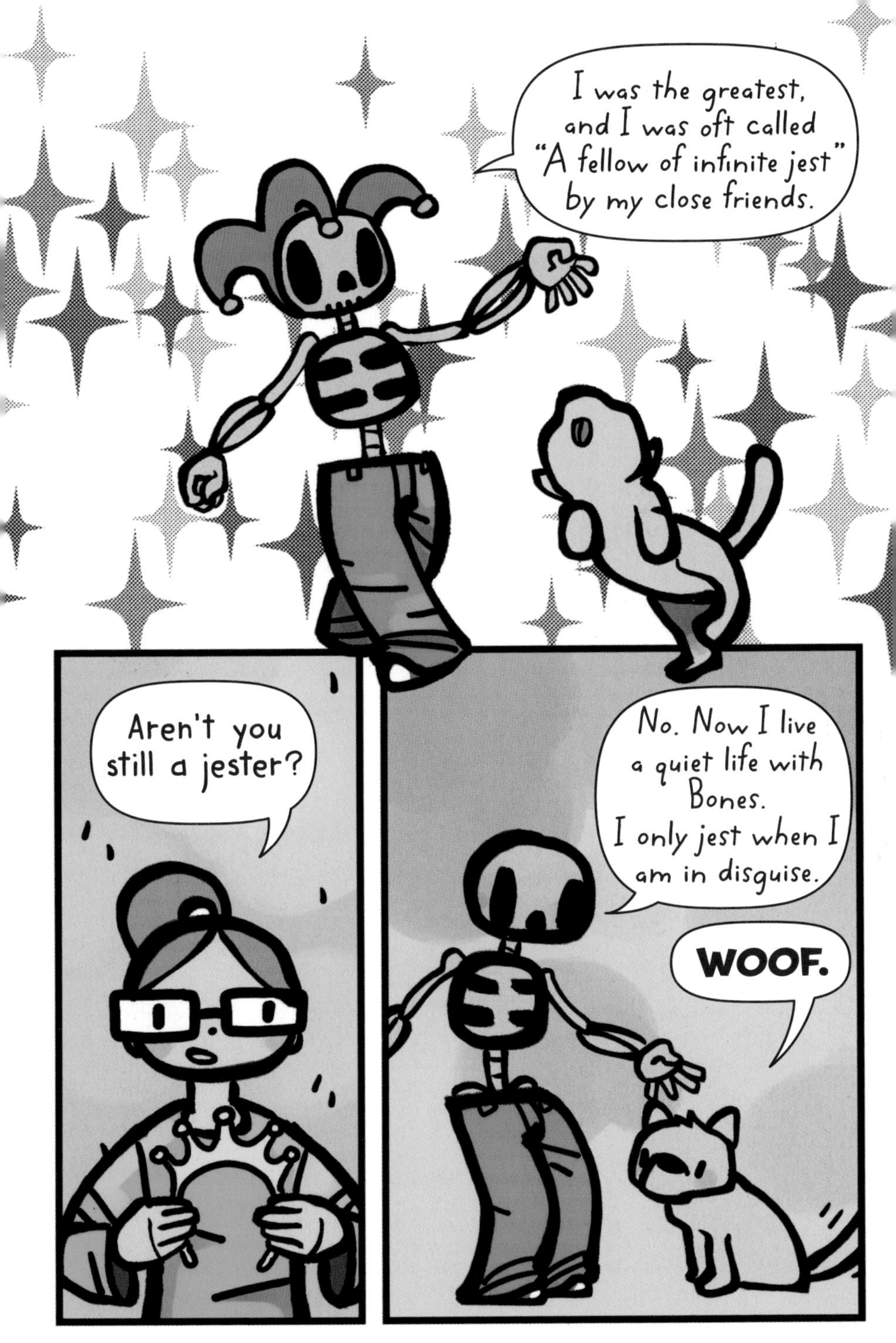

I was the greatest, and I was oft called "A fellow of infinite jest" by my close friends.
Aren't you still a jester?
No. Now I live a quiet life with Bones. I only jest when I am in disguise.
WOOF.

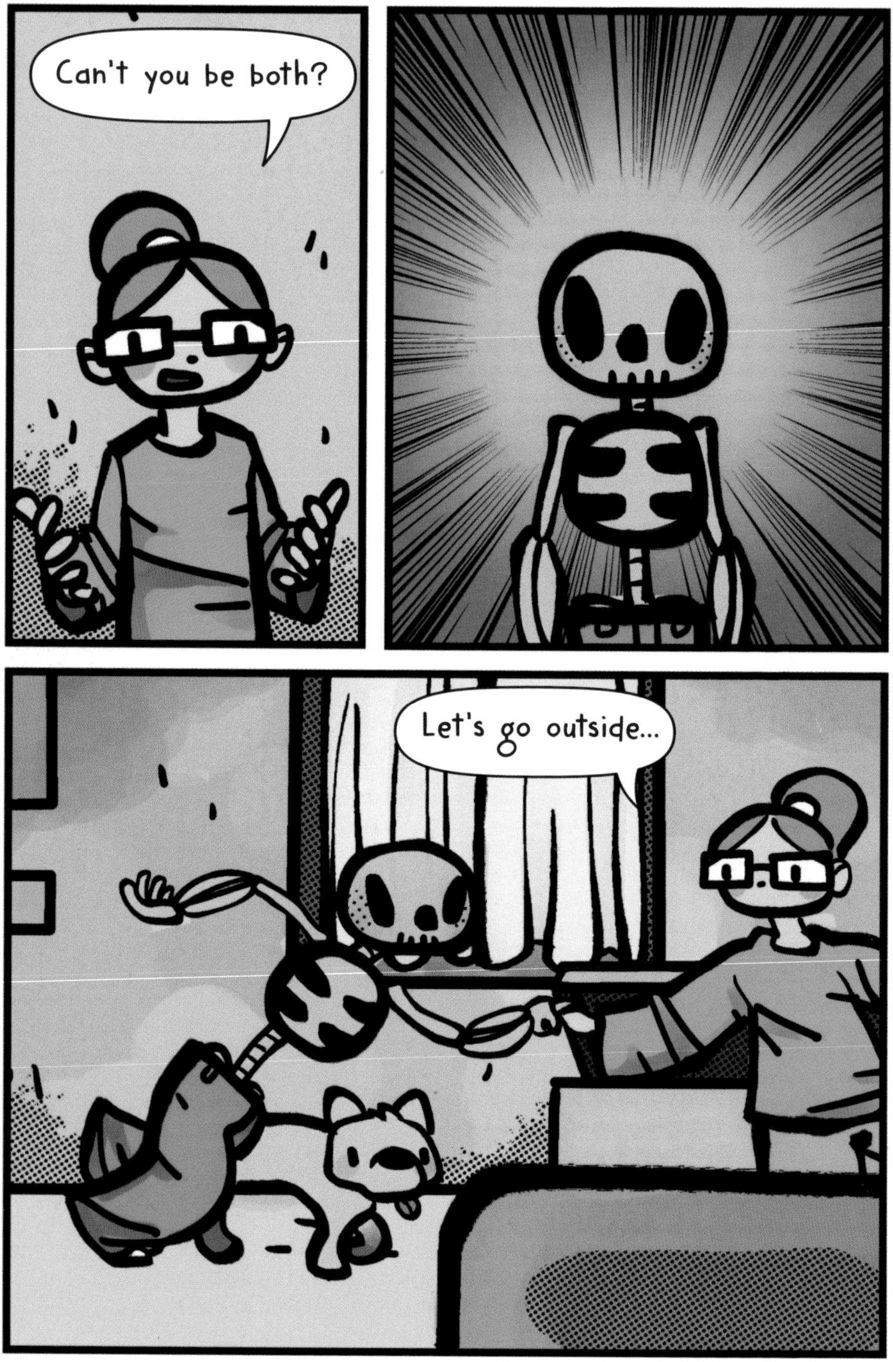
Can't you be both?
Let's go outside...

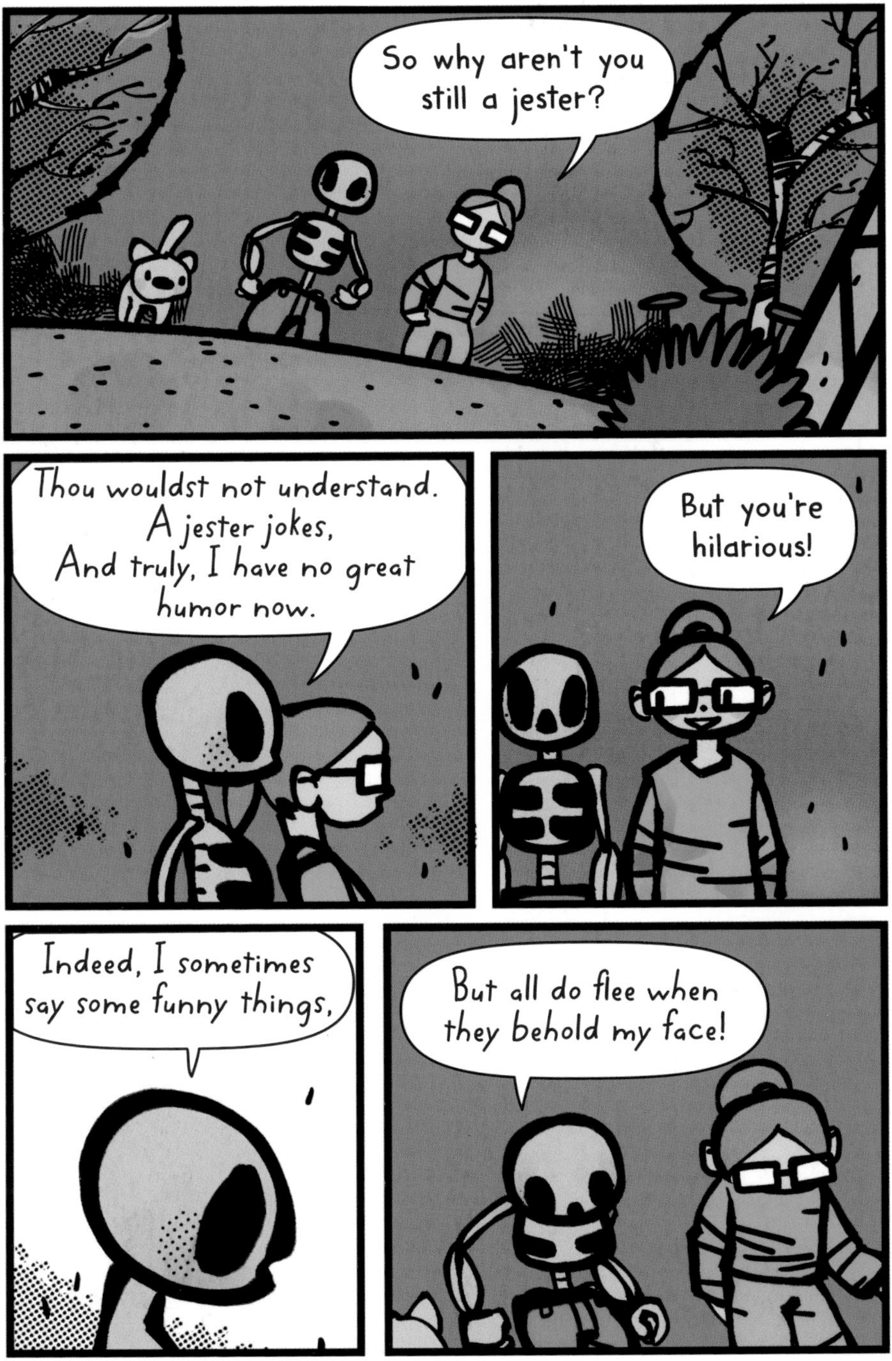
So why aren't you still a jester?
Thou wouldst not understand. A jester jokes, And truly, I have no great humor now.
But you're hilarious!
Indeed, I sometimes say some funny things,
But all do flee when they behold my face!

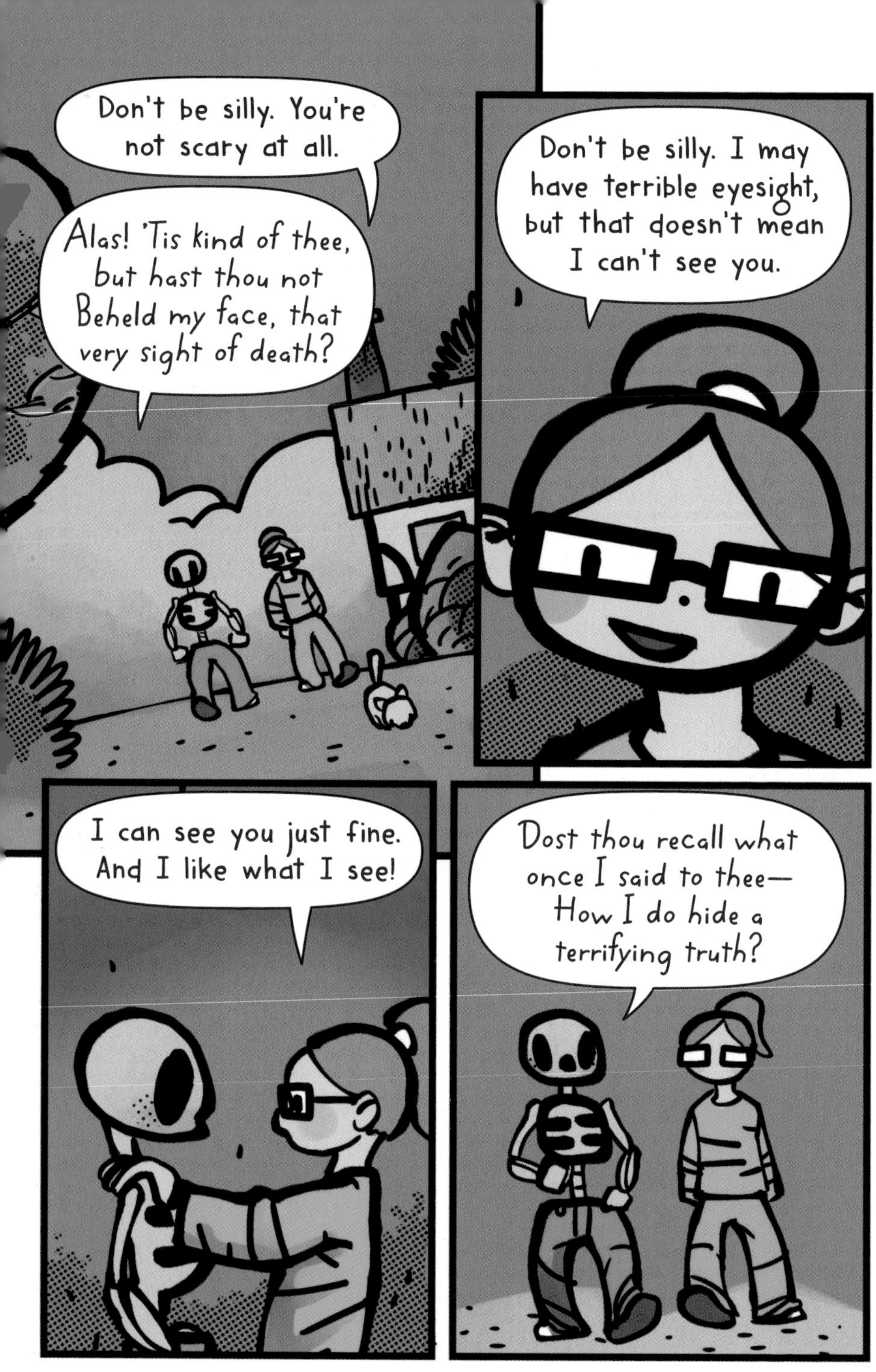
Don't be silly. You're not scary at all.
Alas! 'Tis kind of thee, but hast thou not Beheld my face, that very sight of death?
Don't be silly. I may have terrible eyesight, but that doesn't mean I can't see you.
I can see you just fine. And I like what I see!
Dost thou recall what once I said to thee— How I do hide a terrifying truth?

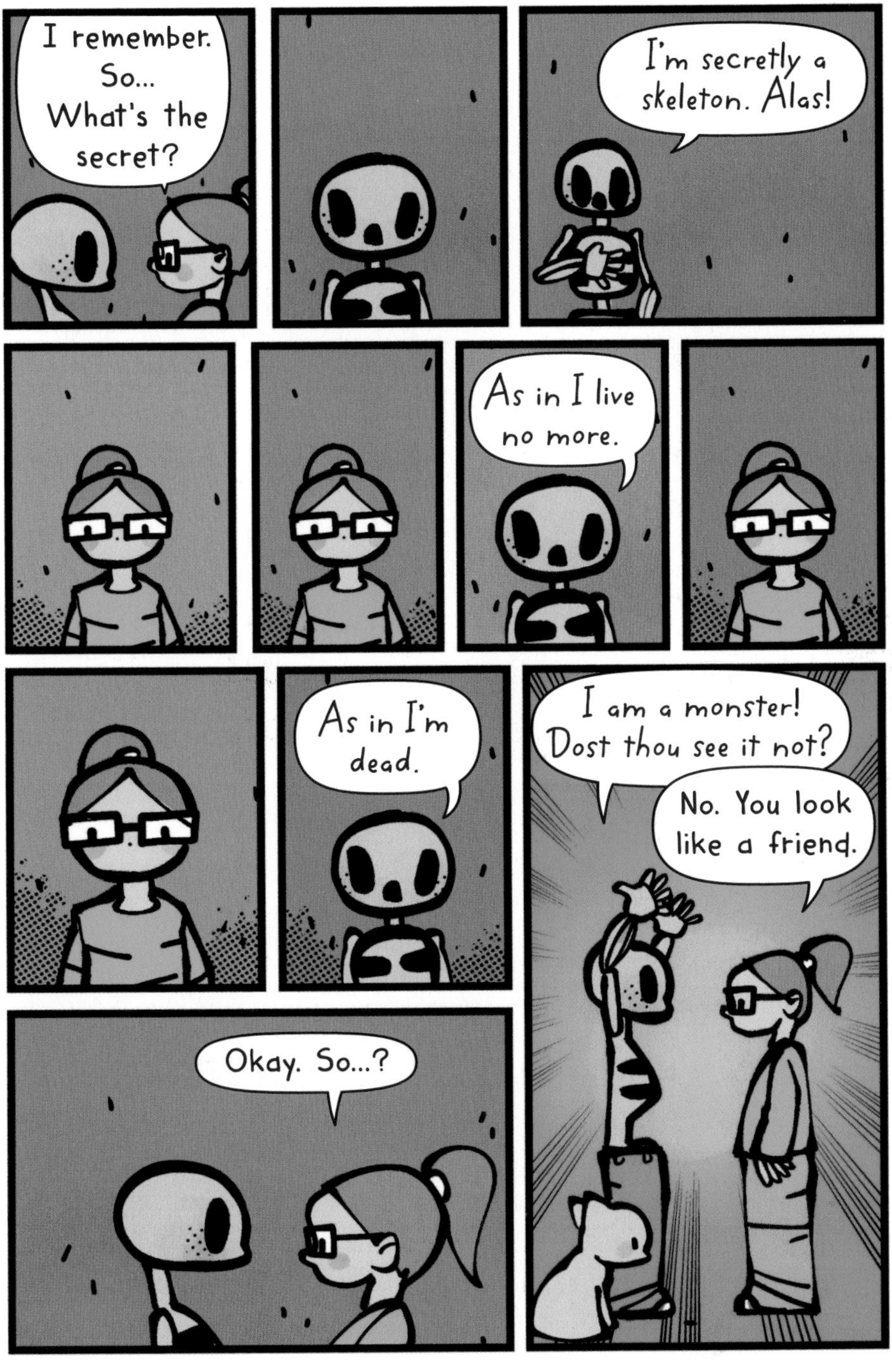
I remember. So... What's the secret?
I'm secretly a skeleton. Alas!
As in I live no more.
As in I'm dead.
I am a monster! Dost thou see it not?
No. You look like a friend.
Okay. So...?

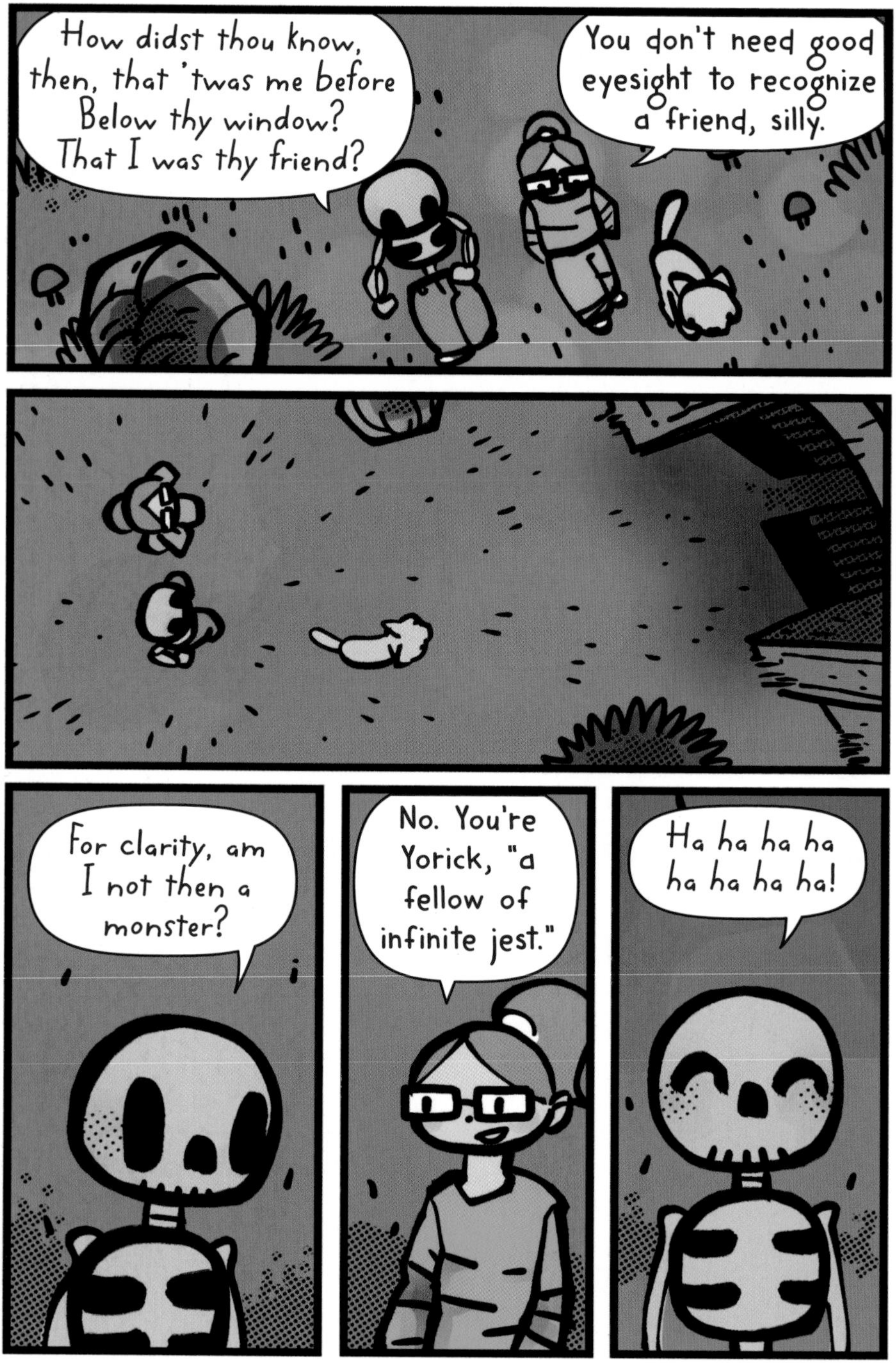
How didst thou know, then, that 'twas me before Below thy window? That I was thy friend?
You don't need good eyesight to recognize a friend, silly.
For clarity, am I not then a monster?
No. You're Yorick, "a fellow of infinite jest."
Ha ha ha ha ha ha ha ha!

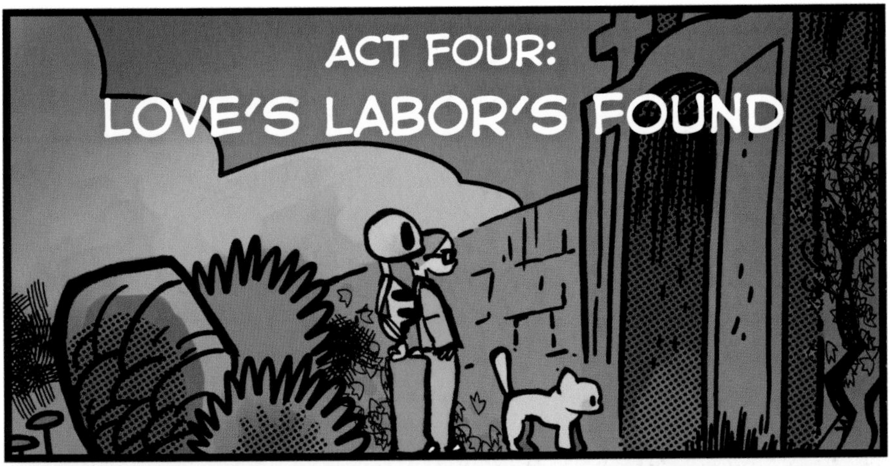
ACT FOUR:
LOVE'S LABOR'S FOUND

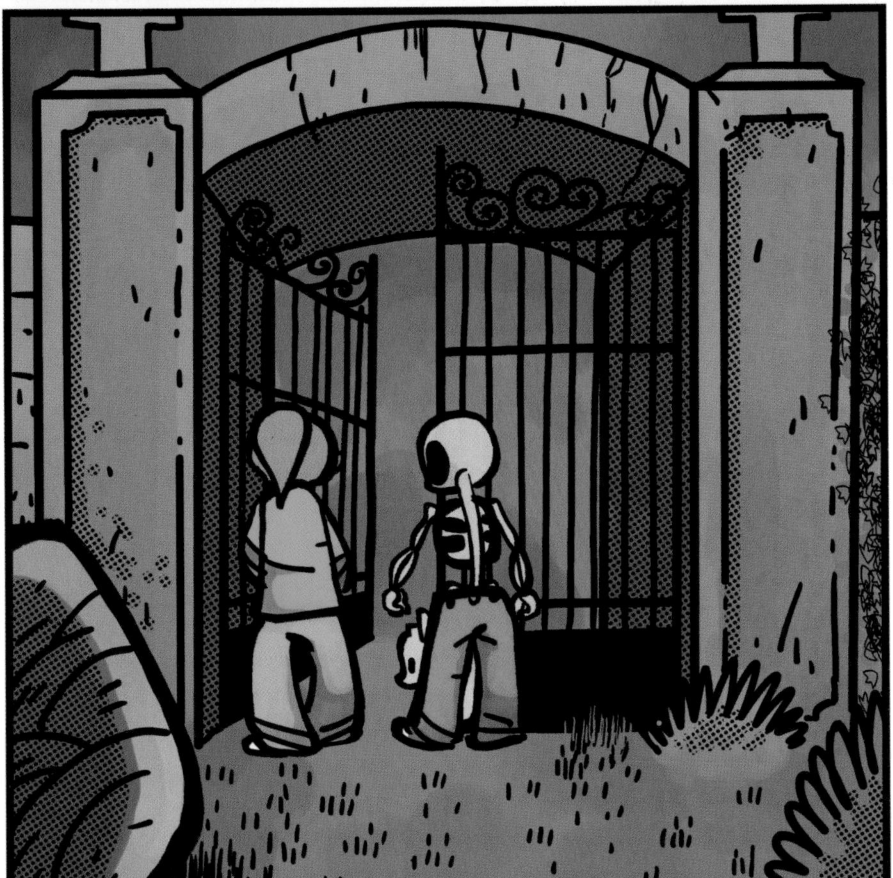

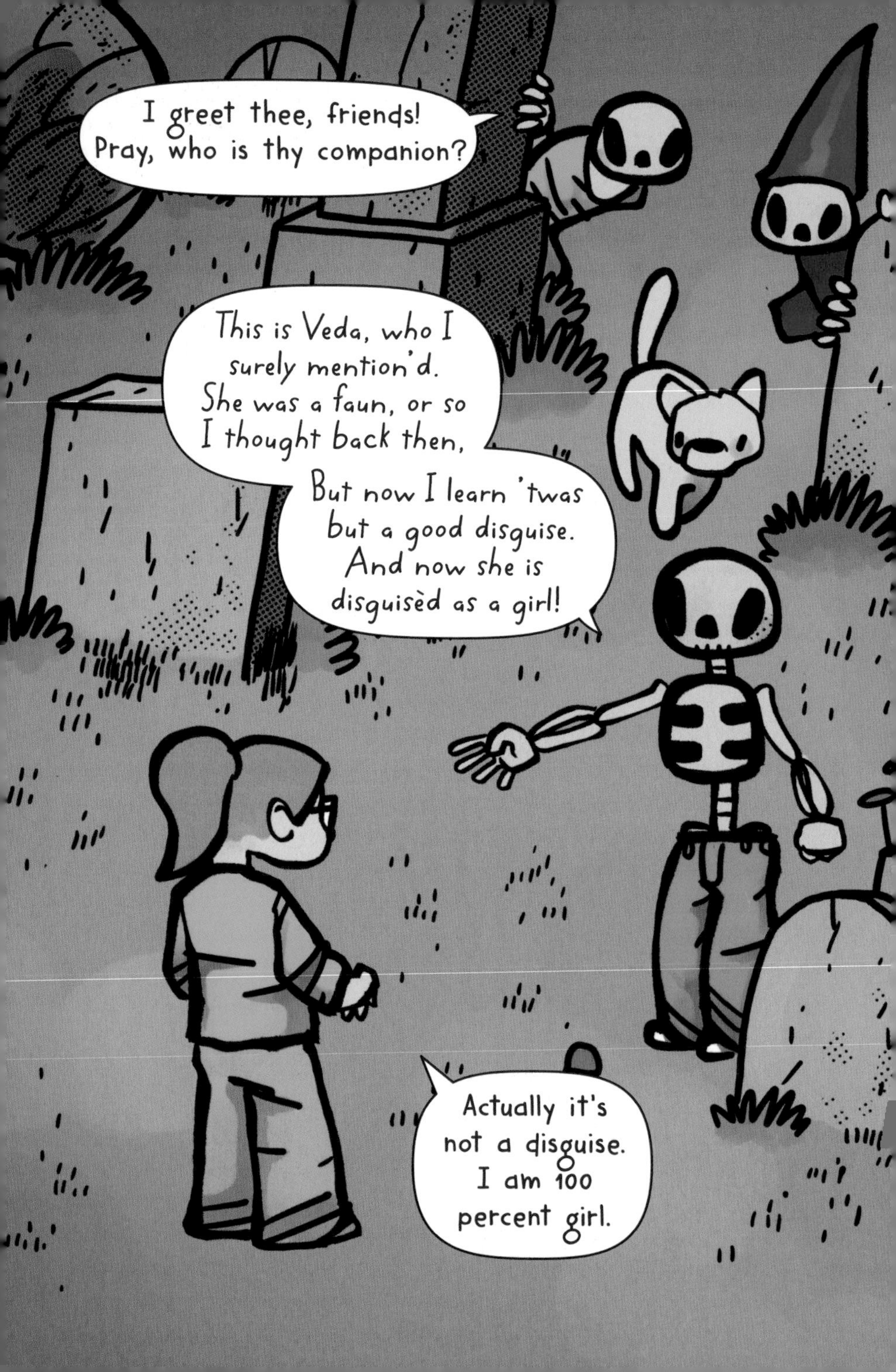

I greet thee, friends! Pray, who is thy companion?
This is Veda, who I surely mention'd. She was a faun, or so I thought back then,
But now I learn 'twas but a good disguise. And now she is disguisèd as a girl!
Actually it's not a disguise. I am 100 percent girl.

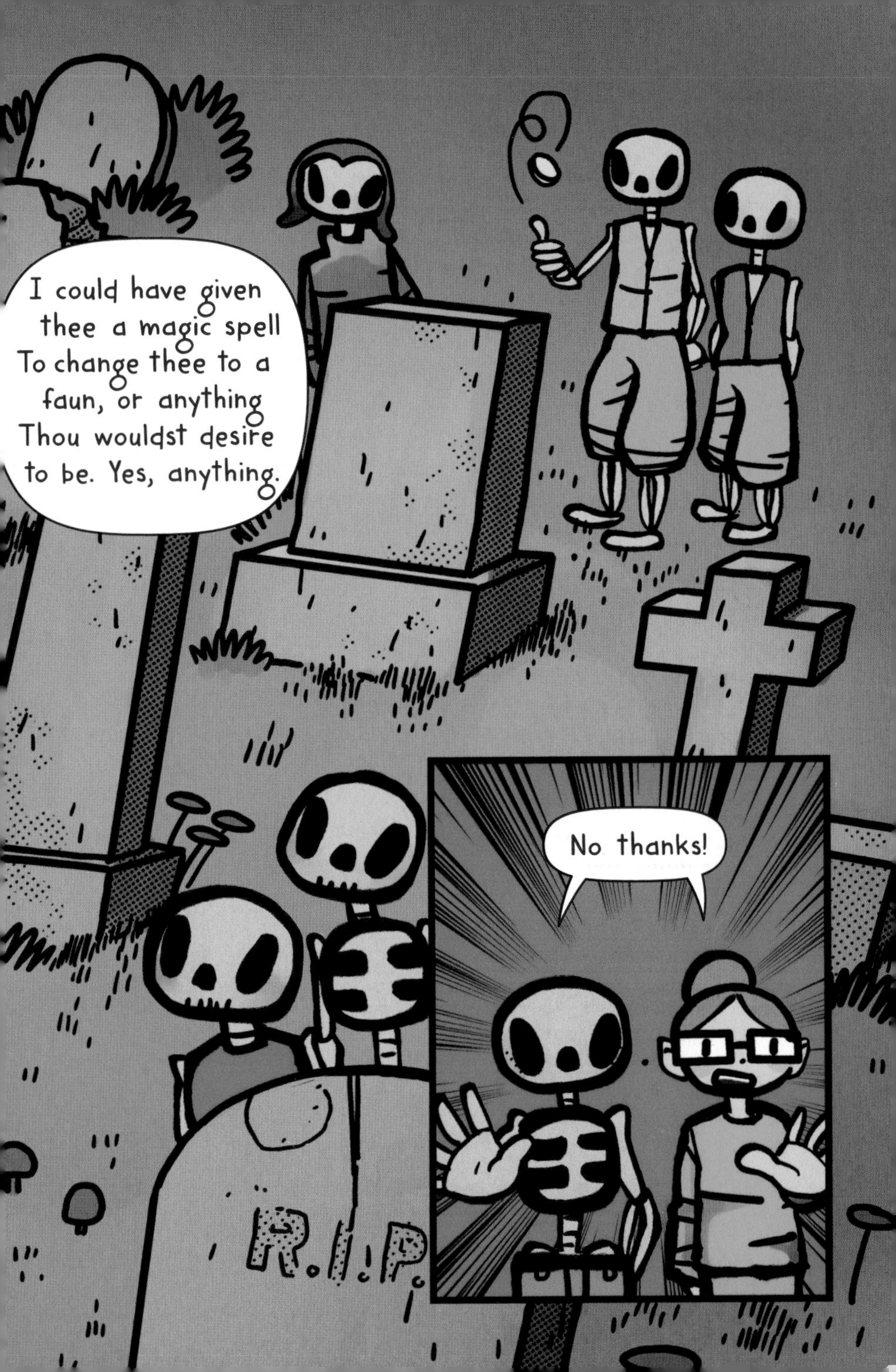
I could have given thee a magic spell To change thee to a faun, or anything Thou wouldst desire to be. Yes, anything.
No thanks!
R.I.P.

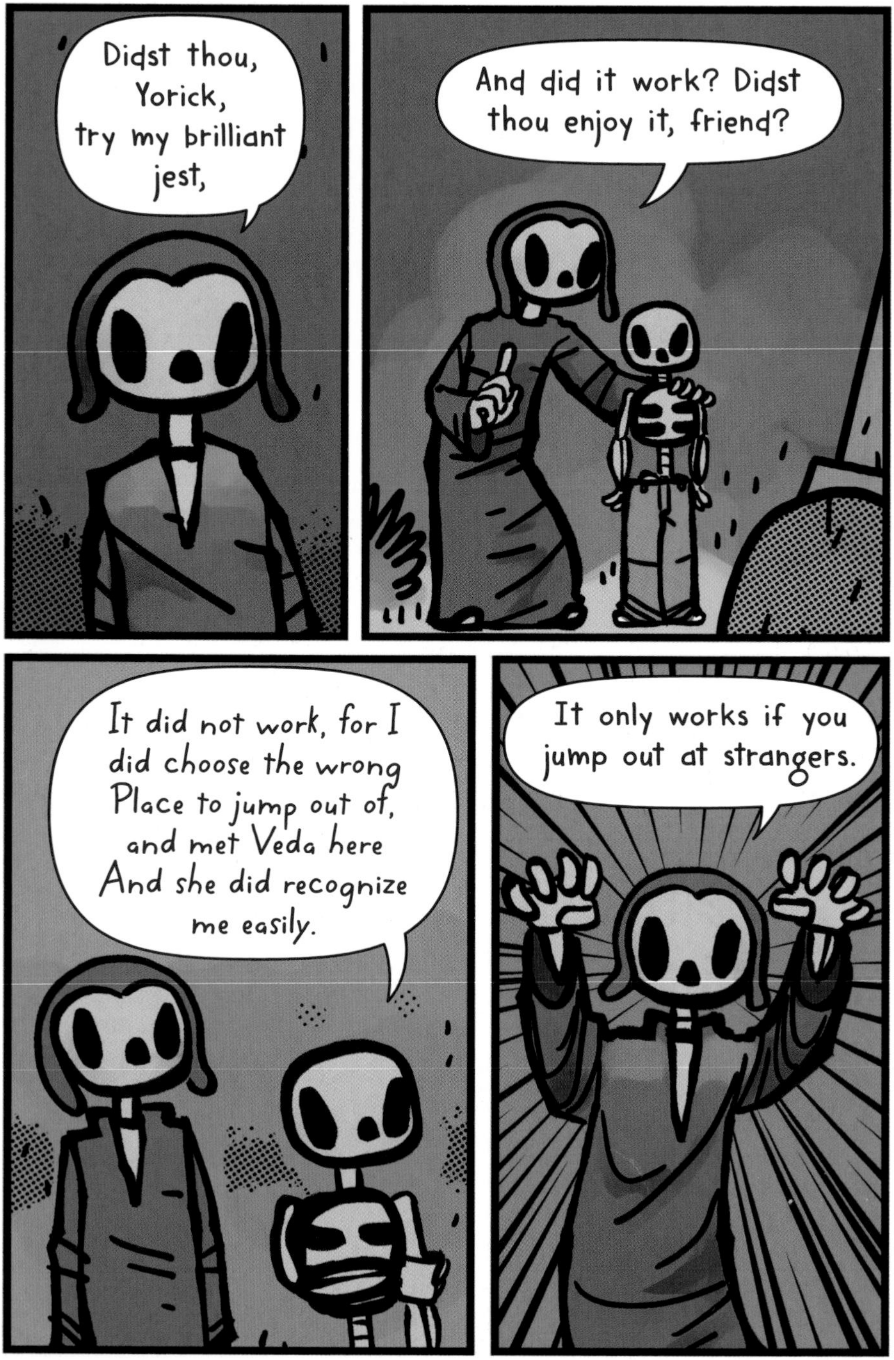
Didst thou, Yorick, try my brilliant jest,
And did it work? Didst thou enjoy it, friend?
It did not work, for I did choose the wrong Place to jump out of, and met Veda here And she did recognize me easily.
It only works if you jump out at strangers.

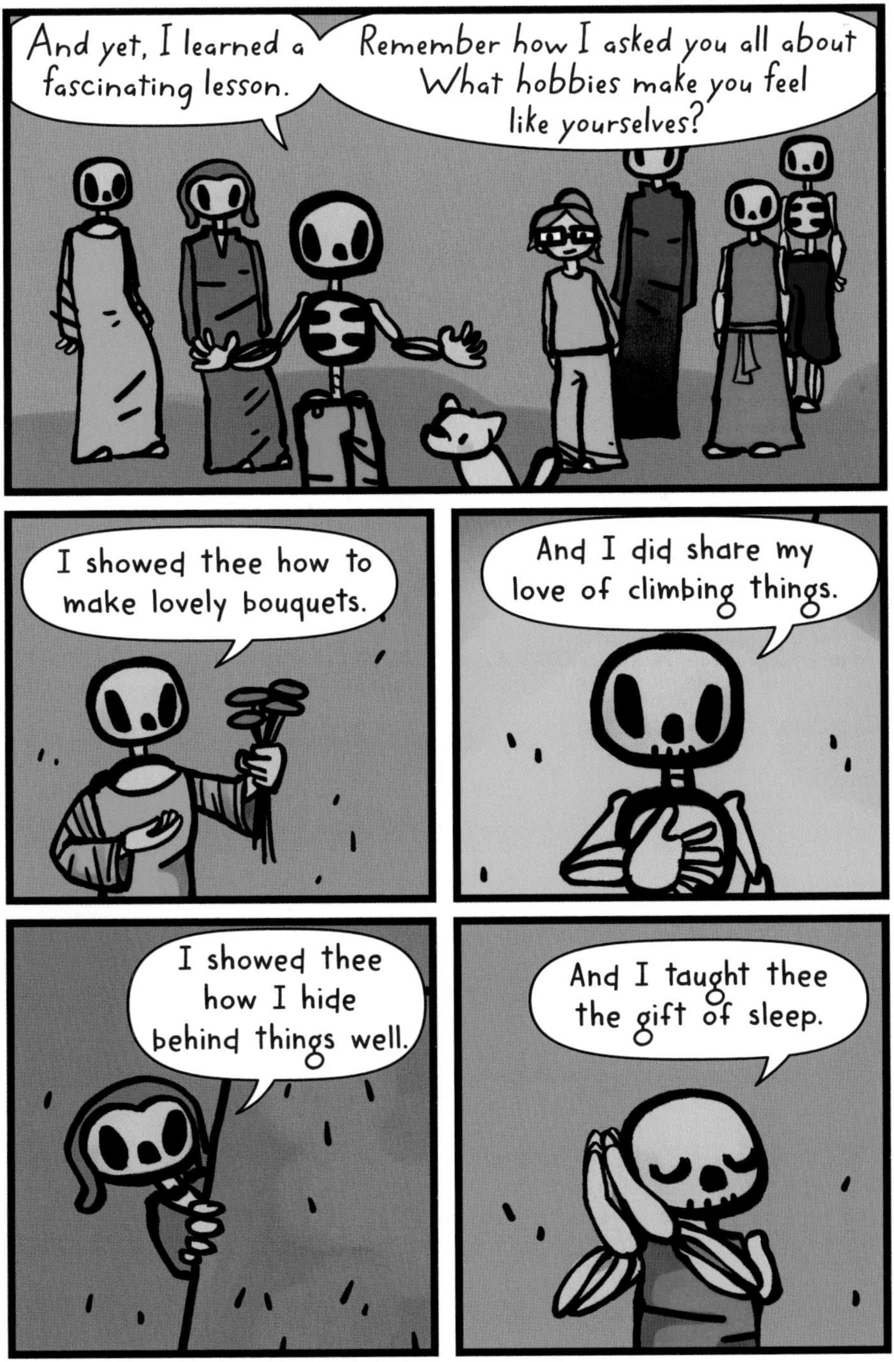

And yet, I learned a fascinating lesson.
Remember how I asked you all about What hobbies make you feel like yourselves?
I showed thee how to make lovely bouquets.
And I did share my love of climbing things.
I showed thee how I hide behind things well.
And I taught thee the gift of sleep.

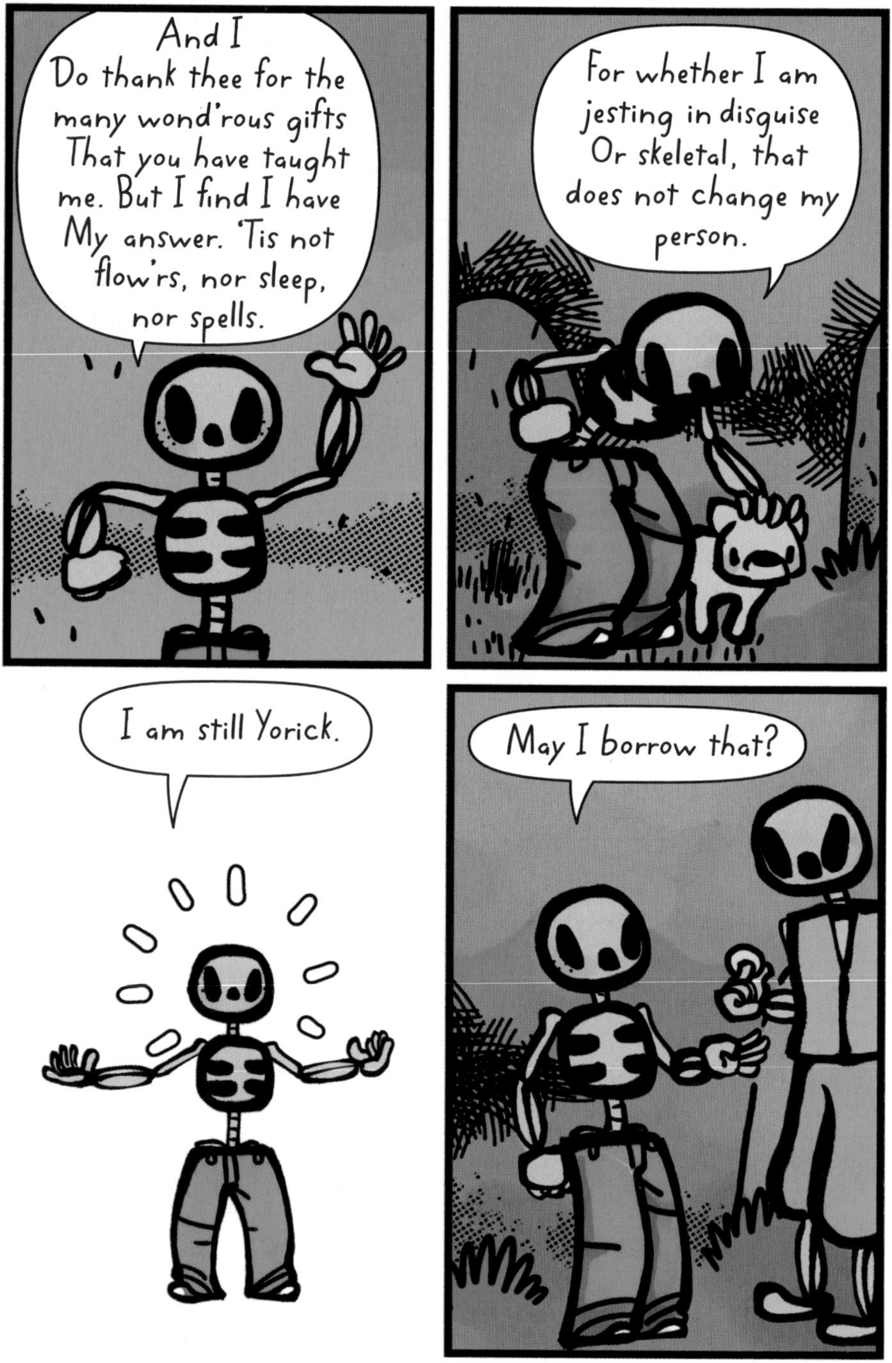
And I
Do thank thee for the many wond'rous gifts
That you have taught me. But I find I have
My answer. 'Tis not flow'rs, nor sleep, nor spells.
For whether I am jesting in disguise
Or skeletal, that does not change my person.
I am still Yorick.
May I borrow that?

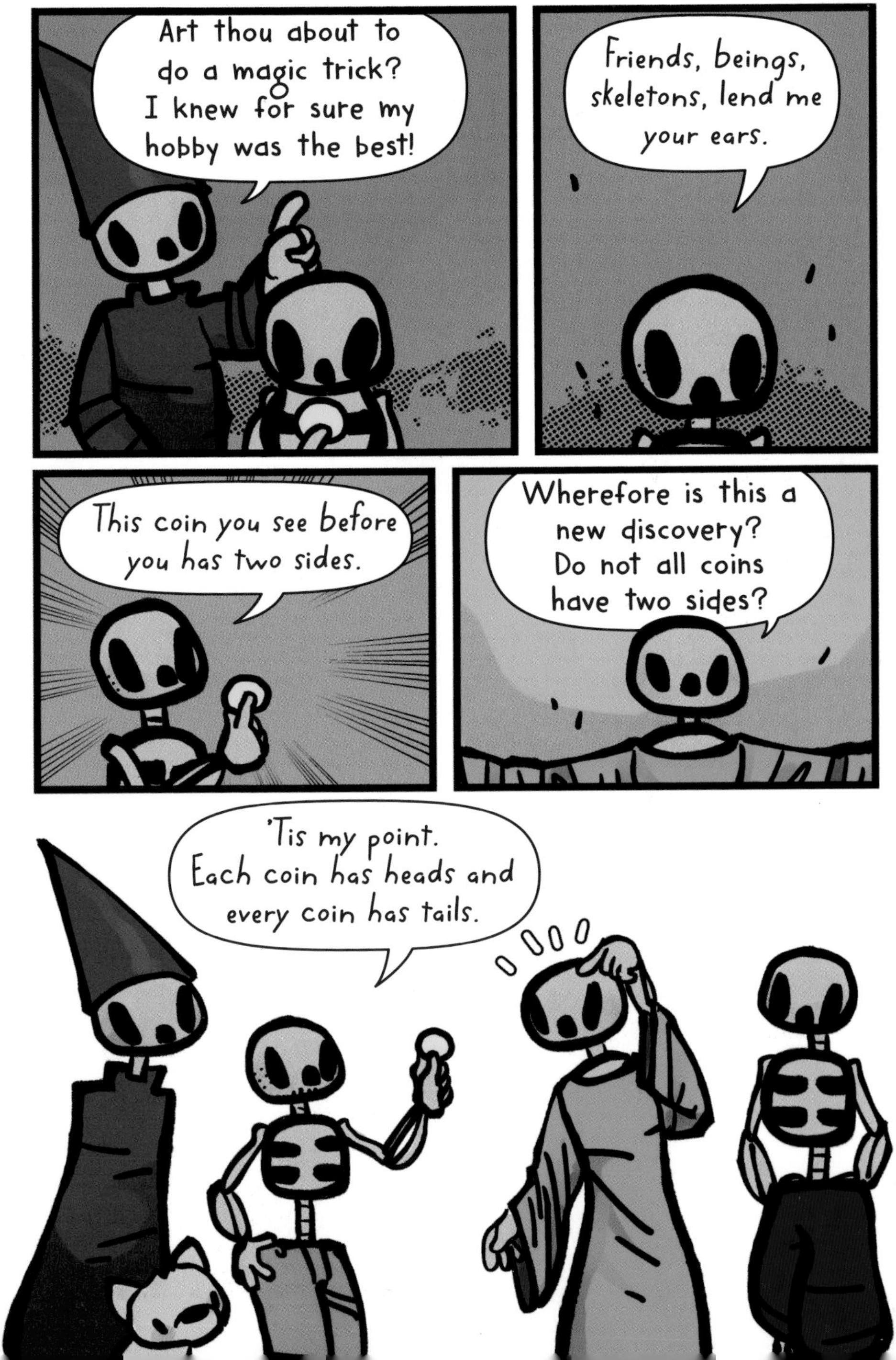
Art thou about to do a magic trick? I knew for sure my hobby was the best!
Friends, beings, skeletons, lend me your ears.
This coin you see before you has two sides.
Wherefore is this a new discovery? Do not all coins have two sides?
'Tis my point. Each coin has heads and every coin has tails.

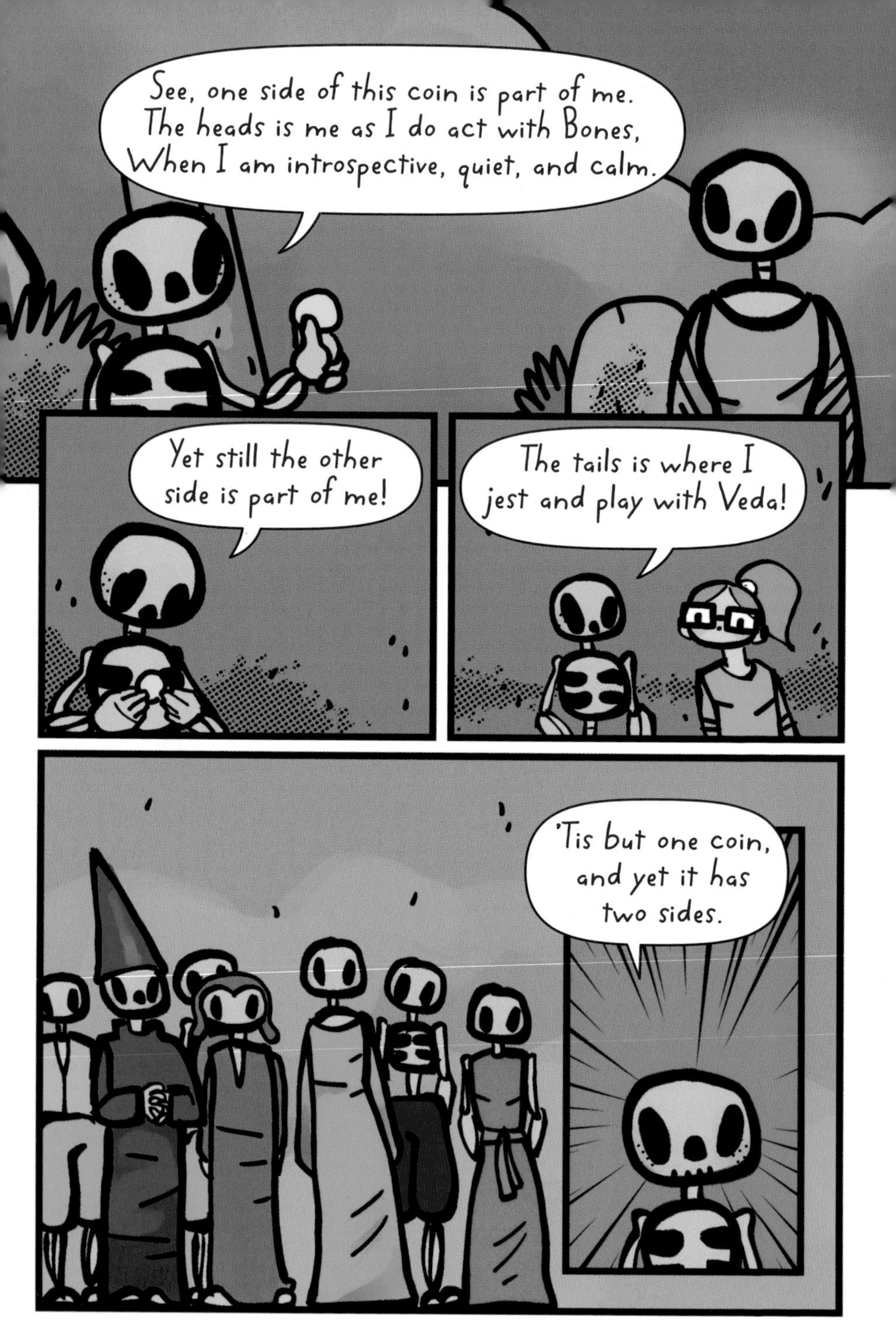

See, one side of this coin is part of me. The heads is me as I do act with Bones, When I am introspective, quiet, and calm.
Yet still the other side is part of me!
The tails is where I jest and play with Veda!
'Tis but one coin, and yet it has two sides.

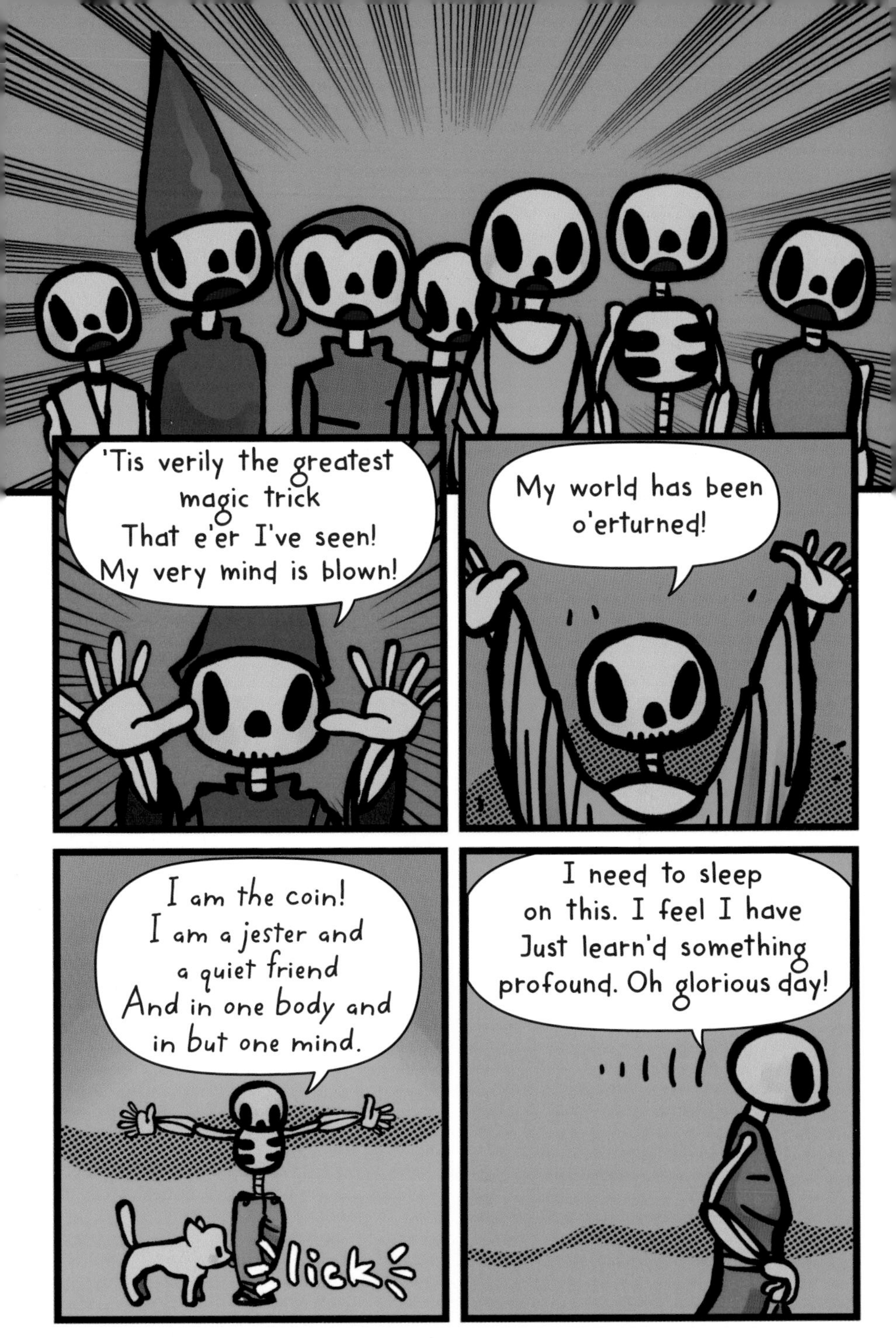
'Tis verily the greatest magic trick
That e'er I've seen!
My very mind is blown!
My world has been o'erturned!
I am the coin!
I am a jester and a quiet friend
And in one body and in but one mind.
lick
I need to sleep on this. I feel I have
Just learn'd something profound. Oh glorious day!

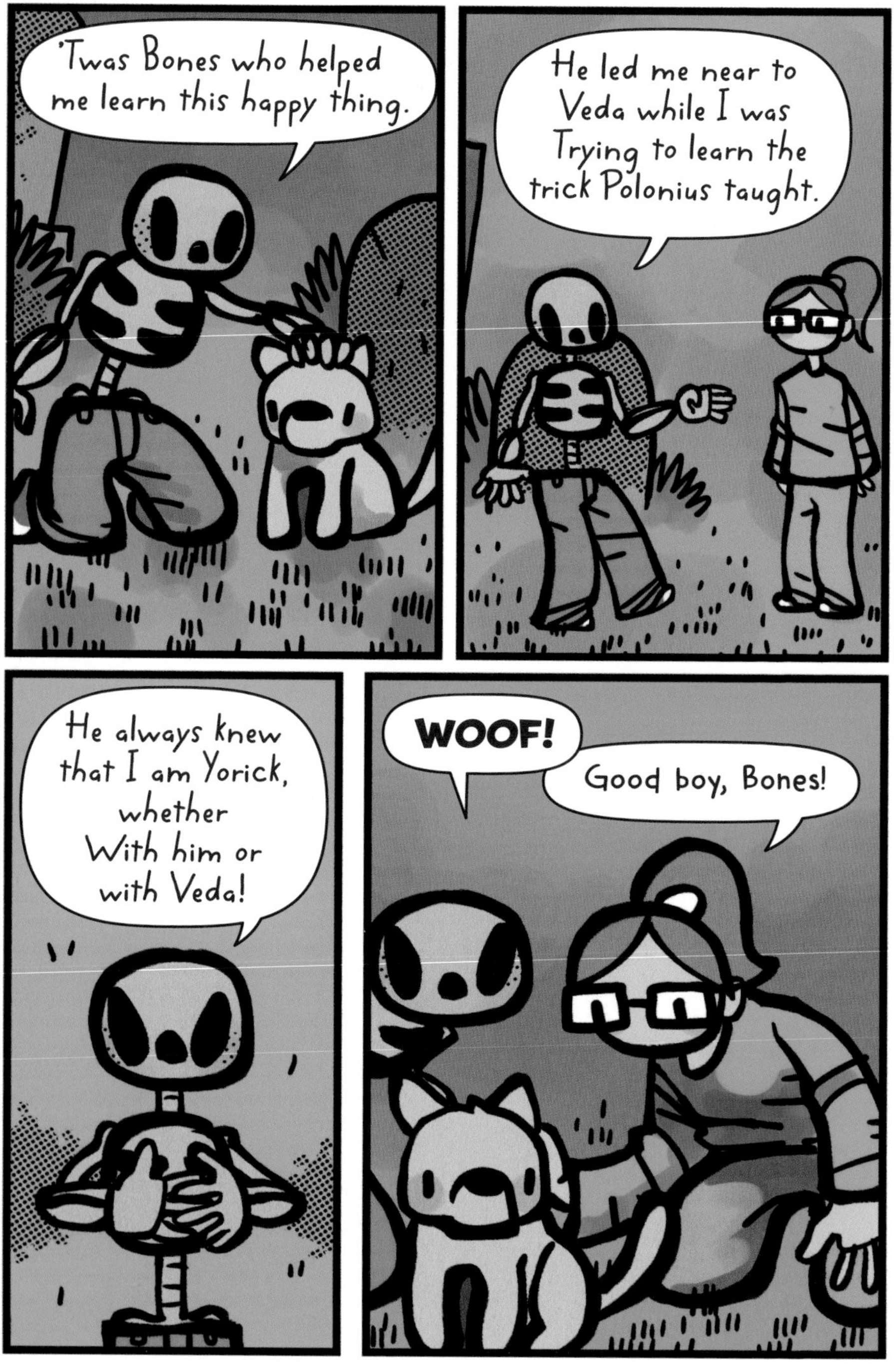
'Twas Bones who helped me learn this happy thing.
He led me near to Veda while I was Trying to learn the trick Polonius taught.
He always knew that I am Yorick, whether With him or with Veda!
WOOF!
Good boy, Bones!

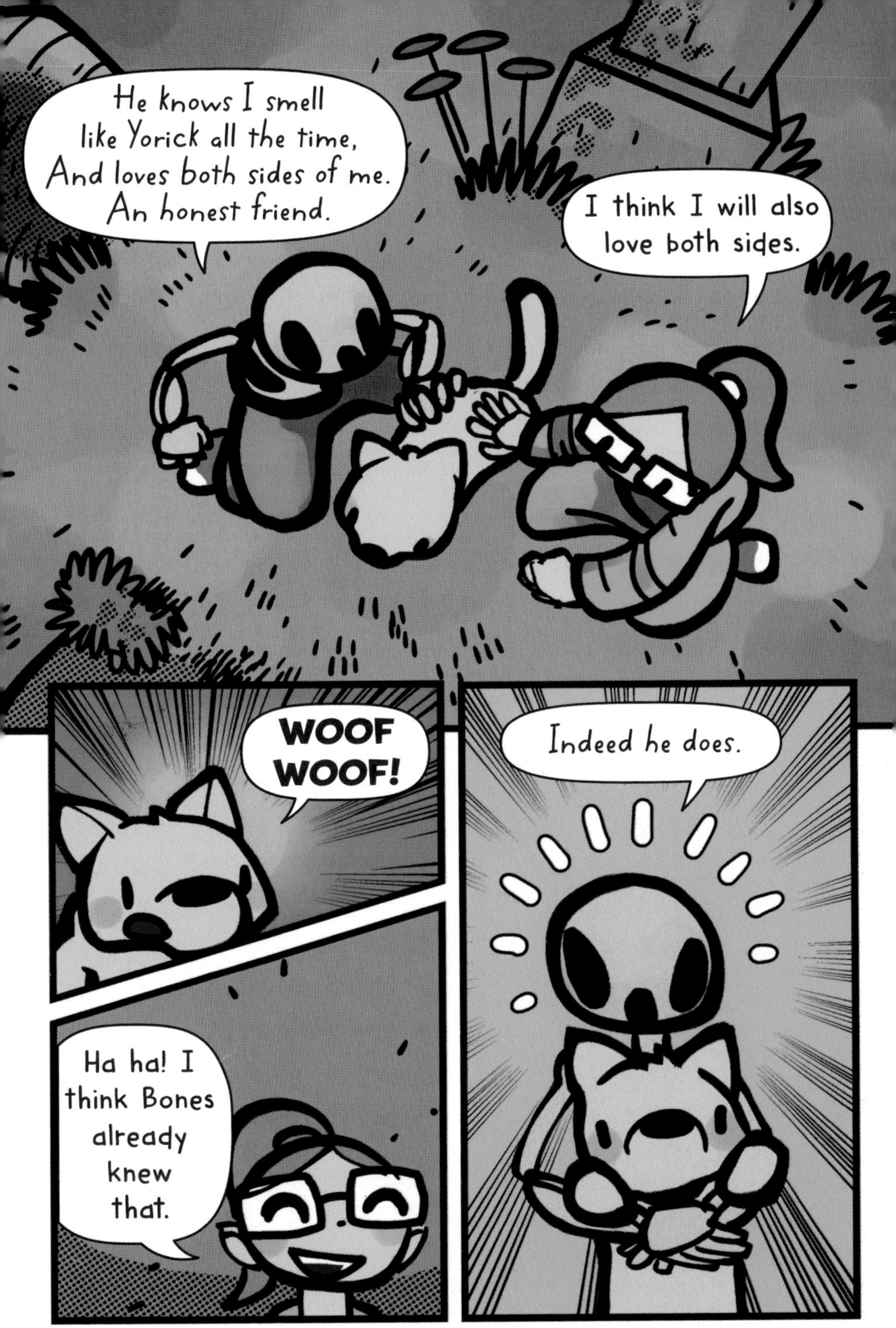
He knows I smell like Yorick all the time, And loves both sides of me. An honest friend.
I think I will also love both sides.
WOOF WOOF!
Ha ha! I think Bones already knew that.
Indeed he does.

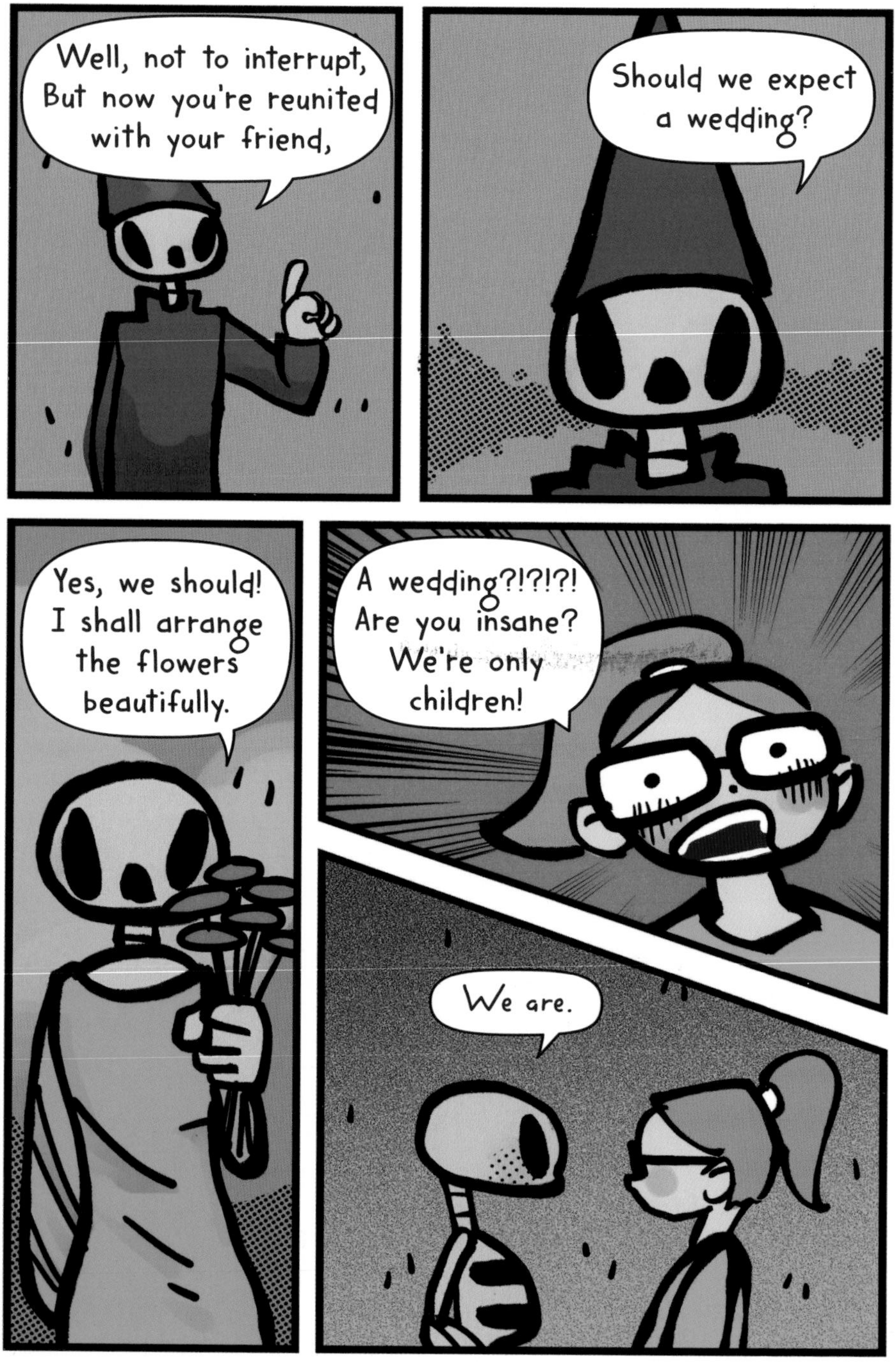
Well, not to interrupt, But now you're reunited with your friend,
Should we expect a wedding?
Yes, we should! I shall arrange the flowers beautifully.
A wedding?!?!?! Are you insane? We're only children!
We are.

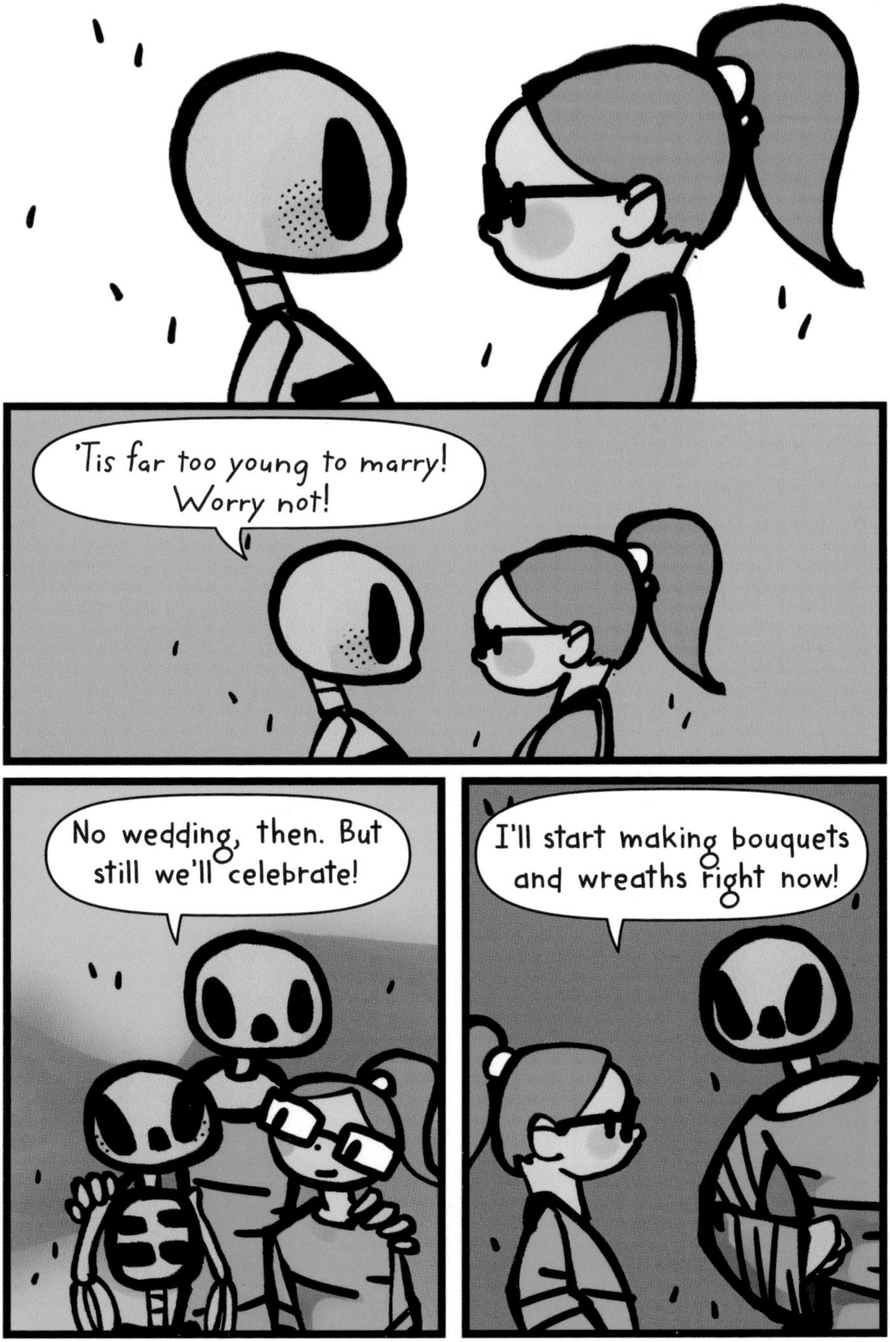
'Tis far too young to marry! Worry not!
No wedding, then. But still we'll celebrate!
I'll start making bouquets and wreaths right now!

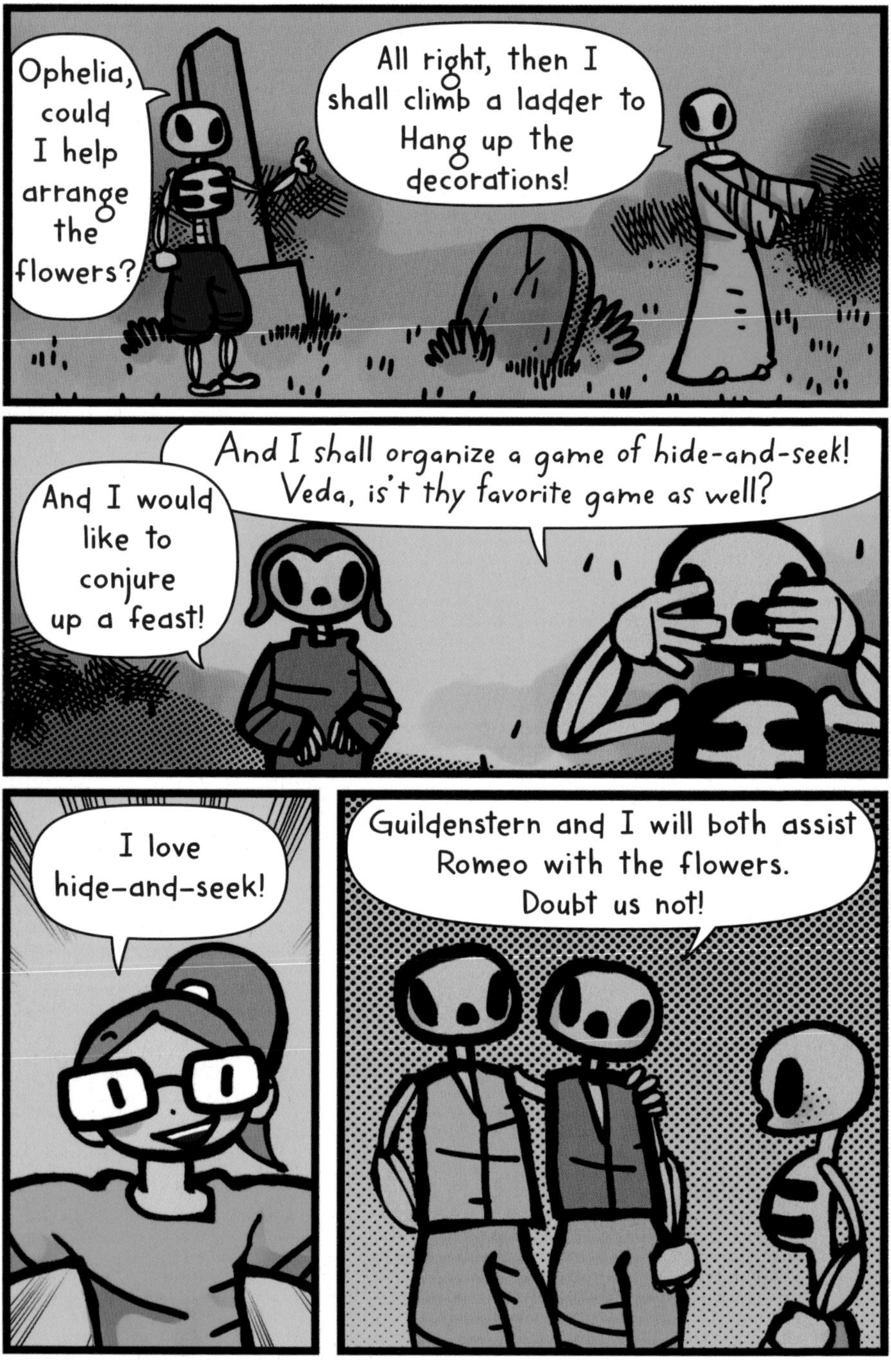
Ophelia, could I help arrange the flowers?
All right, then I shall climb a ladder to Hang up the decorations!
And I shall organize a game of hide-and-seek! Veda, is't thy favorite game as well?
And I would like to conjure up a feast!
I love hide-and-seek!
Guildenstern and I will both assist Romeo with the flowers. Doubt us not!

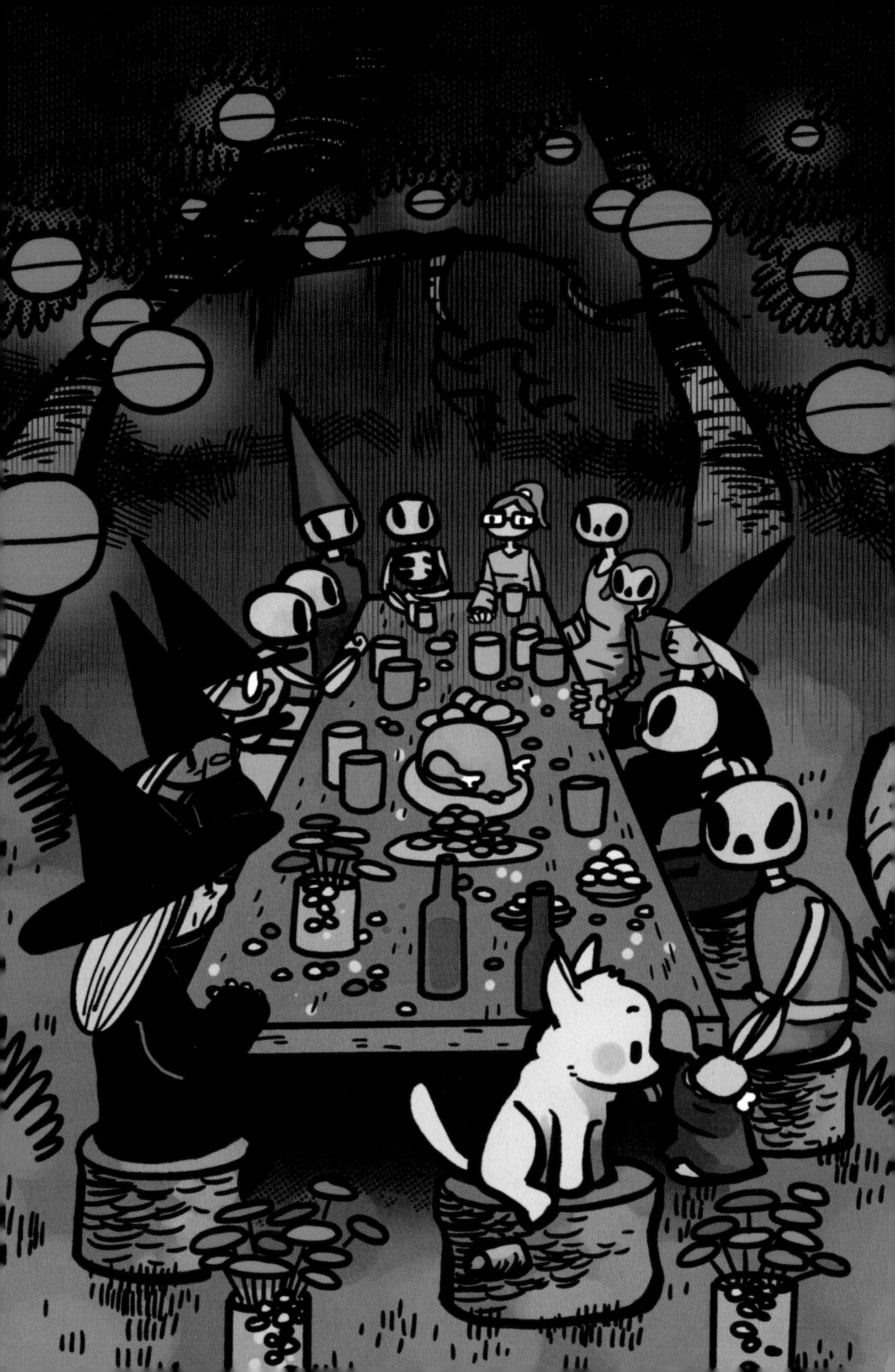

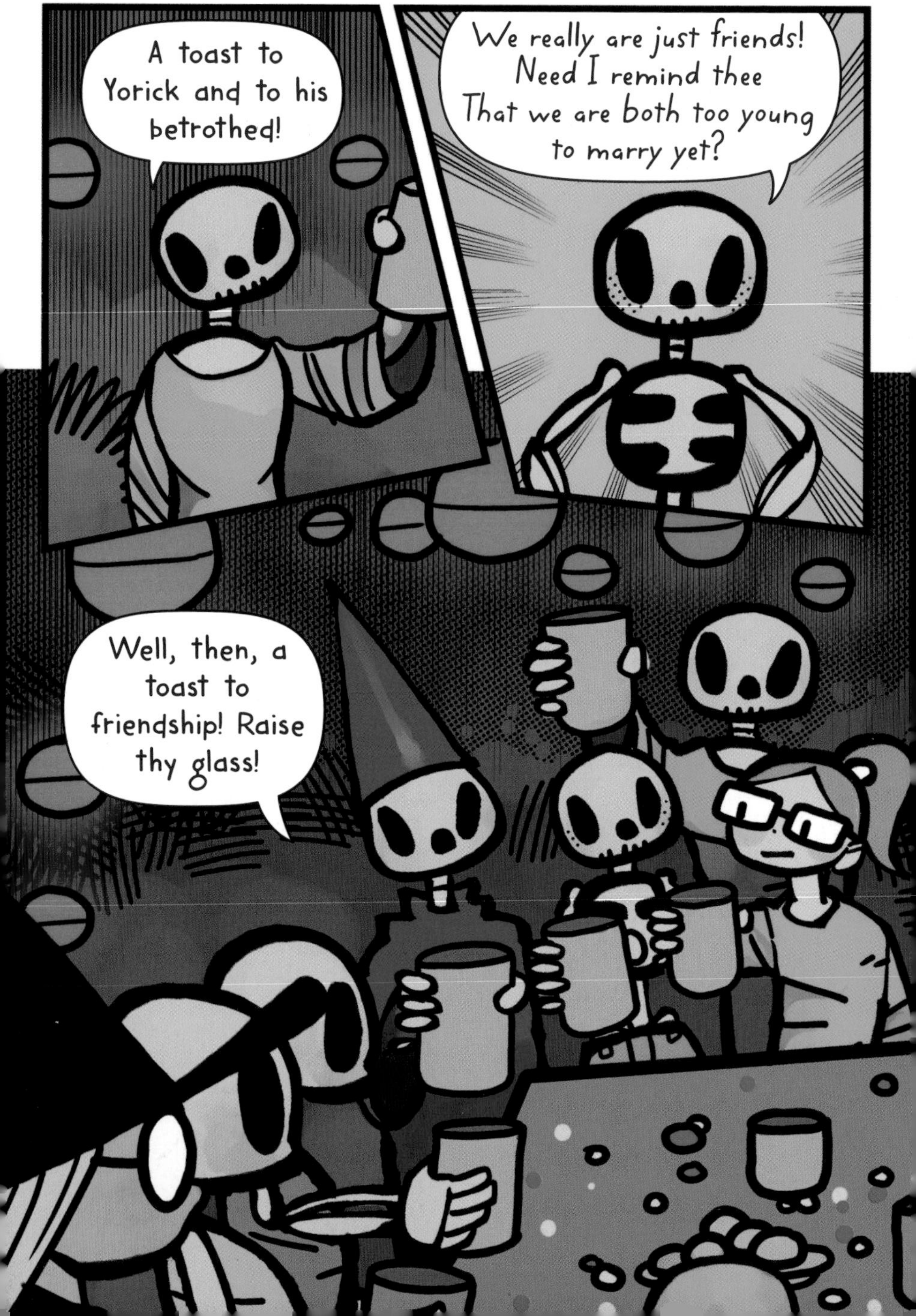
A toast to Yorick and to his betrothed!
We really are just friends! Need I remind thee That we are both too young to marry yet?
Well, then, a toast to friendship! Raise thy glass!

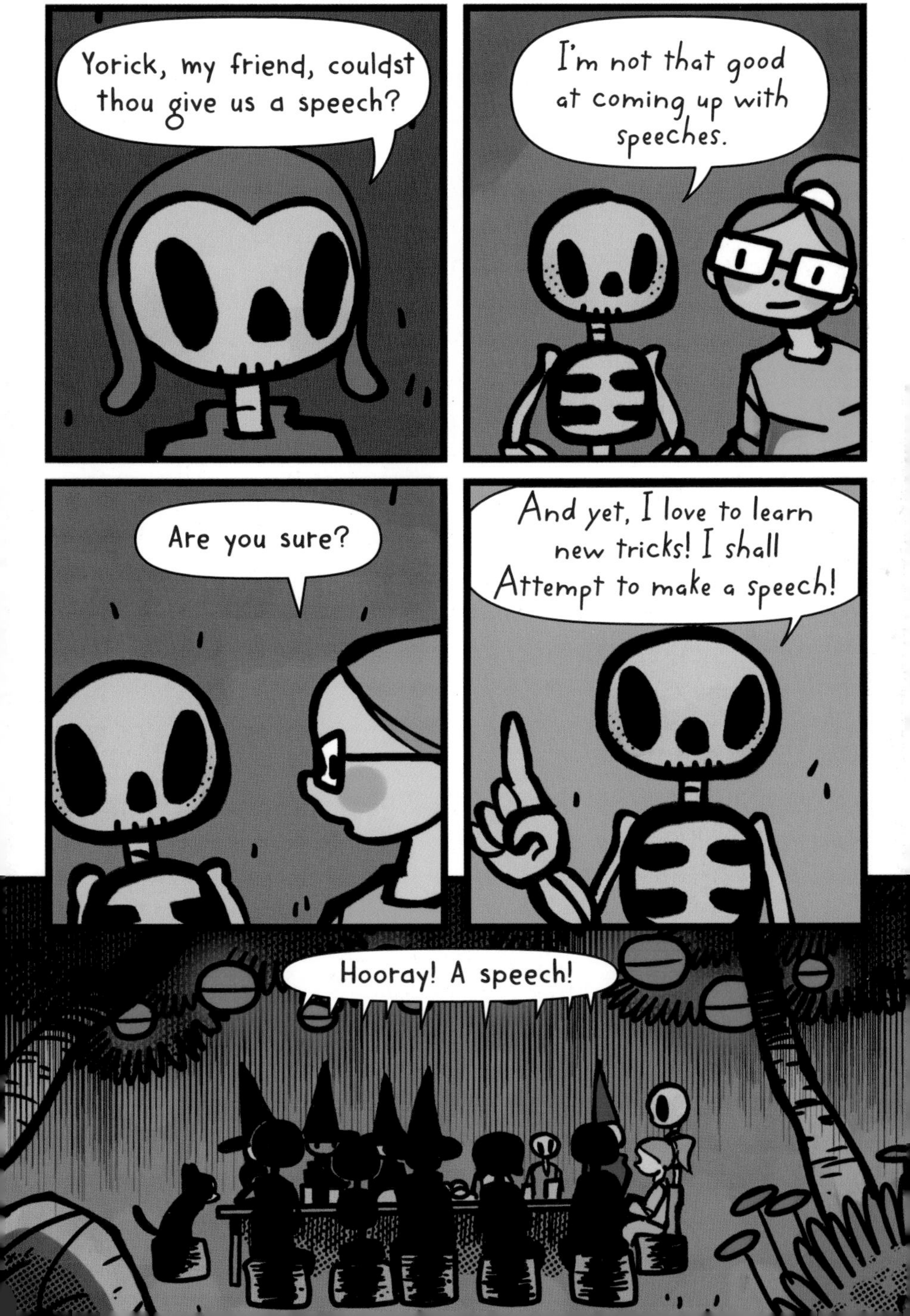
Yorick, my friend, couldst thou give us a speech?
I'm not that good at coming up with speeches.
Are you sure?
And yet, I love to learn new tricks! I shall Attempt to make a speech!
Hooray! A speech!

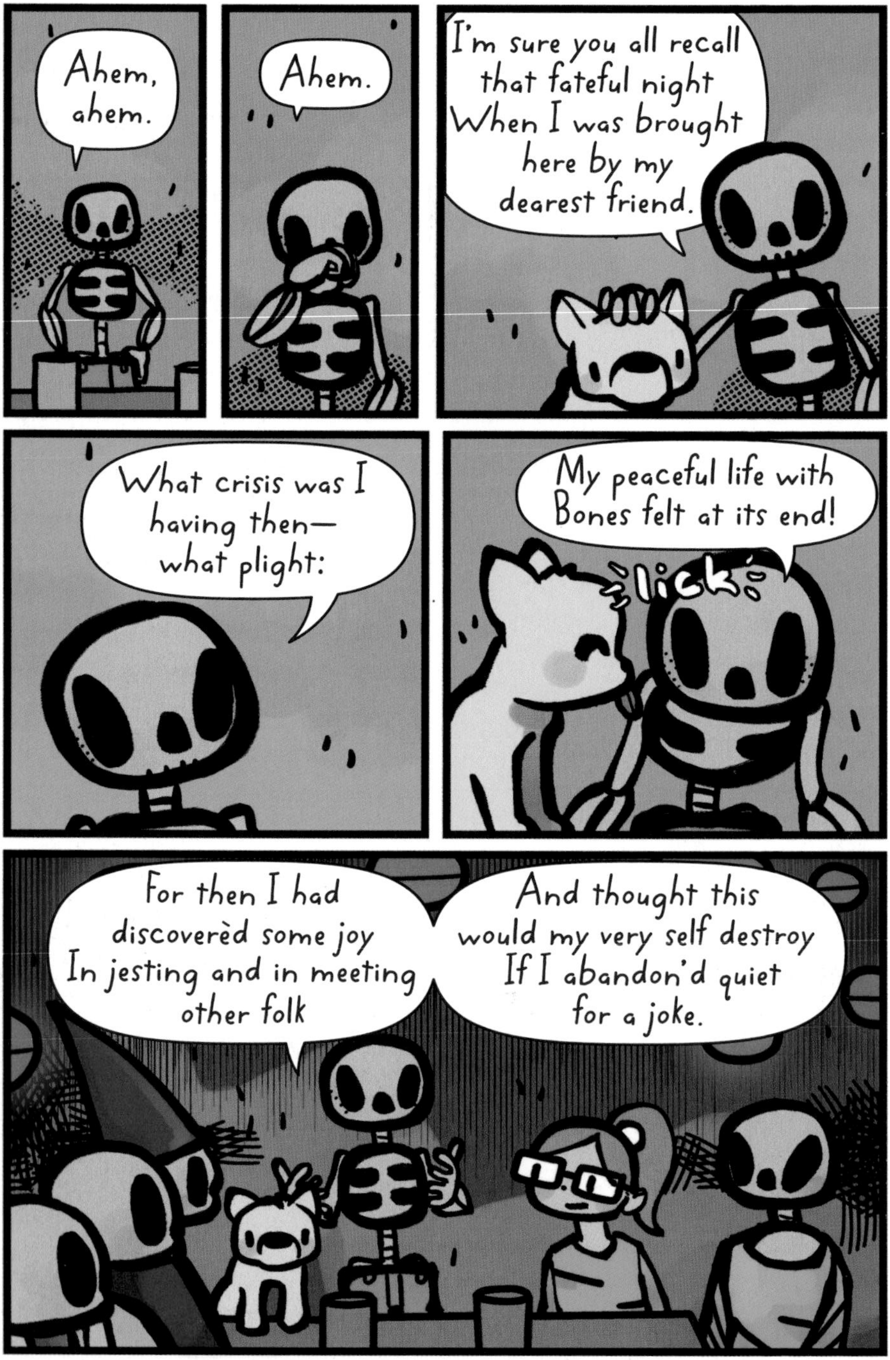
Ahem, ahem.
Ahem.
I'm sure you all recall that fateful night When I was brought here by my dearest friend.
What crisis was I having then— what plight:
My peaceful life with Bones felt at its end!
lick
For then I had discoverèd some joy In jesting and in meeting other folk
And thought this would my very self destroy If I abandon'd quiet for a joke.

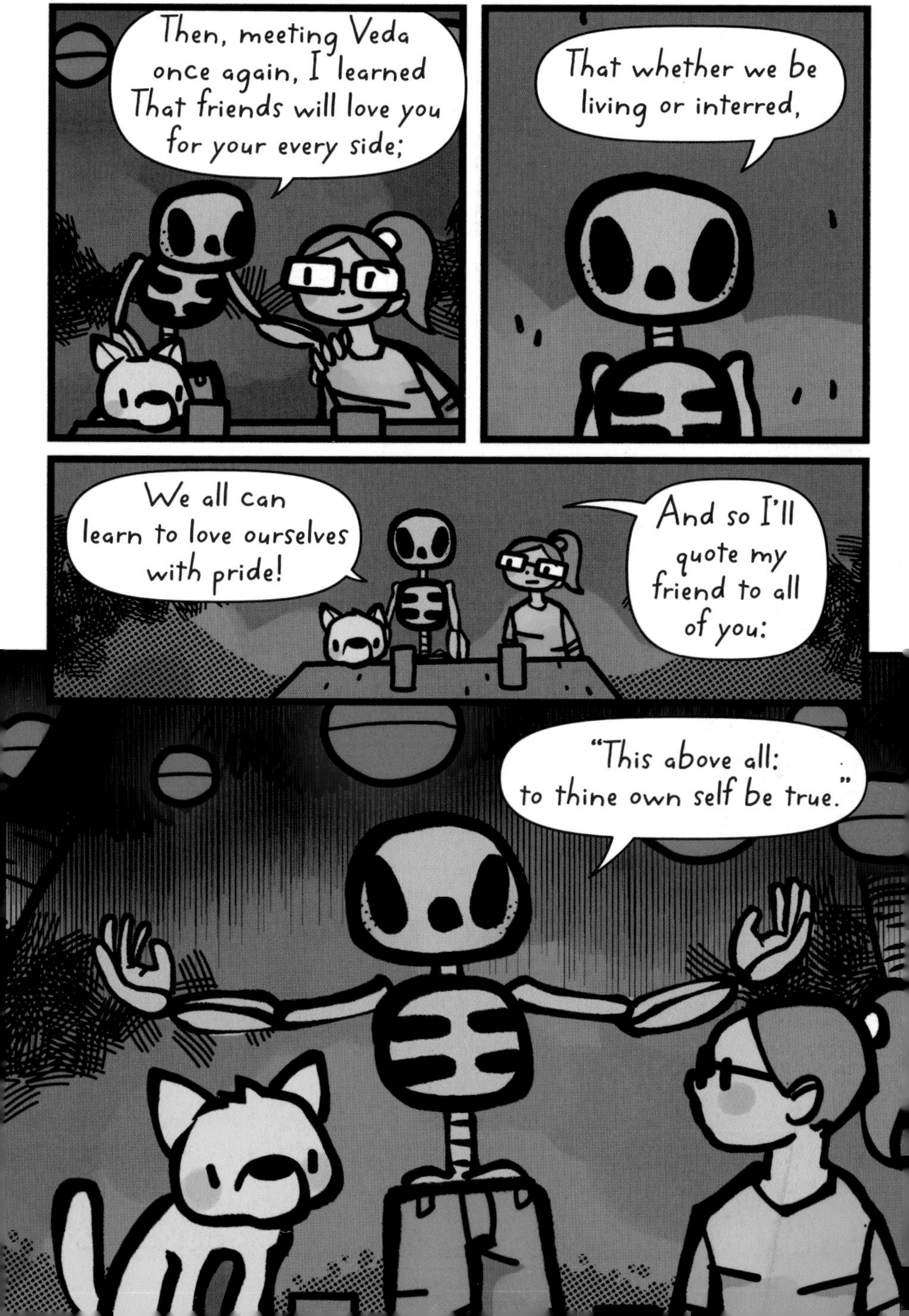

Then, meeting Veda once again, I learned That friends will love you for your every side;
That whether we be living or interred,
We all can learn to love ourselves with pride!
And so I'll quote my friend to all of you:
"This above all: to thine own self be true."

Acknowledgments

Jeremy

The first Yorick and Bones book was published during a global pandemic. This one was created during the pandemic. I would like to thank our AMAZING team at HarperCollins for their hard work and for keeping things on track during such uncertain times. I'm looking at you, Andrew, Erin, David, Bria, Maeve, and Shamin, and everyone else behind the scenes. Thank you to Krista, Scott, Joyce, Rebecca, Mme. Godel, Khalil, M. Brisebois, and M. Beattie for putting kids first. Your dedication to schools and children meant I was able to shift my thoughts regularly back into this book and that was only possible because of you. Thank you to these kids: Alev, Chloë, Esmé, and Hawk, for being early readers of book one—your enthusiasm carried into the creation of this second book. Theo, thanks for laughing at the right places when you finally read book one. And where would I be without you, Heather? Nowhere. Thanks for everything, but especially for being a cheering section when I most need it. And, finally, Hermione: my partner in crime, daughter, cowriter, coconspirator, and fellow Shakespeare nerd. What a joy to share this project with you!

Hermione

First of all, I need to thank Andrew Eliopulos, our amazing editor who made sure this book was awesome. Thank you, Andrew!!! I would also like to thank Paul and Susanne Moniz de Sà for all they taught me about Shakespeare and the theater, and my voice teacher, Wendy Nielsen, for being so supportive even though my writing has nothing to do with singing. Thank you to my friends for being amazing in general. Thank you to my brother for reading the first book even though he would "rather read a dictionary." And thank you to my mom for, you know, being my mom. Finally, I must especially thank my dad for making me part of this project that he's been working on for so long. It's an honor.